PAWS

GABBY GETS IT TOGETHER

MICHELE ASSARASAKORN
NATHAN FAIRBAIRN

RAZORBILL

RAZORBILL

An imprint of Penguin Random House LLC, New York

First published in the United States of America by Razorbill,
an imprint of Penguin Random House LLC, 2022

Copyright © 2022 by Nathan Fairbairn and Michele Assarasakorn

Visit us online at penguinrandomhouse.com.

Library of Congress Cataloging-in-Publication Data is available.
ISBN 9780593351857 (hardcover)
ISBN 9780593351864 (paperback)

Manufactured in China

1   3   5   7   9   10   8   6   4   2

TOPL

Illustrated by Michele Assarasakorn
Written, colored, and lettered by Nathan Fairbairn

Edited by Christopher Hernandez
Design by Maria Fazio

Text set in CCJoeKubert

We acknowledge the support of the Canada Council for the Arts.

Canada Council   Conseil des arts
for the Arts   du Canada

This book is for Lily Ann Fairbairn, without whom PAWS would certainly not exist. The best inspiration, focus group, beta reader, color assistant, and daughter that a father could ever ask for.

—N. F.

To my mom, thank you for never letting me own a "normal" pet. A prairie dog isn't a real dog, but it was cute anyway. And to Selena Goulding and Andrea Scott, for all the belly laughs, tea parties, and two a.m. fries in the bathtub. The little moments in this book would not exist without you guys.

—M. A.

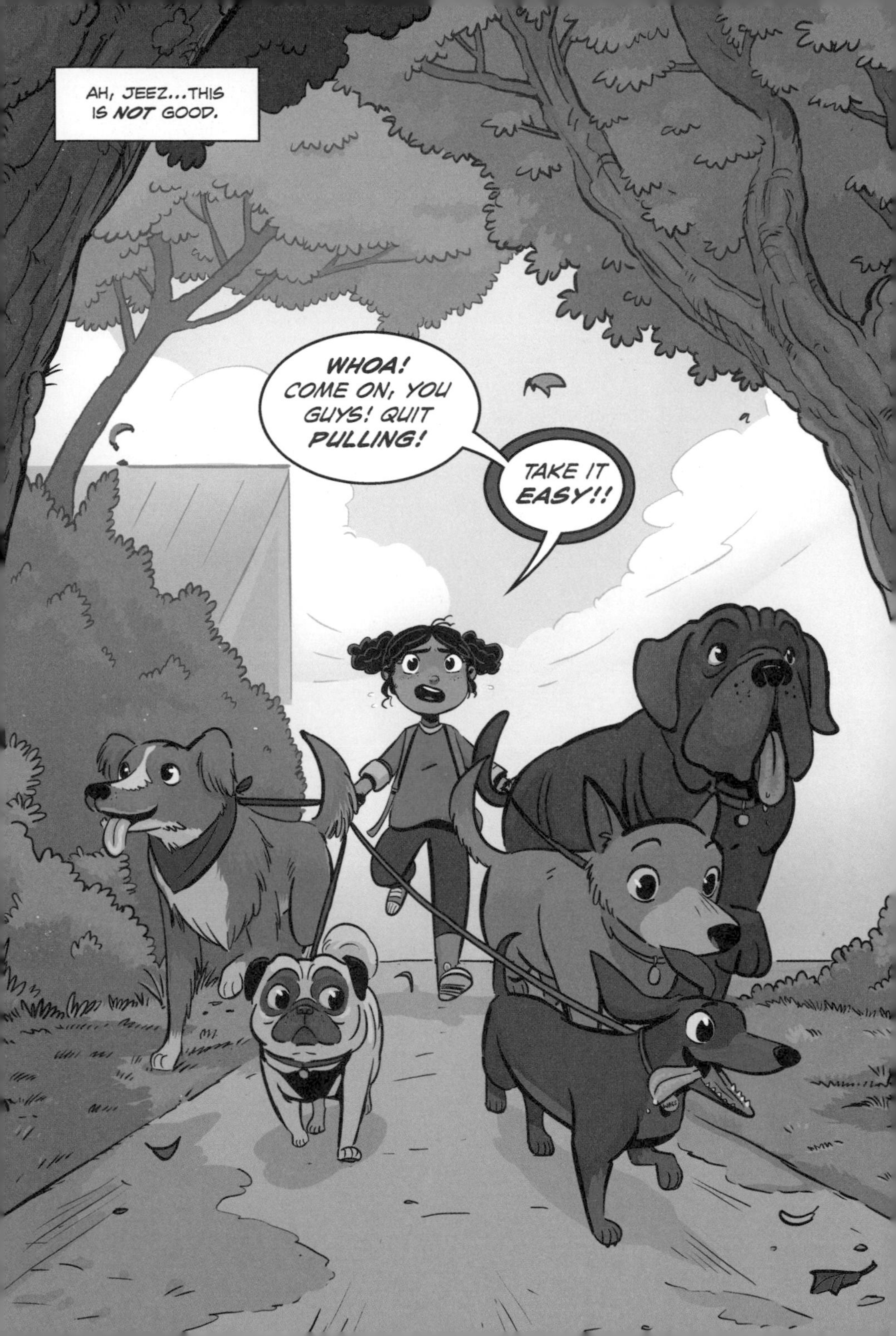
AH, JEEZ...THIS IS *NOT* GOOD.
WHOA! COME ON, YOU GUYS! QUIT *PULLING!*
TAKE IT *EASY!!*

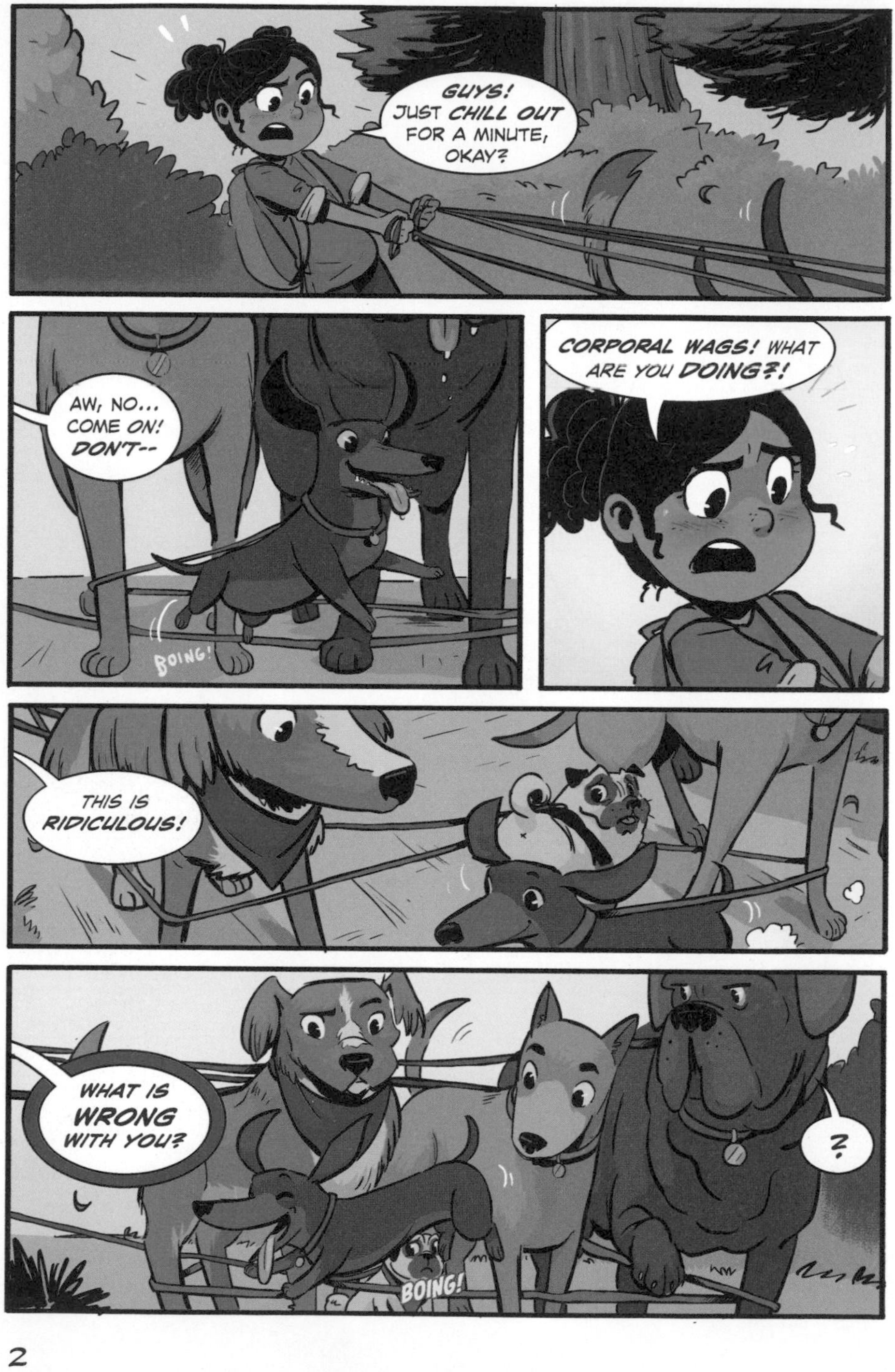
GUYS! JUST CHILL OUT FOR A MINUTE, OKAY?
AW, NO... COME ON! DON'T--
BOING!
CORPORAL WAGS! WHAT ARE YOU DOING?!
THIS IS RIDICULOUS!
WHAT IS WRONG WITH YOU?
?
BOING!

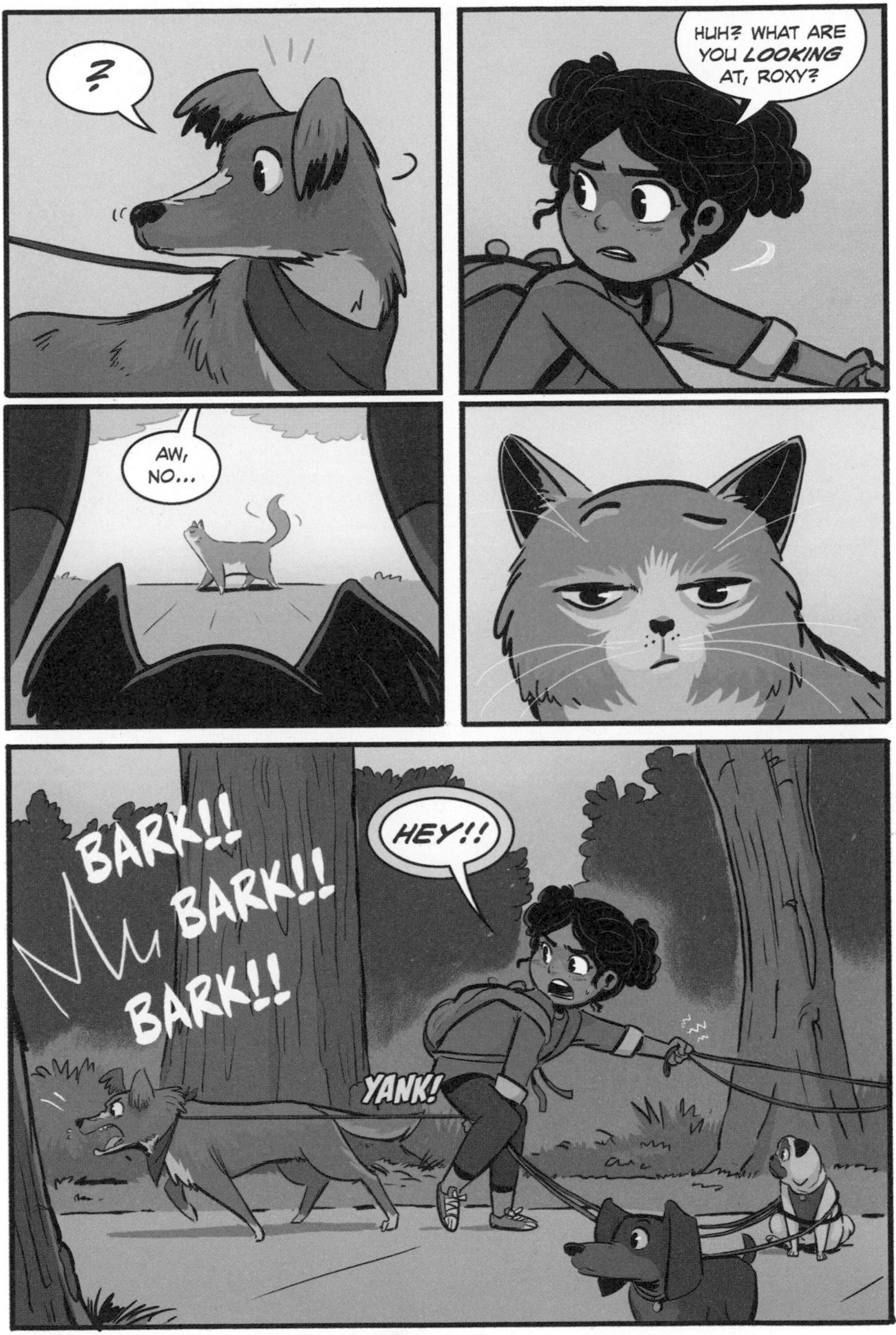
?
HUH? WHAT ARE YOU *LOOKING* AT, ROXY?
AW, NO...
HEY!!
BARK!! BARK!! BARK!!
YANK!

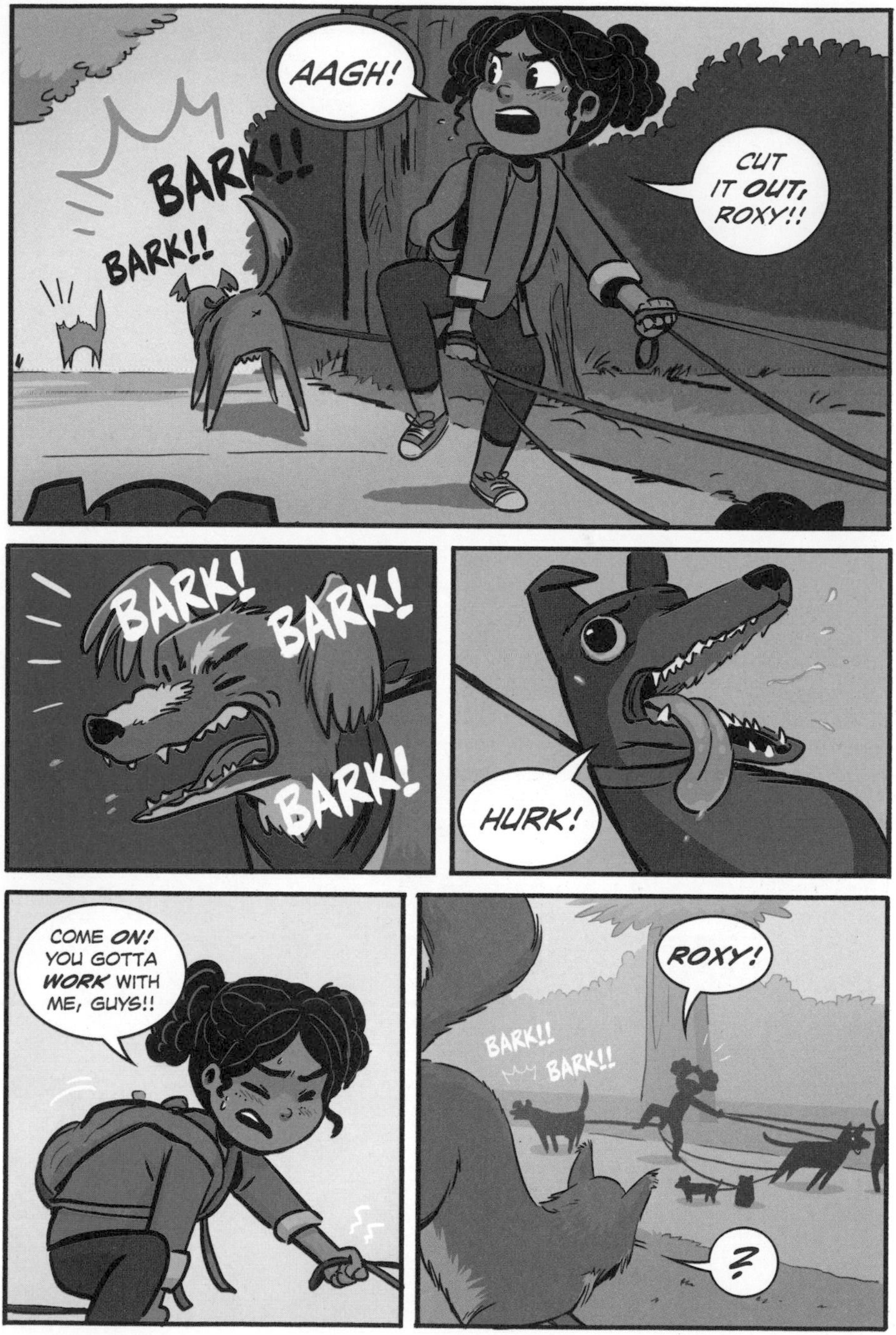
AAGH!
BARK!!
BARK!!
CUT IT OUT, ROXY!!
BARK!
BARK!
BARK!
HURK!
COME ON! YOU GOTTA WORK WITH ME, GUYS!!
ROXY!
BARK!!
BARK!!
?

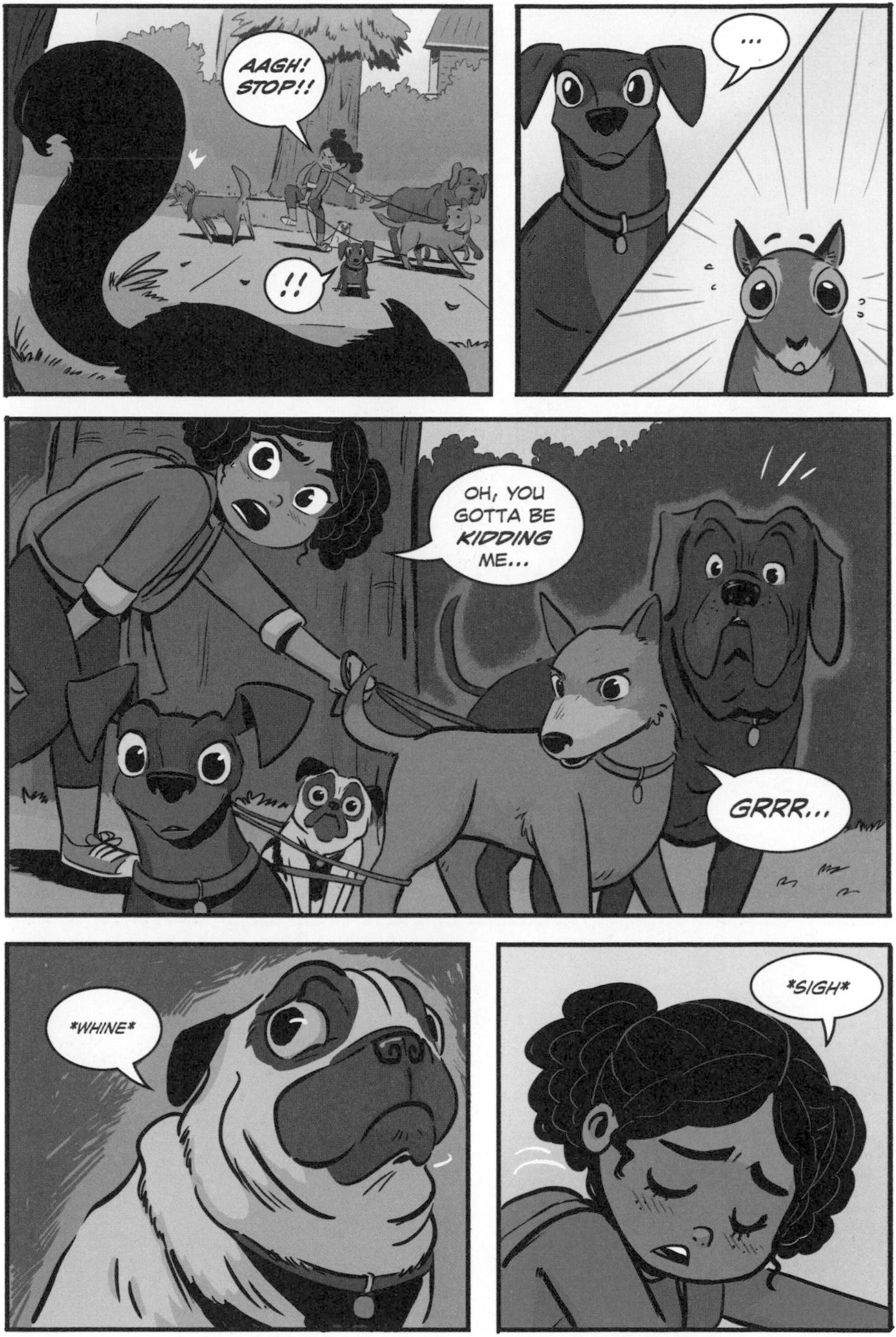
AAGH! STOP!!
!!
...
OH, YOU GOTTA BE KIDDING ME...
GRRR...
WHINE
SIGH

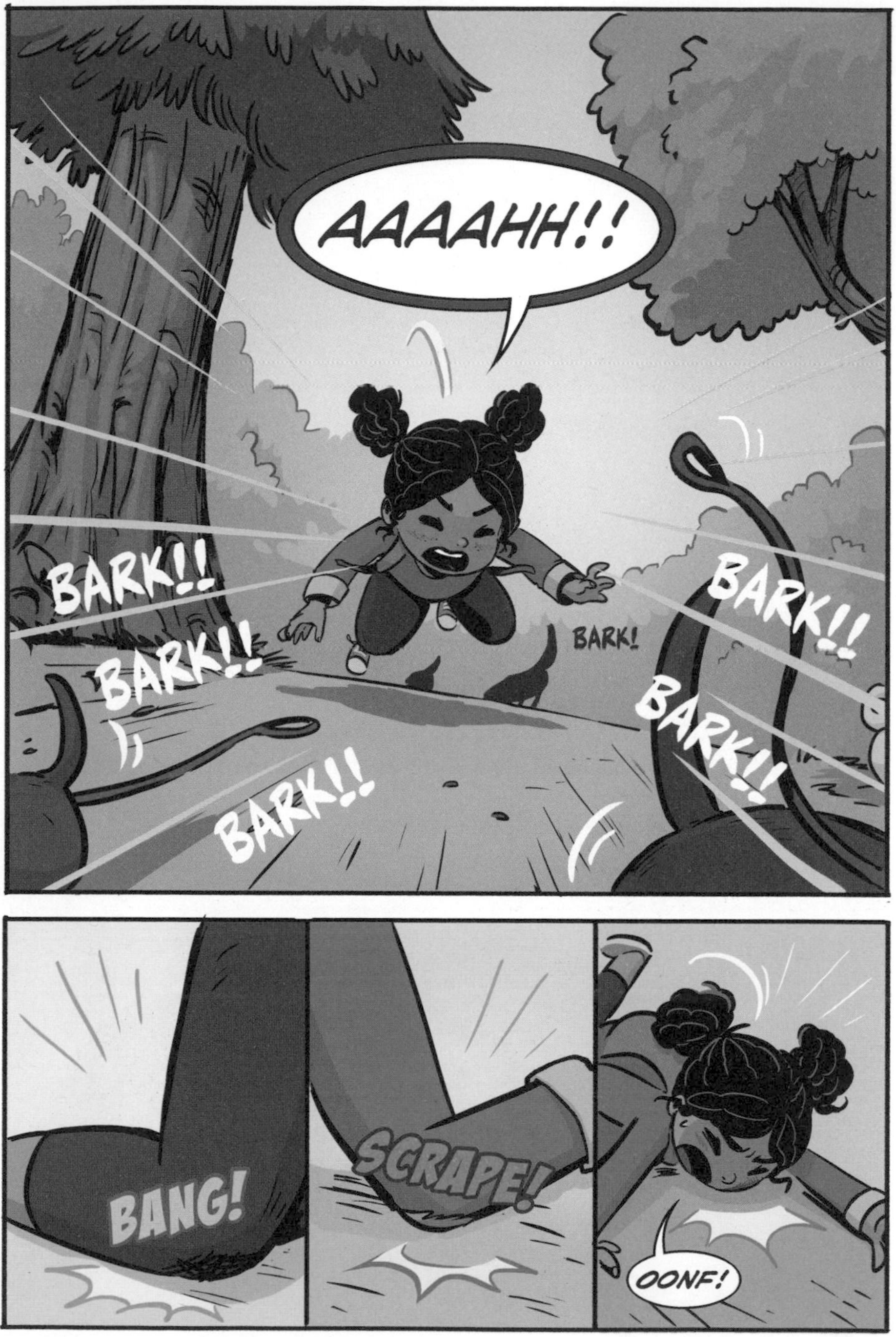
AAAAHH!!
BARK!!
BARK!!
BARK!!
BARK!
BARK!!
BARK!!
BANG!
SCRAPE!
OONF!

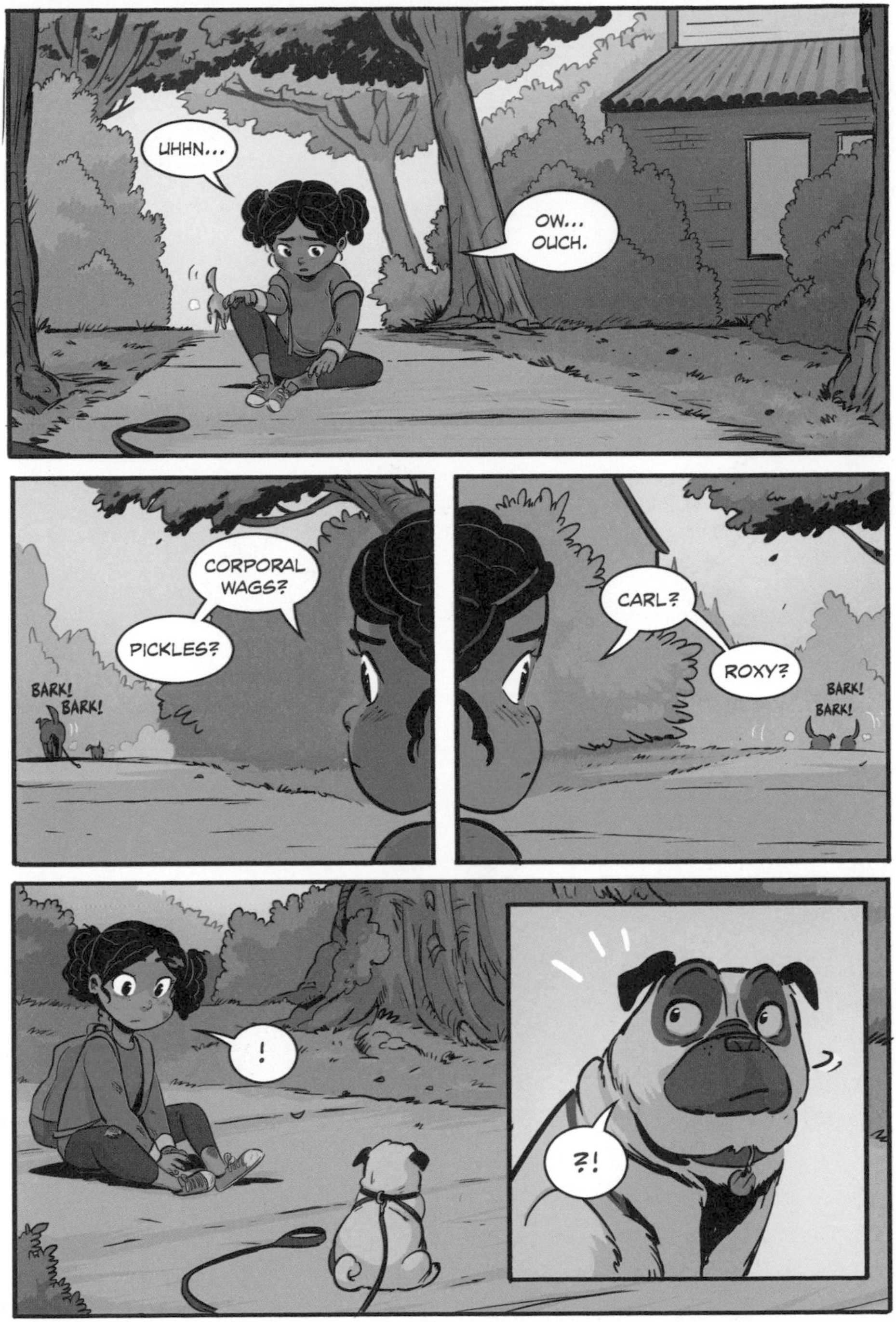
UHHN...
OW... OUCH.
CORPORAL WAGS?
PICKLES?
BARK! BARK!
CARL?
ROXY?
BARK! BARK!
!
?!

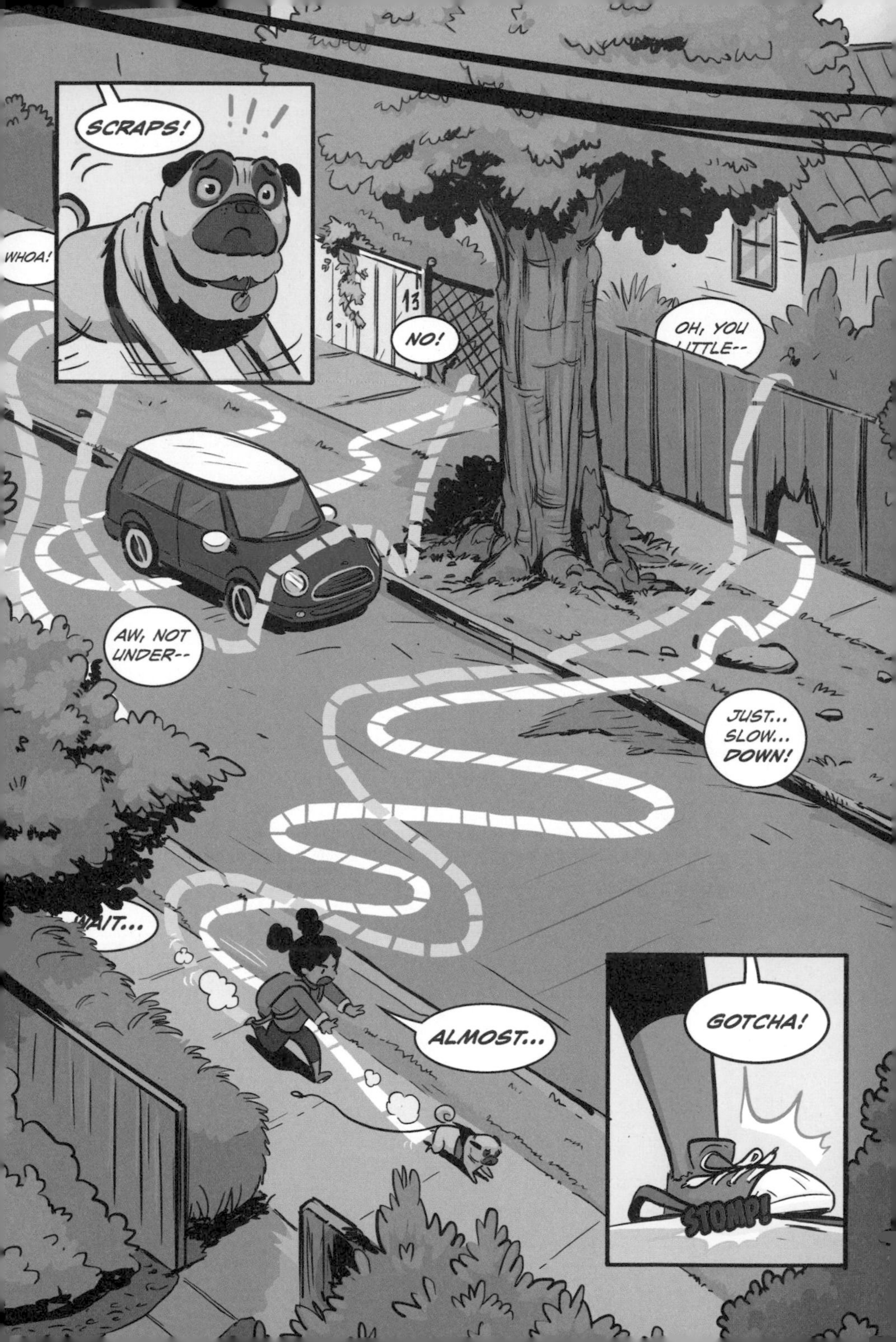
SCRAPS!
!!!
WHOA!
NO!
OH, YOU LITTLE--
AW, NOT UNDER--
JUST... SLOW... DOWN!
WAIT...
ALMOST...
GOTCHA!
STOMP!

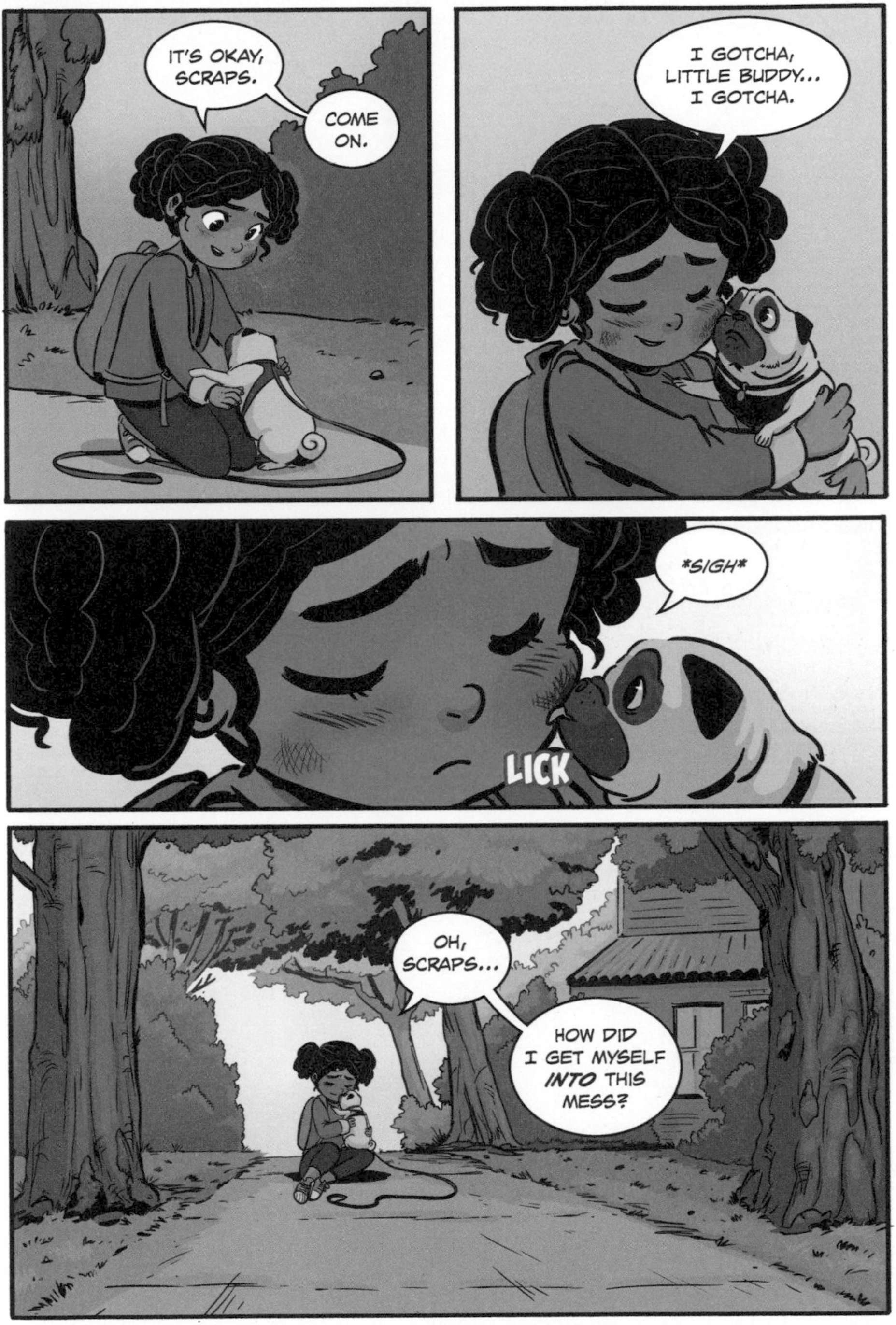
IT'S OKAY, SCRAPS.
COME ON.
I GOTCHA, LITTLE BUDDY... I GOTCHA.
SIGH
LICK
OH, SCRAPS...
HOW DID I GET MYSELF INTO THIS MESS?

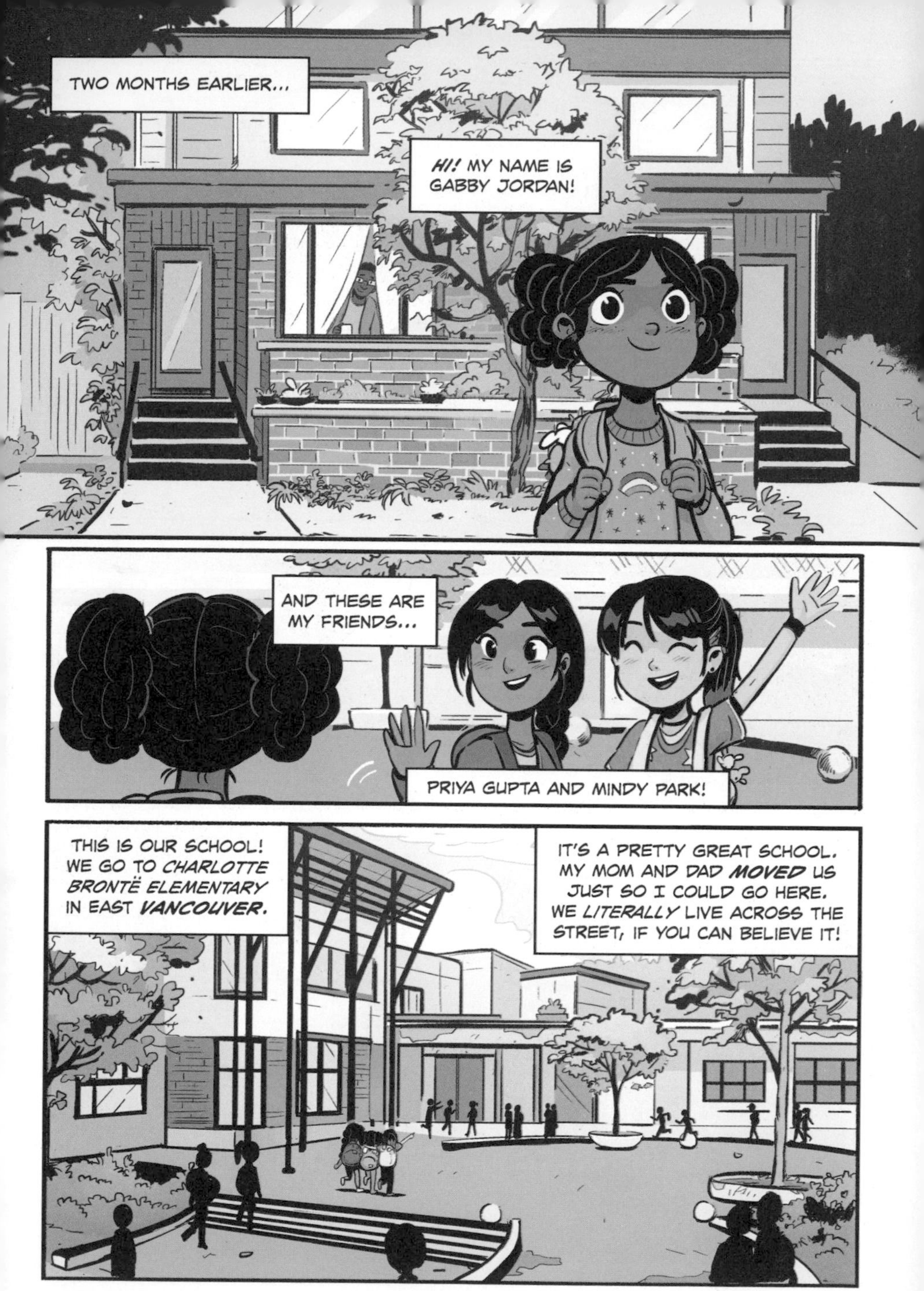
TWO MONTHS EARLIER...
HI! MY NAME IS GABBY JORDAN!
AND THESE ARE MY FRIENDS...
PRIYA GUPTA AND MINDY PARK!
THIS IS OUR SCHOOL! WE GO TO CHARLOTTE BRONTË ELEMENTARY IN EAST VANCOUVER.
IT'S A PRETTY GREAT SCHOOL. MY MOM AND DAD MOVED US JUST SO I COULD GO HERE. WE LITERALLY LIVE ACROSS THE STREET, IF YOU CAN BELIEVE IT!

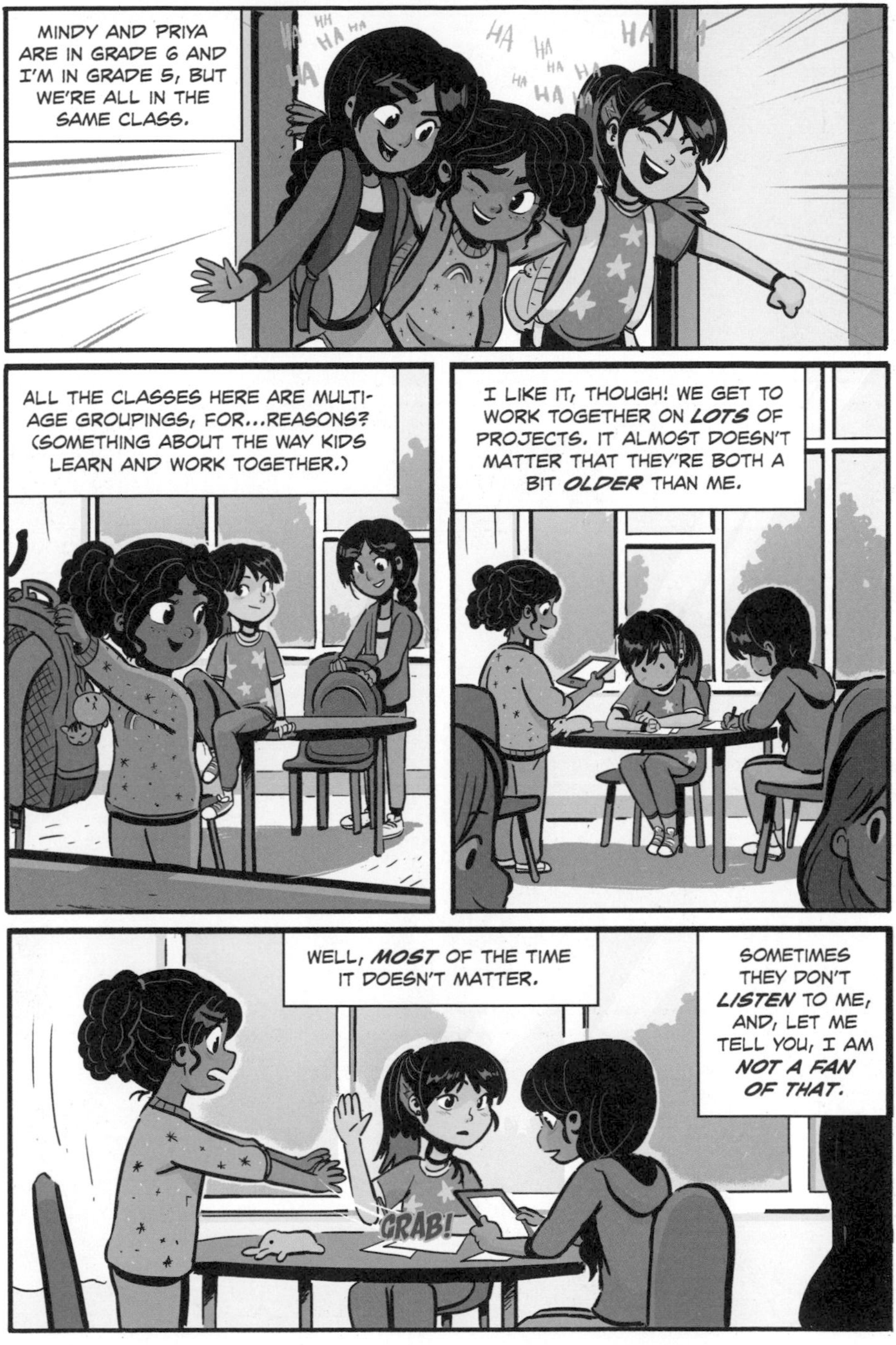
MINDY AND PRIYA ARE IN GRADE 6 AND I'M IN GRADE 5, BUT WE'RE ALL IN THE SAME CLASS.
HA HH HA HA
HA
HA HA HA HA HA HA
HA
ALL THE CLASSES HERE ARE MULTI-AGE GROUPINGS, FOR...REASONS? (SOMETHING ABOUT THE WAY KIDS LEARN AND WORK TOGETHER.)
I LIKE IT, THOUGH! WE GET TO WORK TOGETHER ON *LOTS* OF PROJECTS. IT ALMOST DOESN'T MATTER THAT THEY'RE BOTH A BIT *OLDER* THAN ME.
WELL, *MOST* OF THE TIME IT DOESN'T MATTER.
SOMETIMES THEY DON'T *LISTEN* TO ME, AND, LET ME TELL YOU, I AM *NOT A FAN OF THAT*.
GRAB!

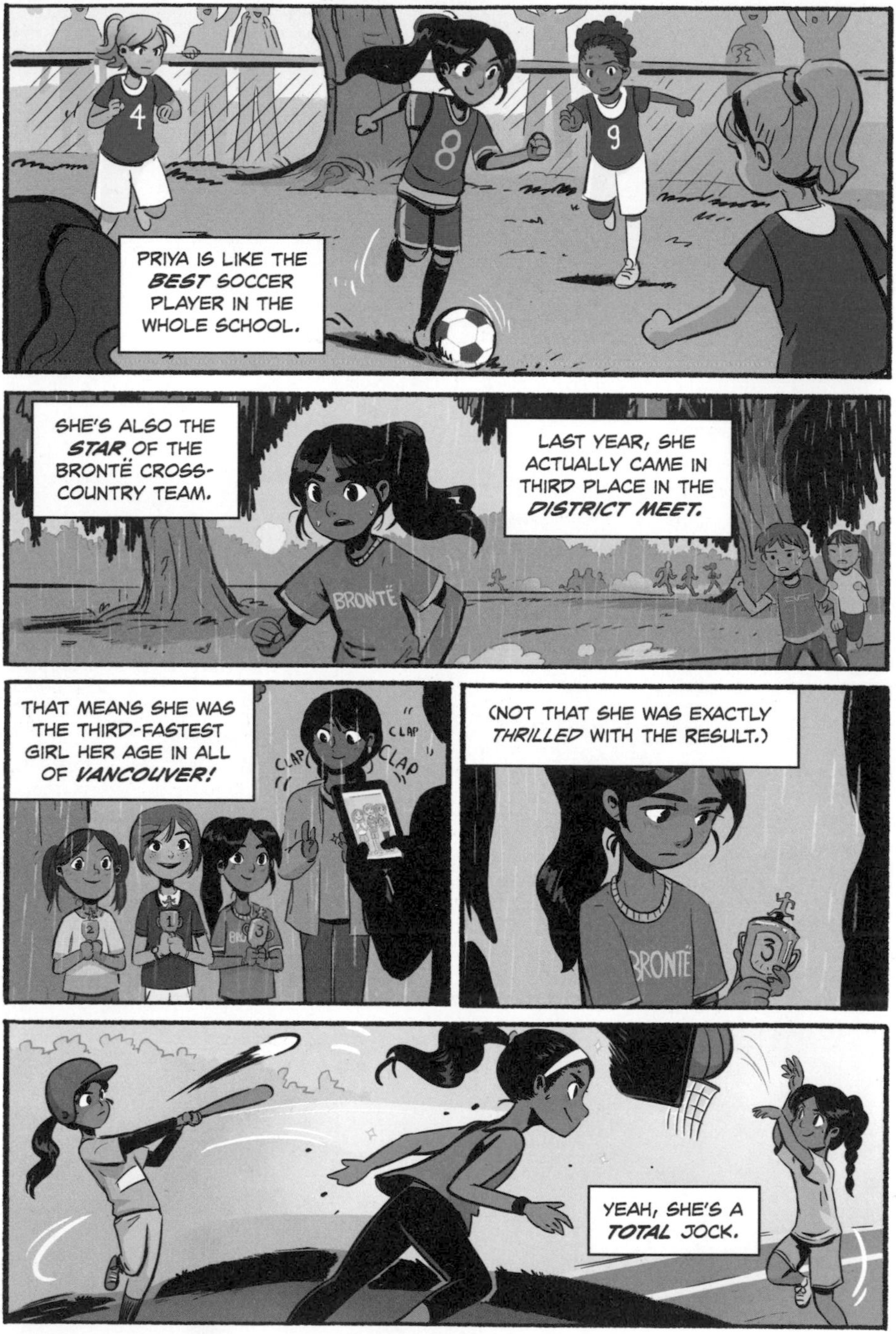
PRIYA IS LIKE THE *BEST* SOCCER PLAYER IN THE WHOLE SCHOOL.
4
8
9
SHE'S ALSO THE *STAR* OF THE BRONTË CROSS-COUNTRY TEAM.
LAST YEAR, SHE ACTUALLY CAME IN THIRD PLACE IN THE *DISTRICT MEET.*
BRONTË
THAT MEANS SHE WAS THE THIRD-FASTEST GIRL HER AGE IN ALL OF *VANCOUVER!*
CLAP
CLAP
CLAP
2
1
3
(NOT THAT SHE WAS EXACTLY *THRILLED* WITH THE RESULT.)
BRONTË
3
YEAH, SHE'S A *TOTAL* JOCK.

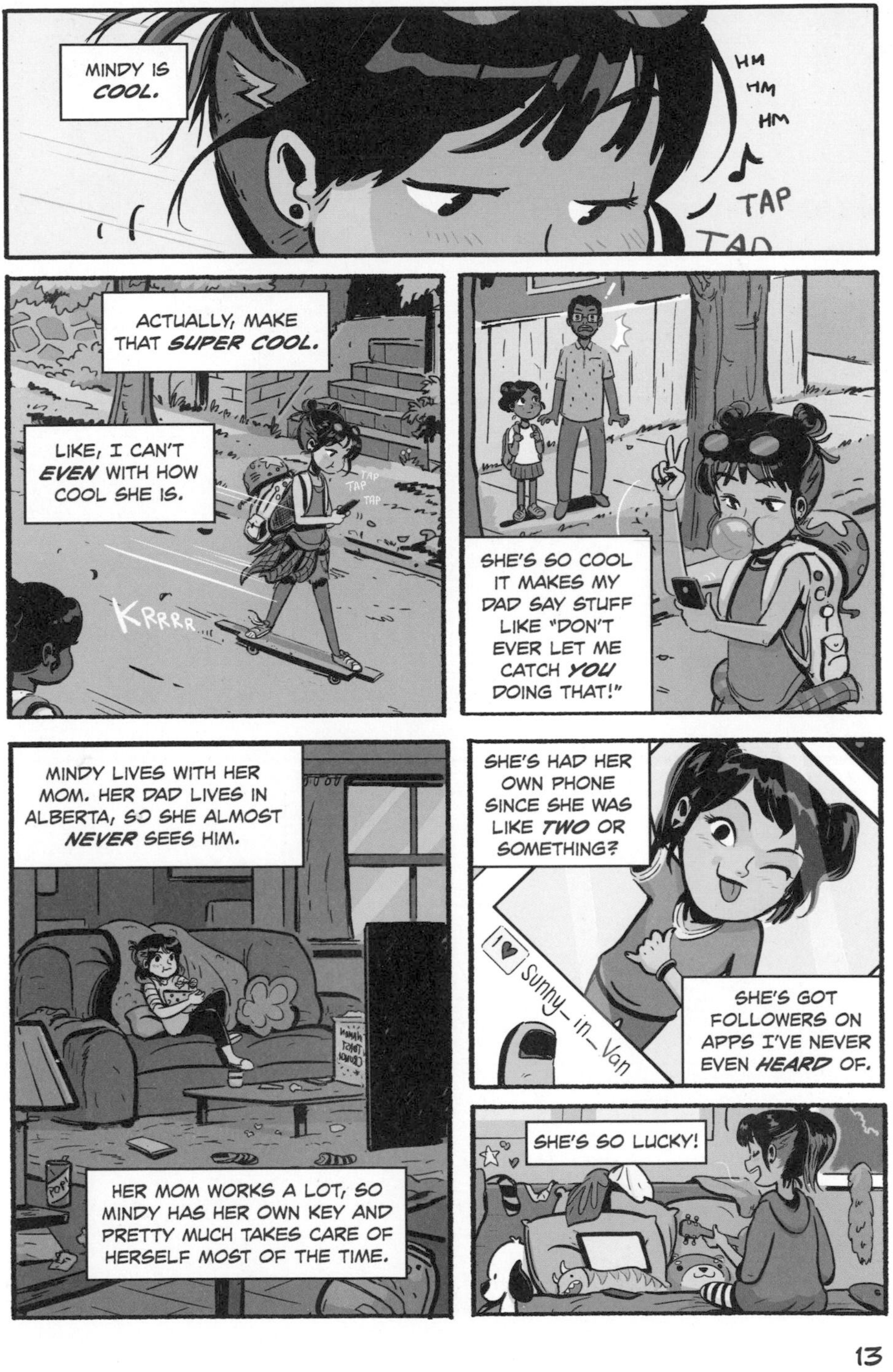
MINDY IS COOL.
HM
HM
HM
TAP
ACTUALLY, MAKE THAT SUPER COOL.
LIKE, I CAN'T EVEN WITH HOW COOL SHE IS.
TAP
TAP
TAP
KRRRR
SHE'S SO COOL IT MAKES MY DAD SAY STUFF LIKE "DON'T EVER LET ME CATCH YOU DOING THAT!"
MINDY LIVES WITH HER MOM. HER DAD LIVES IN ALBERTA, SO SHE ALMOST NEVER SEES HIM.
HER MOM WORKS A LOT, SO MINDY HAS HER OWN KEY AND PRETTY MUCH TAKES CARE OF HERSELF MOST OF THE TIME.
SHE'S HAD HER OWN PHONE SINCE SHE WAS LIKE TWO OR SOMETHING?
Sunny_in_Van
SHE'S GOT FOLLOWERS ON APPS I'VE NEVER EVEN HEARD OF.
SHE'S SO LUCKY!

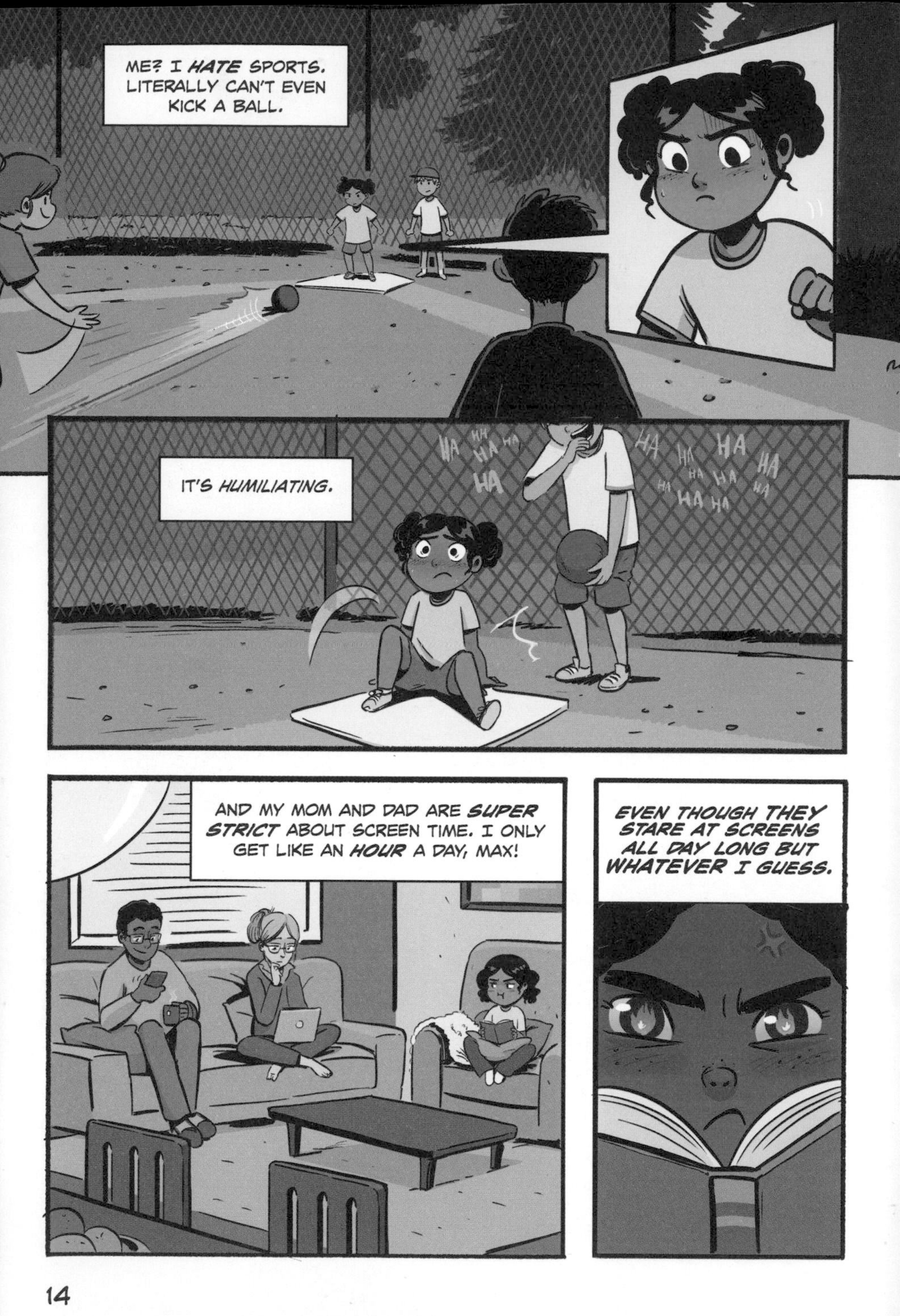
ME? I HATE SPORTS. LITERALLY CAN'T EVEN KICK A BALL.
IT'S HUMILIATING.
HA HA HA HA HA
HA HA HA HA HA HA HA HA HA HA
AND MY MOM AND DAD ARE SUPER STRICT ABOUT SCREEN TIME. I ONLY GET LIKE AN HOUR A DAY, MAX!
EVEN THOUGH THEY STARE AT SCREENS ALL DAY LONG BUT WHATEVER I GUESS.

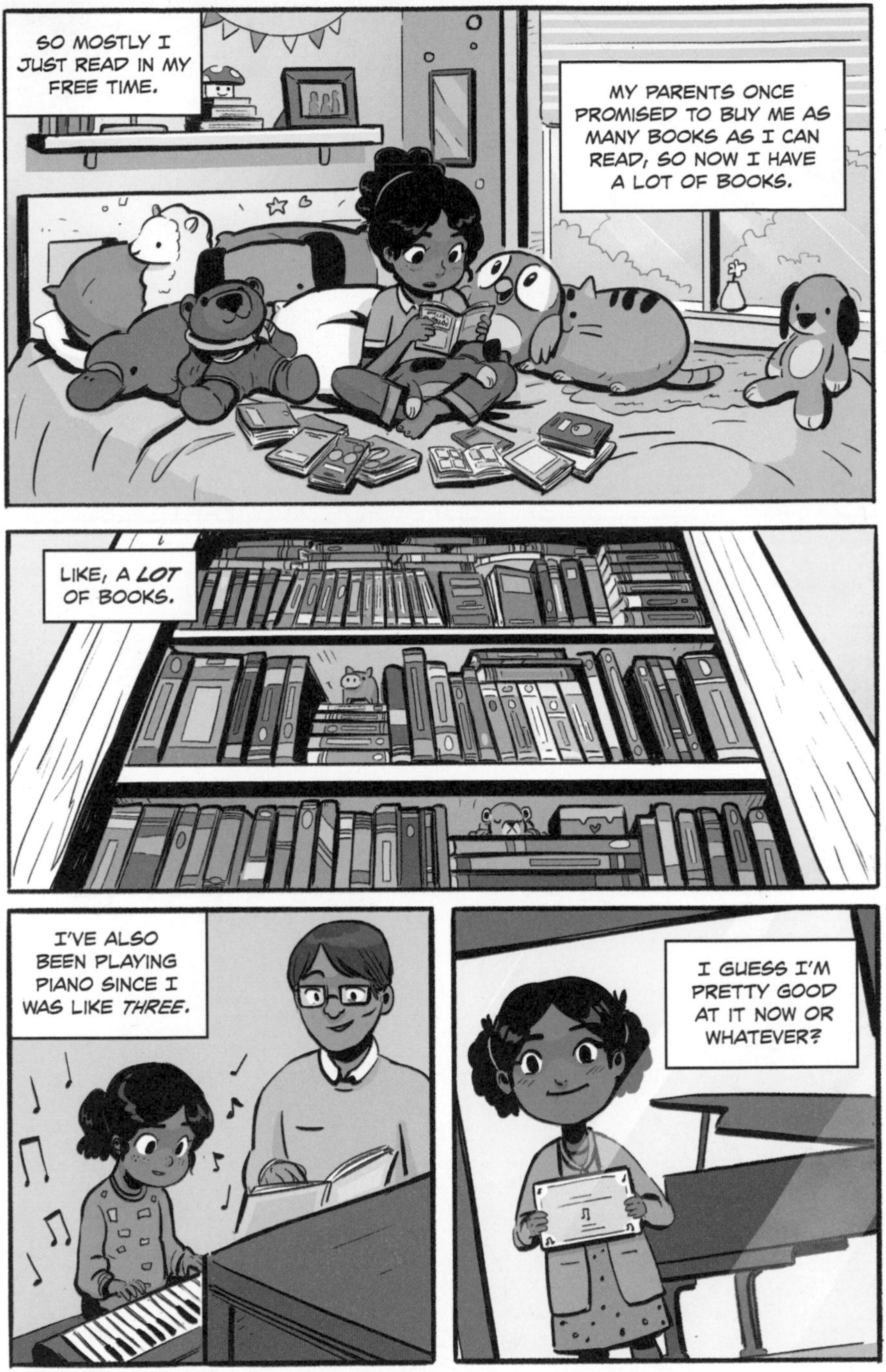
SO MOSTLY I JUST READ IN MY FREE TIME.
MY PARENTS ONCE PROMISED TO BUY ME AS MANY BOOKS AS I CAN READ, SO NOW I HAVE A LOT OF BOOKS.
LIKE, A *LOT* OF BOOKS.
I'VE ALSO BEEN PLAYING PIANO SINCE I WAS LIKE *THREE*.
I GUESS I'M PRETTY GOOD AT IT NOW OR WHATEVER?

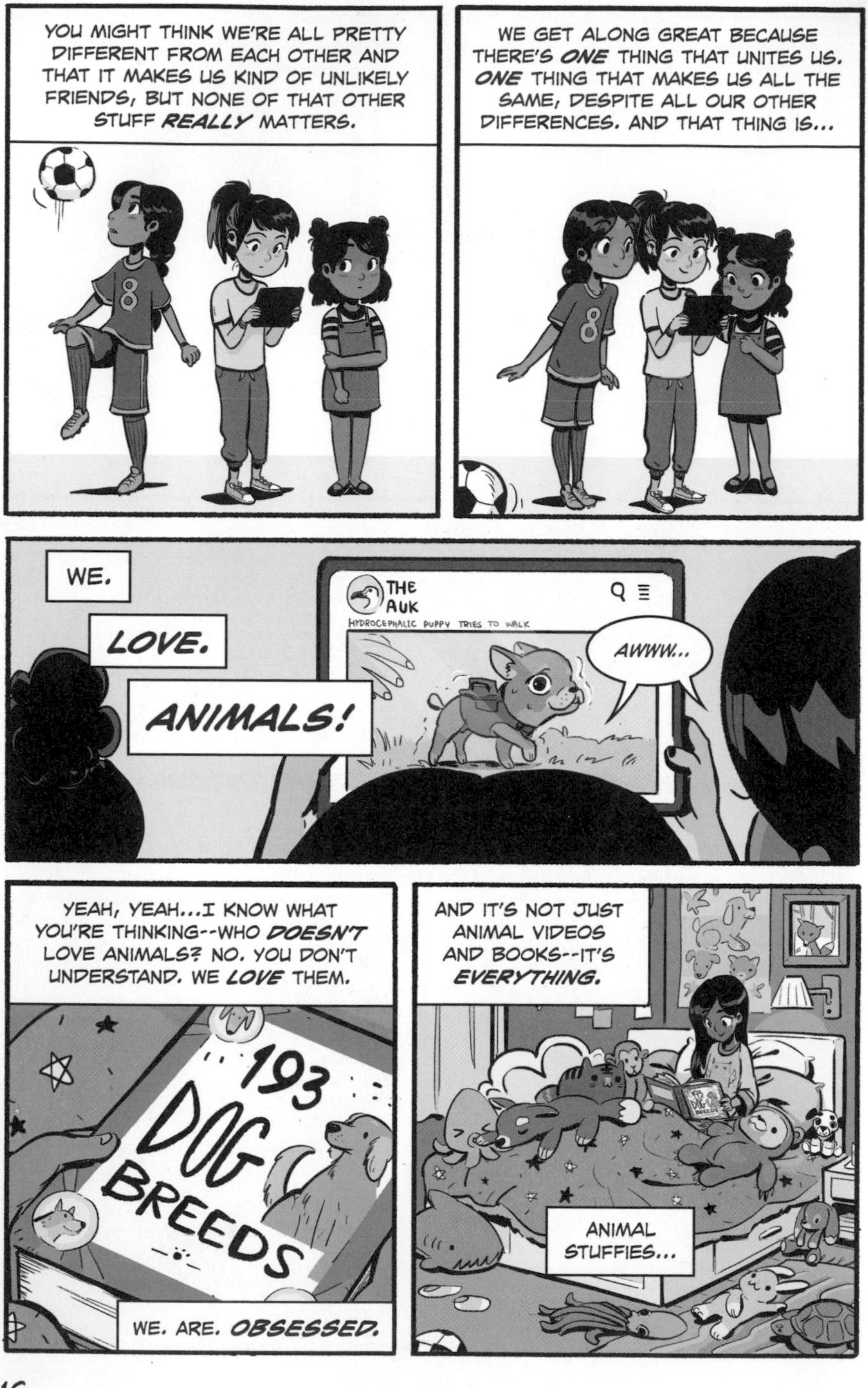
YOU MIGHT THINK WE'RE ALL PRETTY DIFFERENT FROM EACH OTHER AND THAT IT MAKES US KIND OF UNLIKELY FRIENDS, BUT NONE OF THAT OTHER STUFF REALLY MATTERS.
WE GET ALONG GREAT BECAUSE THERE'S ONE THING THAT UNITES US. ONE THING THAT MAKES US ALL THE SAME, DESPITE ALL OUR OTHER DIFFERENCES. AND THAT THING IS...
WE.
LOVE.
ANIMALS!
THE AUK
HYDROCEPHALIC PUPPY TRIES TO WALK
AWWW...
YEAH, YEAH...I KNOW WHAT YOU'RE THINKING--WHO DOESN'T LOVE ANIMALS? NO. YOU DON'T UNDERSTAND. WE LOVE THEM.
193 DOG BREEDS
WE. ARE. OBSESSED.
AND IT'S NOT JUST ANIMAL VIDEOS AND BOOKS--IT'S EVERYTHING.
ANIMAL STUFFIES...

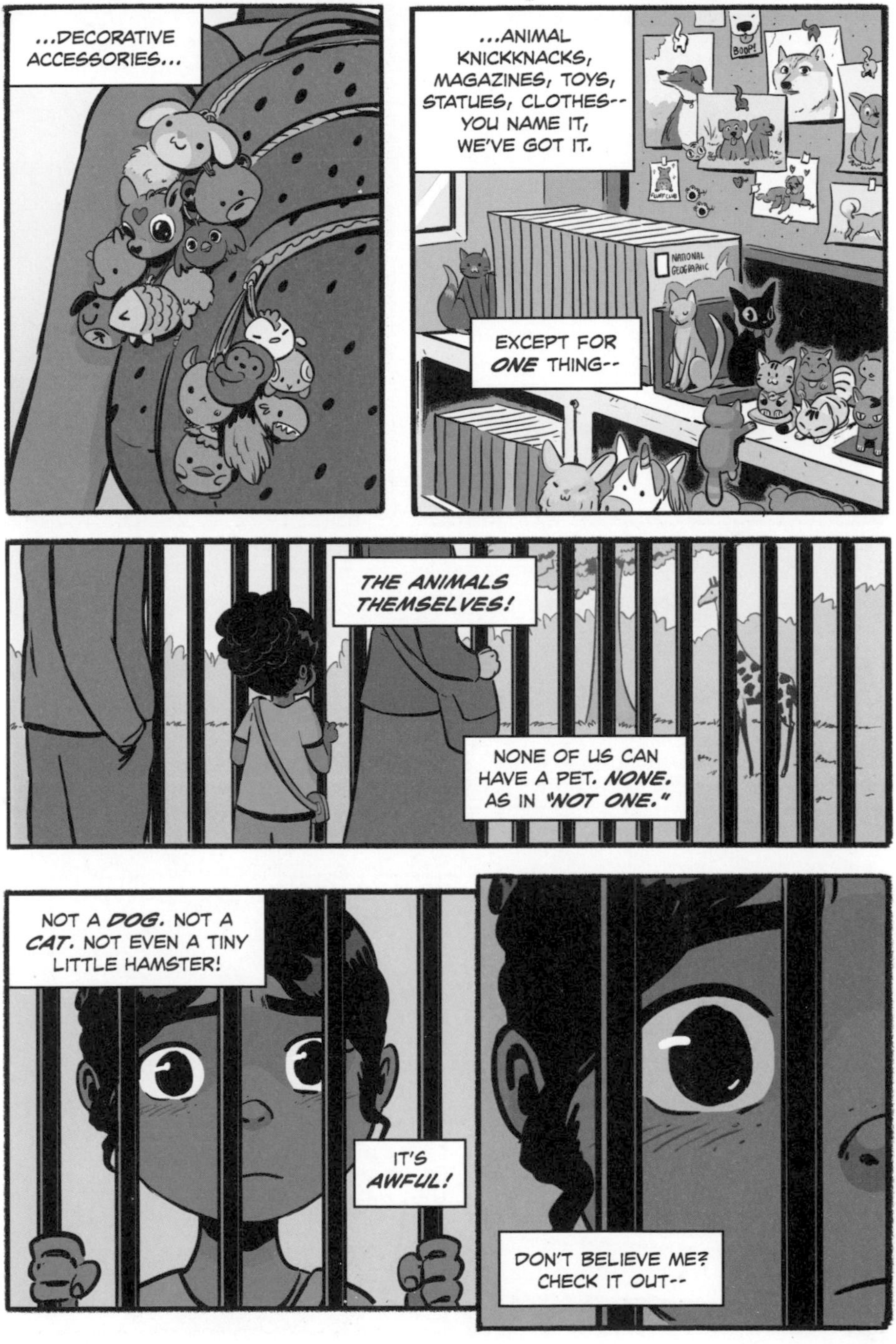
...DECORATIVE ACCESSORIES...
...ANIMAL KNICKKNACKS, MAGAZINES, TOYS, STATUES, CLOTHES-- YOU NAME IT, WE'VE GOT IT.
BOOP!
NATIONAL GEOGRAPHIC
EXCEPT FOR *ONE* THING--
THE ANIMALS THEMSELVES!
NONE OF US CAN HAVE A PET. *NONE.* AS IN *"NOT ONE."*
NOT A *DOG.* NOT A *CAT.* NOT EVEN A TINY LITTLE HAMSTER!
IT'S *AWFUL!*
DON'T BELIEVE ME? CHECK IT OUT--

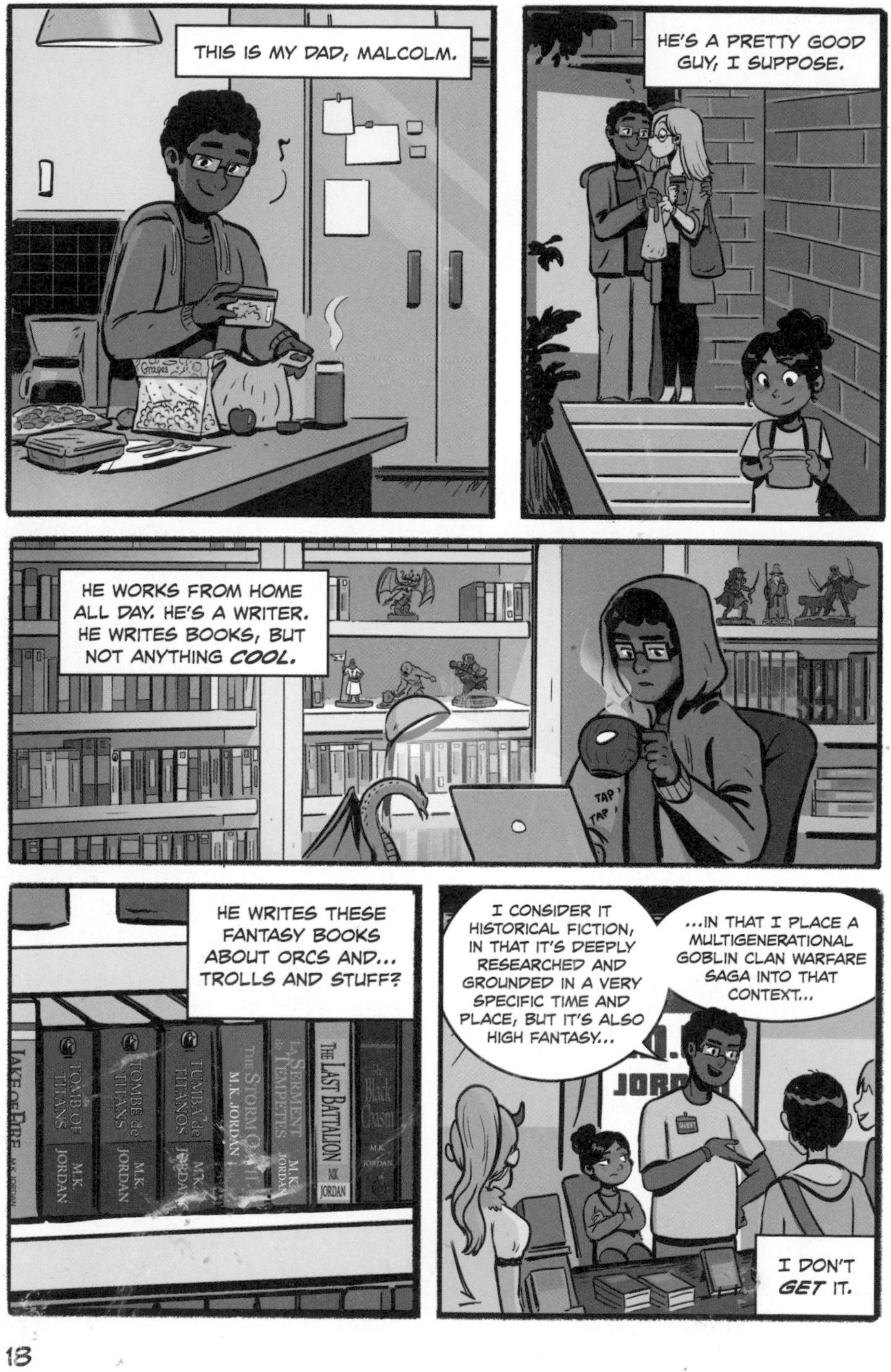
THIS IS MY DAD, MALCOLM.
Grapes
HE'S A PRETTY GOOD GUY, I SUPPOSE.
HE WORKS FROM HOME ALL DAY. HE'S A WRITER. HE WRITES BOOKS, BUT NOT ANYTHING *COOL.*
TAP TAP
HE WRITES THESE FANTASY BOOKS ABOUT ORCS AND... TROLLS AND STUFF?
TOMB OF TITANS M.K. JORDAN
TOMBE de TITANS M.K. JORDAN
TUMBA de TITANOS
THE LAST BATTALION M.K. JORDAN
I CONSIDER IT HISTORICAL FICTION, IN THAT IT'S DEEPLY RESEARCHED AND GROUNDED IN A VERY SPECIFIC TIME AND PLACE, BUT IT'S ALSO HIGH FANTASY...
...IN THAT I PLACE A MULTIGENERATIONAL GOBLIN CLAN WARFARE SAGA INTO THAT CONTEXT...
JORDAN
I DON'T *GET* IT.

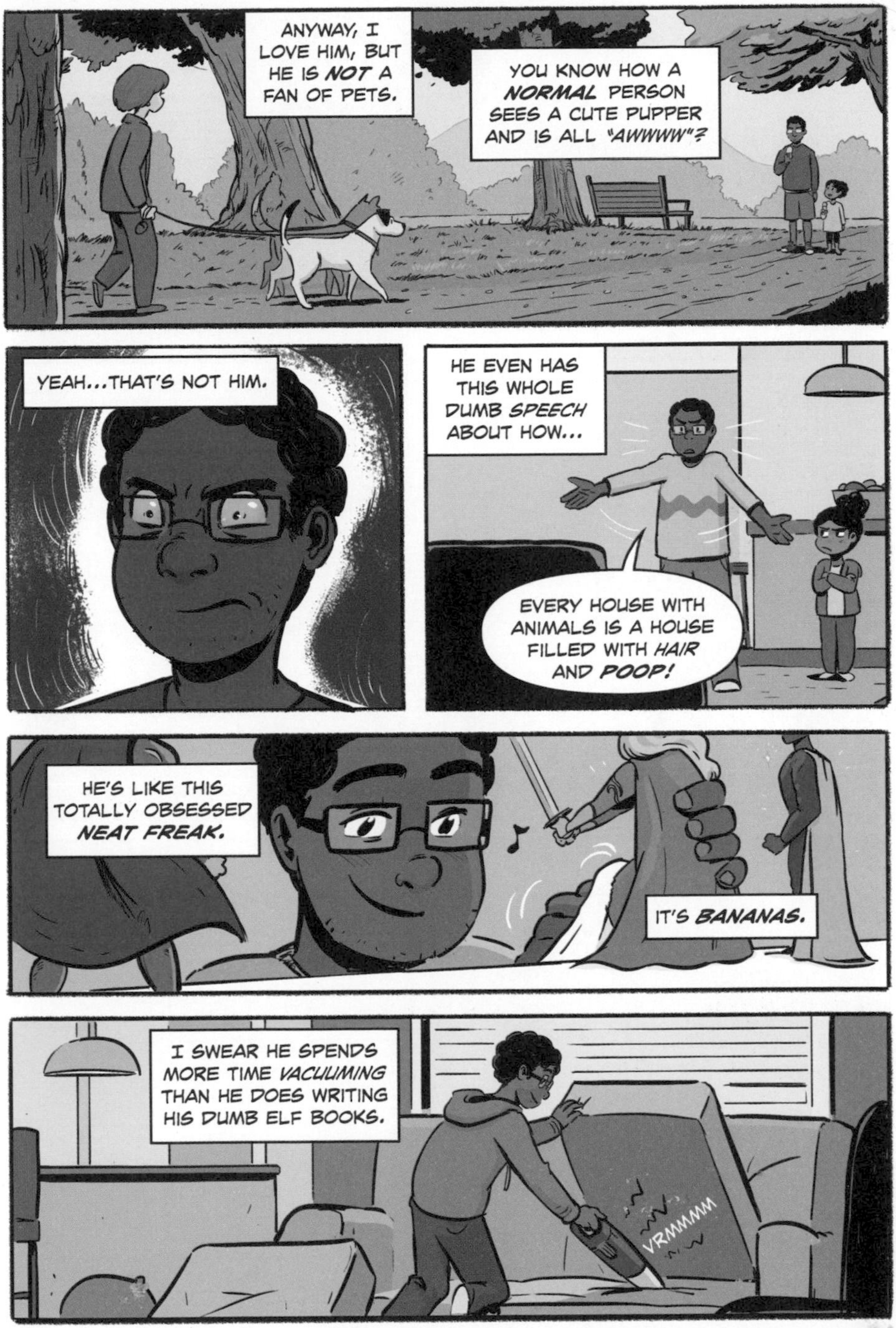
ANYWAY, I LOVE HIM, BUT HE IS NOT A FAN OF PETS.
YOU KNOW HOW A NORMAL PERSON SEES A CUTE PUPPER AND IS ALL "AWWWW"?
YEAH...THAT'S NOT HIM.
HE EVEN HAS THIS WHOLE DUMB SPEECH ABOUT HOW...
EVERY HOUSE WITH ANIMALS IS A HOUSE FILLED WITH HAIR AND POOP!
HE'S LIKE THIS TOTALLY OBSESSED NEAT FREAK.
IT'S BANANAS.
I SWEAR HE SPENDS MORE TIME VACUUMING THAN HE DOES WRITING HIS DUMB ELF BOOKS.
VRMMMM

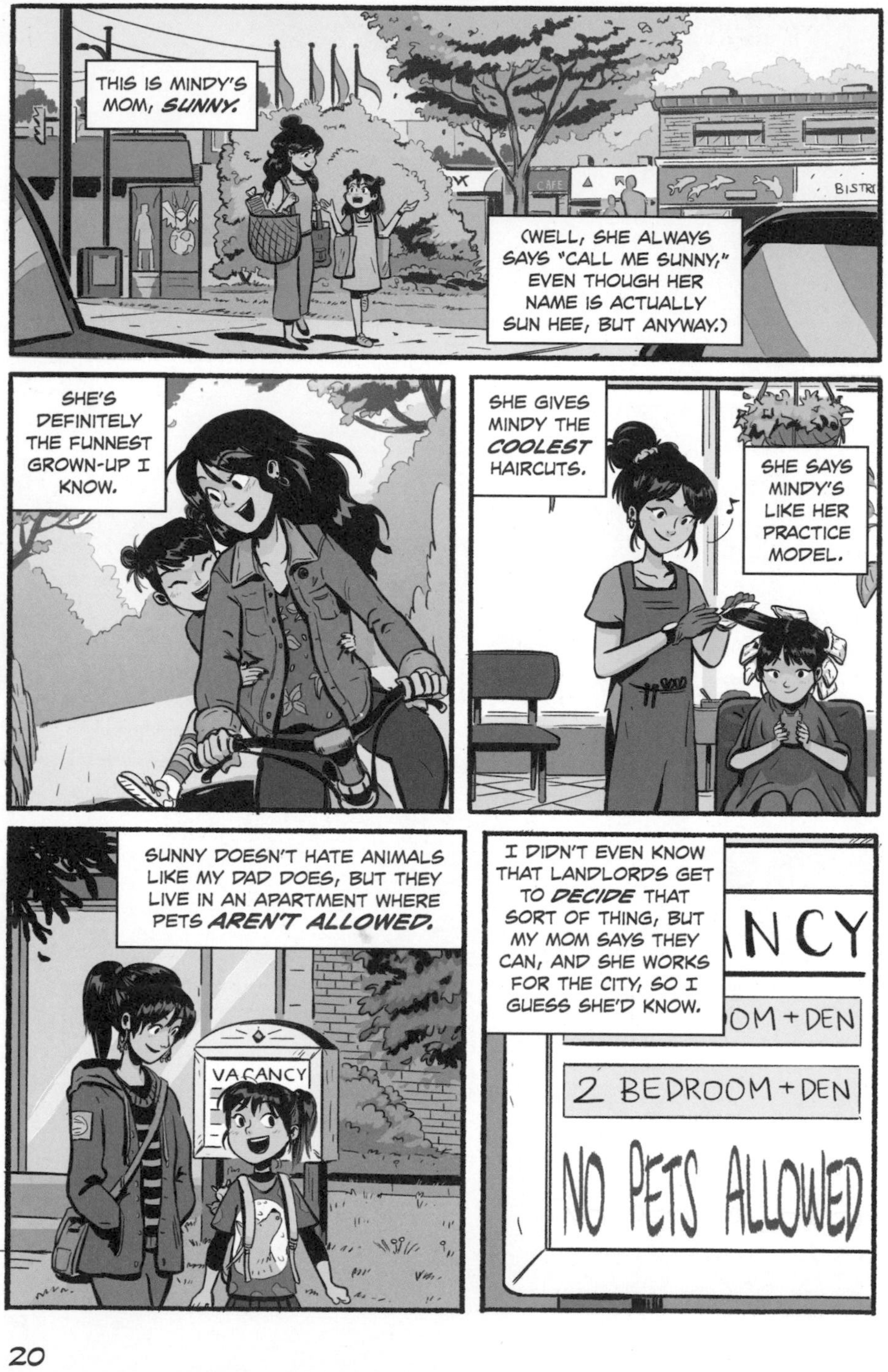
THIS IS MINDY'S MOM, SUNNY.
CAFE
(WELL, SHE ALWAYS SAYS "CALL ME SUNNY," EVEN THOUGH HER NAME IS ACTUALLY SUN HEE, BUT ANYWAY.)
SHE'S DEFINITELY THE FUNNEST GROWN-UP I KNOW.
SHE GIVES MINDY THE COOLEST HAIRCUTS.
SHE SAYS MINDY'S LIKE HER PRACTICE MODEL.
SUNNY DOESN'T HATE ANIMALS LIKE MY DAD DOES, BUT THEY LIVE IN AN APARTMENT WHERE PETS AREN'T ALLOWED.
VACANCY
I DIDN'T EVEN KNOW THAT LANDLORDS GET TO DECIDE THAT SORT OF THING, BUT MY MOM SAYS THEY CAN, AND SHE WORKS FOR THE CITY, SO I GUESS SHE'D KNOW.
ANCY
OM + DEN
2 BEDROOM + DEN
NO PETS ALLOWED

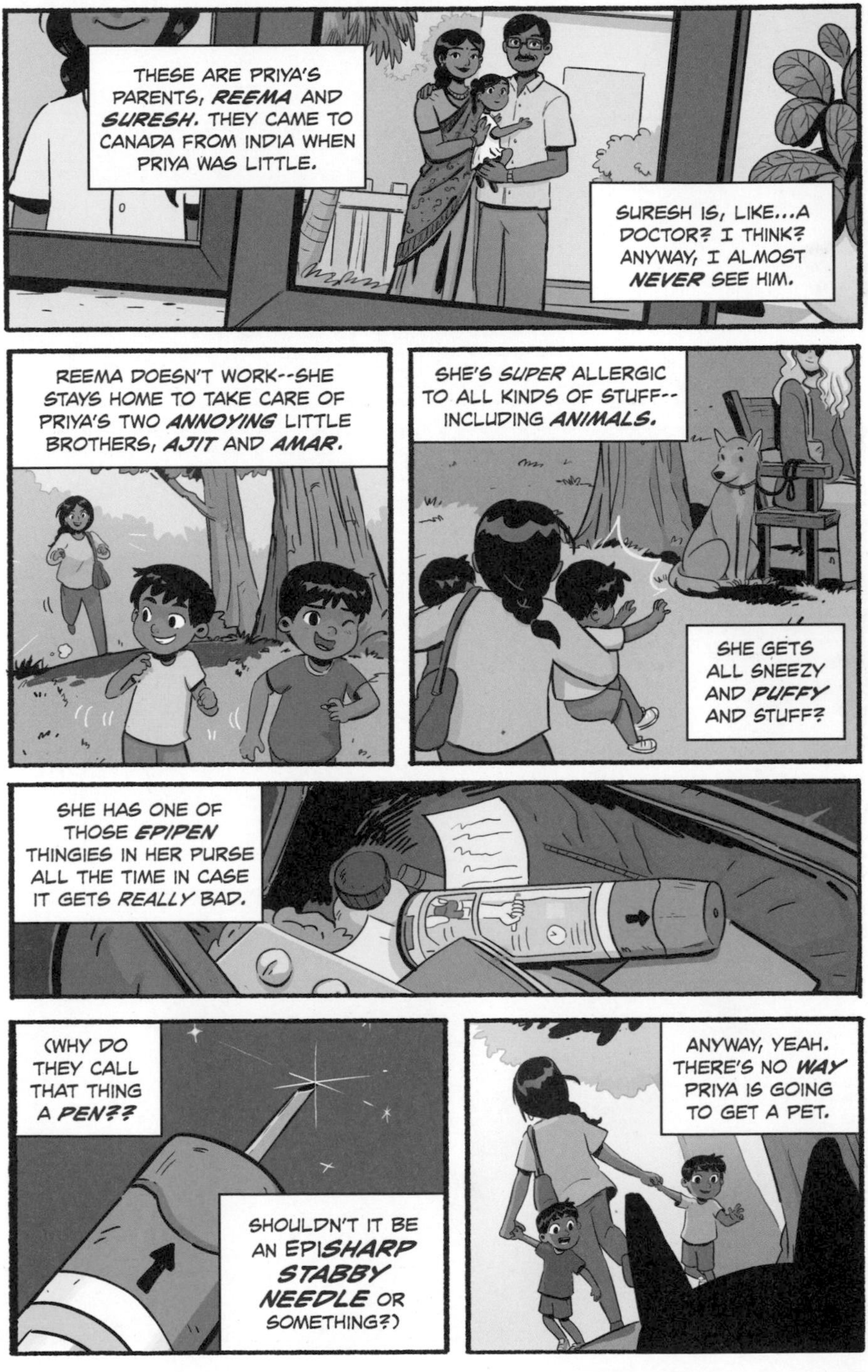
THESE ARE PRIYA'S PARENTS, REEMA AND SURESH. THEY CAME TO CANADA FROM INDIA WHEN PRIYA WAS LITTLE.
SURESH IS, LIKE...A DOCTOR? I THINK? ANYWAY, I ALMOST NEVER SEE HIM.
REEMA DOESN'T WORK--SHE STAYS HOME TO TAKE CARE OF PRIYA'S TWO ANNOYING LITTLE BROTHERS, AJIT AND AMAR.
SHE'S SUPER ALLERGIC TO ALL KINDS OF STUFF--INCLUDING ANIMALS.
SHE GETS ALL SNEEZY AND PUFFY AND STUFF?
SHE HAS ONE OF THOSE EPIPEN THINGIES IN HER PURSE ALL THE TIME IN CASE IT GETS REALLY BAD.
(WHY DO THEY CALL THAT THING A PEN??
SHOULDN'T IT BE AN EPISHARP STABBY NEEDLE OR SOMETHING?)
ANYWAY, YEAH. THERE'S NO WAY PRIYA IS GOING TO GET A PET.

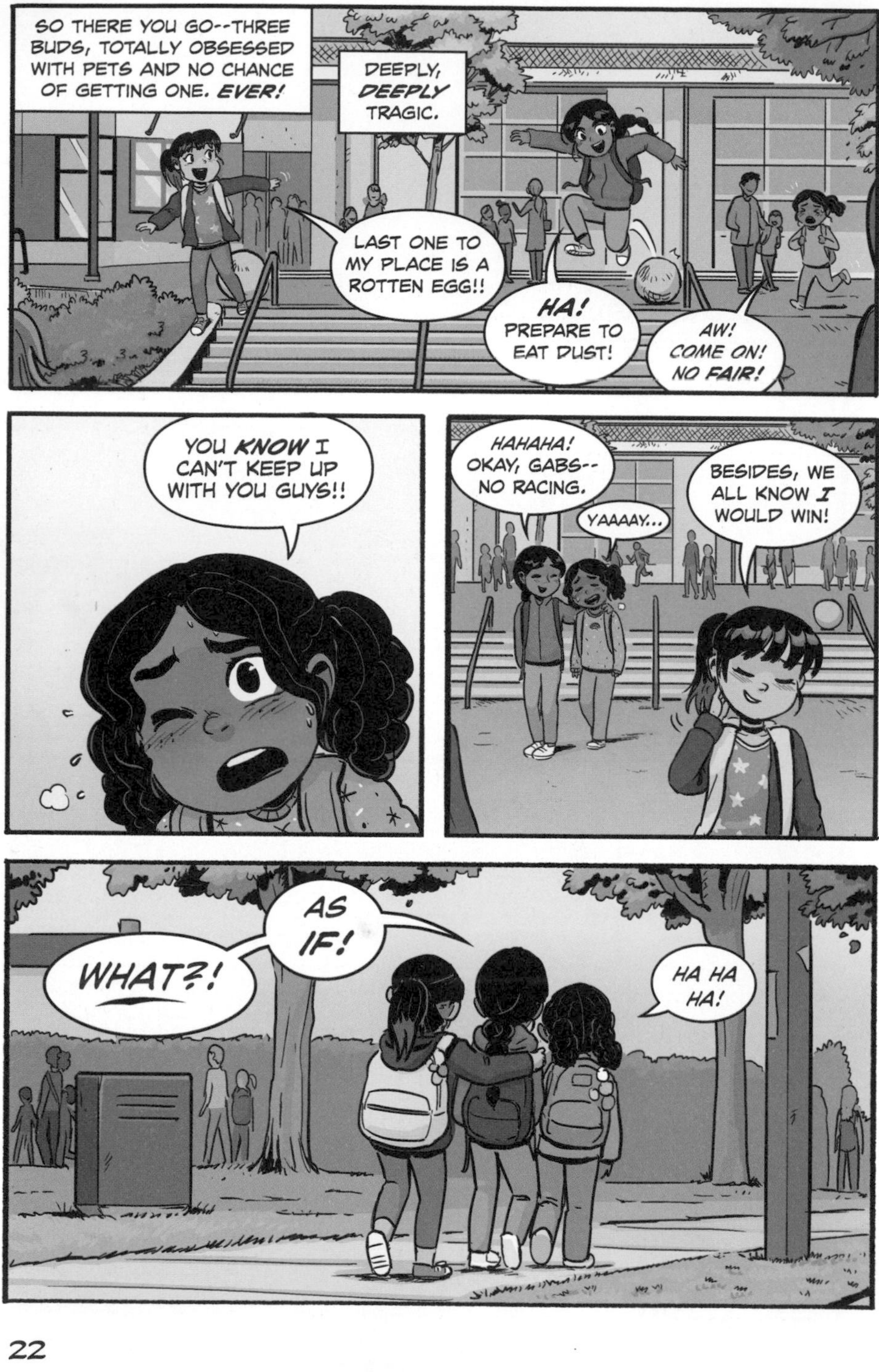
SO THERE YOU GO--THREE BUDS, TOTALLY OBSESSED WITH PETS AND NO CHANCE OF GETTING ONE. *EVER!*
DEEPLY, *DEEPLY* TRAGIC.
LAST ONE TO MY PLACE IS A ROTTEN EGG!!
HA! PREPARE TO EAT DUST!
AW! COME ON! NO FAIR!
YOU *KNOW* I CAN'T KEEP UP WITH YOU GUYS!!
HAHAHA! OKAY, GABS-- NO RACING.
YAAAAY...
BESIDES, WE ALL KNOW *I* WOULD WIN!
WHAT?!
AS IF!
HA HA HA!

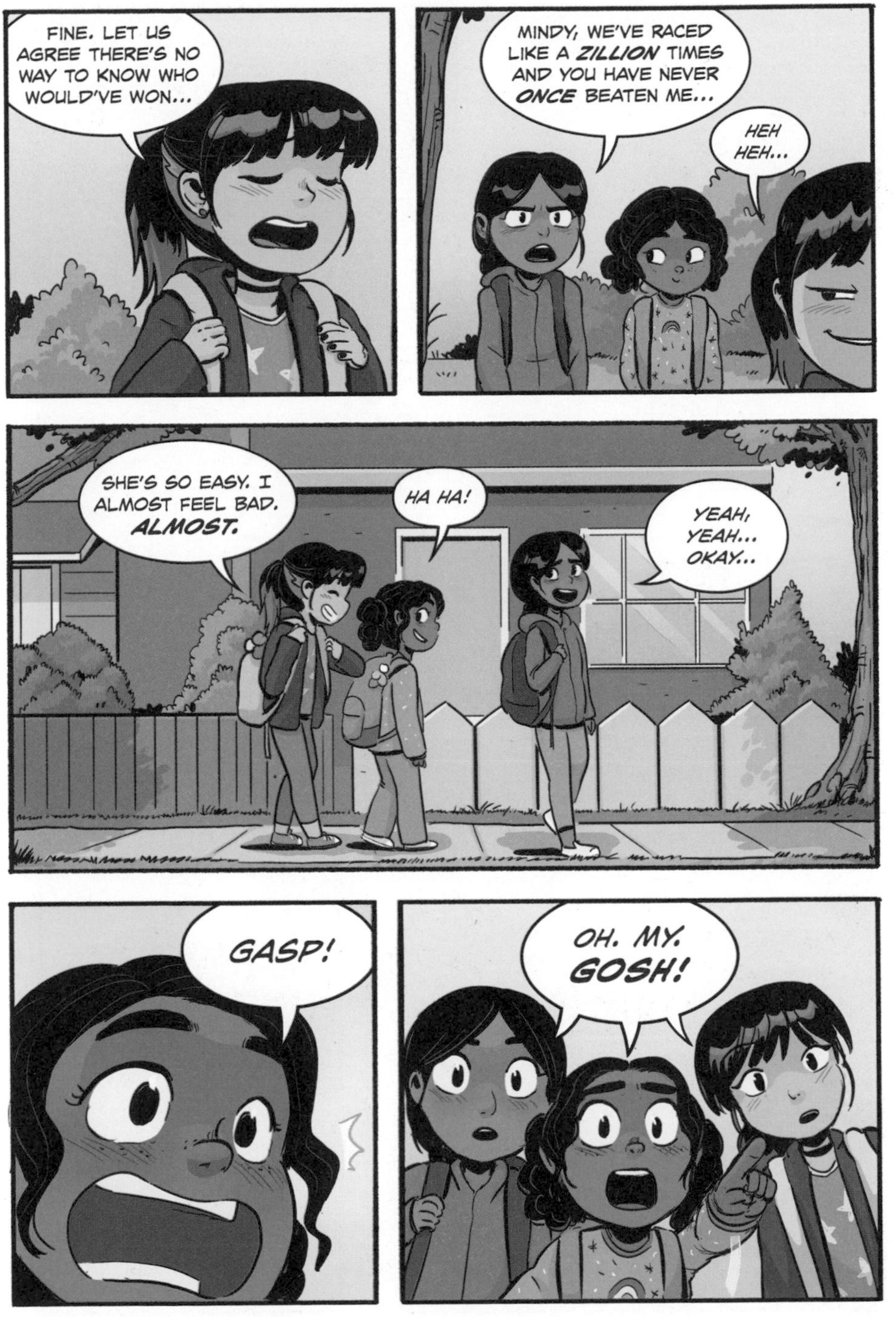
FINE. LET US AGREE THERE'S NO WAY TO KNOW WHO WOULD'VE WON...
MINDY, WE'VE RACED LIKE A ZILLION TIMES AND YOU HAVE NEVER ONCE BEATEN ME...
HEH HEH...
SHE'S SO EASY. I ALMOST FEEL BAD. ALMOST.
HA HA!
YEAH, YEAH... OKAY...
GASP!
OH. MY. GOSH!

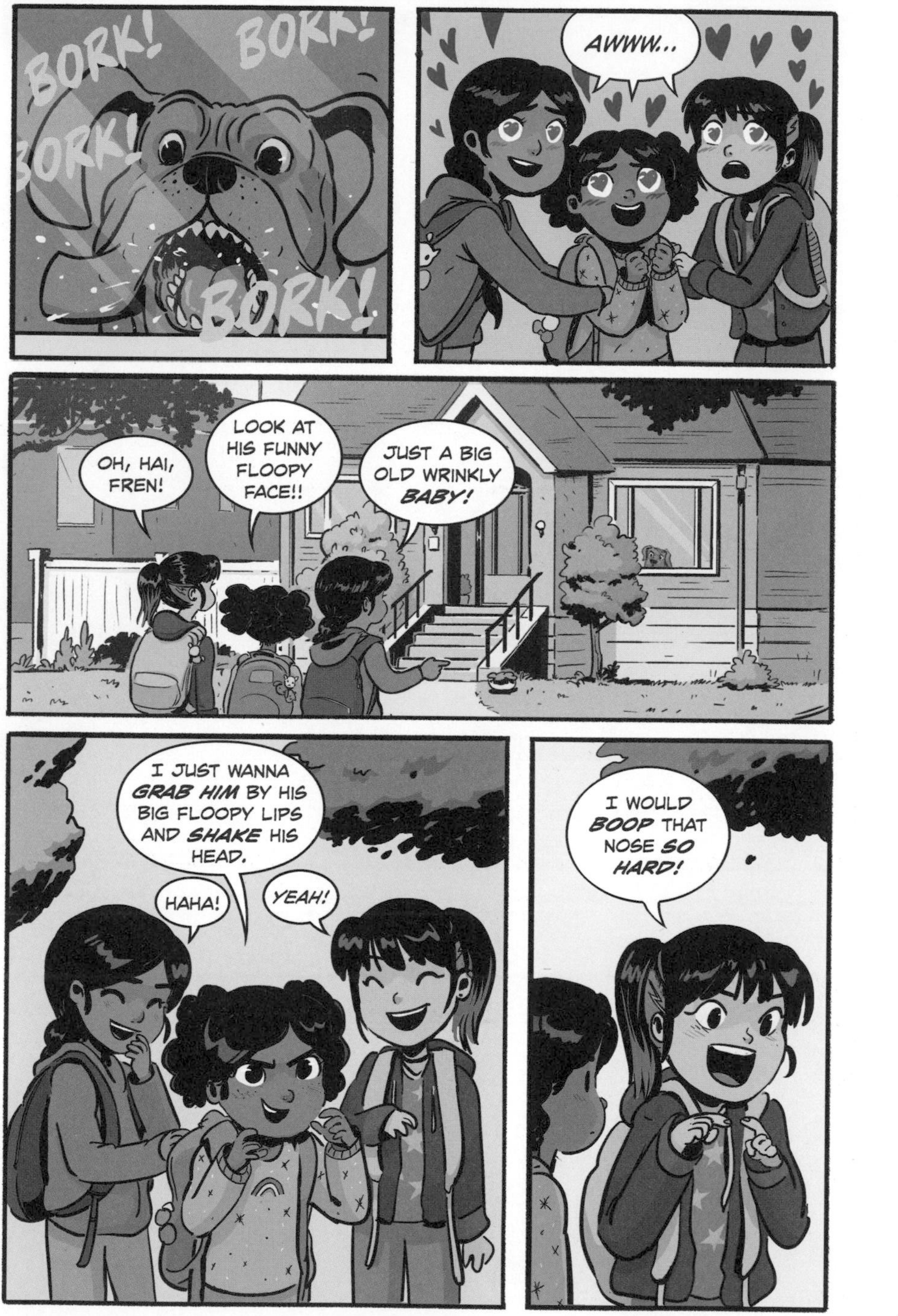
BORK! BORK!
BORK!
BORK!
AWWW...
OH, HAI, FREN!
LOOK AT HIS FUNNY FLOOPY FACE!!
JUST A BIG OLD WRINKLY *BABY!*
I JUST WANNA *GRAB HIM* BY HIS BIG FLOOPY LIPS AND *SHAKE* HIS HEAD.
HAHA!
YEAH!
I WOULD *BOOP* THAT NOSE *SO HARD!*

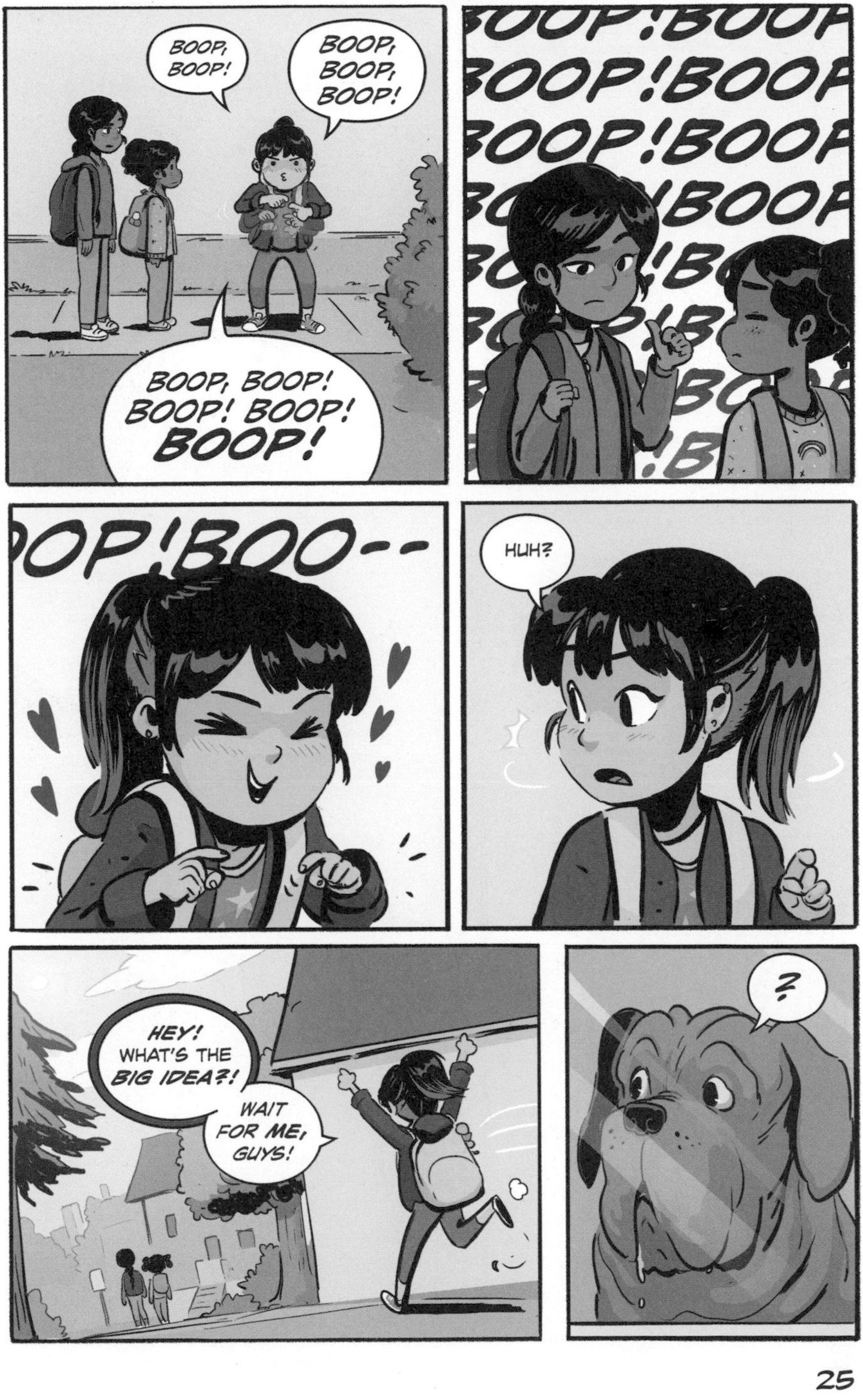
BOOP, BOOP!
BOOP, BOOP, BOOP!
BOOP, BOOP! BOOP! BOOP! BOOP!
BOOP!BOOP BOOP!BOOP BOOP!BOOP
OOP!BOO--
HUH?
HEY! WHAT'S THE BIG IDEA?!
WAIT FOR ME, GUYS!
?

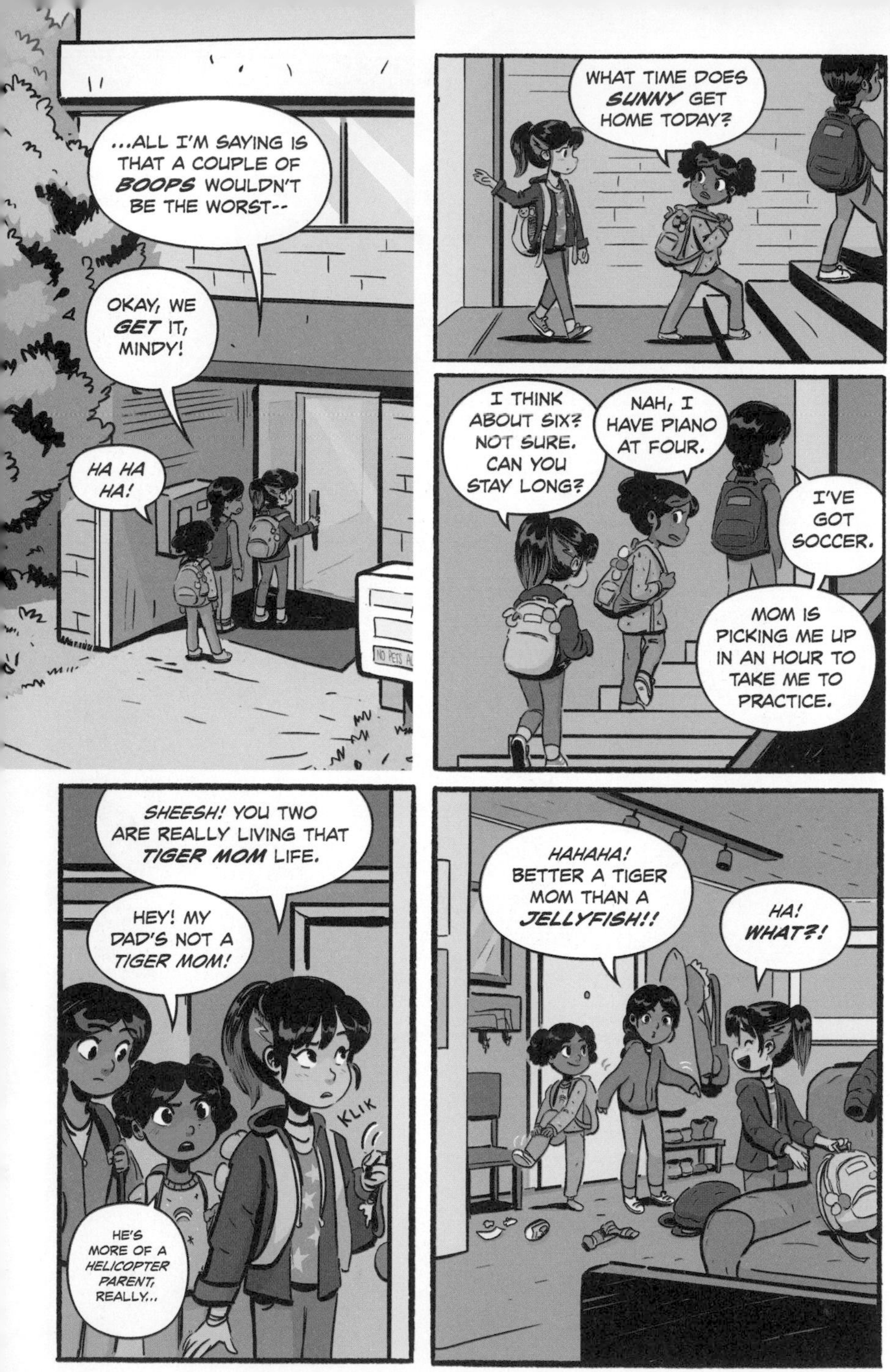
...ALL I'M SAYING IS THAT A COUPLE OF BOOPS WOULDN'T BE THE WORST--
OKAY, WE GET IT, MINDY!
HA HA HA!
NO PETS AL
WHAT TIME DOES SUNNY GET HOME TODAY?
I THINK ABOUT SIX? NOT SURE. CAN YOU STAY LONG?
NAH, I HAVE PIANO AT FOUR.
I'VE GOT SOCCER.
MOM IS PICKING ME UP IN AN HOUR TO TAKE ME TO PRACTICE.
SHEESH! YOU TWO ARE REALLY LIVING THAT TIGER MOM LIFE.
HEY! MY DAD'S NOT A TIGER MOM!
KLIK
HE'S MORE OF A HELICOPTER PARENT, REALLY...
HAHAHA! BETTER A TIGER MOM THAN A JELLYFISH!!
HA! WHAT?!

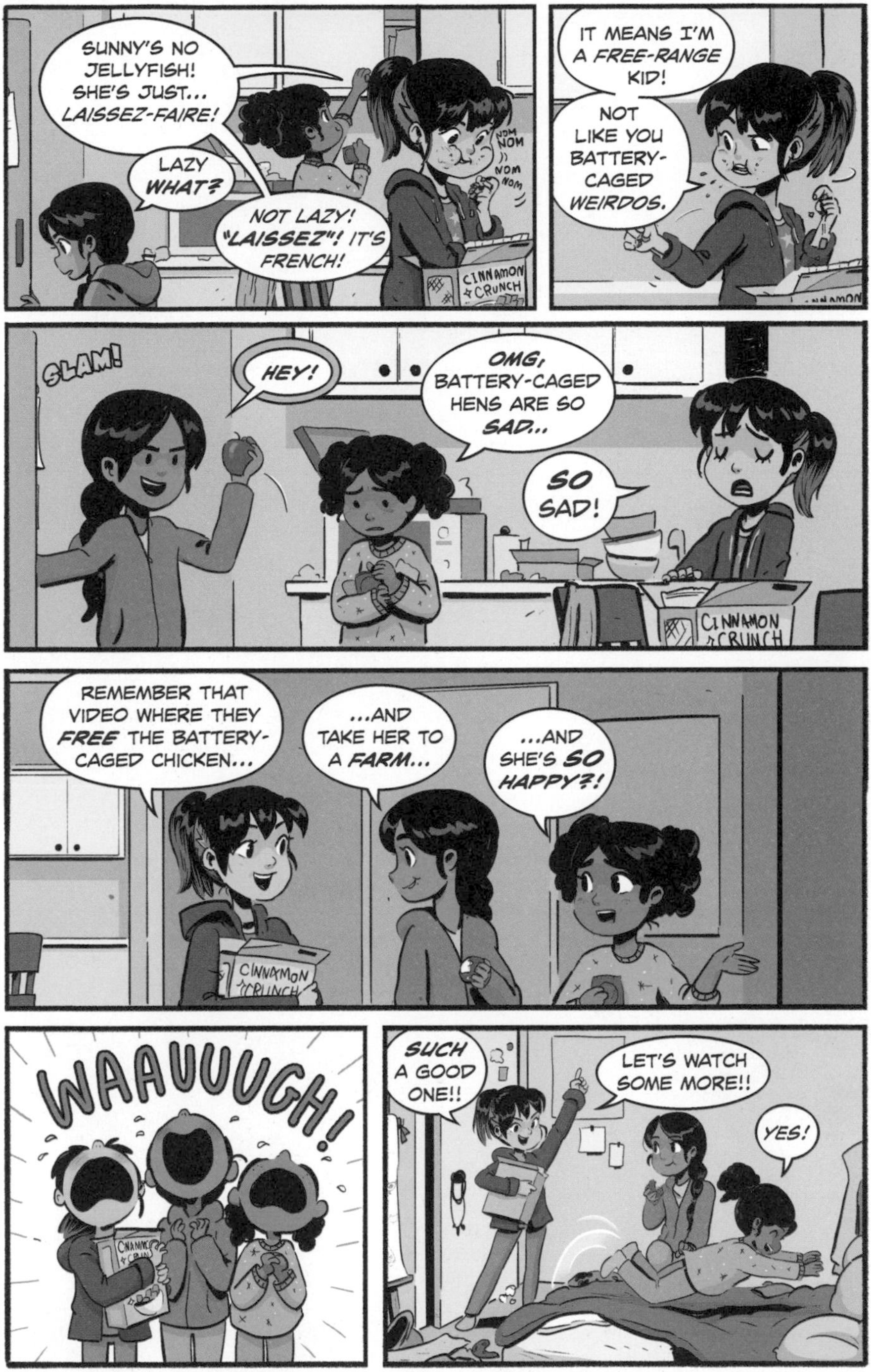
SUNNY'S NO JELLYFISH! SHE'S JUST... LAISSEZ-FAIRE!
LAZY WHAT?
NOT LAZY! "LAISSEZ"! IT'S FRENCH!
NOM NOM
NOM NOM
CINNAMON CRUNCH
IT MEANS I'M A FREE-RANGE KID!
NOT LIKE YOU BATTERY-CAGED WEIRDOS.
SLAM!
HEY!
OMG, BATTERY-CAGED HENS ARE SO SAD...
SO SAD!
CINNAMON CRUNCH
REMEMBER THAT VIDEO WHERE THEY FREE THE BATTERY-CAGED CHICKEN...
...AND TAKE HER TO A FARM...
...AND SHE'S SO HAPPY?!
CINNAMON CRUNCH
WAAUUUGH!
SUCH A GOOD ONE!!
LET'S WATCH SOME MORE!!
YES!

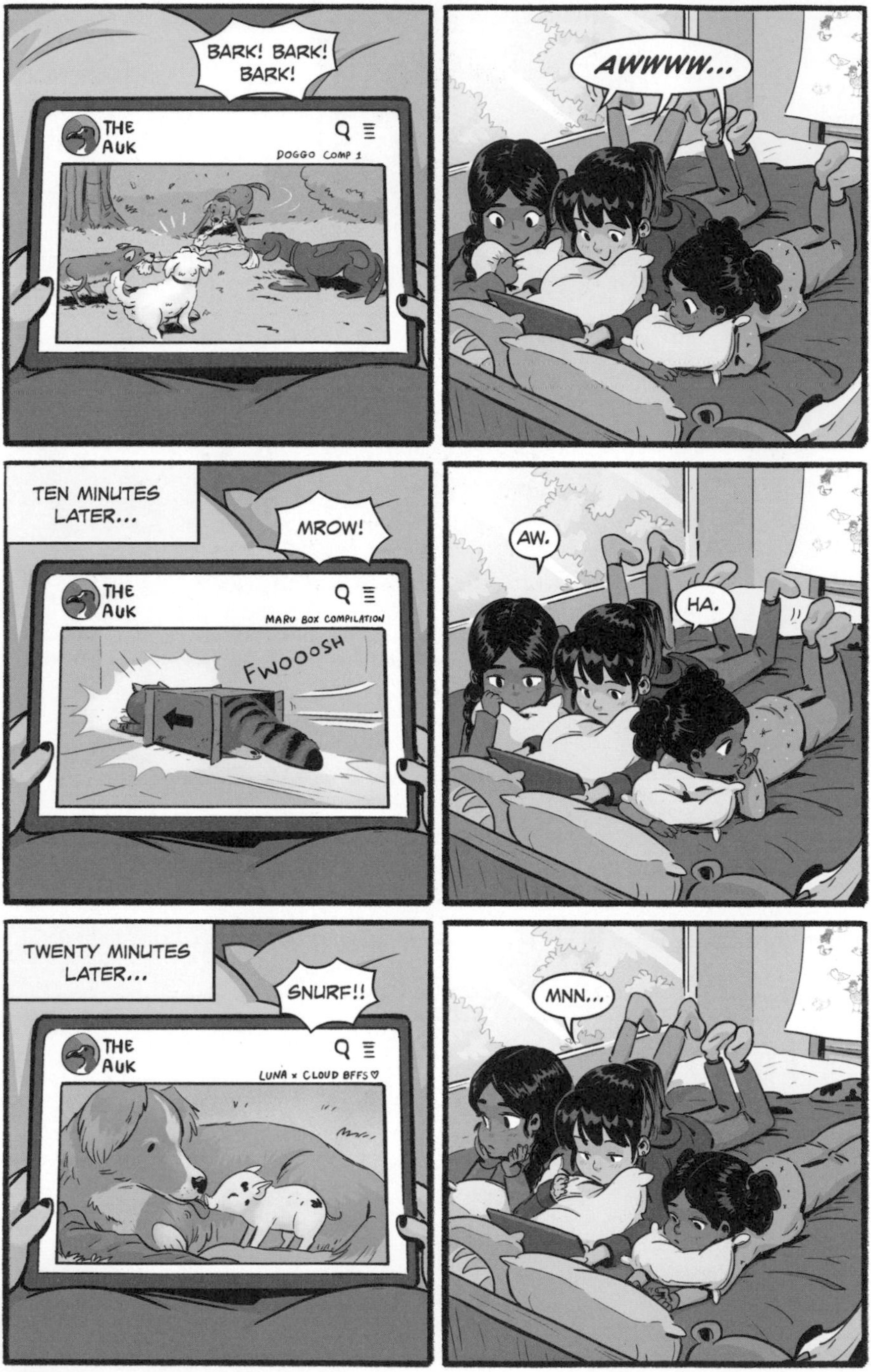

BARK! BARK! BARK!
THE AUK
DOGGO COMP 1
AWWWW...
TEN MINUTES LATER...
MROW!
THE AUK
MARU BOX COMPILATION
FWOOOSH
AW.
HA.
TWENTY MINUTES LATER...
SNURF!!
THE AUK
LUNA × CLOUD BFFS ♡
MNN...

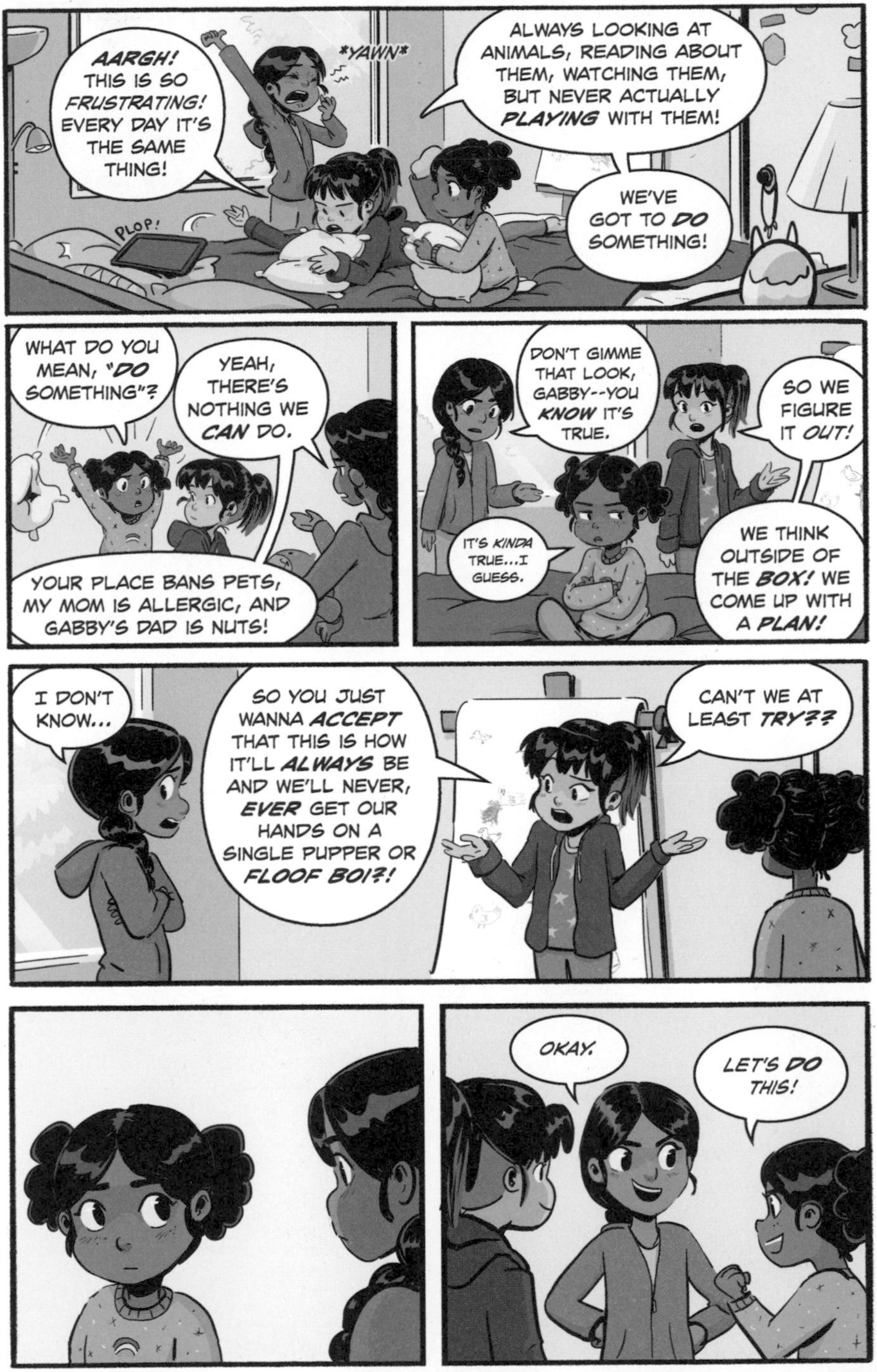
AARGH! THIS IS SO FRUSTRATING! EVERY DAY IT'S THE SAME THING!
YAWN
ALWAYS LOOKING AT ANIMALS, READING ABOUT THEM, WATCHING THEM, BUT NEVER ACTUALLY PLAYING WITH THEM!
PLOP!
WE'VE GOT TO DO SOMETHING!
WHAT DO YOU MEAN, "DO SOMETHING"?
YEAH, THERE'S NOTHING WE CAN DO.
YOUR PLACE BANS PETS, MY MOM IS ALLERGIC, AND GABBY'S DAD IS NUTS!
DON'T GIMME THAT LOOK, GABBY--YOU KNOW IT'S TRUE.
IT'S KINDA TRUE...I GUESS.
SO WE FIGURE IT OUT!
WE THINK OUTSIDE OF THE BOX! WE COME UP WITH A PLAN!
I DON'T KNOW...
SO YOU JUST WANNA ACCEPT THAT THIS IS HOW IT'LL ALWAYS BE AND WE'LL NEVER, EVER GET OUR HANDS ON A SINGLE PUPPER OR FLOOF BOI?!
CAN'T WE AT LEAST TRY??
OKAY.
LET'S DO THIS!

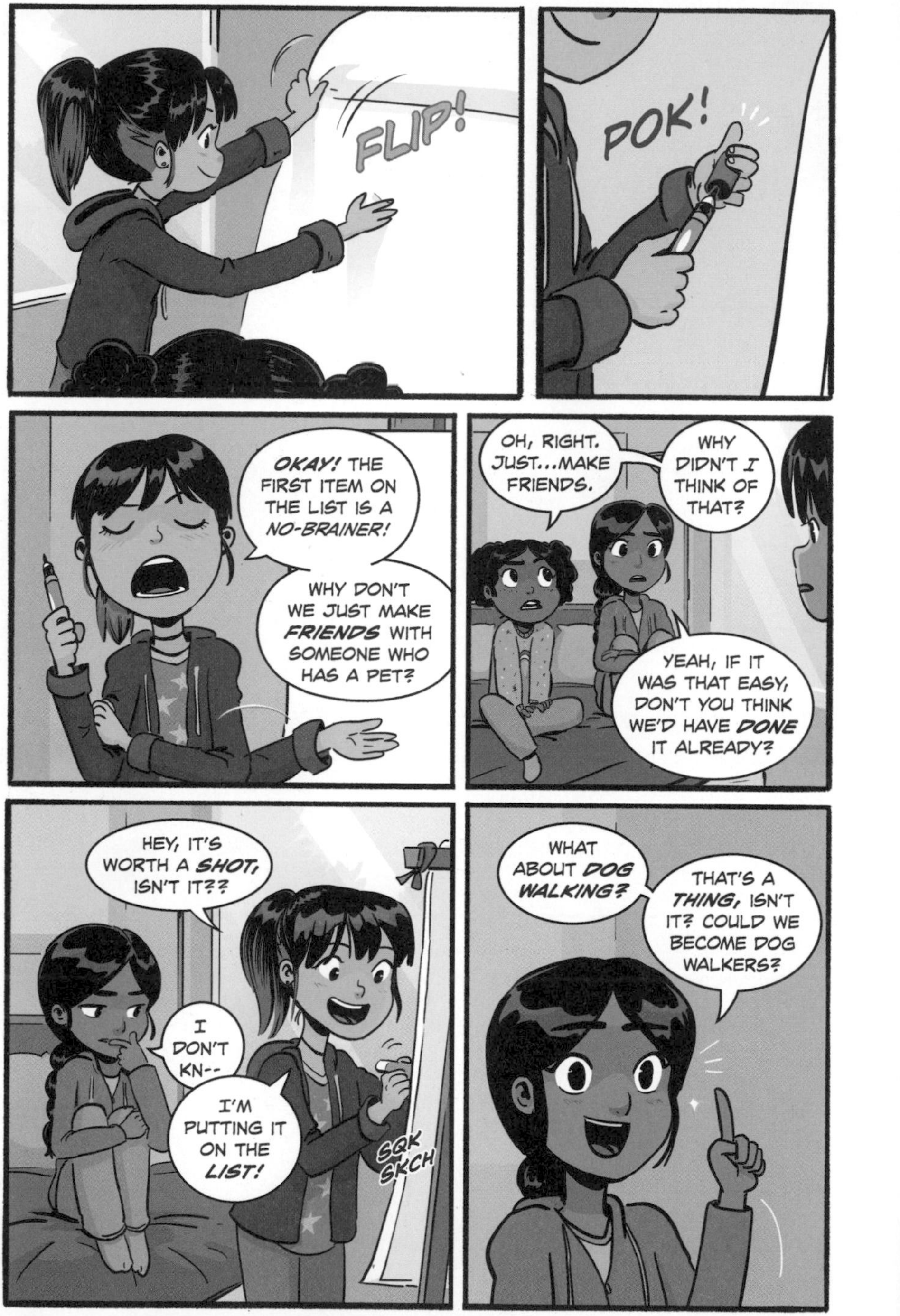
FLIP!
POK!
OKAY! THE FIRST ITEM ON THE LIST IS A NO-BRAINER!
WHY DON'T WE JUST MAKE FRIENDS WITH SOMEONE WHO HAS A PET?
OH, RIGHT. JUST...MAKE FRIENDS.
WHY DIDN'T I THINK OF THAT?
YEAH, IF IT WAS THAT EASY, DON'T YOU THINK WE'D HAVE DONE IT ALREADY?
HEY, IT'S WORTH A SHOT, ISN'T IT??
I DON'T KN--
I'M PUTTING IT ON THE LIST!
SQK SKCH
WHAT ABOUT DOG WALKING?
THAT'S A THING, ISN'T IT? COULD WE BECOME DOG WALKERS?

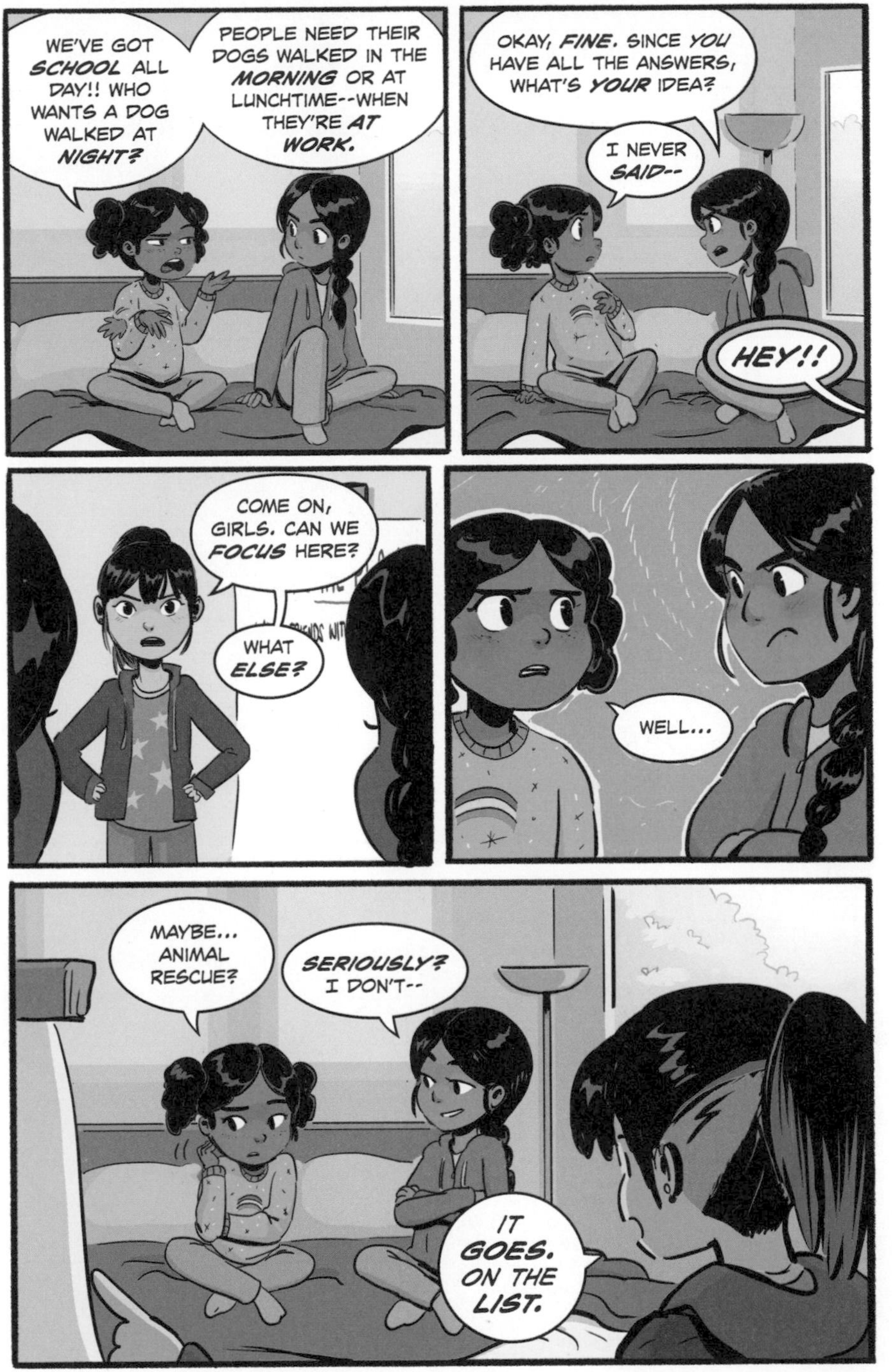
WE'VE GOT *SCHOOL* ALL DAY!! WHO WANTS A DOG WALKED AT *NIGHT?*
PEOPLE NEED THEIR DOGS WALKED IN THE *MORNING* OR AT LUNCHTIME--WHEN THEY'RE *AT WORK.*
OKAY, *FINE.* SINCE *YOU* HAVE ALL THE ANSWERS, WHAT'S *YOUR* IDEA?
I NEVER *SAID--*
HEY!!
COME ON, GIRLS. CAN WE *FOCUS* HERE?
WHAT *ELSE?*
WELL...
MAYBE... ANIMAL RESCUE?
SERIOUSLY? I DON'T--
IT *GOES.* ON THE *LIST.*

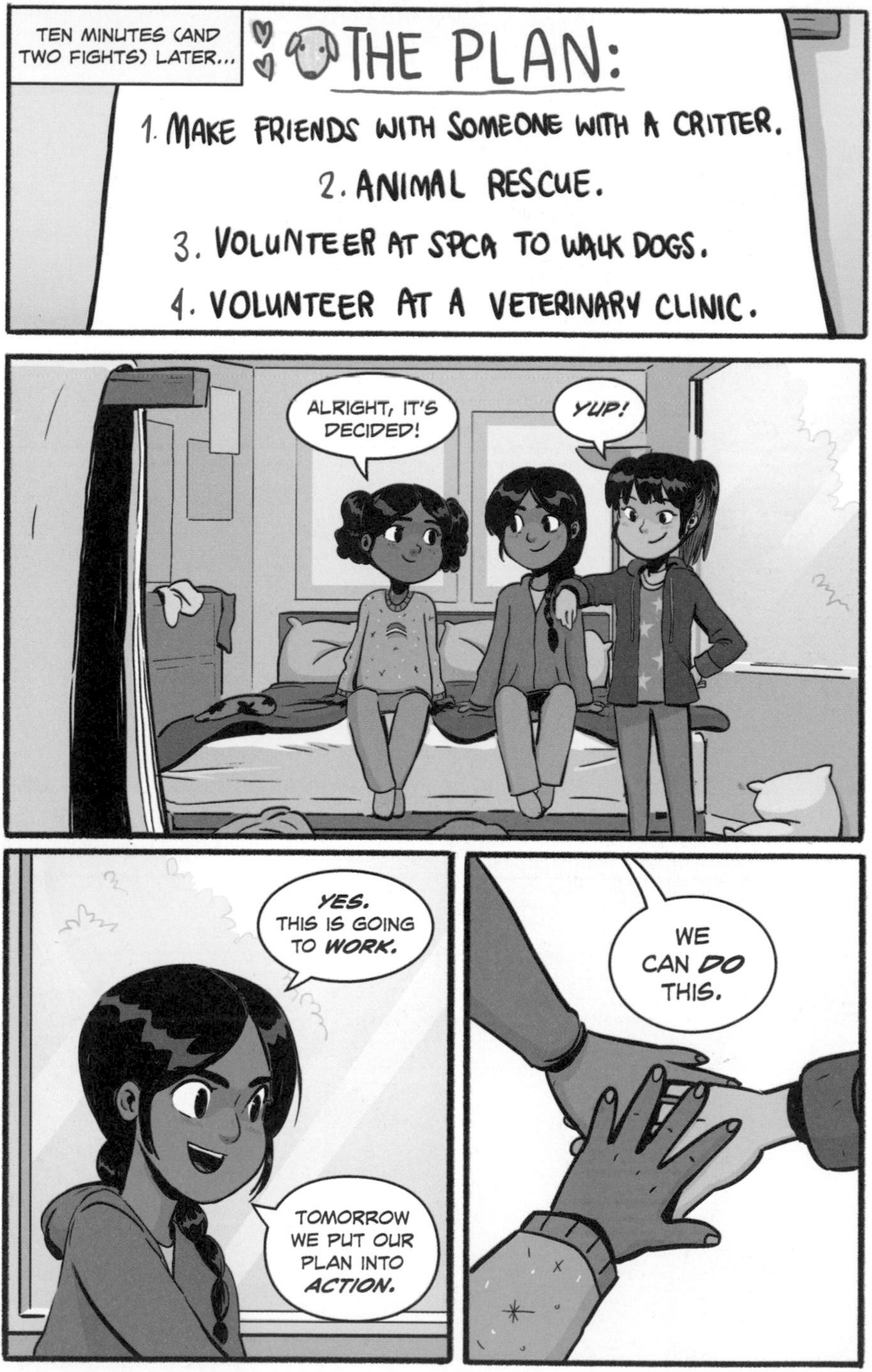
TEN MINUTES (AND TWO FIGHTS) LATER...
THE PLAN:
1. MAKE FRIENDS WITH SOMEONE WITH A CRITTER.
2. ANIMAL RESCUE.
3. VOLUNTEER AT SPCA TO WALK DOGS.
4. VOLUNTEER AT A VETERINARY CLINIC.
ALRIGHT, IT'S DECIDED!
YUP!
YES. THIS IS GOING TO *WORK.*
TOMORROW WE PUT OUR PLAN INTO *ACTION.*
WE CAN *DO* THIS.

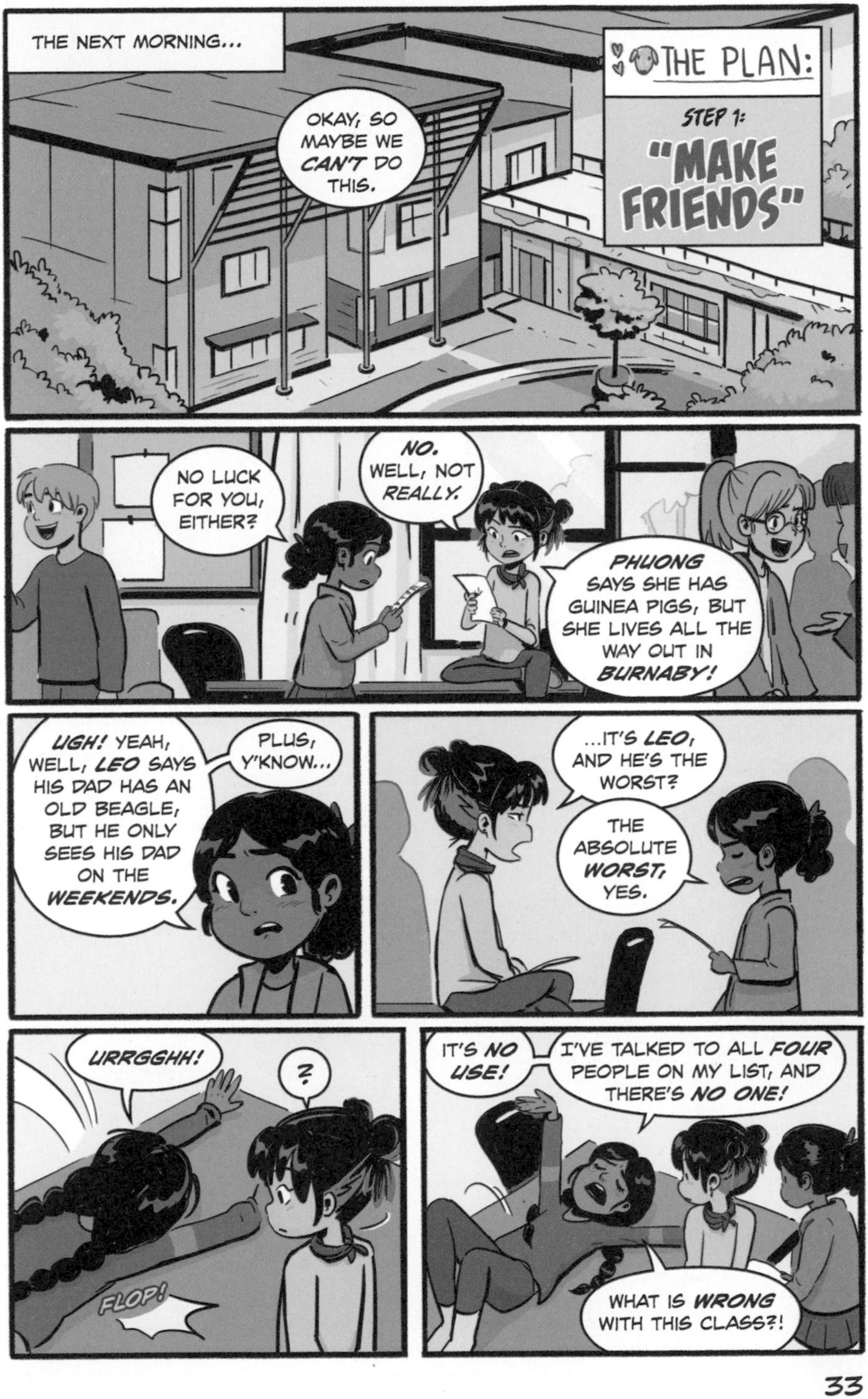
THE NEXT MORNING...
THE PLAN:
STEP 1:
"MAKE FRIENDS"
OKAY, SO MAYBE WE CAN'T DO THIS.
NO LUCK FOR YOU, EITHER?
NO. WELL, NOT REALLY.
PHUONG SAYS SHE HAS GUINEA PIGS, BUT SHE LIVES ALL THE WAY OUT IN BURNABY!
UGH! YEAH, WELL, LEO SAYS HIS DAD HAS AN OLD BEAGLE, BUT HE ONLY SEES HIS DAD ON THE WEEKENDS.
PLUS, Y'KNOW...
...IT'S LEO, AND HE'S THE WORST?
THE ABSOLUTE WORST, YES.
URRGGHH!
?
FLOP!
IT'S NO USE!
I'VE TALKED TO ALL FOUR PEOPLE ON MY LIST, AND THERE'S NO ONE!
WHAT IS WRONG WITH THIS CLASS?!

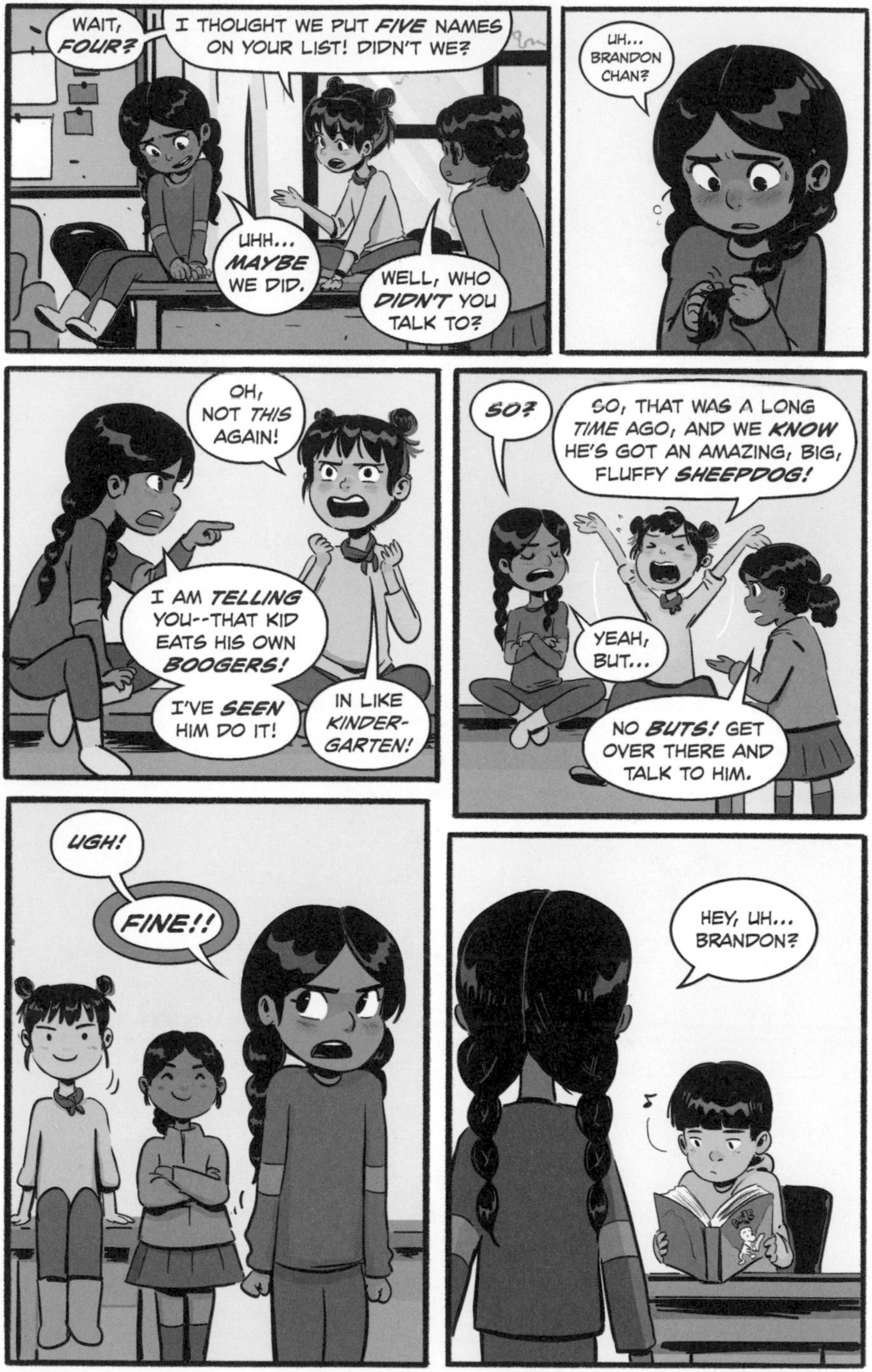
WAIT, *FOUR?*
I THOUGHT WE PUT *FIVE* NAMES ON YOUR LIST! DIDN'T WE?
UHH... *MAYBE* WE DID.
WELL, WHO *DIDN'T* YOU TALK TO?
UH... BRANDON CHAN?
OH, NOT *THIS* AGAIN!
I AM *TELLING* YOU--THAT KID EATS HIS OWN *BOOGERS!*
I'VE *SEEN* HIM DO IT!
IN LIKE *KINDERGARTEN!*
SO?
SO, THAT WAS A LONG *TIME* AGO, AND WE *KNOW* HE'S GOT AN AMAZING, BIG, FLUFFY *SHEEPDOG!*
YEAH, BUT...
NO *BUTS!* GET OVER THERE AND TALK TO HIM.
UGH!
FINE!!
HEY, UH... BRANDON?

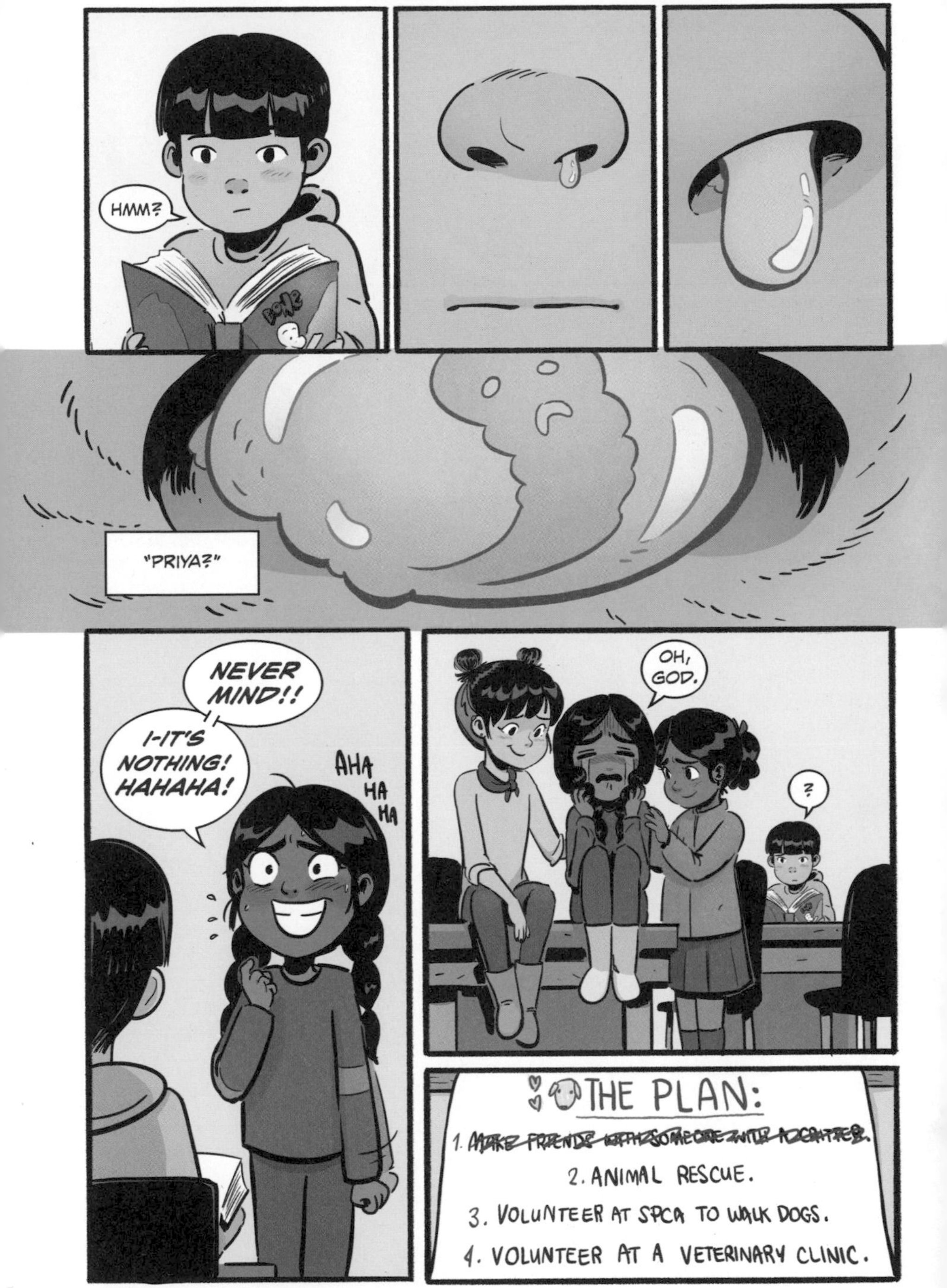
HMM?
"PRIYA?"
NEVER MIND!!
I-IT'S NOTHING! HAHAHA!
AHA HA HA
OH, GOD.
?
THE PLAN:
1. ~~MAKE FRIENDS WITH SOMEONE WITH A CRITTER.~~
2. ANIMAL RESCUE.
3. VOLUNTEER AT SPCA TO WALK DOGS.
4. VOLUNTEER AT A VETERINARY CLINIC.

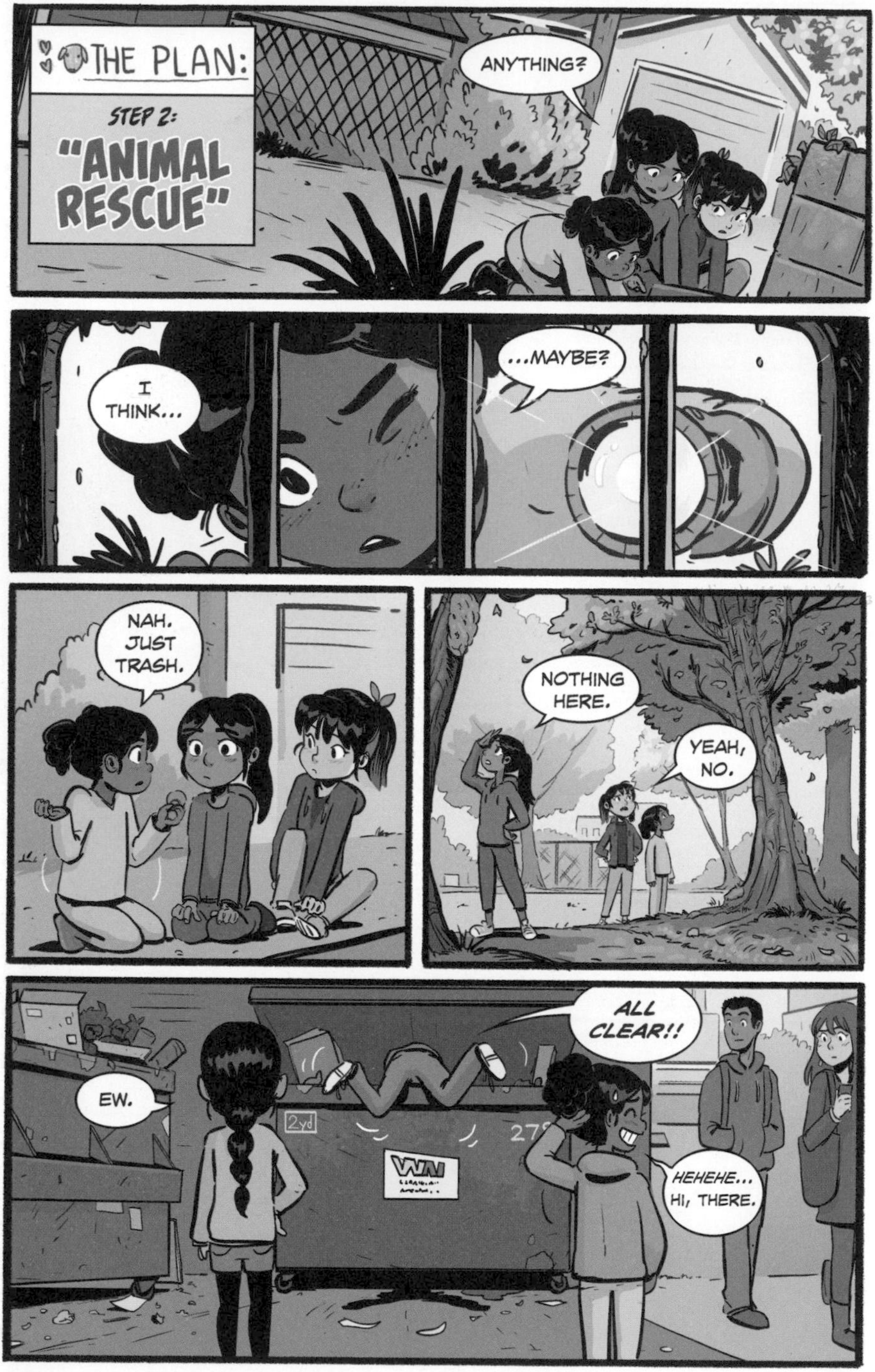
THE PLAN:
STEP 2:
"ANIMAL RESCUE"
ANYTHING?
I THINK...
...MAYBE?
NAH. JUST TRASH.
NOTHING HERE.
YEAH, NO.
ALL CLEAR!!
EW.
HEHEHE... HI, THERE.

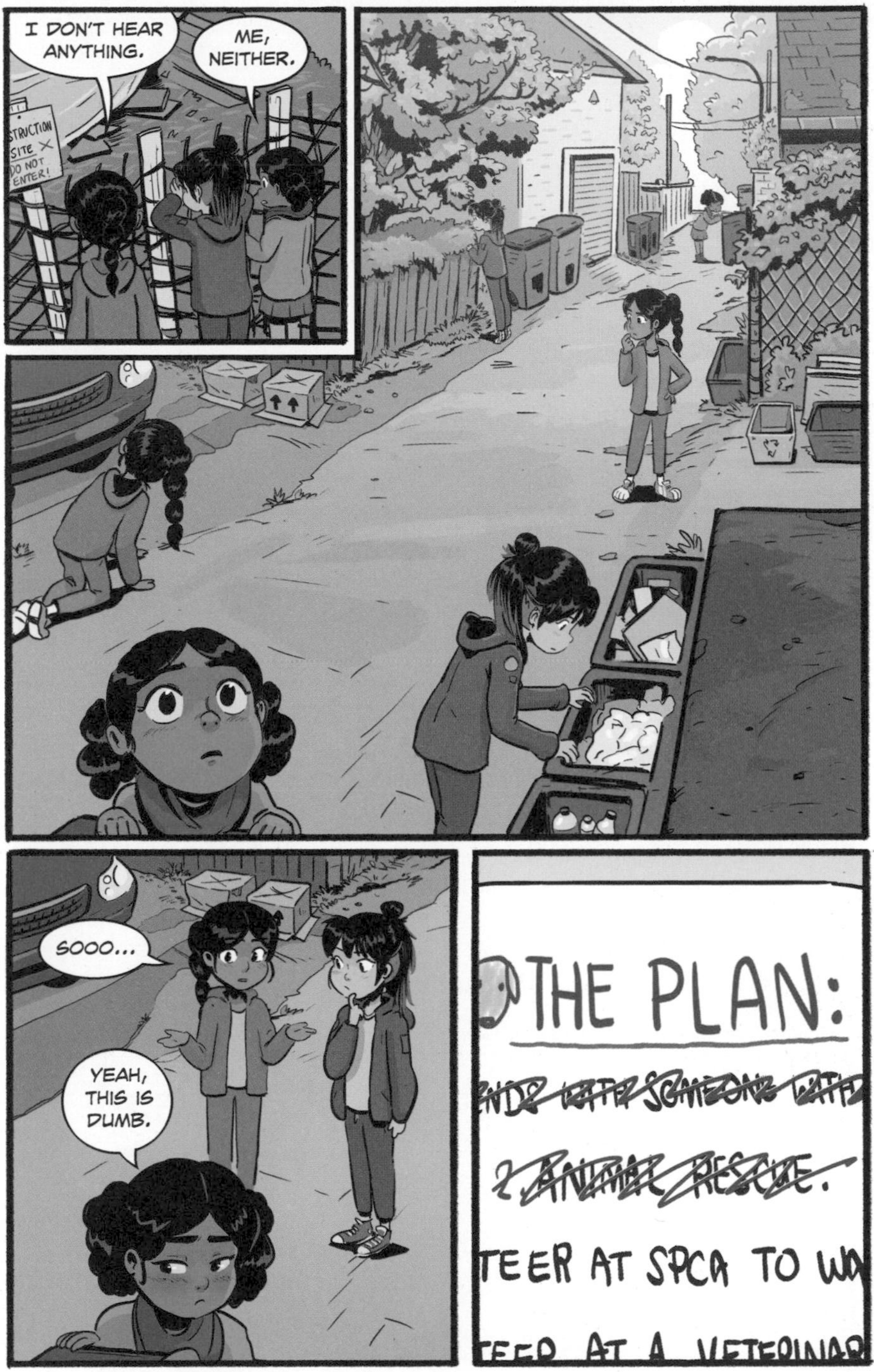
I DON'T HEAR ANYTHING.
ME, NEITHER.
STRUCTION SITE DO NOT ENTER!
SOOO...
YEAH, THIS IS DUMB.
THE PLAN:
TEER AT SPCA TO WA
TEER AT A VETERINAR

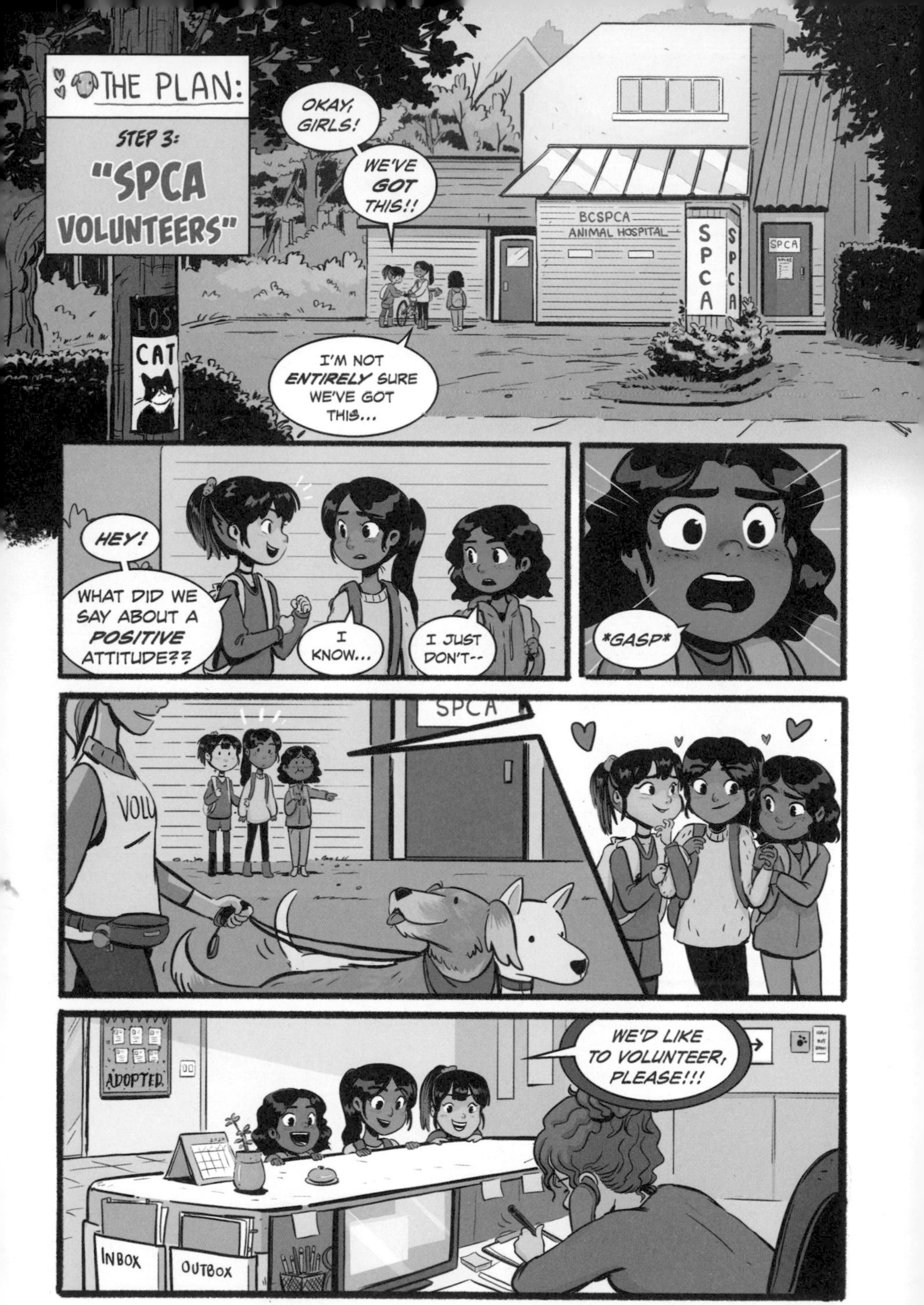
THE PLAN:
STEP 3:
"SPCA VOLUNTEERS"
OKAY, GIRLS!
WE'VE GOT THIS!!
BCSPCA ANIMAL HOSPITAL
SPCA
SPCA
SPCA
LOST CAT
I'M NOT ENTIRELY SURE WE'VE GOT THIS...
HEY!
WHAT DID WE SAY ABOUT A POSITIVE ATTITUDE??
I KNOW...
I JUST DON'T--
GASP
SPCA
VOLU
ADOPTED
WE'D LIKE TO VOLUNTEER, PLEASE!!!
INBOX
OUTBOX

CURRENTLY WE'VE RECEIVED THE MAXIMUM NUMBER OF APPLICATIONS THAT WE CAN PROCESS...

OUTBOX

BUT YOU CAN FILL OUT THIS FORM...

AND WE'LL BE DOING A NEW INTAKE IN APRIL--

VOLUNTEER APPLICATION

THUNK!

APRIL?!

OH, I'M SORRY, GIRLS. I DIDN'T EVEN LOOK!

I'M JUST SO BUSY RIGHT NOW...

...BUT I'M AFRAID YOU NEED TO BE NINETEEN TO VOLUNTEER HERE, ANYWAY.

OH.

OKAY...

💜🐾THE PLAN:
1. ~~MAKE FRIENDS WITH SOMEONE WITH A COMPUTER~~
2. ~~ANIMAL RESCUE~~
3. ~~VOLUNTEER AT SPCA TO WALK DOGS.~~
4. VOLUNTEER AT A VETERINARY CLINIC

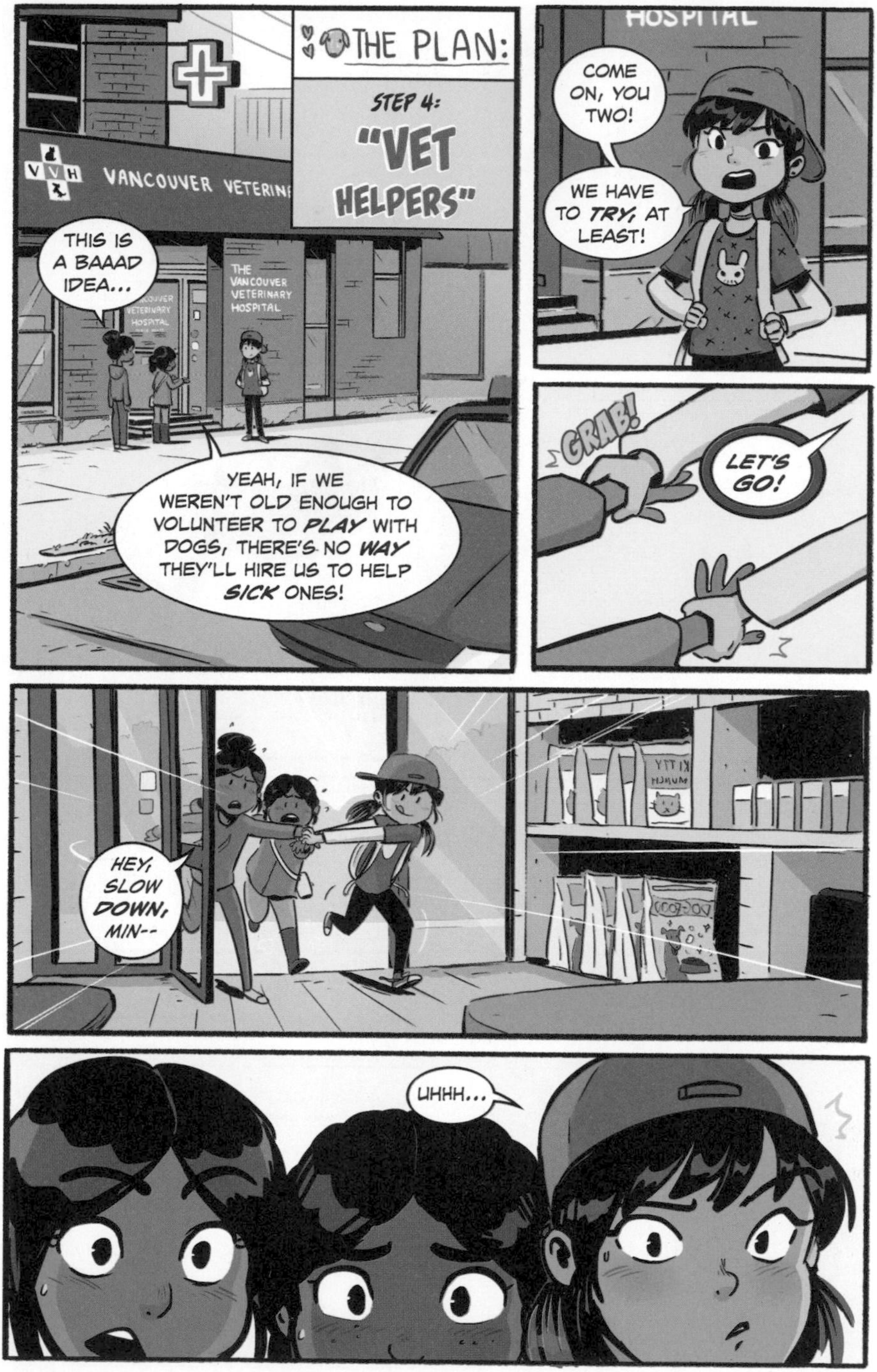
THE PLAN:
STEP 4:
"VET HELPERS"
VANCOUVER VETERINA
VVH
THE VANCOUVER VETERINARY HOSPITAL
THIS IS A BAAAD IDEA...
YEAH, IF WE WEREN'T OLD ENOUGH TO VOLUNTEER TO PLAY WITH DOGS, THERE'S NO WAY THEY'LL HIRE US TO HELP SICK ONES!
HOSPITAL
COME ON, YOU TWO!
WE HAVE TO TRY, AT LEAST!
GRAB!
LET'S GO!
KITTY MUNCH
HEY, SLOW DOWN, MIN--
UHHH...

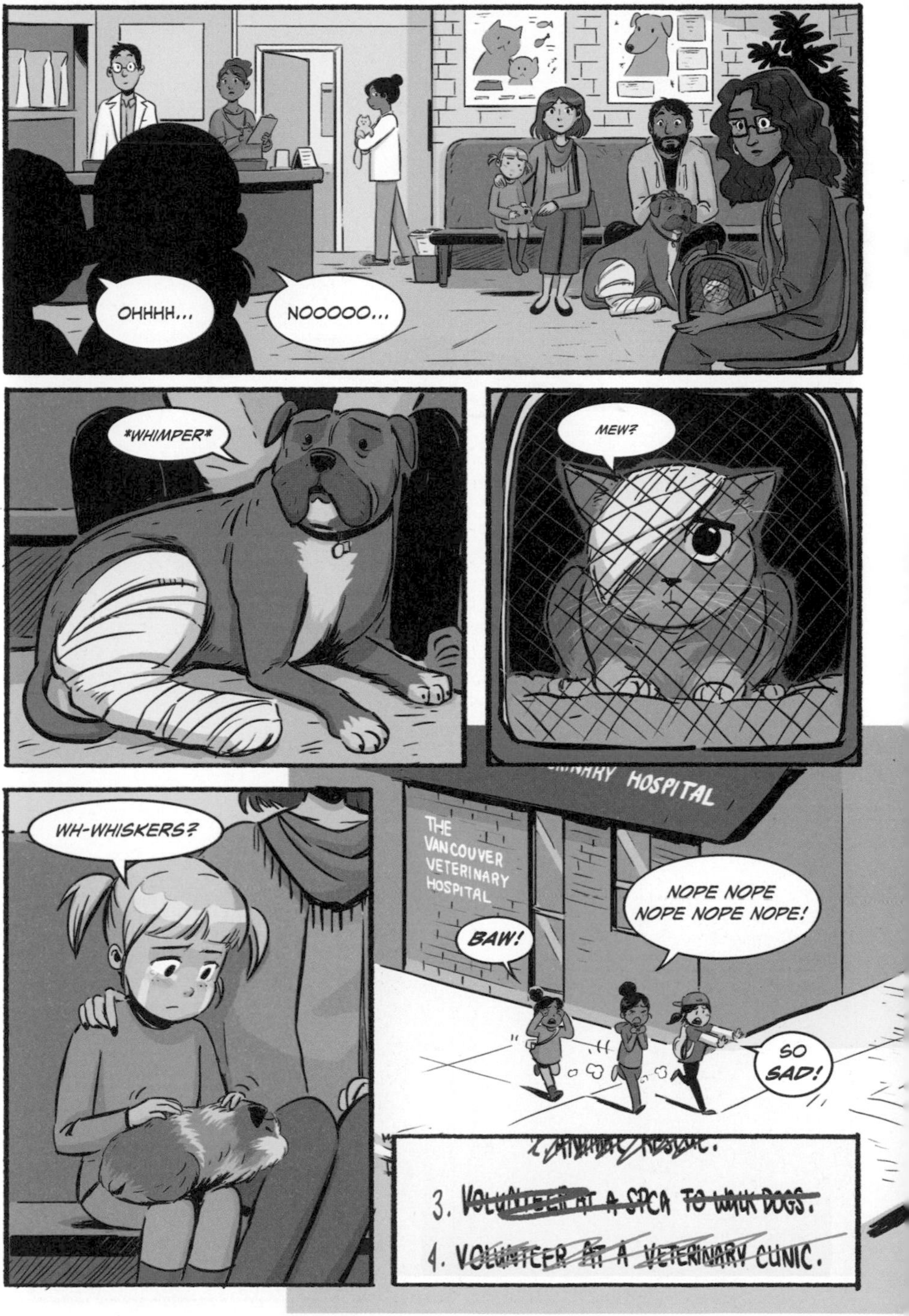
OHHHH...
NOOOOO...
WHIMPER
MEW?
WH-WHISKERS?
THE VANCOUVER VETERINARY HOSPITAL
BAW!
NOPE NOPE NOPE NOPE NOPE!
SO SAD!
3. VOLUNTEER AT A SPCA TO WALK DOGS.
4. VOLUNTEER AT A VETERINARY CLINIC.

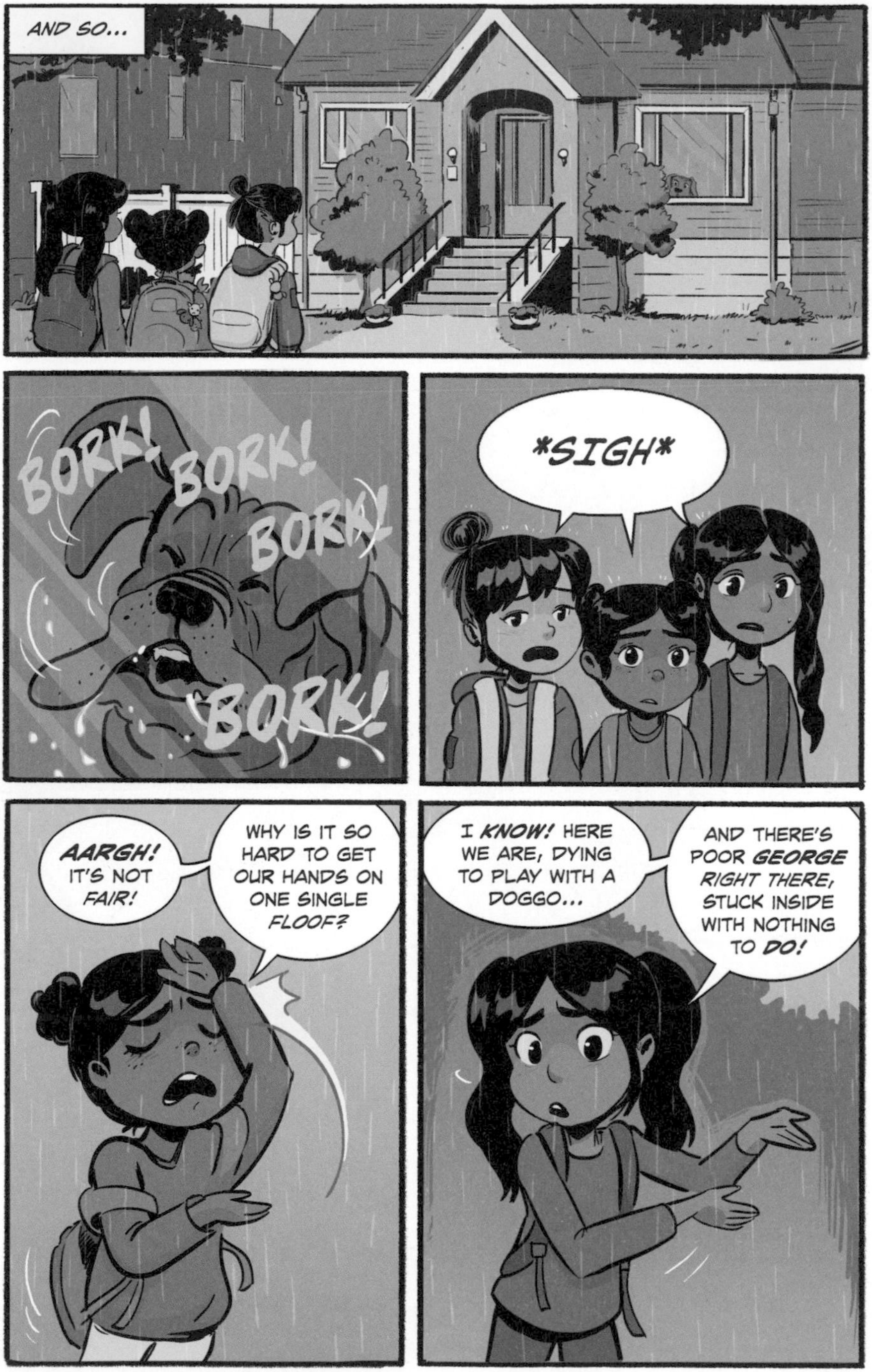
AND SO...
BORK! BORK! BORK! BORK!
SIGH
AARGH! IT'S NOT FAIR!
WHY IS IT SO HARD TO GET OUR HANDS ON ONE SINGLE FLOOF?
I KNOW! HERE WE ARE, DYING TO PLAY WITH A DOGGO...
AND THERE'S POOR GEORGE RIGHT THERE, STUCK INSIDE WITH NOTHING TO DO!

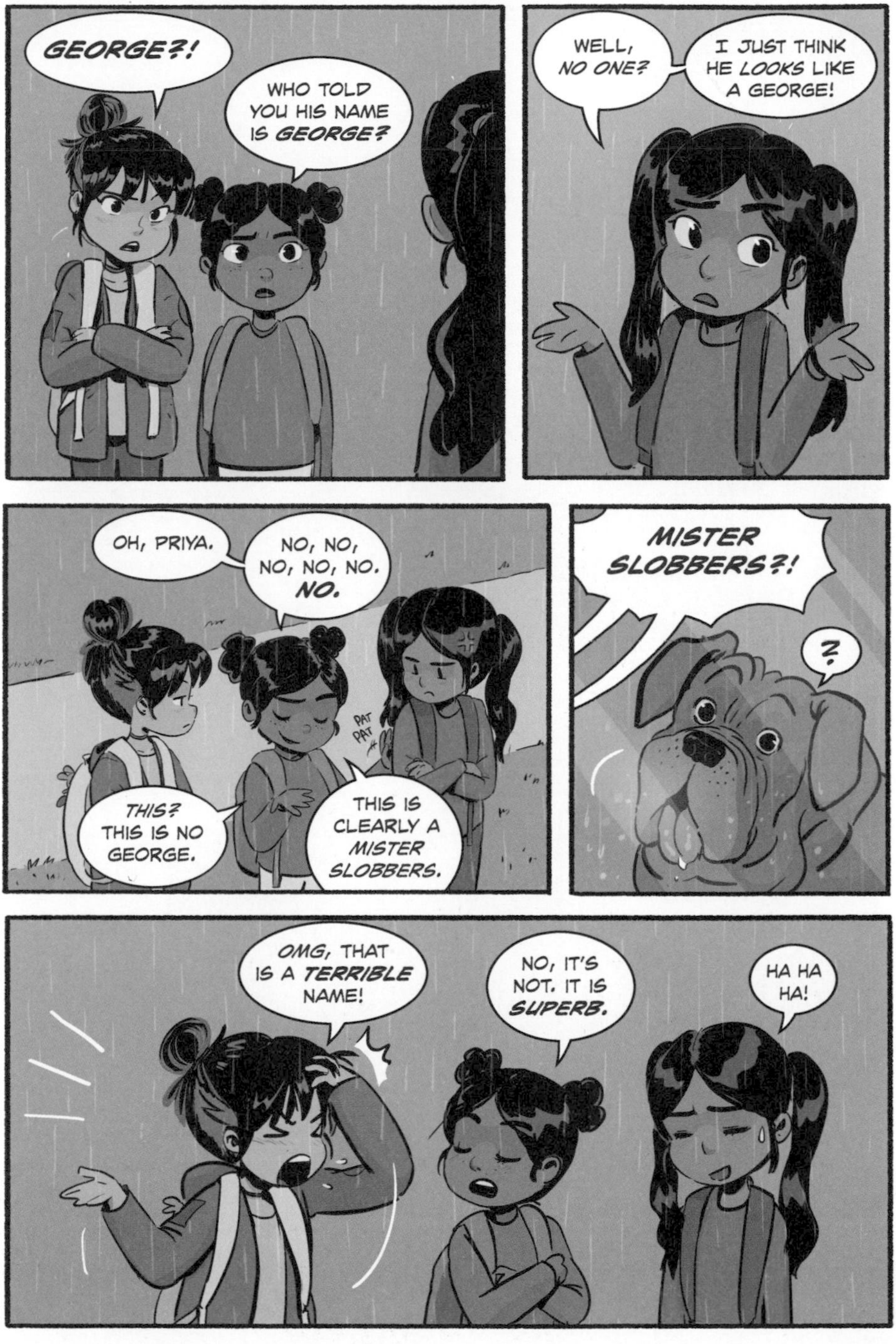
GEORGE?!
WHO TOLD YOU HIS NAME IS GEORGE?
WELL, NO ONE?
I JUST THINK HE LOOKS LIKE A GEORGE!
OH, PRIYA.
NO, NO, NO, NO, NO. NO.
THIS? THIS IS NO GEORGE.
PAT PAT
THIS IS CLEARLY A MISTER SLOBBERS.
MISTER SLOBBERS?!
?
OMG, THAT IS A TERRIBLE NAME!
NO, IT'S NOT. IT IS SUPERB.
HA HA HA!

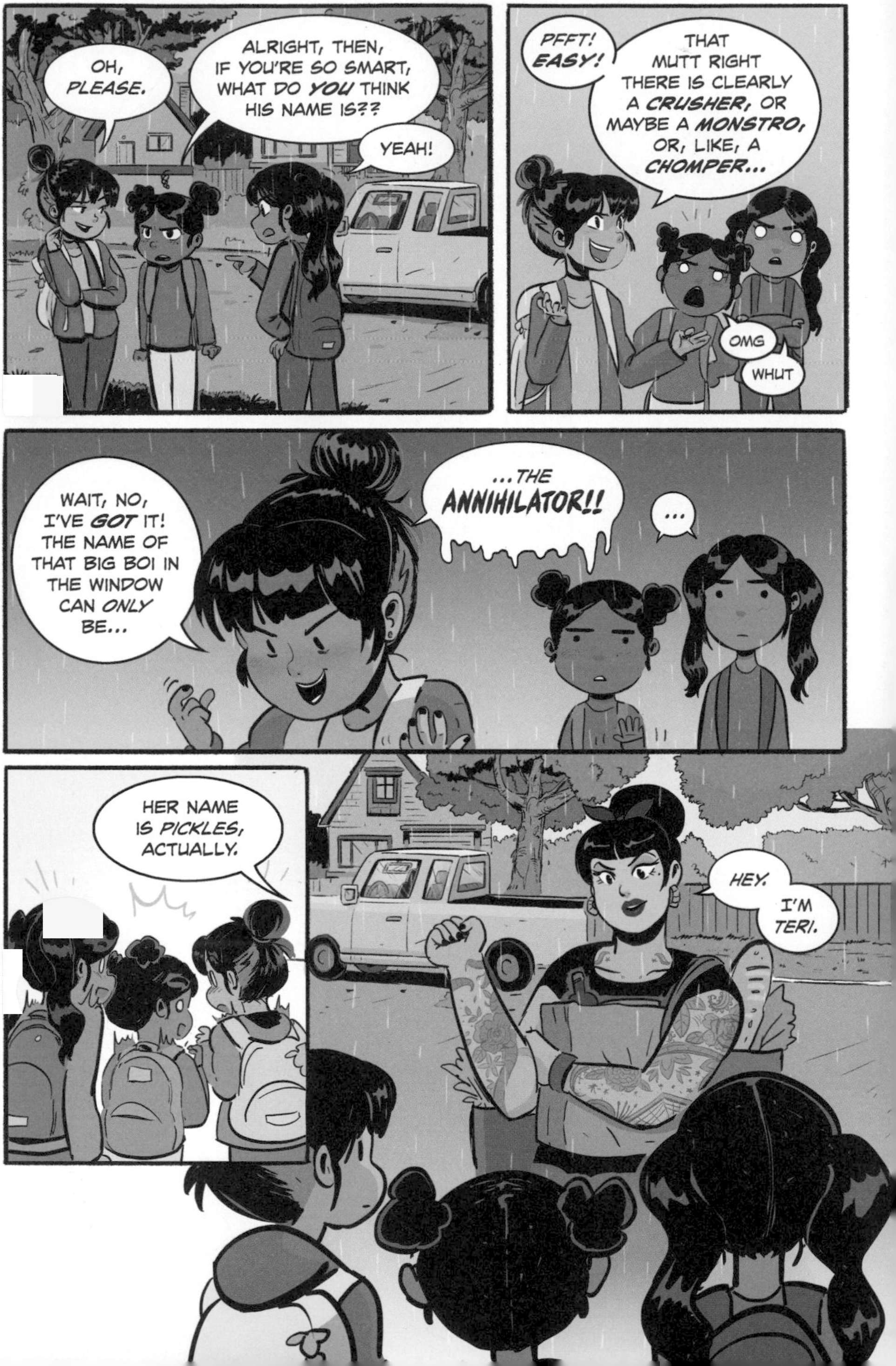
OH, PLEASE.
ALRIGHT, THEN, IF YOU'RE SO SMART, WHAT DO YOU THINK HIS NAME IS??
YEAH!
PFFT! EASY!
THAT MUTT RIGHT THERE IS CLEARLY A CRUSHER, OR MAYBE A MONSTRO, OR, LIKE, A CHOMPER...
OMG
WHUT
WAIT, NO, I'VE GOT IT! THE NAME OF THAT BIG BOI IN THE WINDOW CAN ONLY BE...
...THE ANNIHILATOR!!
...
HER NAME IS PICKLES, ACTUALLY.
HEY.
I'M TERI.

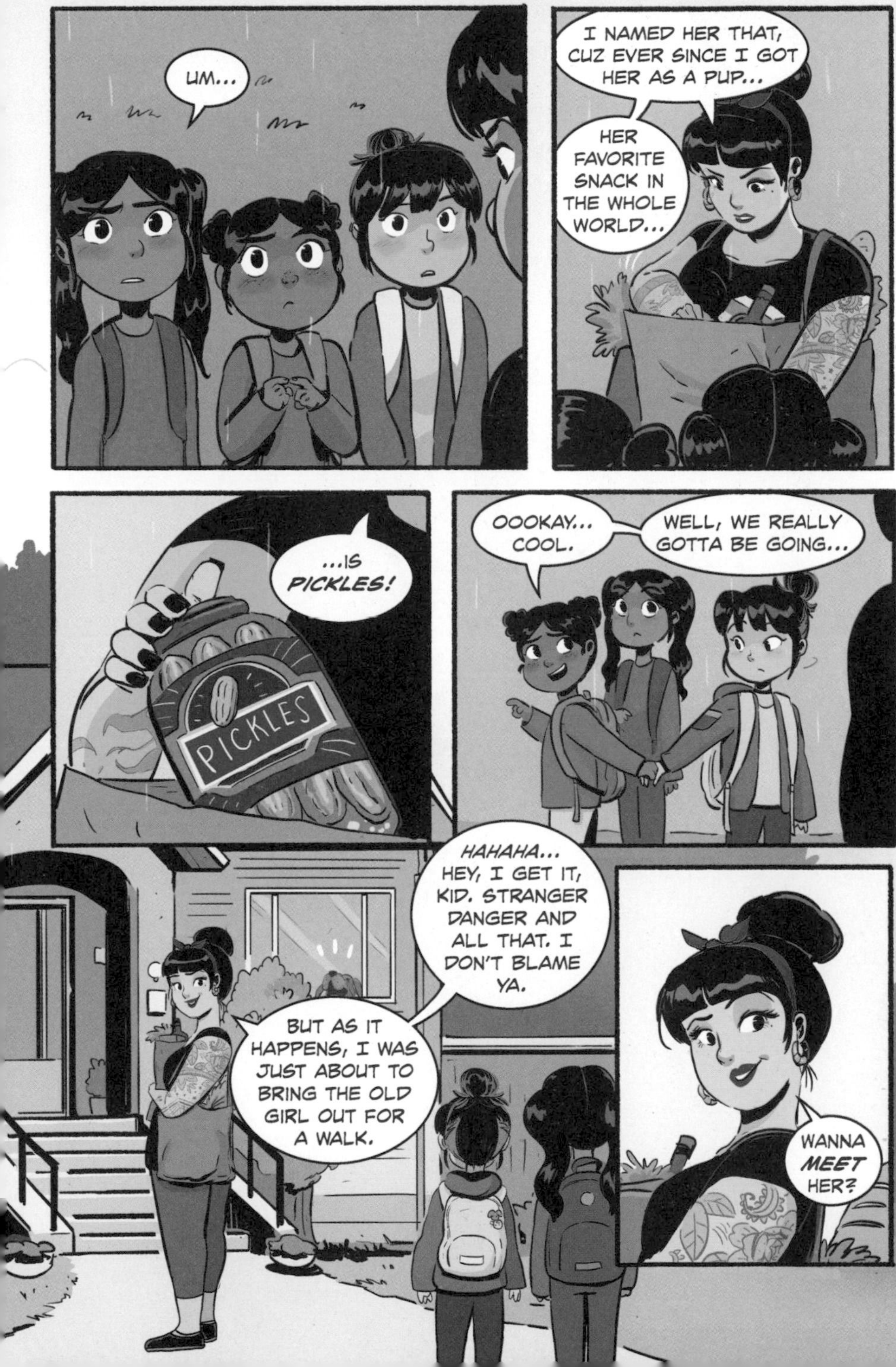
UM...
I NAMED HER THAT, CUZ EVER SINCE I GOT HER AS A PUP...
HER FAVORITE SNACK IN THE WHOLE WORLD...
...IS *PICKLES!*
PICKLES
OOOKAY... COOL.
WELL, WE REALLY GOTTA BE GOING...
HAHAHA... HEY, I GET IT, KID. STRANGER DANGER AND ALL THAT. I DON'T BLAME YA.
BUT AS IT HAPPENS, I WAS JUST ABOUT TO BRING THE OLD GIRL OUT FOR A WALK.
WANNA *MEET* HER?

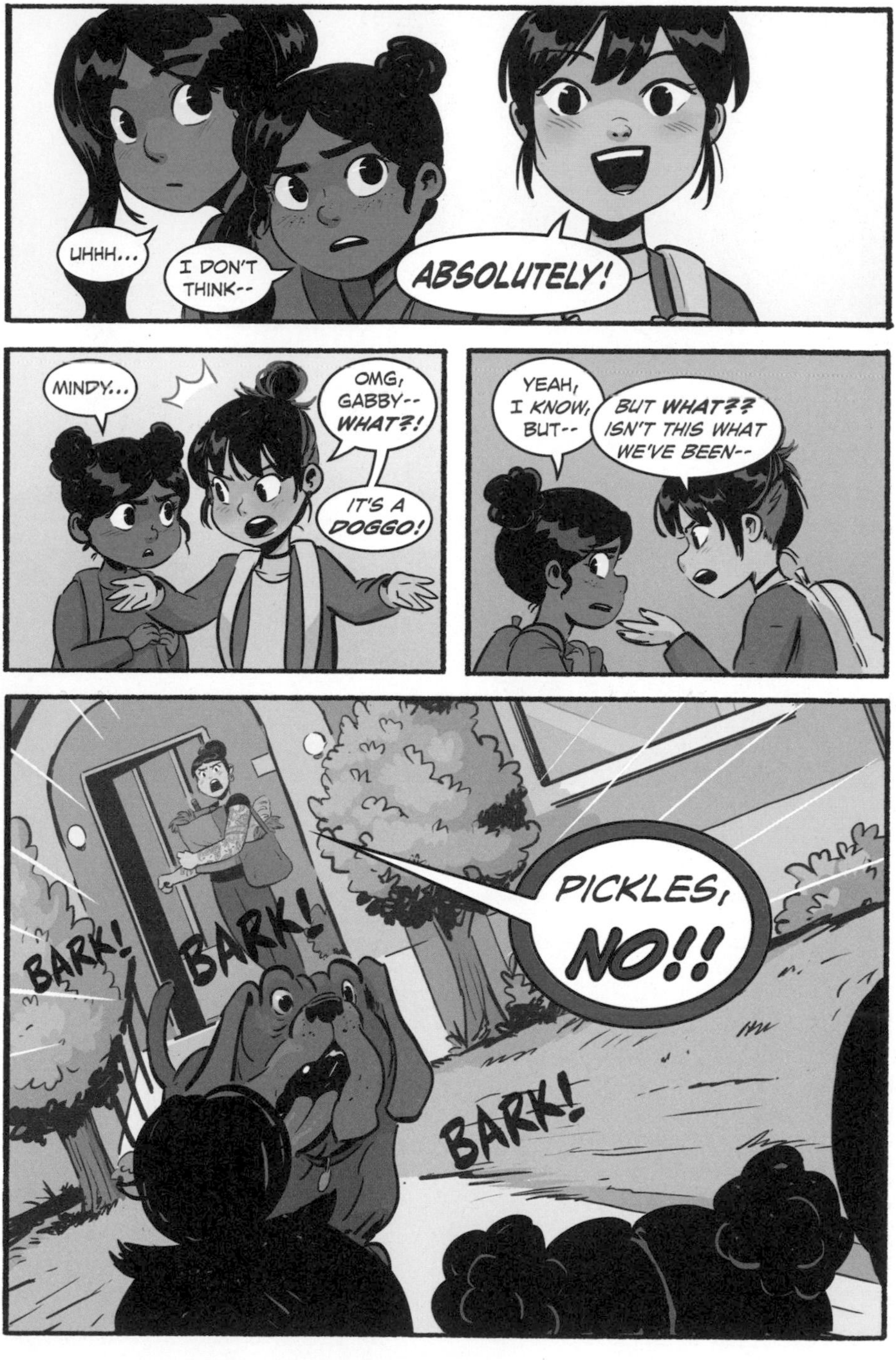
UHHH...
I DON'T THINK--
ABSOLUTELY!
MINDY...
OMG, GABBY--WHAT?!
IT'S A DOGGO!
YEAH, I KNOW, BUT--
BUT WHAT?? ISN'T THIS WHAT WE'VE BEEN--
PICKLES, NO!!
BARK!
BARK!
BARK!

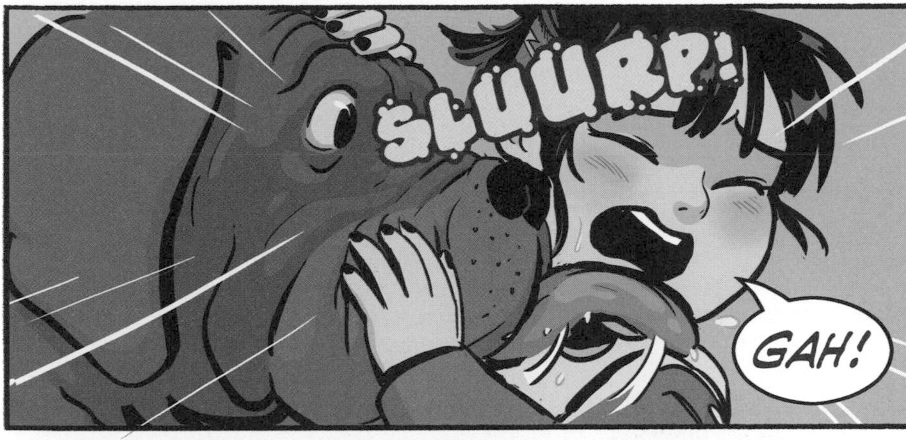
SLUURP!
GAH!

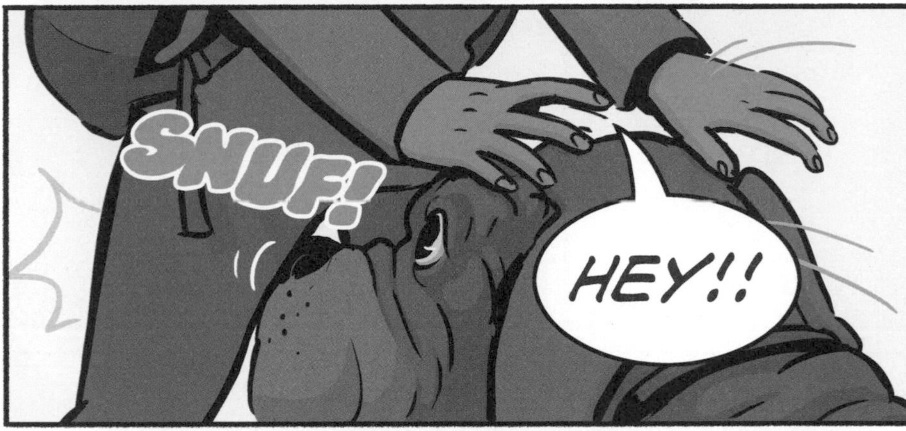
SNUF!
HEY!!

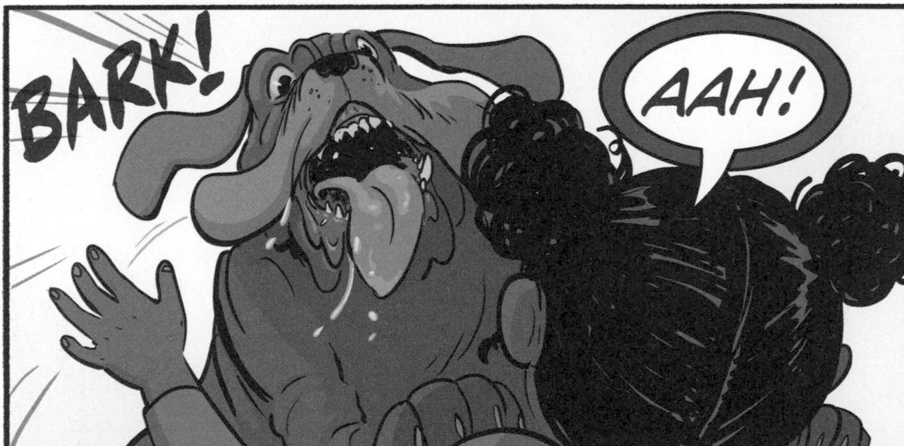
BARK!
AAH!

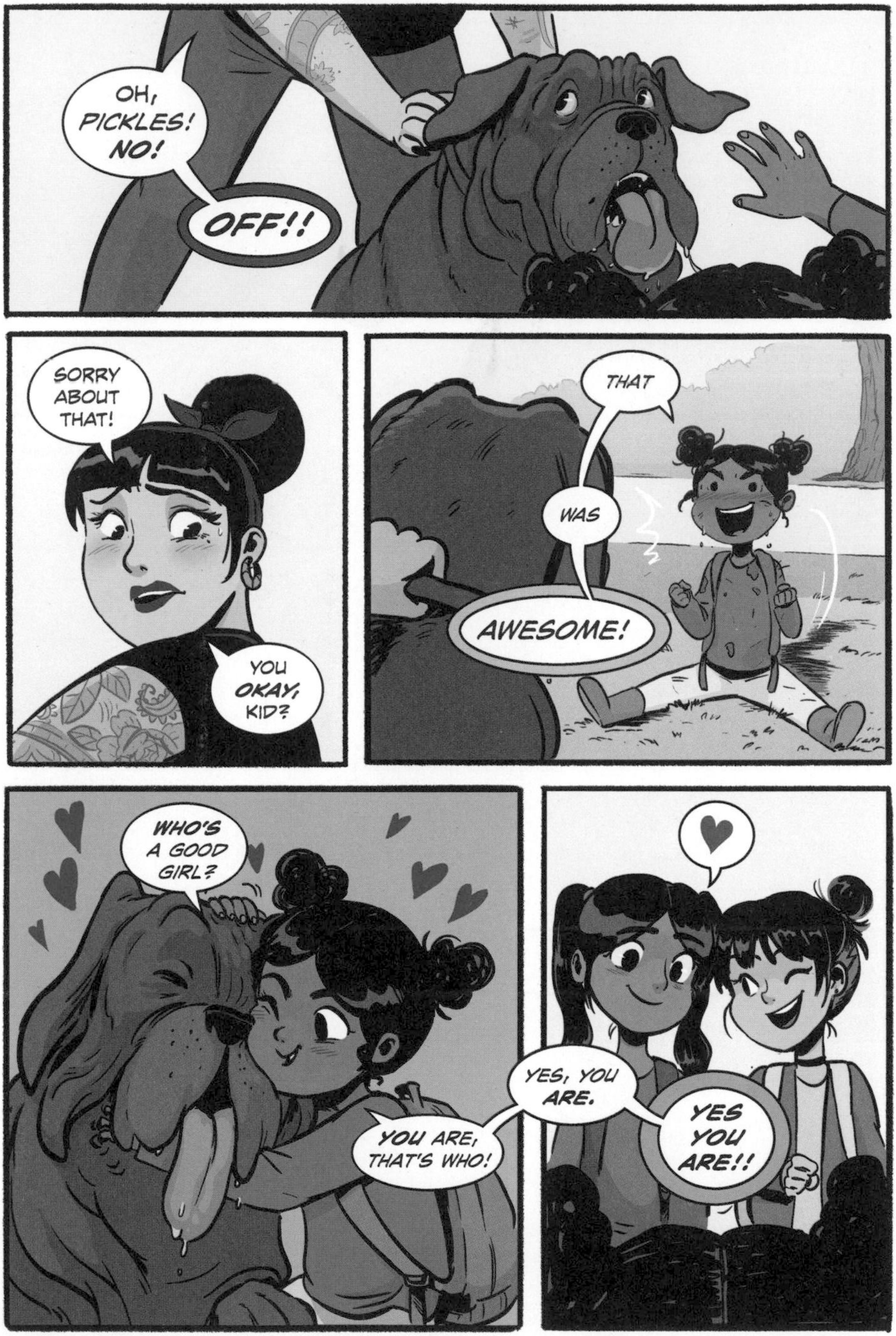
OH, PICKLES! NO!
OFF!!
SORRY ABOUT THAT!
YOU OKAY, KID?
THAT
WAS
AWESOME!
WHO'S A GOOD GIRL?
YOU ARE, THAT'S WHO!
YES, YOU ARE.
YES YOU ARE!!

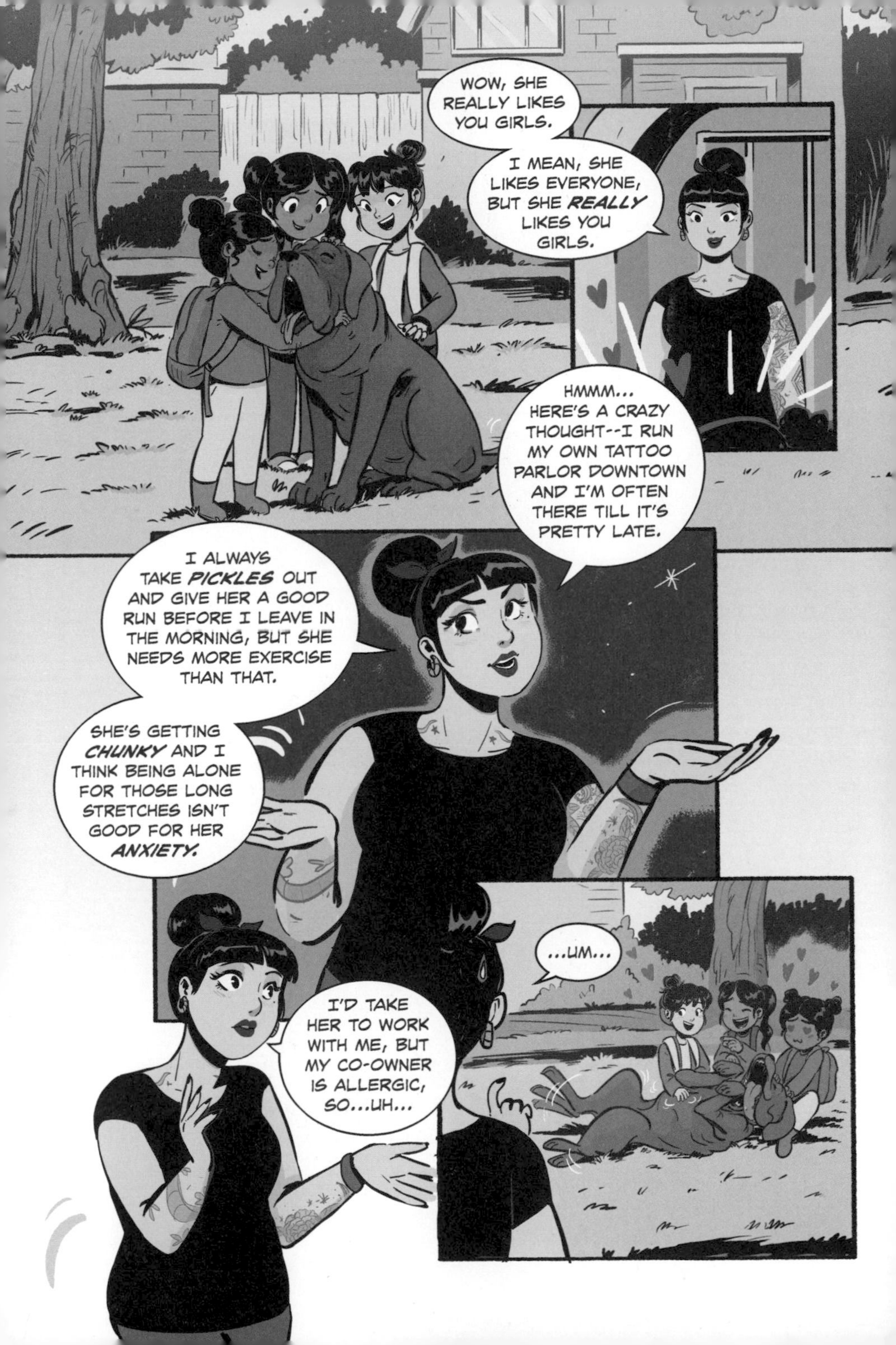
WOW, SHE REALLY LIKES YOU GIRLS.
I MEAN, SHE LIKES EVERYONE, BUT SHE *REALLY* LIKES YOU GIRLS.
HMMM... HERE'S A CRAZY THOUGHT--I RUN MY OWN TATTOO PARLOR DOWNTOWN AND I'M OFTEN THERE TILL IT'S PRETTY LATE.
I ALWAYS TAKE *PICKLES* OUT AND GIVE HER A GOOD RUN BEFORE I LEAVE IN THE MORNING, BUT SHE NEEDS MORE EXERCISE THAN THAT.
SHE'S GETTING *CHUNKY* AND I THINK BEING ALONE FOR THOSE LONG STRETCHES ISN'T GOOD FOR HER *ANXIETY.*
I'D TAKE HER TO WORK WITH ME, BUT MY CO-OWNER IS ALLERGIC, SO...UH...
...UM...

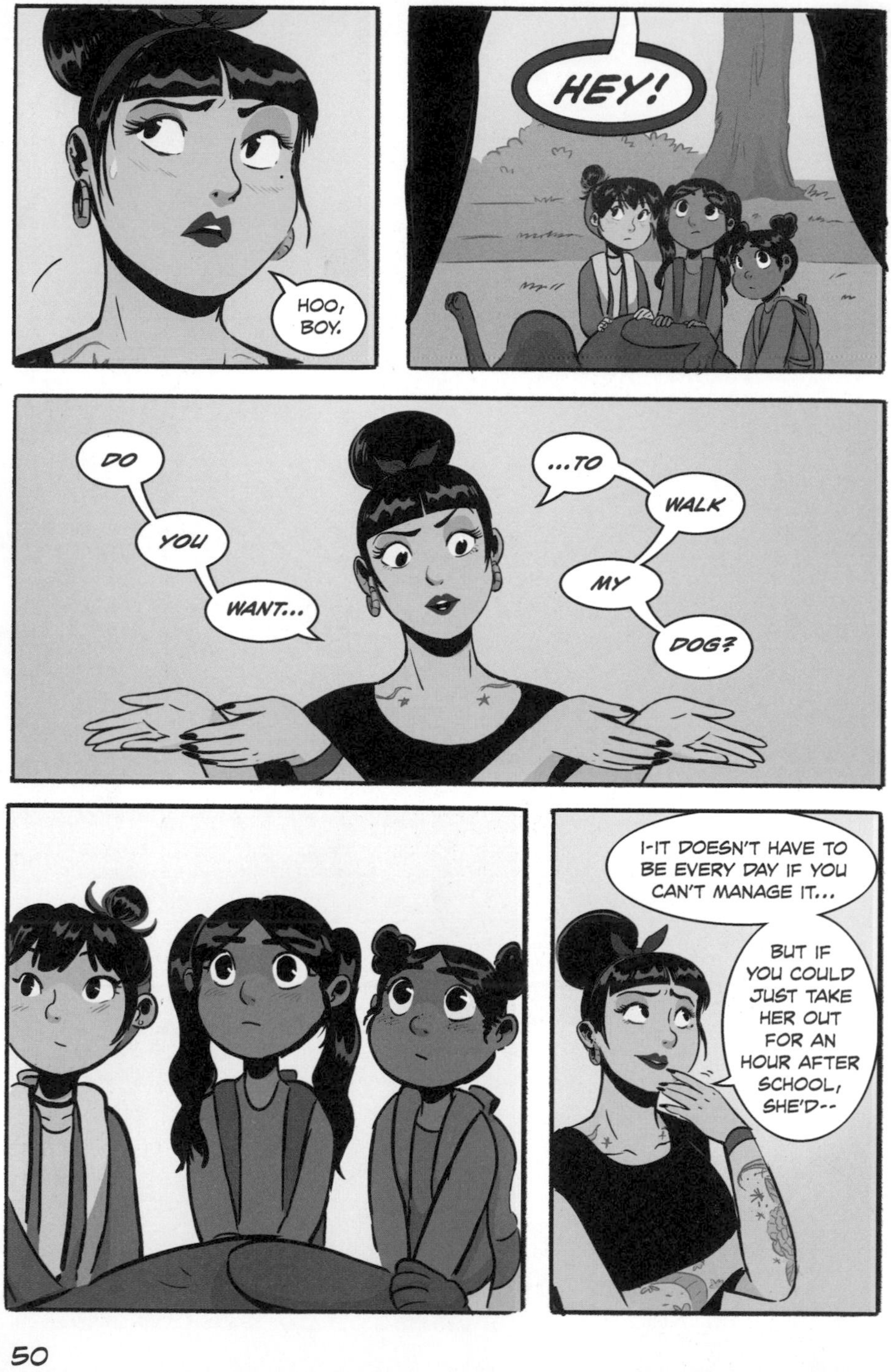
HOO, BOY.
HEY!
DO
YOU
WANT...
...TO
WALK
MY
DOG?
I-IT DOESN'T HAVE TO BE EVERY DAY IF YOU CAN'T MANAGE IT...
BUT IF YOU COULD JUST TAKE HER OUT FOR AN HOUR AFTER SCHOOL, SHE'D--

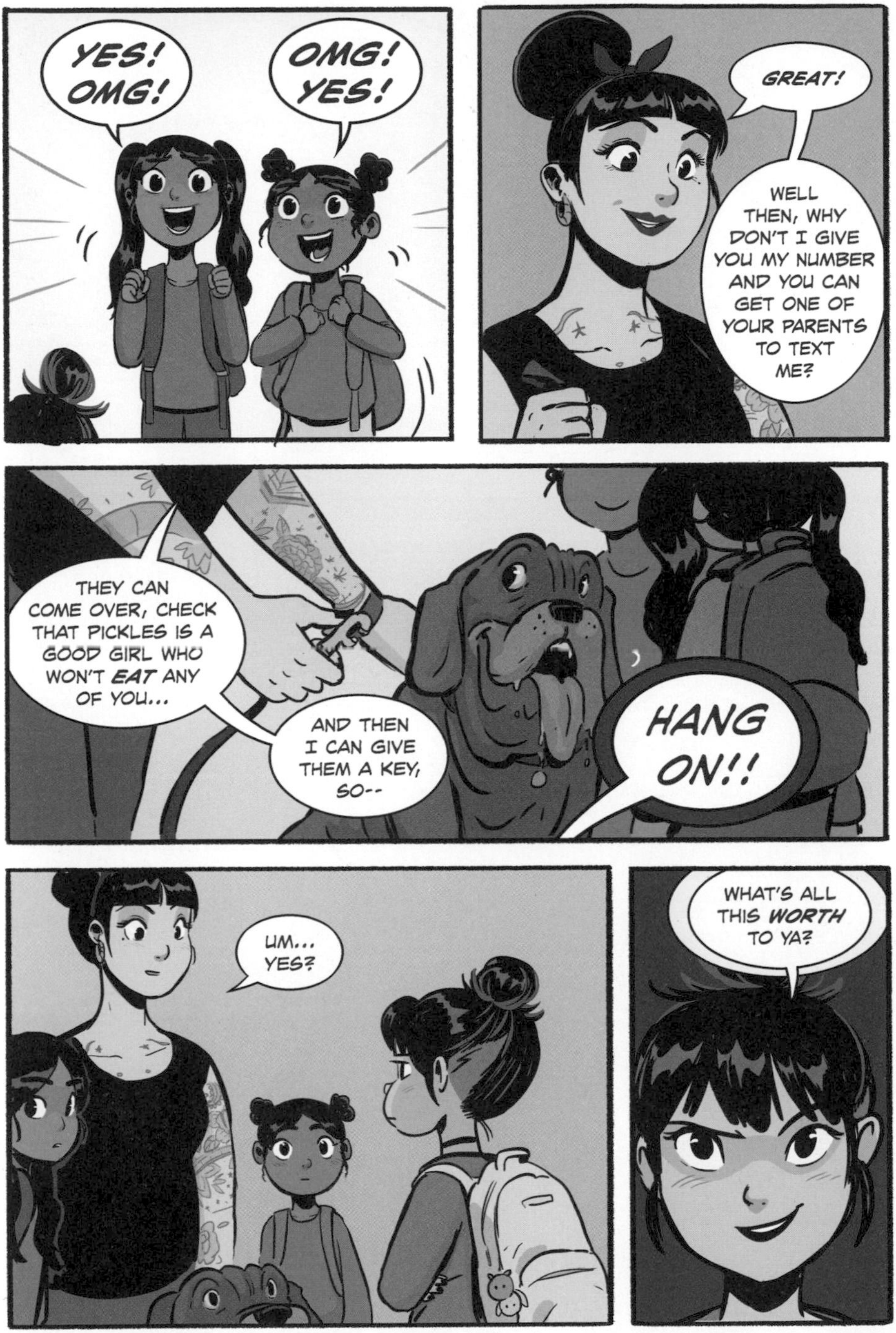
YES! OMG!
OMG! YES!
GREAT!
WELL THEN, WHY DON'T I GIVE YOU MY NUMBER AND YOU CAN GET ONE OF YOUR PARENTS TO TEXT ME?
THEY CAN COME OVER, CHECK THAT PICKLES IS A GOOD GIRL WHO WON'T *EAT* ANY OF YOU...
AND THEN I CAN GIVE THEM A KEY, SO--
HANG ON!!
UM... YES?
WHAT'S ALL THIS *WORTH* TO YA?

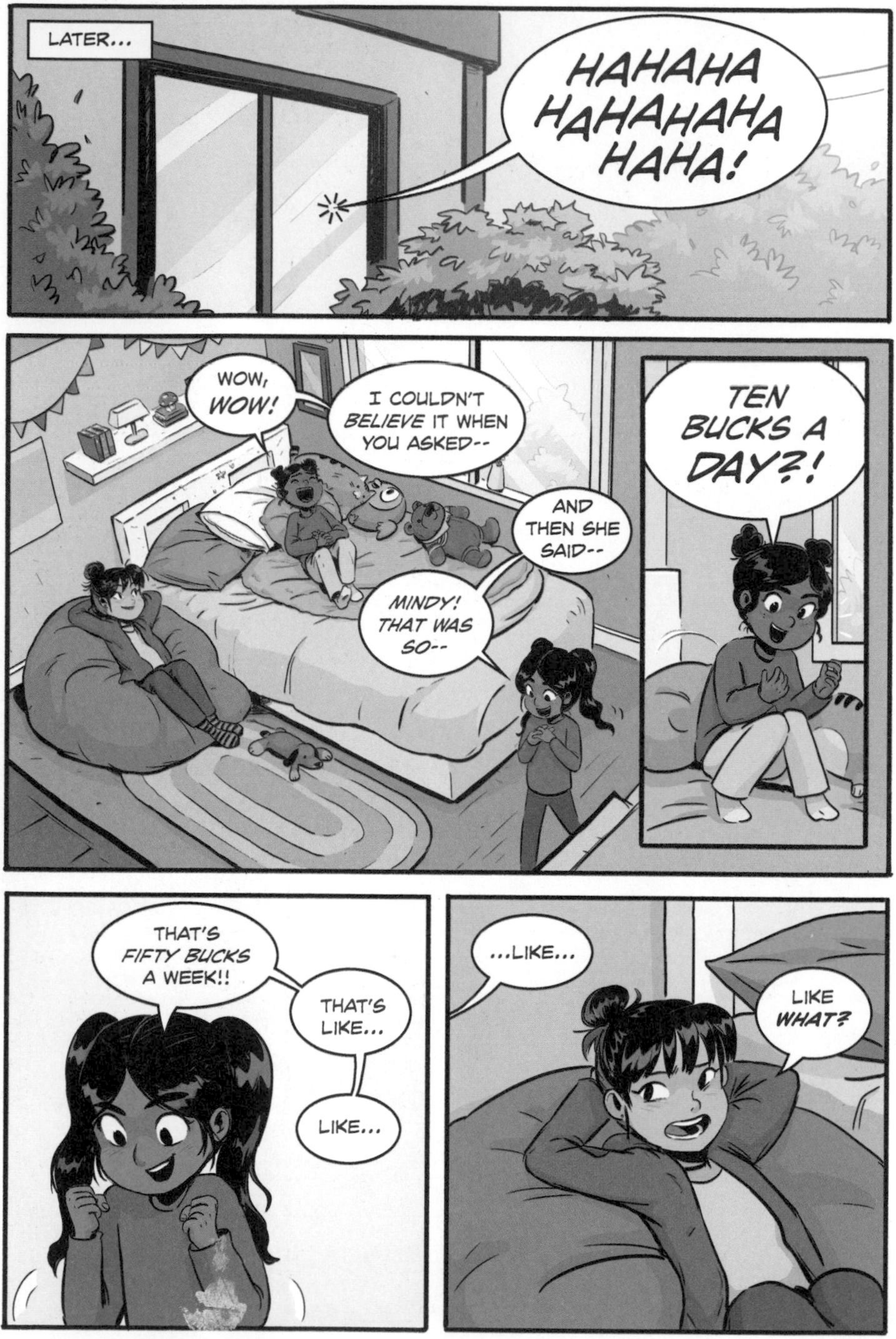
LATER...
HAHAHA HAHAHAHA HAHA!
WOW, *WOW!*
I COULDN'T *BELIEVE* IT WHEN YOU ASKED--
AND THEN SHE SAID--
MINDY! THAT WAS SO--
TEN BUCKS A DAY?!
THAT'S *FIFTY BUCKS* A WEEK!!
THAT'S LIKE...
LIKE...
...LIKE...
LIKE *WHAT?*

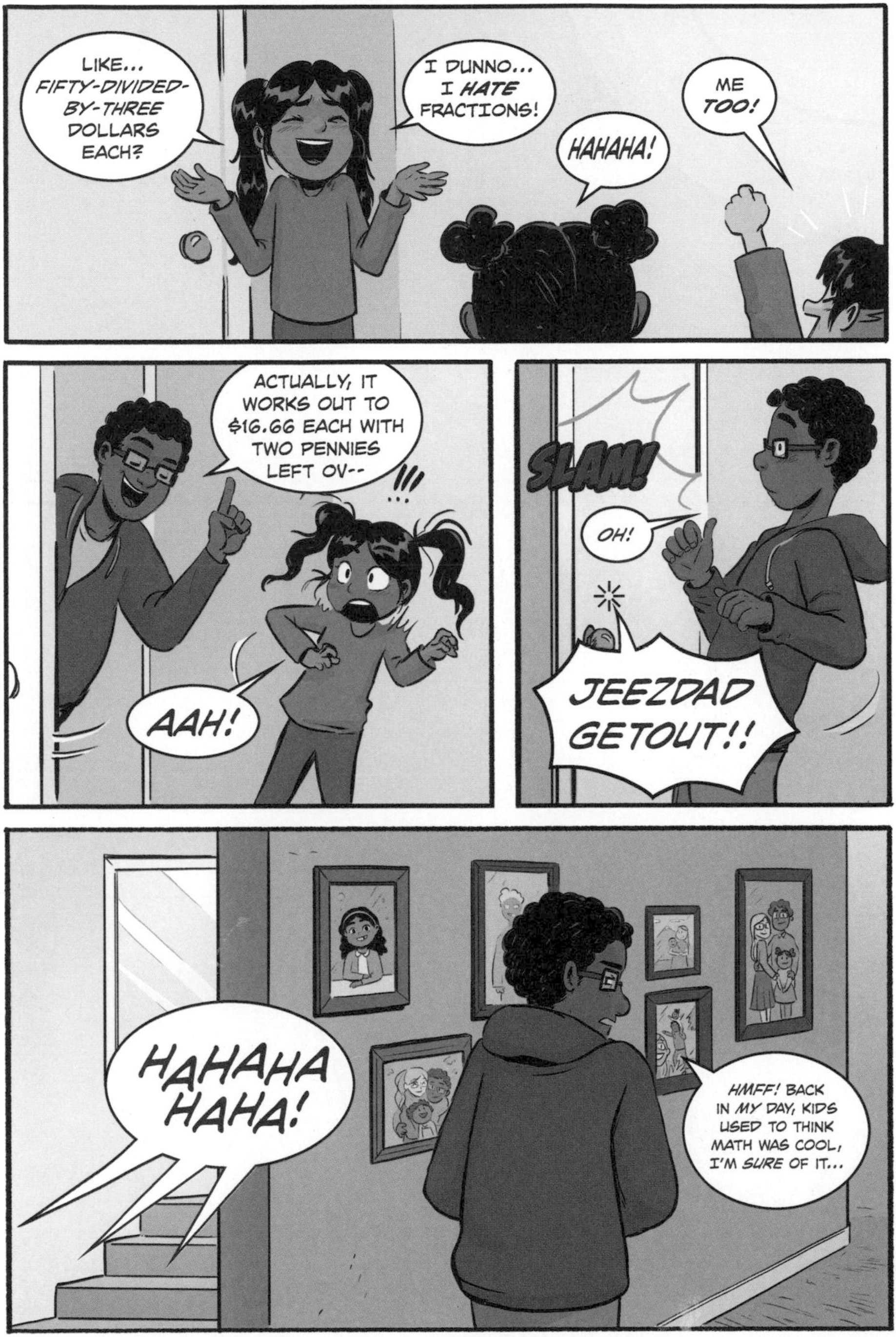
LIKE... FIFTY-DIVIDED-BY-THREE DOLLARS EACH?
I DUNNO... I HATE FRACTIONS!
HAHAHA!
ME TOO!
ACTUALLY, IT WORKS OUT TO $16.66 EACH WITH TWO PENNIES LEFT OV--
!!!
...
AAH!
SLAM!
OH!
JEEZDAD GETOUT!!
HAHAHA HAHA!
HMFF! BACK IN MY DAY, KIDS USED TO THINK MATH WAS COOL, I'M SURE OF IT...

HAHA HA!
OMG, GABBY-- YOUR DAD IS SUCH A *NERD!*
NO, HE'S *NOT!* HE'S A ***GEEK!***
THERE'S A DIFFERENCE, YOU KNOW...
HAHA! OKAY, FINE.
SO YOUR PARENTS CAN *DEFINITELY* GO PICK UP A KEY FROM TERI TONIGHT?
FLOP!
THAT'S WHAT DAD SAID, YEAH!
WOW! I CAN'T BELIEVE IT.
I KNOW! IT'S LIKE A DREAM!
IT'S *PERFECT.*
IN LESS THAN TWENTY-FOUR HOURS, WE'LL HAVE OUR OWN ***DOGGO*** TO PLAY WITH!
WELL, TO TAKE ***CARE*** OF...
SURE, SURE, THAT'S WHAT I MEAN.

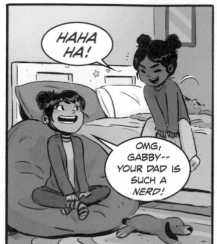

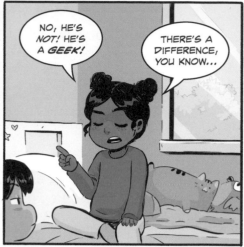

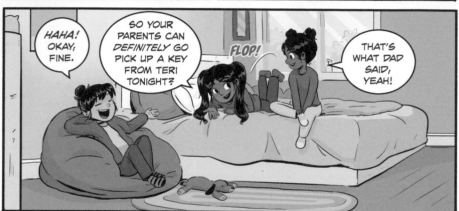

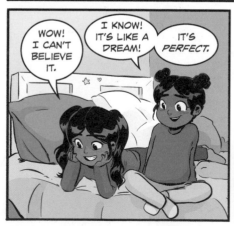

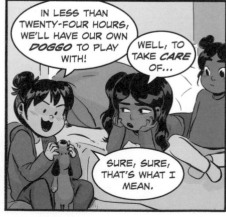

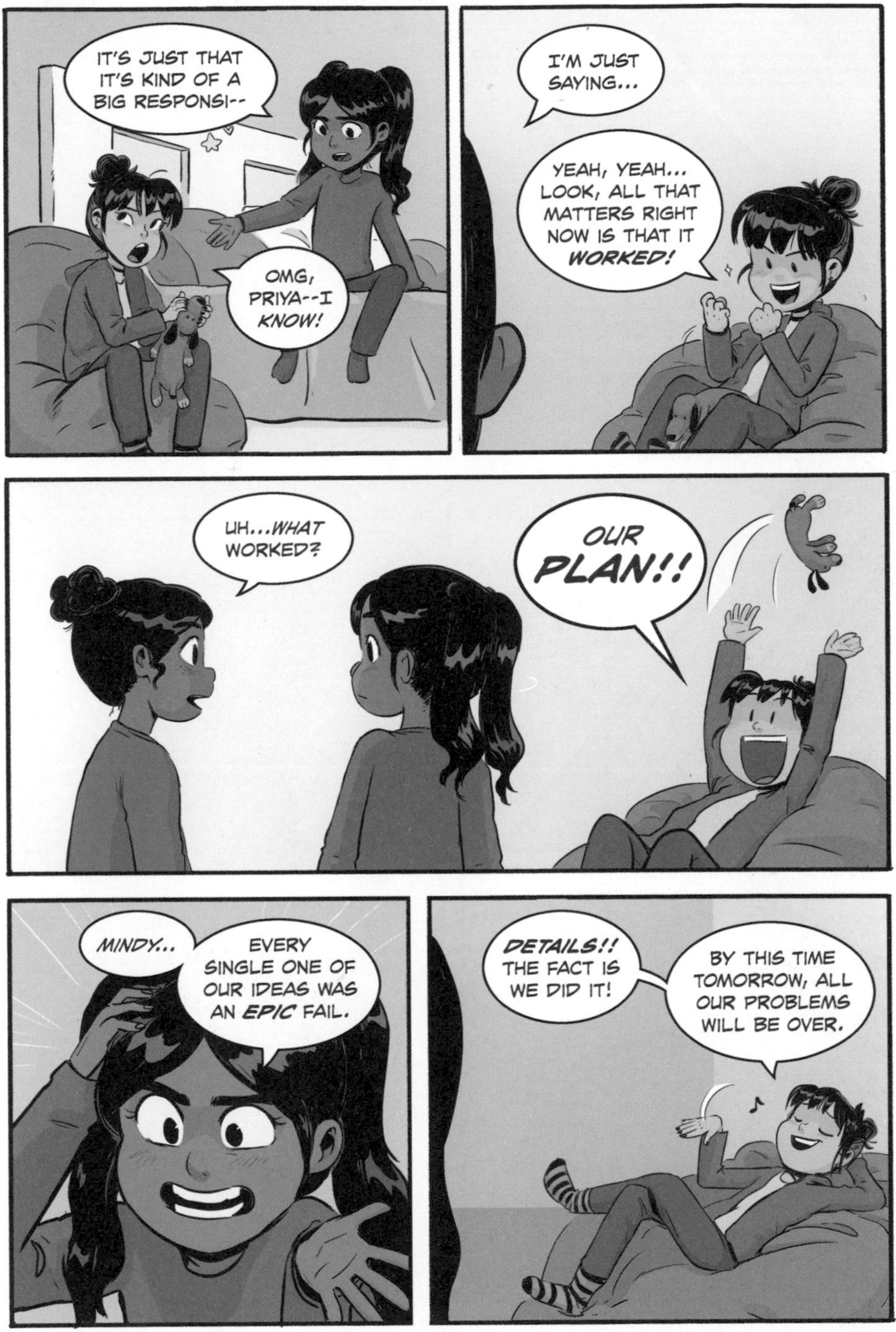
IT'S JUST THAT IT'S KIND OF A BIG RESPONSI--
OMG, PRIYA--I KNOW!
I'M JUST SAYING...
YEAH, YEAH... LOOK, ALL THAT MATTERS RIGHT NOW IS THAT IT WORKED!
UH...WHAT WORKED?
OUR PLAN!!
MINDY...
EVERY SINGLE ONE OF OUR IDEAS WAS AN EPIC FAIL.
DETAILS!! THE FACT IS WE DID IT!
BY THIS TIME TOMORROW, ALL OUR PROBLEMS WILL BE OVER.

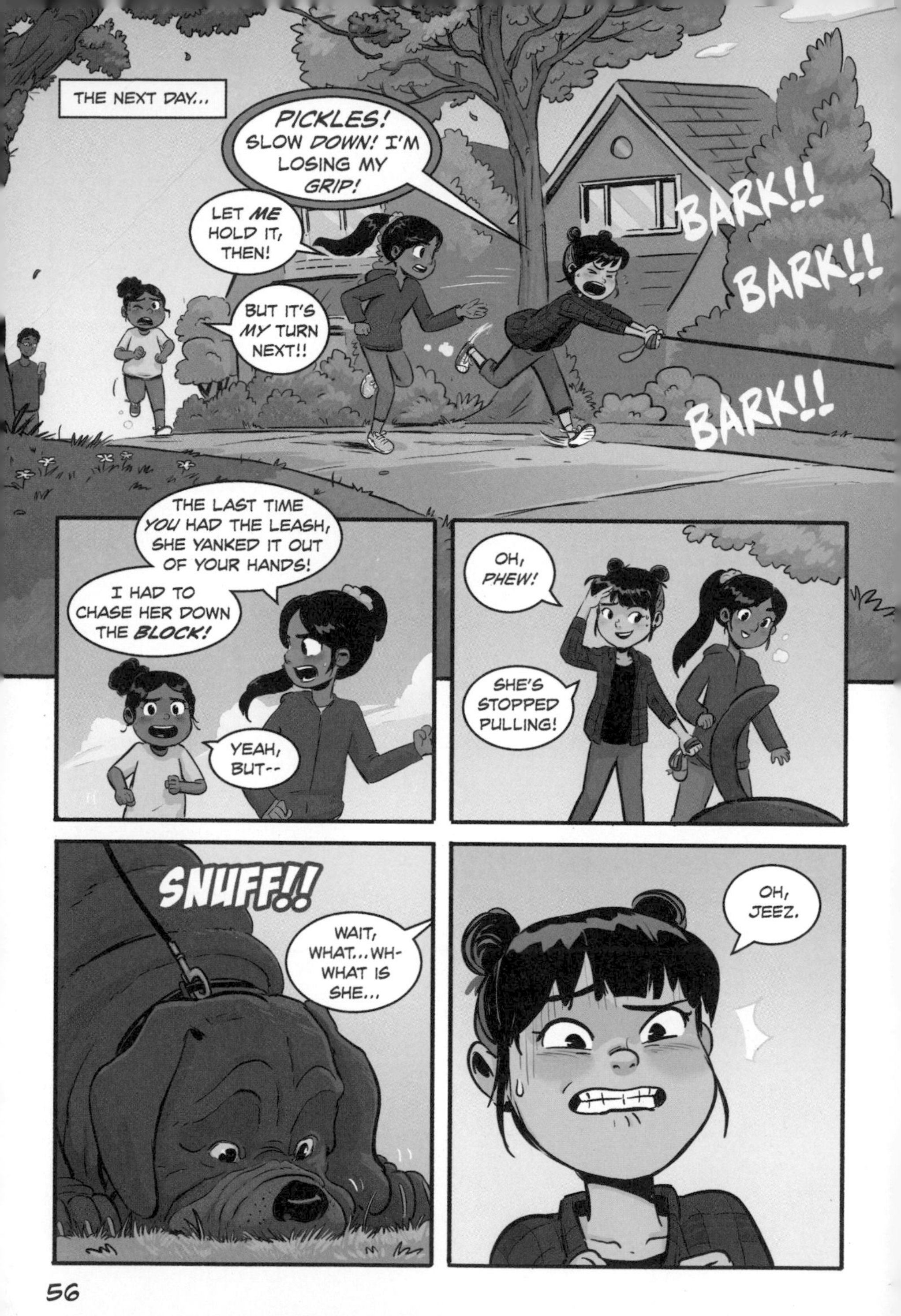
THE NEXT DAY...
PICKLES! SLOW DOWN! I'M LOSING MY GRIP!
LET ME HOLD IT, THEN!
BUT IT'S MY TURN NEXT!!
BARK!!
BARK!!
BARK!!
THE LAST TIME YOU HAD THE LEASH, SHE YANKED IT OUT OF YOUR HANDS!
I HAD TO CHASE HER DOWN THE BLOCK!
YEAH, BUT--
OH, PHEW!
SHE'S STOPPED PULLING!
SNUFF!!
WAIT, WHAT...WH-WHAT IS SHE...
OH, JEEZ.

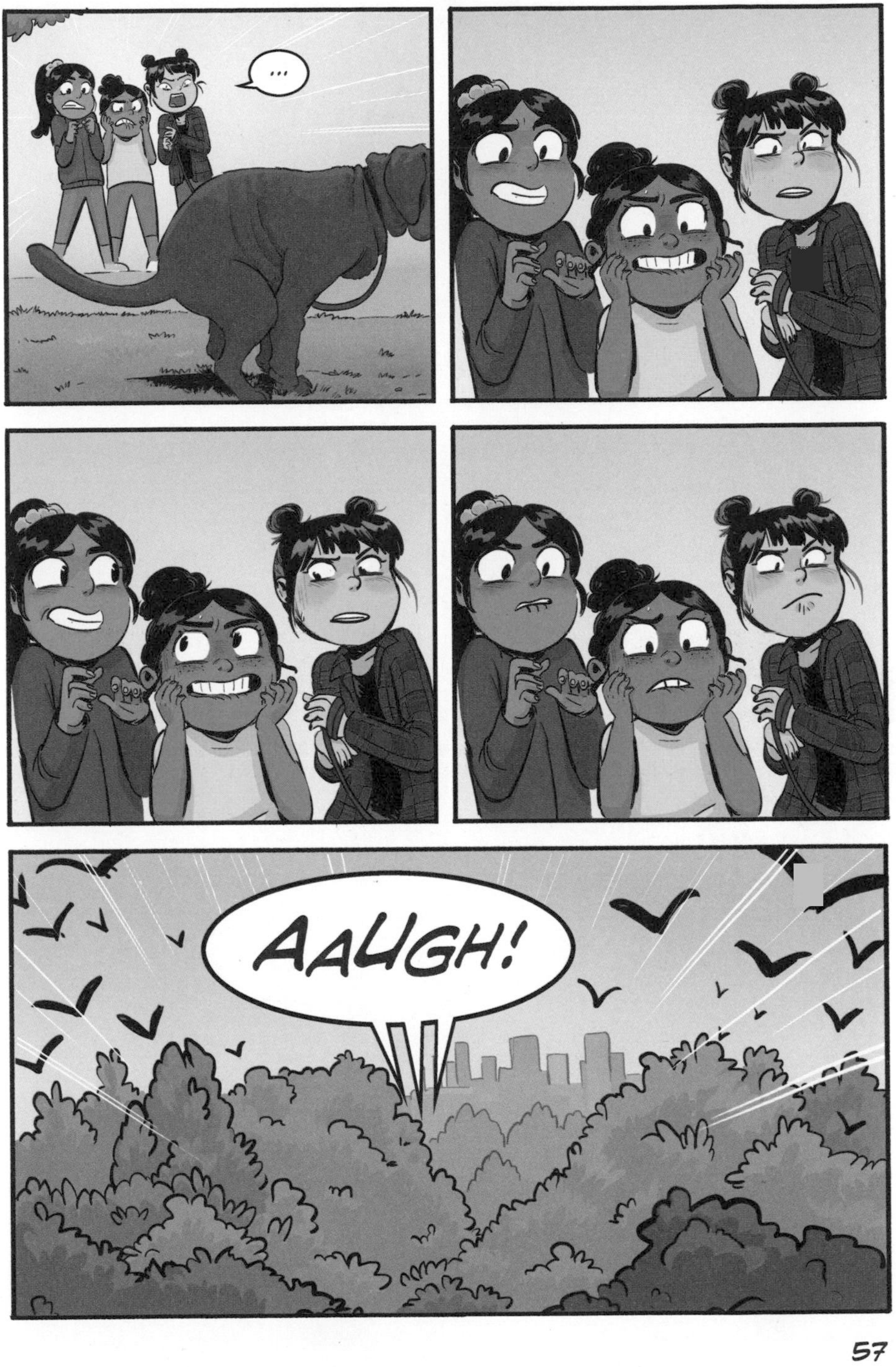
...
AAUGH!

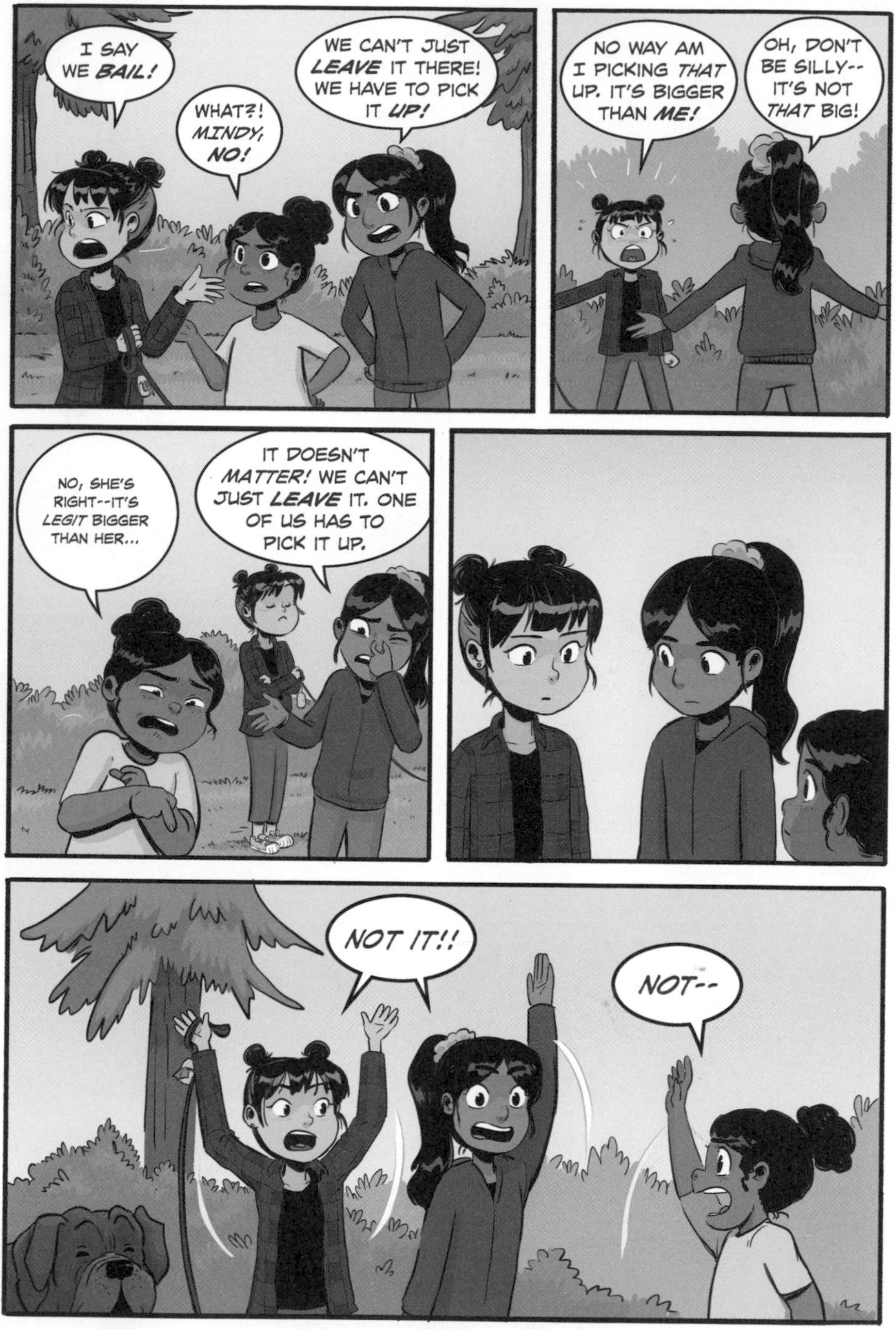
I SAY WE BAIL!
WHAT?! MINDY, NO!
WE CAN'T JUST LEAVE IT THERE! WE HAVE TO PICK IT UP!
NO WAY AM I PICKING THAT UP. IT'S BIGGER THAN ME!
OH, DON'T BE SILLY--IT'S NOT THAT BIG!
NO, SHE'S RIGHT--IT'S LEGIT BIGGER THAN HER...
IT DOESN'T MATTER! WE CAN'T JUST LEAVE IT. ONE OF US HAS TO PICK IT UP.
NOT IT!!
NOT--

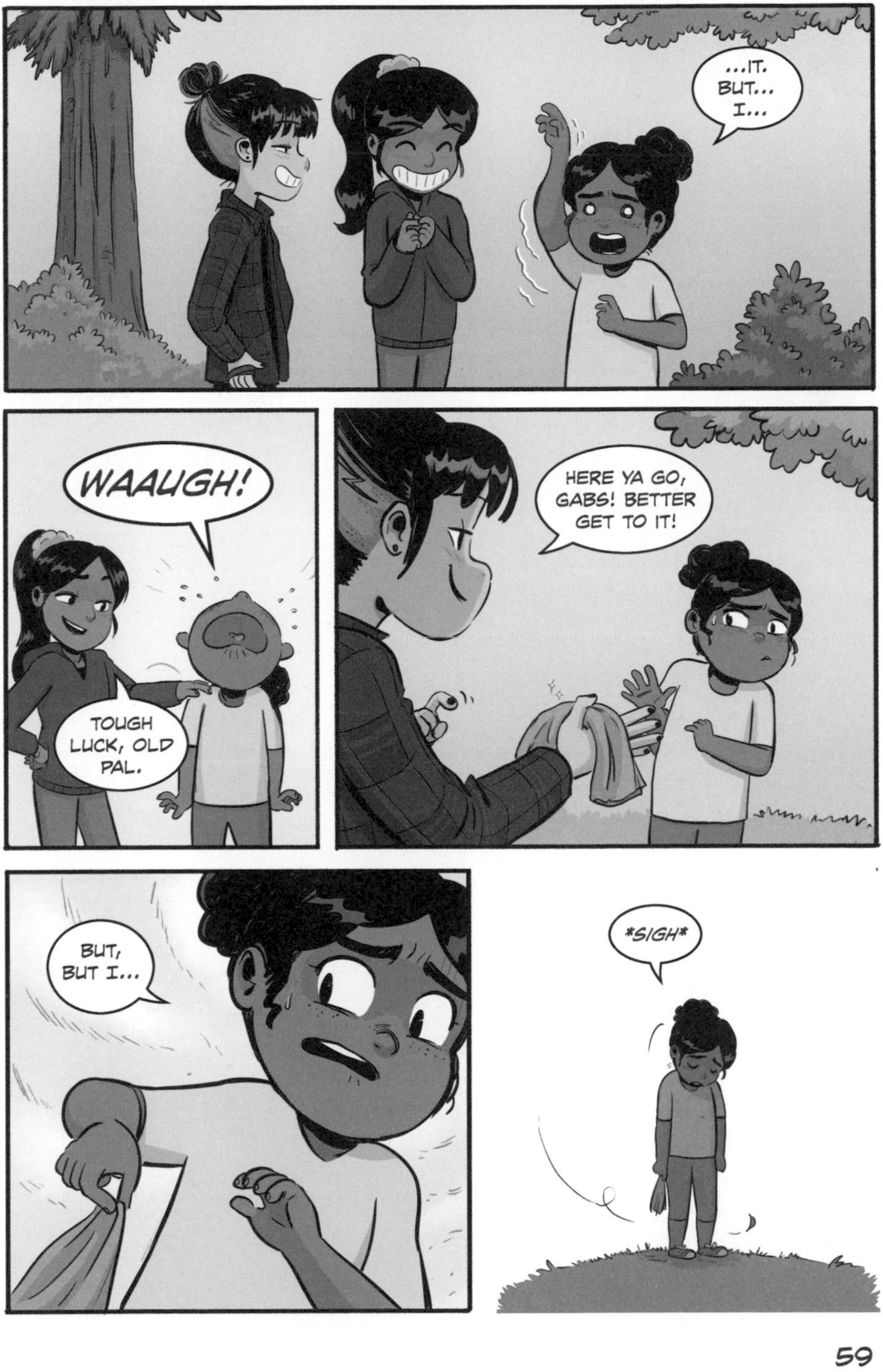

...IT. BUT... I...
WAAUGH!
TOUGH LUCK, OLD PAL.
HERE YA GO, GABS! BETTER GET TO IT!
BUT, BUT I...
SIGH

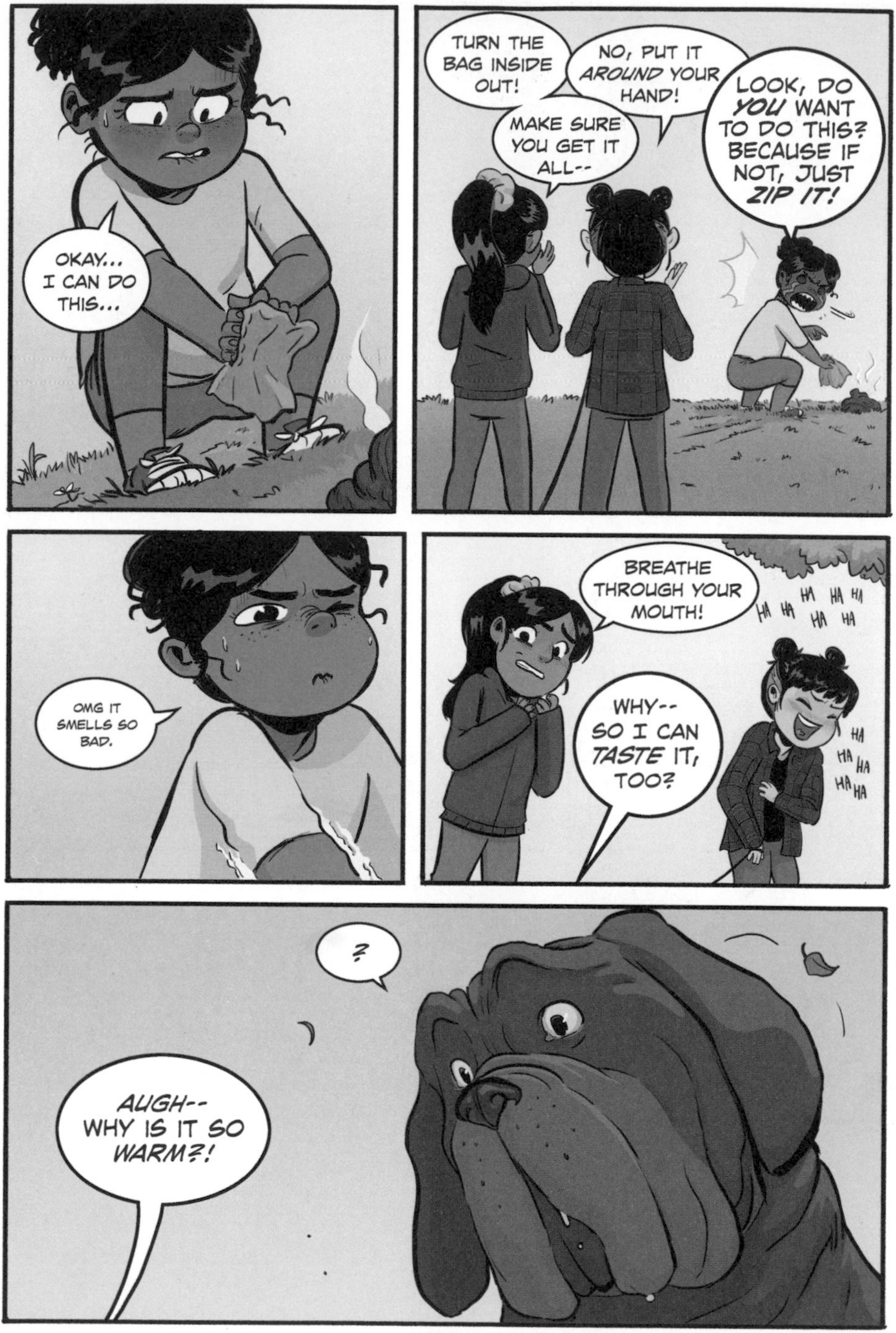
OKAY...
I CAN DO THIS...
TURN THE BAG INSIDE OUT!
NO, PUT IT AROUND YOUR HAND!
MAKE SURE YOU GET IT ALL--
LOOK, DO YOU WANT TO DO THIS? BECAUSE IF NOT, JUST ZIP IT!
OMG IT SMELLS SO BAD.
BREATHE THROUGH YOUR MOUTH!
HA HA HA HA HA HA HA
WHY-- SO I CAN TASTE IT, TOO?
HA HA HA HA HA
?
AUGH-- WHY IS IT SO WARM?!

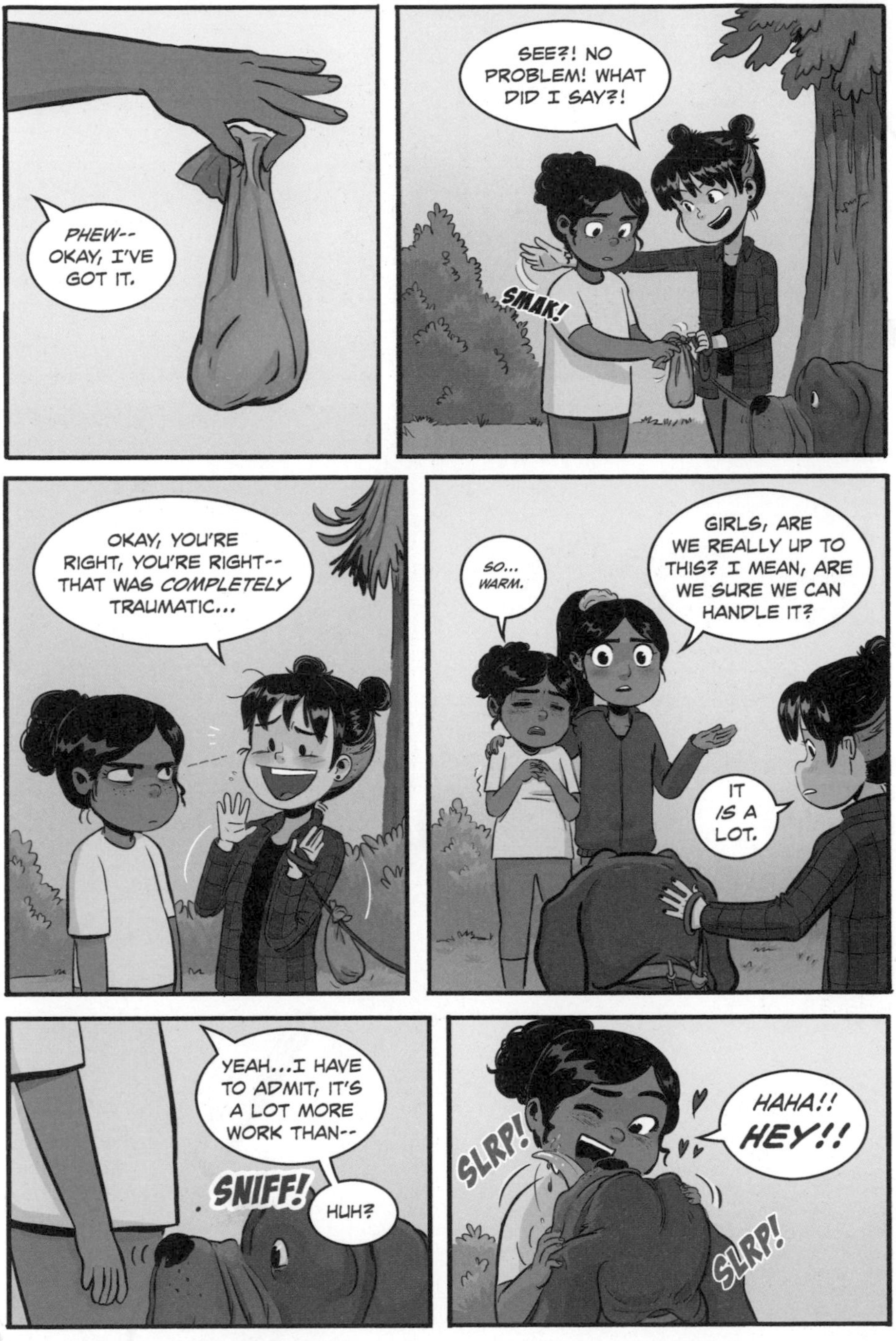
PHEW--
OKAY, I'VE
GOT IT.
SEE?! NO
PROBLEM! WHAT
DID I SAY?!
SMAK!
OKAY, YOU'RE
RIGHT, YOU'RE RIGHT--
THAT WAS *COMPLETELY*
TRAUMATIC...
SO...
WARM.
GIRLS, ARE
WE REALLY UP TO
THIS? I MEAN, ARE
WE SURE WE CAN
HANDLE IT?
IT
IS A
LOT.
YEAH...I HAVE
TO ADMIT, IT'S
A LOT MORE
WORK THAN--
SNIFF!
HUH?
SLRP!
HAHA!!
HEY!!
SLRP!

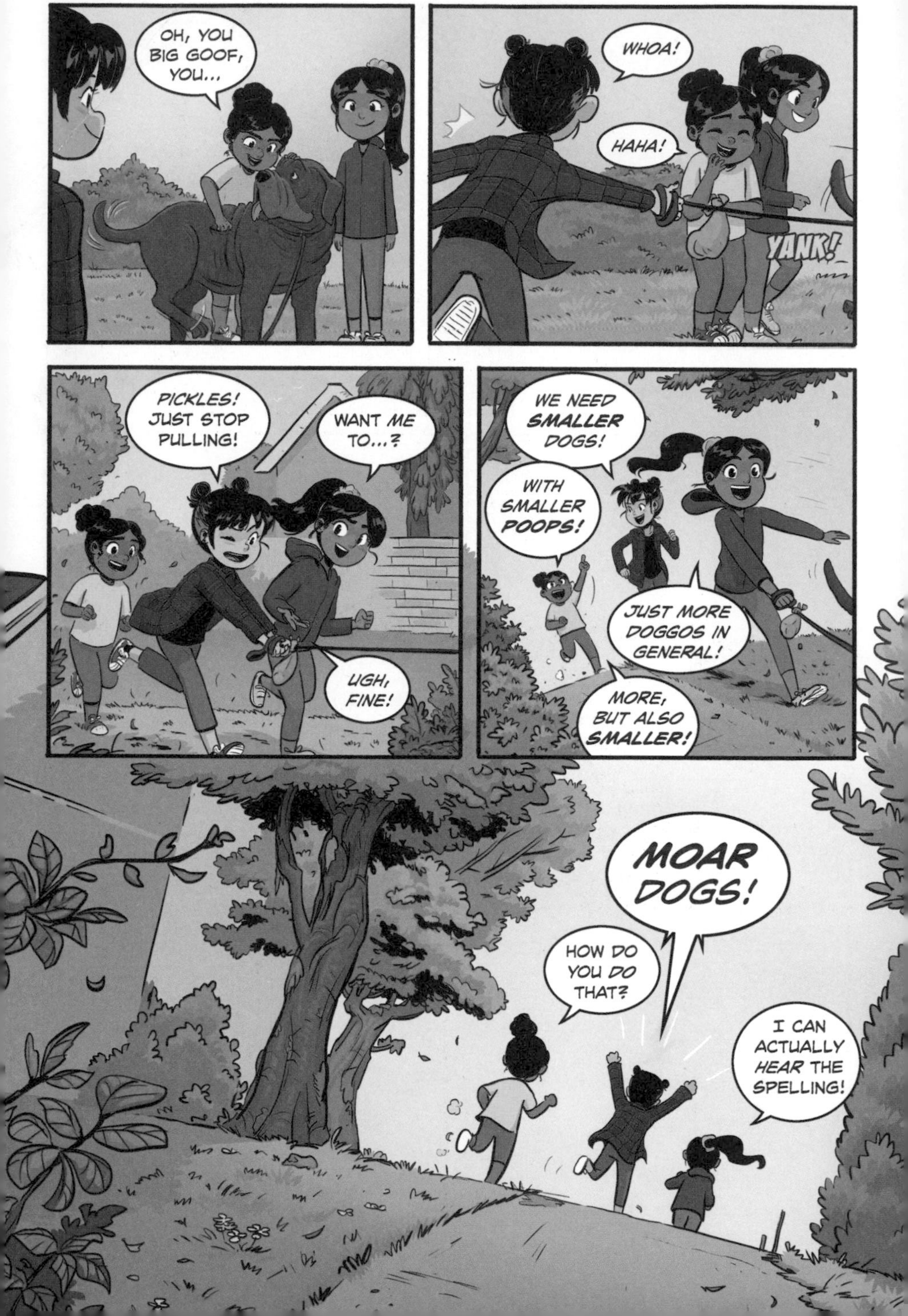
OH, YOU BIG GOOF, YOU...
WHOA!
HAHA!
YANK!
PICKLES! JUST STOP PULLING!
WANT ME TO...?
UGH, FINE!
WE NEED SMALLER DOGS!
WITH SMALLER POOPS!
JUST MORE DOGGOS IN GENERAL!
MORE, BUT ALSO SMALLER!
MOAR DOGS!
HOW DO YOU DO THAT?
I CAN ACTUALLY HEAR THE SPELLING!

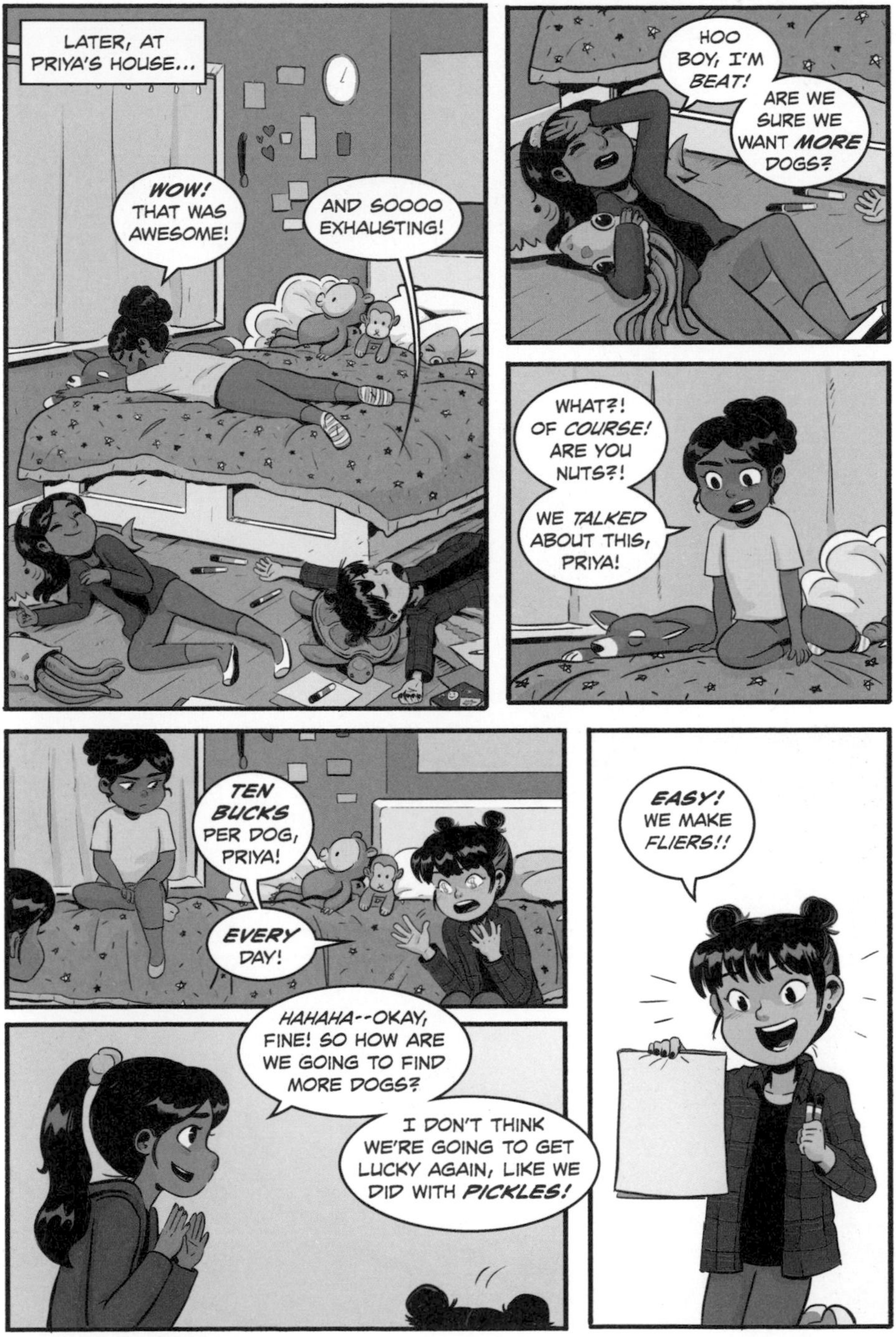
LATER, AT PRIYA'S HOUSE...
WOW! THAT WAS AWESOME!
AND SOOOO EXHAUSTING!
HOO BOY, I'M BEAT!
ARE WE SURE WE WANT MORE DOGS?
WHAT?! OF COURSE! ARE YOU NUTS?!
WE TALKED ABOUT THIS, PRIYA!
TEN BUCKS PER DOG, PRIYA!
EVERY DAY!
HAHAHA--OKAY, FINE! SO HOW ARE WE GOING TO FIND MORE DOGS?
I DON'T THINK WE'RE GOING TO GET LUCKY AGAIN, LIKE WE DID WITH PICKLES!
EASY! WE MAKE FLIERS!!

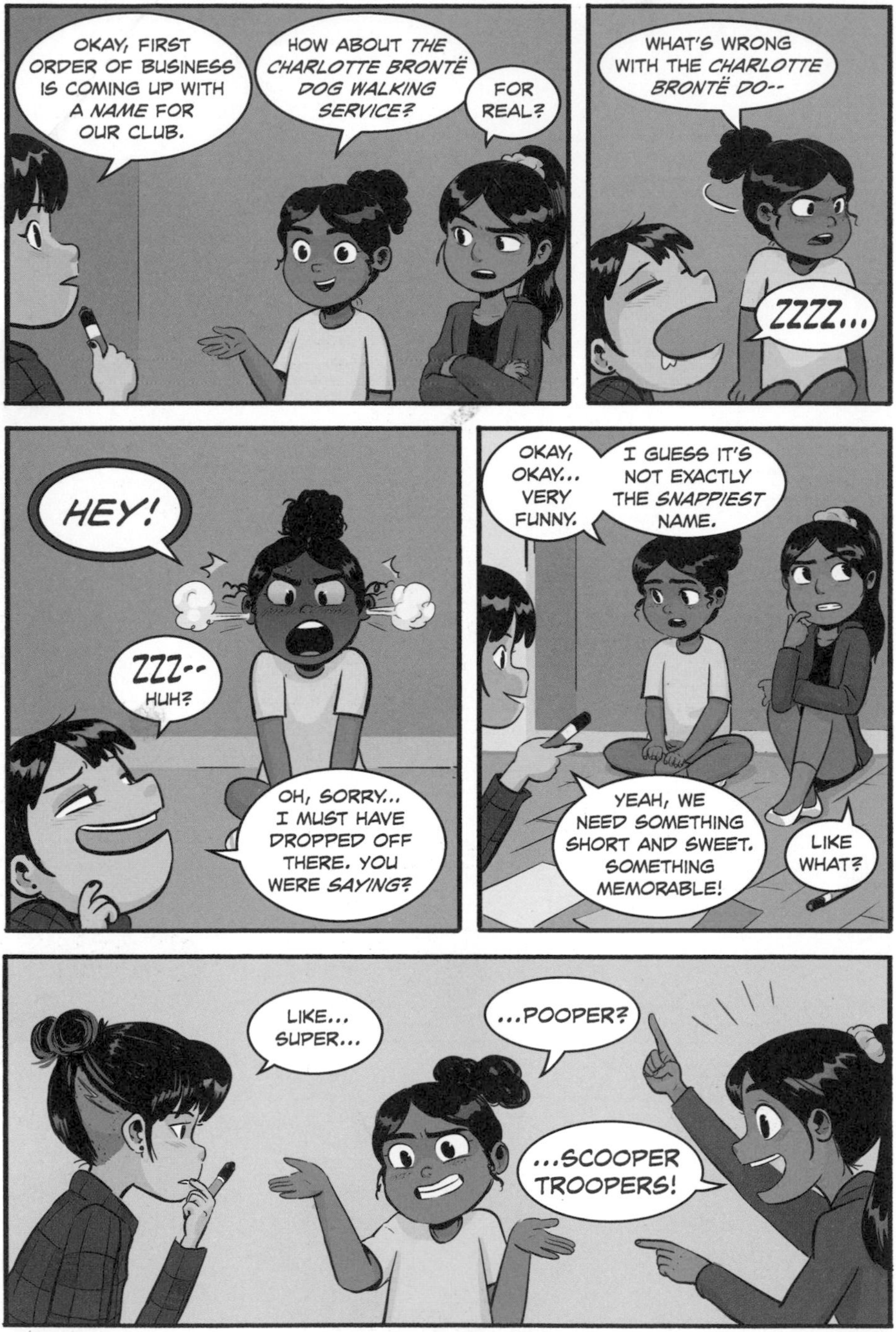
OKAY, FIRST ORDER OF BUSINESS IS COMING UP WITH A *NAME* FOR OUR CLUB.
HOW ABOUT *THE CHARLOTTE BRONTË DOG WALKING SERVICE*?
FOR REAL?
WHAT'S WRONG WITH THE *CHARLOTTE BRONTË DO--*
ZZZZ...
HEY!
ZZZ-- HUH?
OH, SORRY... I MUST HAVE DROPPED OFF THERE. YOU WERE *SAYING*?
OKAY, OKAY... VERY FUNNY.
I GUESS IT'S NOT EXACTLY THE *SNAPPIEST* NAME.
YEAH, WE NEED SOMETHING SHORT AND SWEET. SOMETHING MEMORABLE!
LIKE WHAT?
LIKE... SUPER...
...POOPER?
...SCOOPER TROOPERS!

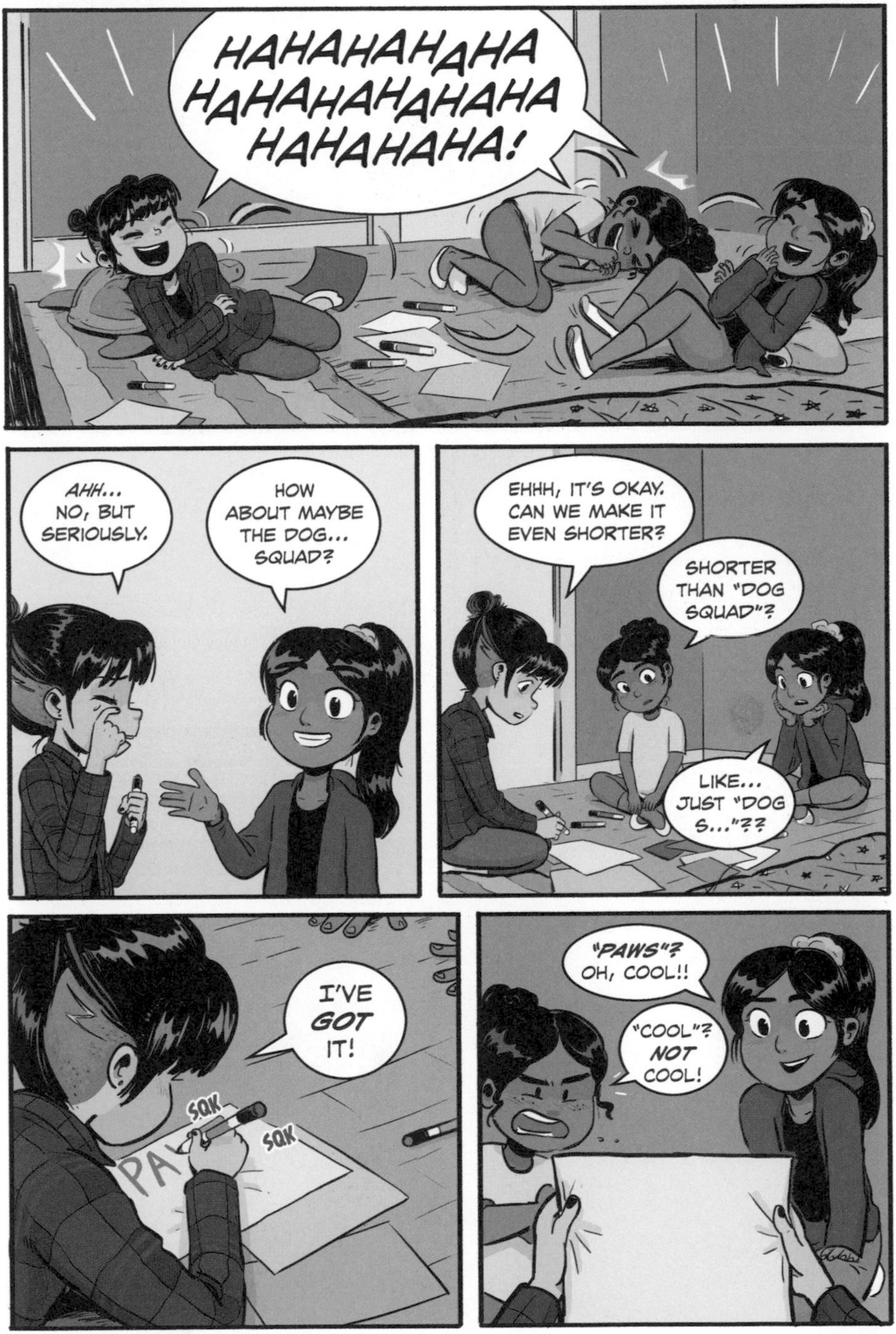
HAHAHAHAHA HAHAHAHAHAHA HAHAHAHA!
AHH... NO, BUT SERIOUSLY.
HOW ABOUT MAYBE THE DOG... SQUAD?
EHHH, IT'S OKAY. CAN WE MAKE IT EVEN SHORTER?
SHORTER THAN "DOG SQUAD"?
LIKE... JUST "DOG S..."??
I'VE *GOT* IT!
SQK
SQK
PA
"PAWS"? OH, COOL!!
"COOL"? *NOT* COOL!

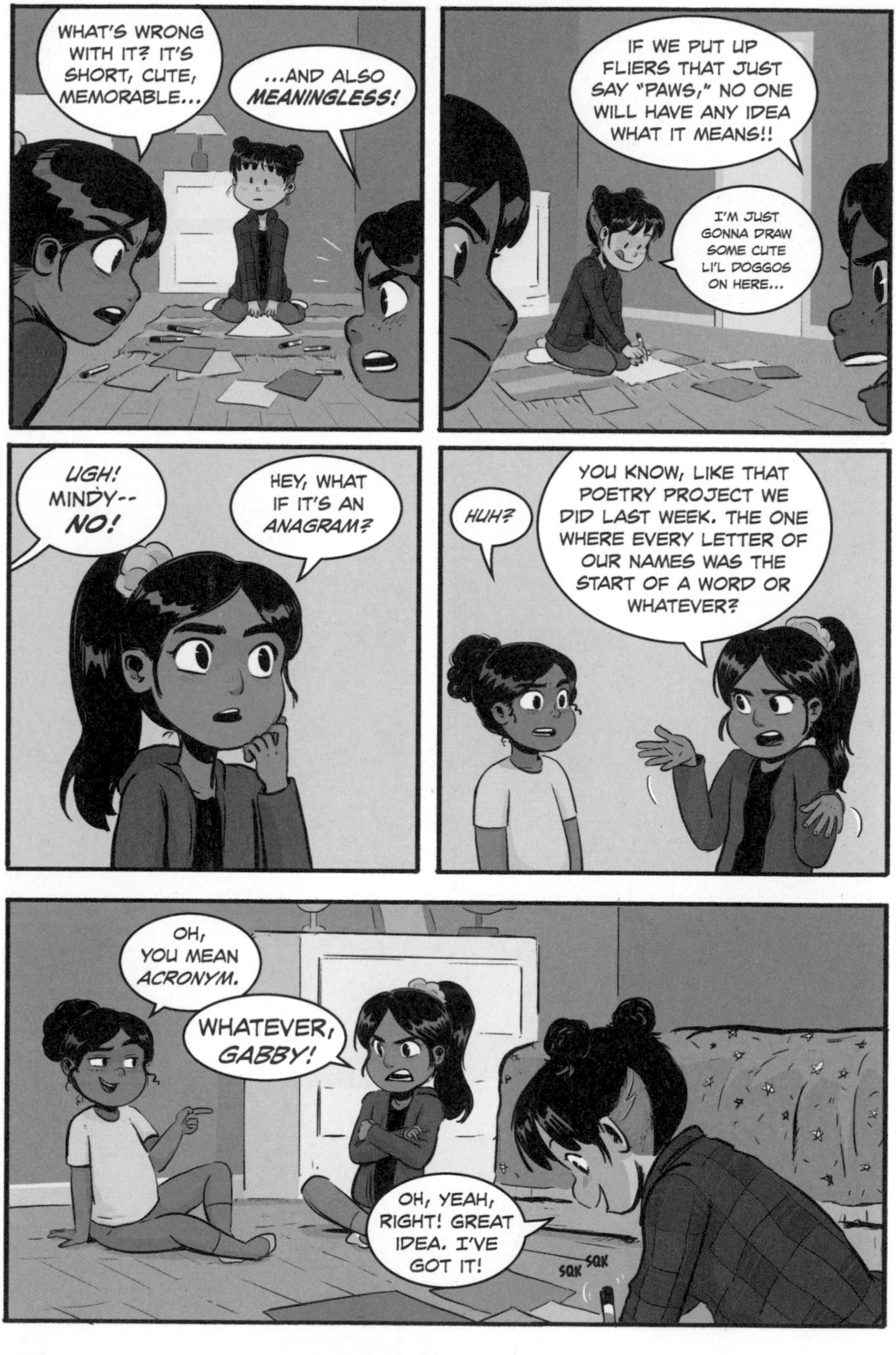
WHAT'S WRONG WITH IT? IT'S SHORT, CUTE, MEMORABLE...
...AND ALSO MEANINGLESS!
IF WE PUT UP FLIERS THAT JUST SAY "PAWS," NO ONE WILL HAVE ANY IDEA WHAT IT MEANS!!
I'M JUST GONNA DRAW SOME CUTE LI'L DOGGOS ON HERE...
UGH! MINDY-- NO!
HEY, WHAT IF IT'S AN ANAGRAM?
HUH?
YOU KNOW, LIKE THAT POETRY PROJECT WE DID LAST WEEK. THE ONE WHERE EVERY LETTER OF OUR NAMES WAS THE START OF A WORD OR WHATEVER?
OH, YOU MEAN ACRONYM.
WHATEVER, GABBY!
OH, YEAH, RIGHT! GREAT IDEA. I'VE GOT IT!
SQK SQK

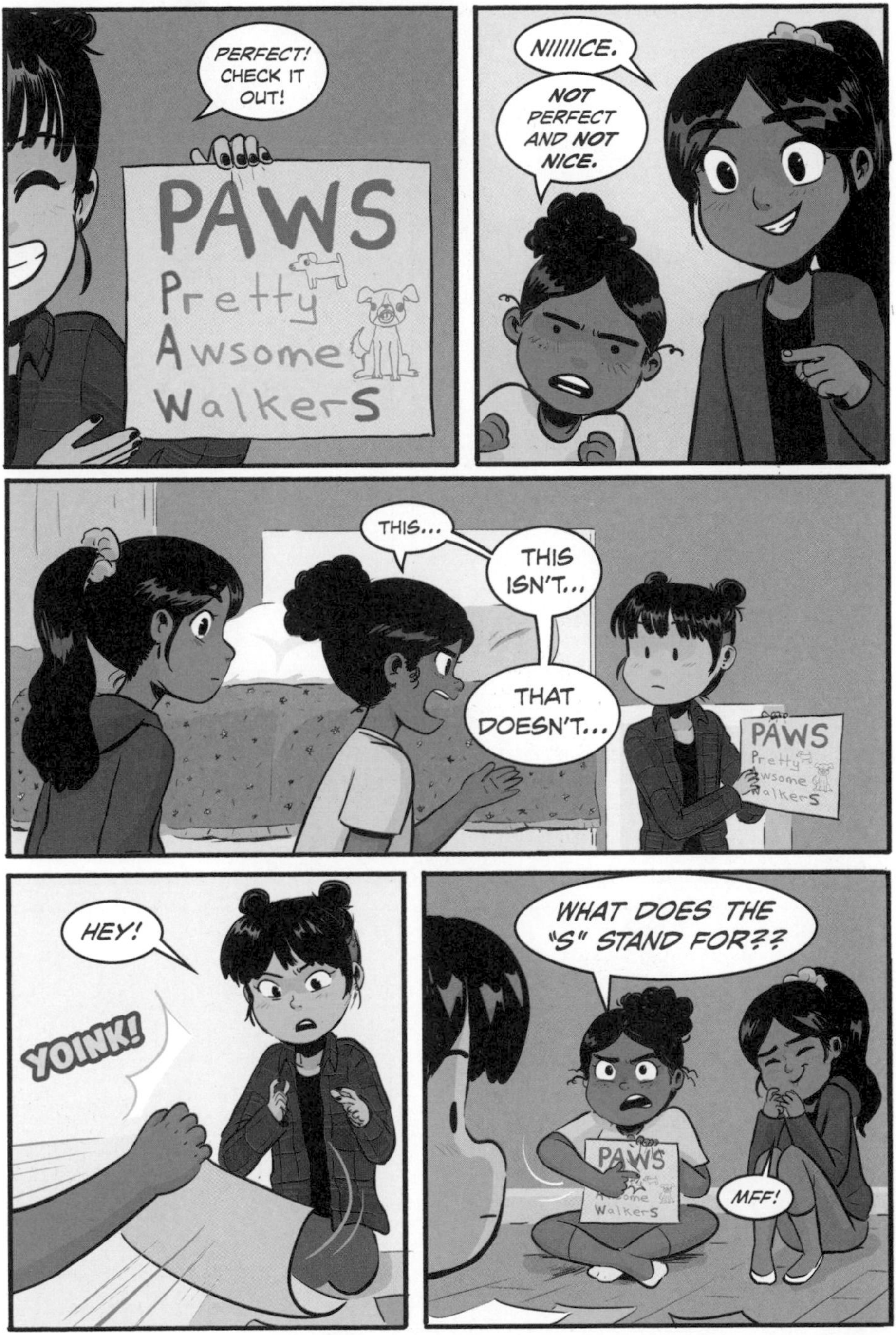
PERFECT! CHECK IT OUT!
PAWS
Pretty
Awsome
WalkerS
NIIIIICE.
NOT PERFECT AND NOT NICE.
THIS...
THIS ISN'T...
THAT DOESN'T...
PAWS
Pretty
Awsome
WalkerS
HEY!
YOINK!
WHAT DOES THE "S" STAND FOR??
PAWS
Awsome
WalkerS
MFF!

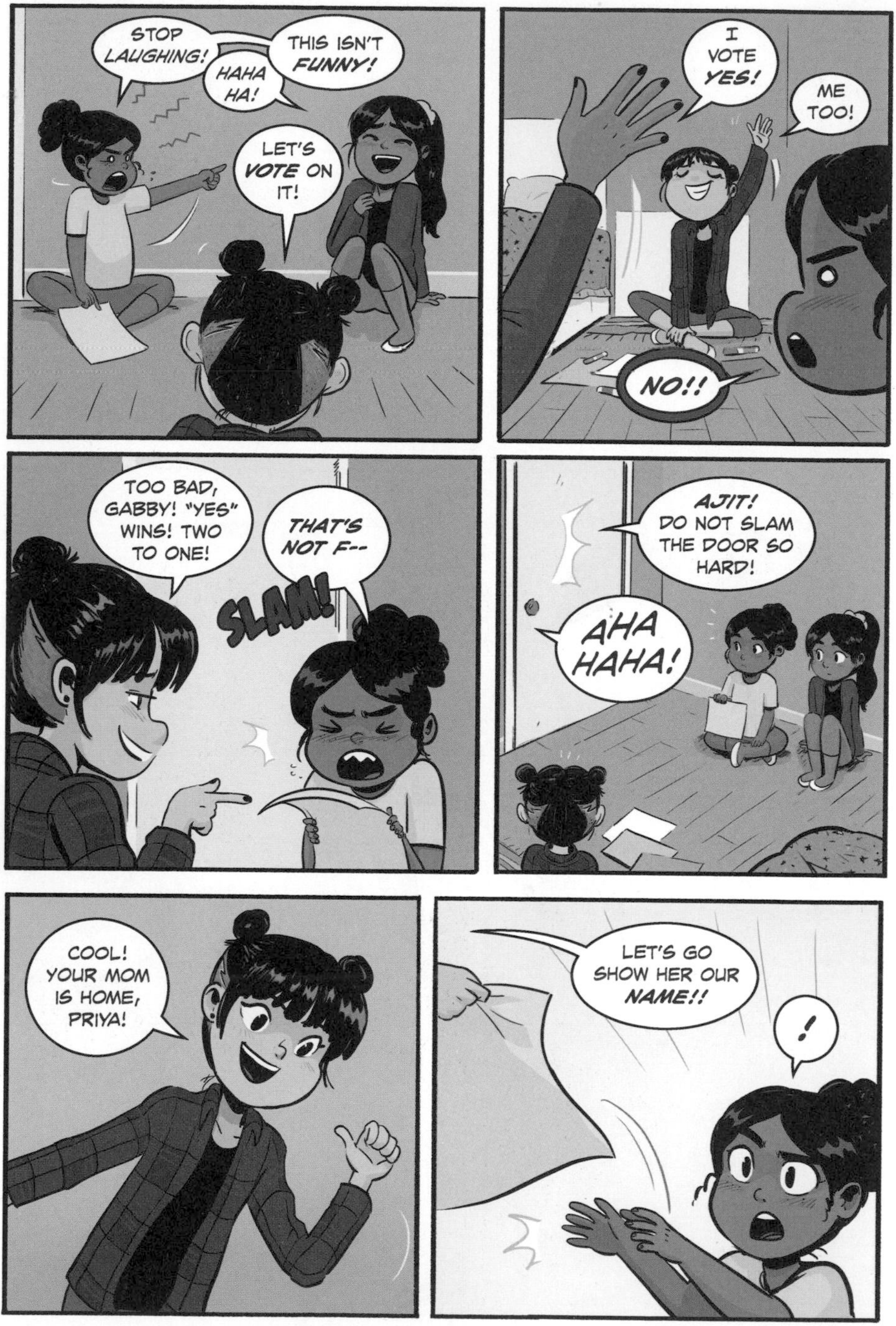
STOP LAUGHING!
HAHA HA!
THIS ISN'T *FUNNY!*
LET'S *VOTE* ON IT!
I VOTE *YES!*
ME TOO!
NO!!
TOO BAD, GABBY! "YES" WINS! TWO TO ONE!
THAT'S NOT F--
SLAM!
AJIT! DO NOT SLAM THE DOOR SO HARD!
AHA HAHA!
COOL! YOUR MOM IS HOME, PRIYA!
LET'S GO SHOW HER OUR *NAME!!*
!

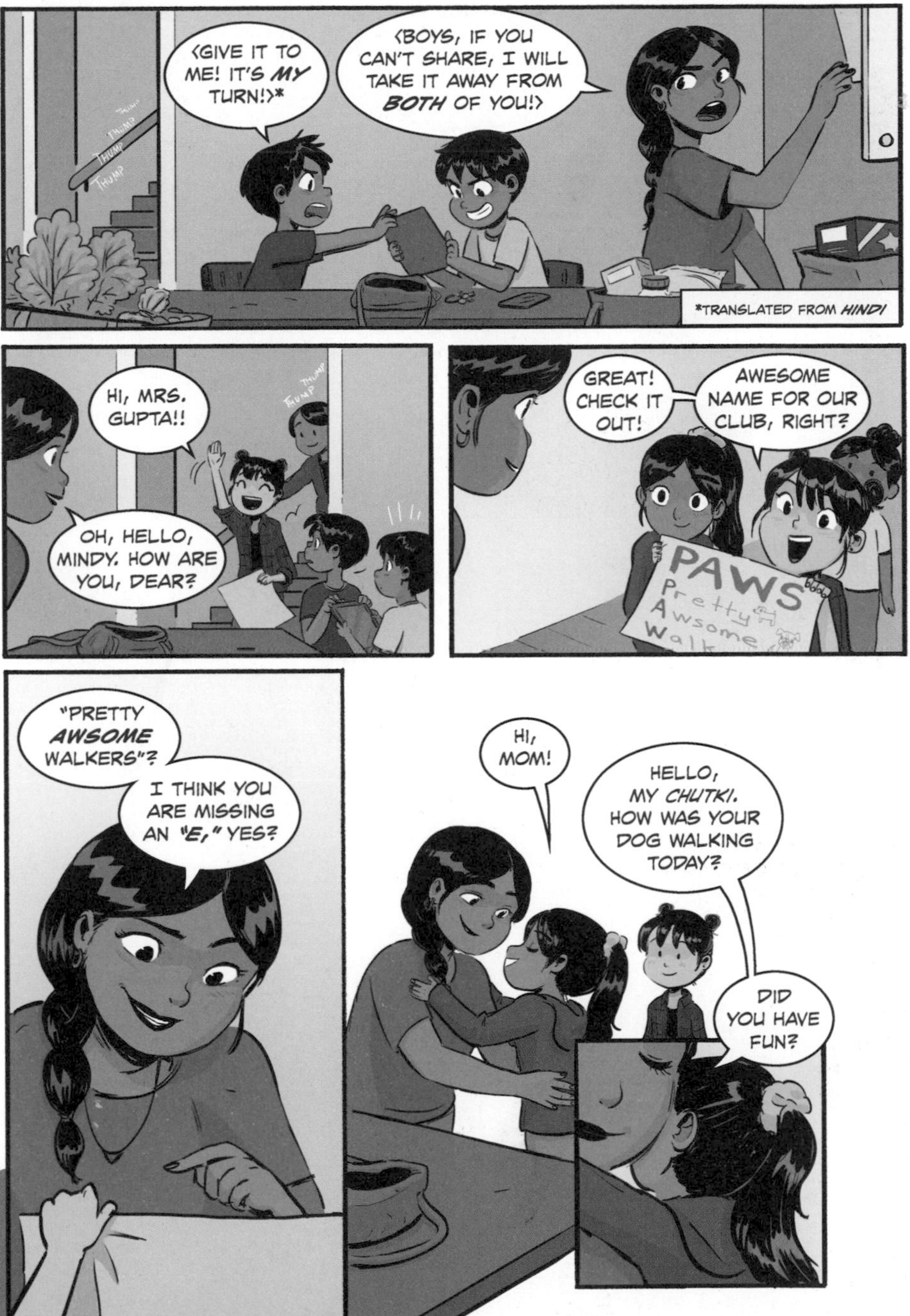

THUMP THUMP THUMP THUMP
‹GIVE IT TO ME! IT'S *MY* TURN!›*
‹BOYS, IF YOU CAN'T SHARE, I WILL TAKE IT AWAY FROM *BOTH* OF YOU!›
*TRANSLATED FROM *HINDI*
THUMP THUMP
HI, MRS. GUPTA!!
OH, HELLO, MINDY. HOW ARE YOU, DEAR?
GREAT! CHECK IT OUT!
AWESOME NAME FOR OUR CLUB, RIGHT?
PAWS Pretty Awsome Walk
"PRETTY *AWSOME* WALKERS"?
I THINK YOU ARE MISSING AN *"E,"* YES?
HI, MOM!
HELLO, MY *CHUTKI*. HOW WAS YOUR DOG WALKING TODAY?
DID YOU HAVE FUN?

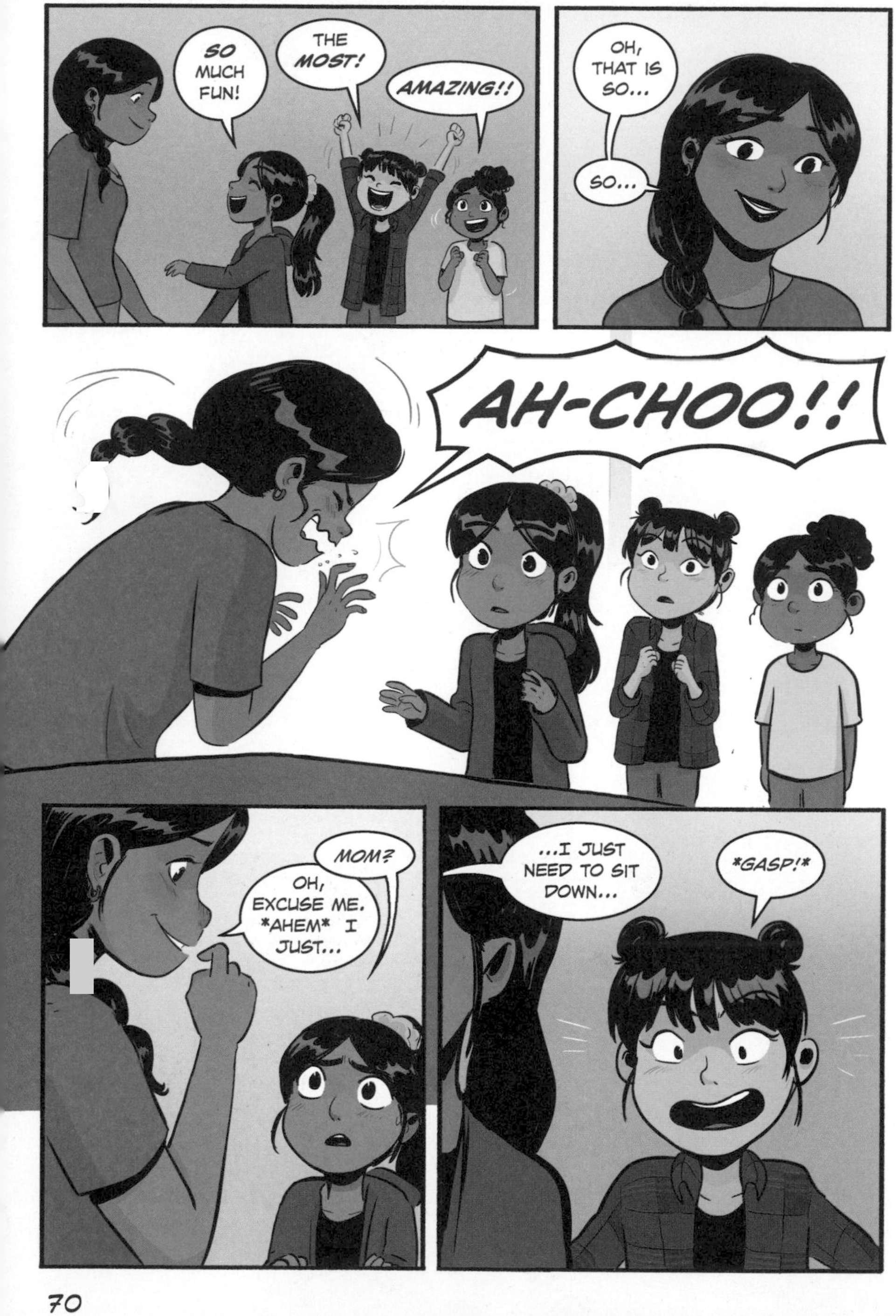
SO MUCH FUN!
THE MOST!
AMAZING!!
OH, THAT IS SO...
SO...
AH-CHOO!!
MOM?
OH, EXCUSE ME. *AHEM* I JUST...
...I JUST NEED TO SIT DOWN...
GASP!

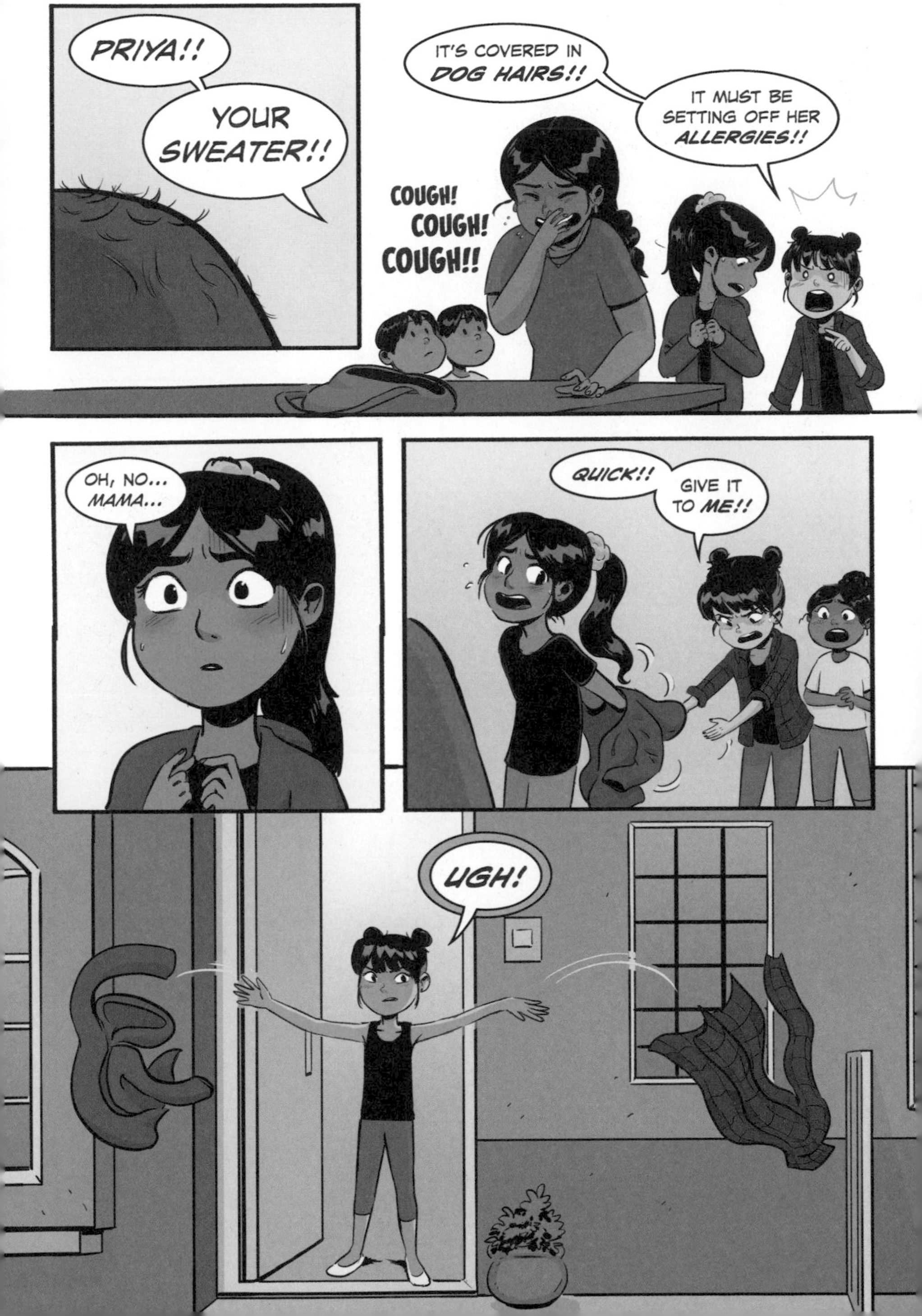
PRIYA!!
YOUR SWEATER!!
IT'S COVERED IN DOG HAIRS!!
IT MUST BE SETTING OFF HER ALLERGIES!!
COUGH! COUGH! COUGH!!
OH, NO... MAMA...
QUICK!!
GIVE IT TO ME!!
UGH!

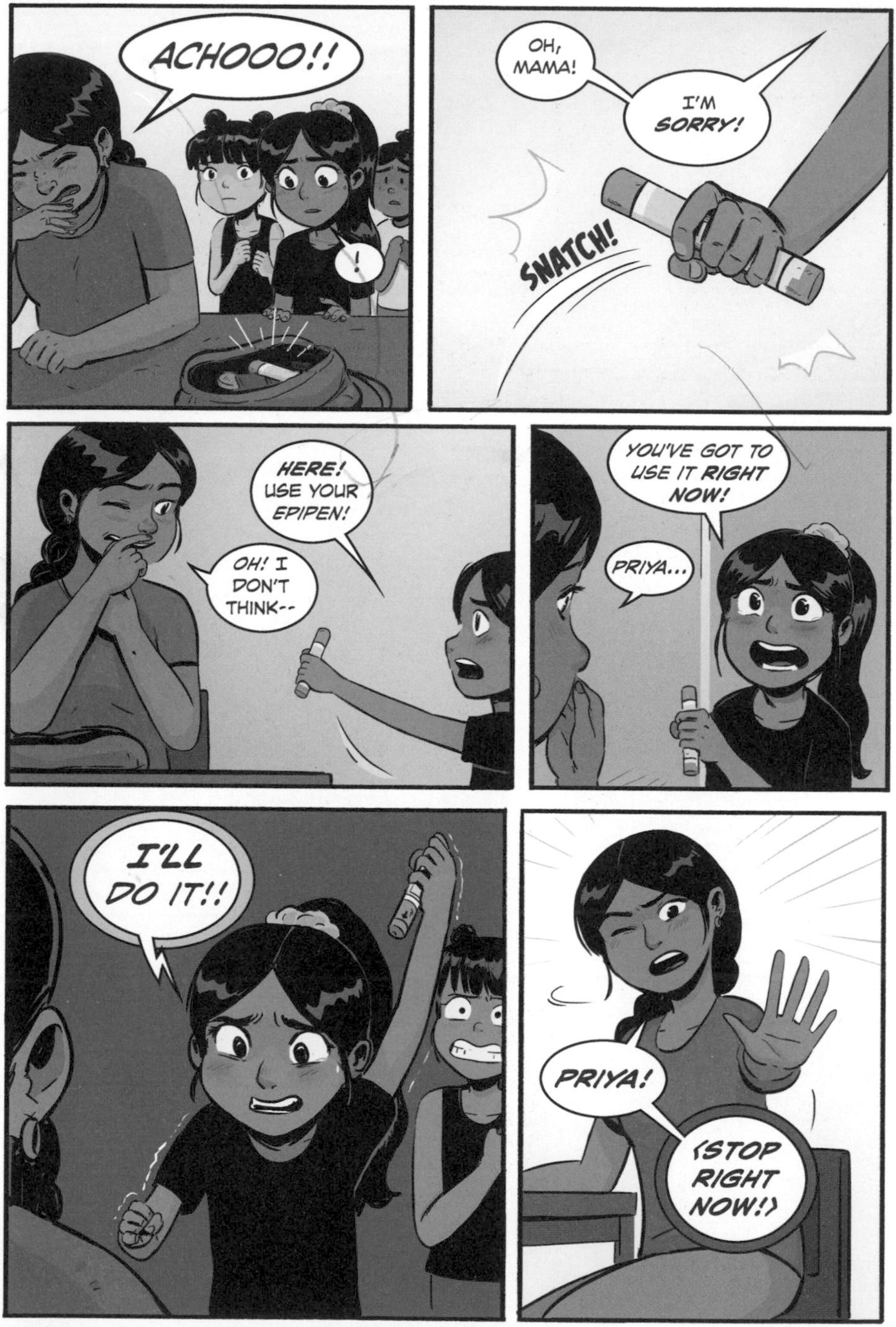
ACHOOO!!
!
OH, MAMA!
I'M SORRY!
SNATCH!
HERE! USE YOUR EPIPEN!
OH! I DON'T THINK--
YOU'VE GOT TO USE IT RIGHT NOW!
PRIYA...
I'LL DO IT!!
PRIYA!
‹STOP RIGHT NOW!›

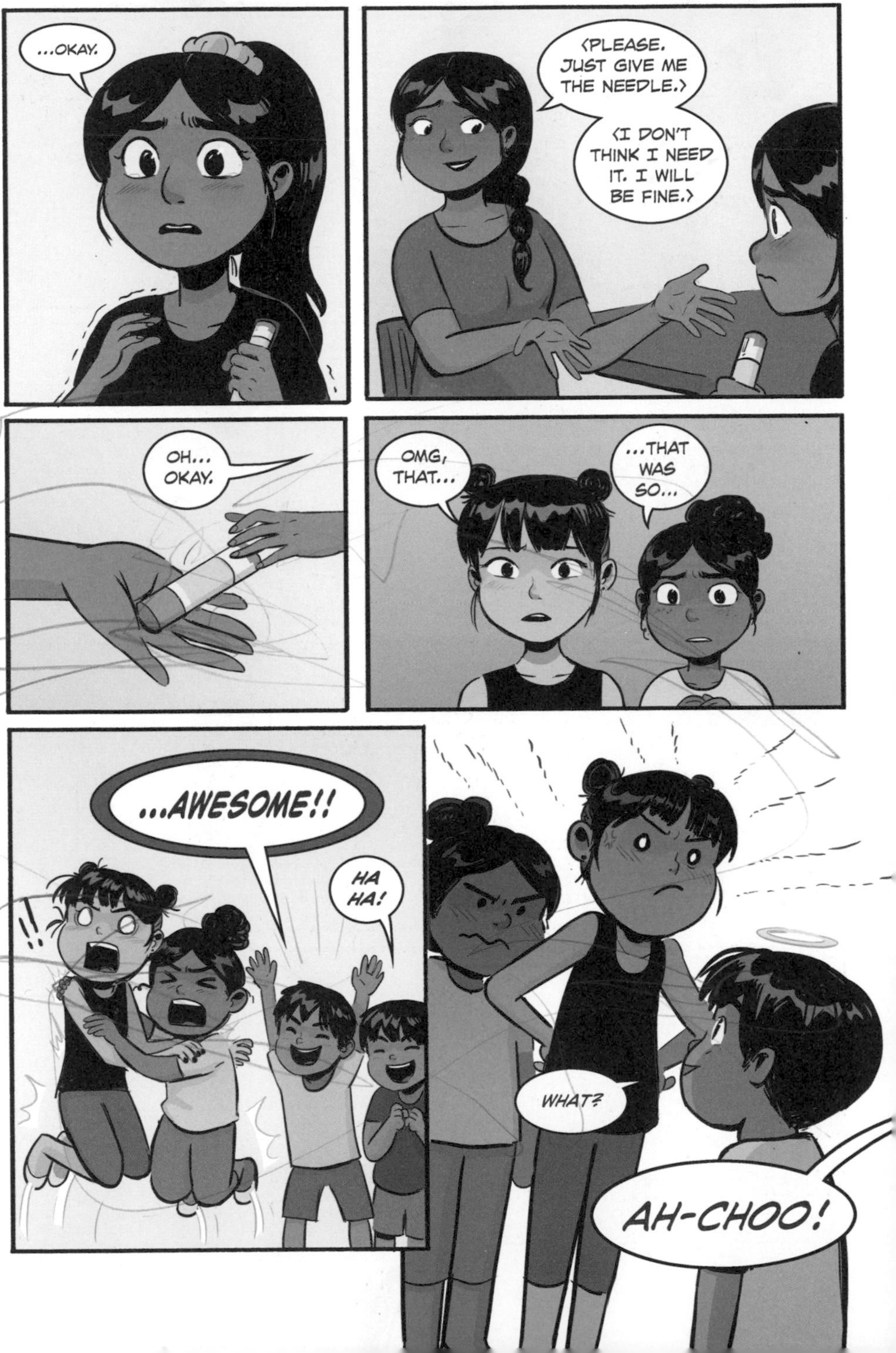
...OKAY.
<PLEASE. JUST GIVE ME THE NEEDLE.>
<I DON'T THINK I NEED IT. I WILL BE FINE.>
OH... OKAY.
OMG, THAT...
...THAT WAS SO...
...AWESOME!!
HA HA!
WHAT?
AH-CHOO!

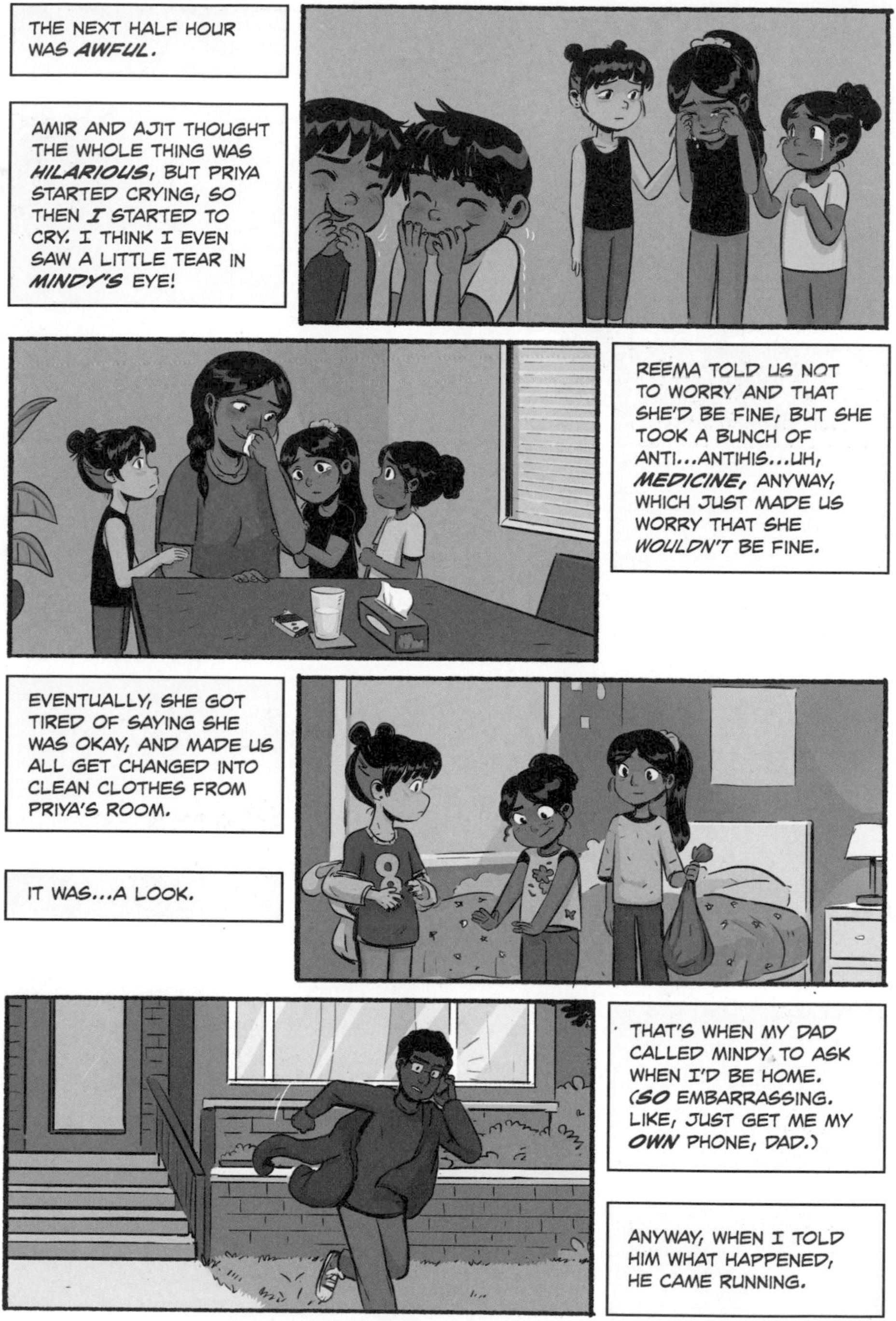
THE NEXT HALF HOUR WAS AWFUL.
AMIR AND AJIT THOUGHT THE WHOLE THING WAS HILARIOUS, BUT PRIYA STARTED CRYING, SO THEN I STARTED TO CRY. I THINK I EVEN SAW A LITTLE TEAR IN MINDY'S EYE!
REEMA TOLD US NOT TO WORRY AND THAT SHE'D BE FINE, BUT SHE TOOK A BUNCH OF ANTI...ANTIHIS...UH, MEDICINE, ANYWAY, WHICH JUST MADE US WORRY THAT SHE WOULDN'T BE FINE.
EVENTUALLY, SHE GOT TIRED OF SAYING SHE WAS OKAY, AND MADE US ALL GET CHANGED INTO CLEAN CLOTHES FROM PRIYA'S ROOM.
IT WAS...A LOOK.
THAT'S WHEN MY DAD CALLED MINDY TO ASK WHEN I'D BE HOME. (SO EMBARRASSING. LIKE, JUST GET ME MY OWN PHONE, DAD.)
ANYWAY, WHEN I TOLD HIM WHAT HAPPENED, HE CAME RUNNING.

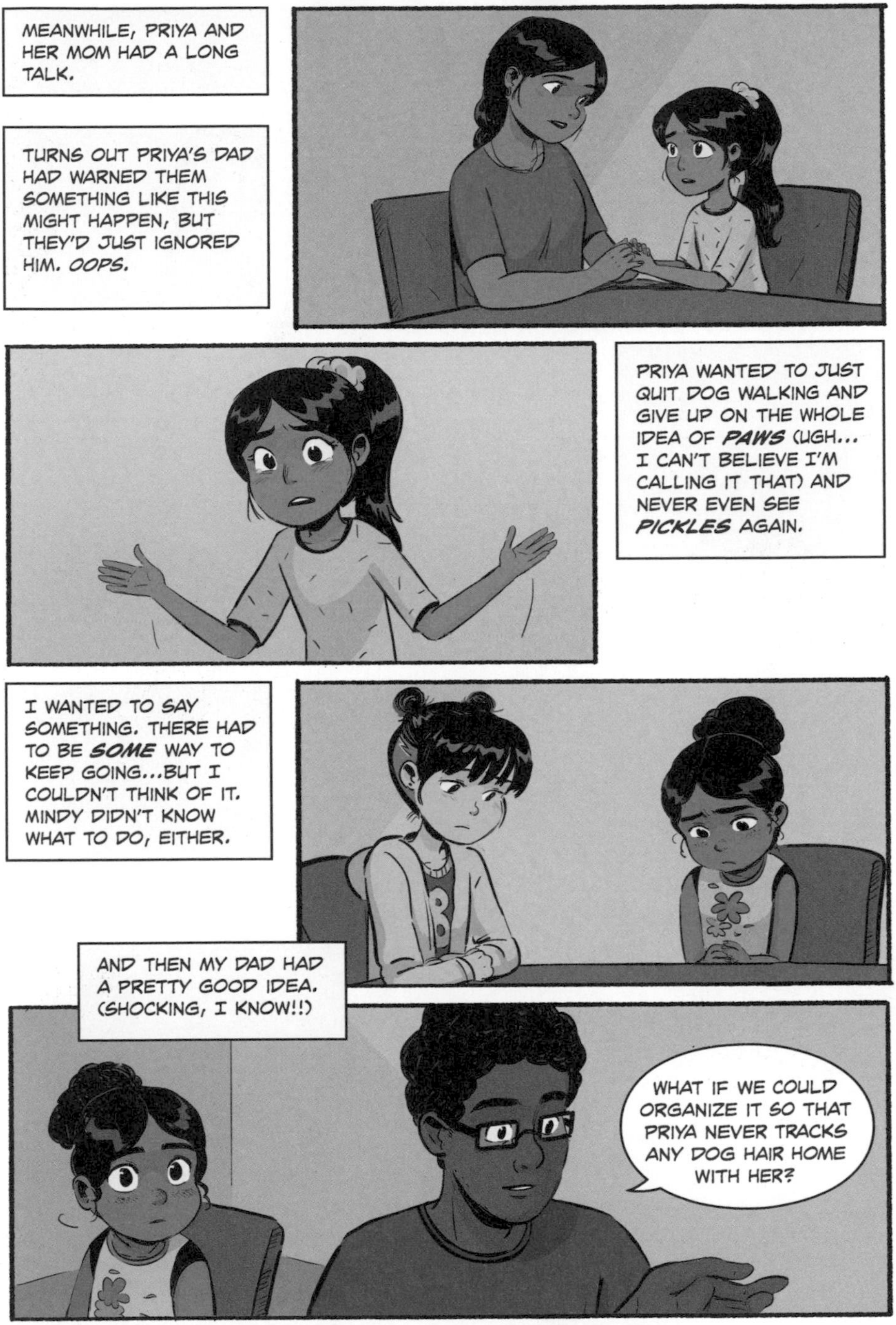
MEANWHILE, PRIYA AND HER MOM HAD A LONG TALK.
TURNS OUT PRIYA'S DAD HAD WARNED THEM SOMETHING LIKE THIS MIGHT HAPPEN, BUT THEY'D JUST IGNORED HIM. *OOPS.*
PRIYA WANTED TO JUST QUIT DOG WALKING AND GIVE UP ON THE WHOLE IDEA OF ***PAWS*** (UGH... I CAN'T BELIEVE I'M CALLING IT THAT) AND NEVER EVEN SEE ***PICKLES*** AGAIN.
I WANTED TO SAY SOMETHING. THERE HAD TO BE ***SOME*** WAY TO KEEP GOING...BUT I COULDN'T THINK OF IT. MINDY DIDN'T KNOW WHAT TO DO, EITHER.
AND THEN MY DAD HAD A PRETTY GOOD IDEA. (SHOCKING, I KNOW!!)
WHAT IF WE COULD ORGANIZE IT SO THAT PRIYA NEVER TRACKS ANY DOG HAIR HOME WITH HER?

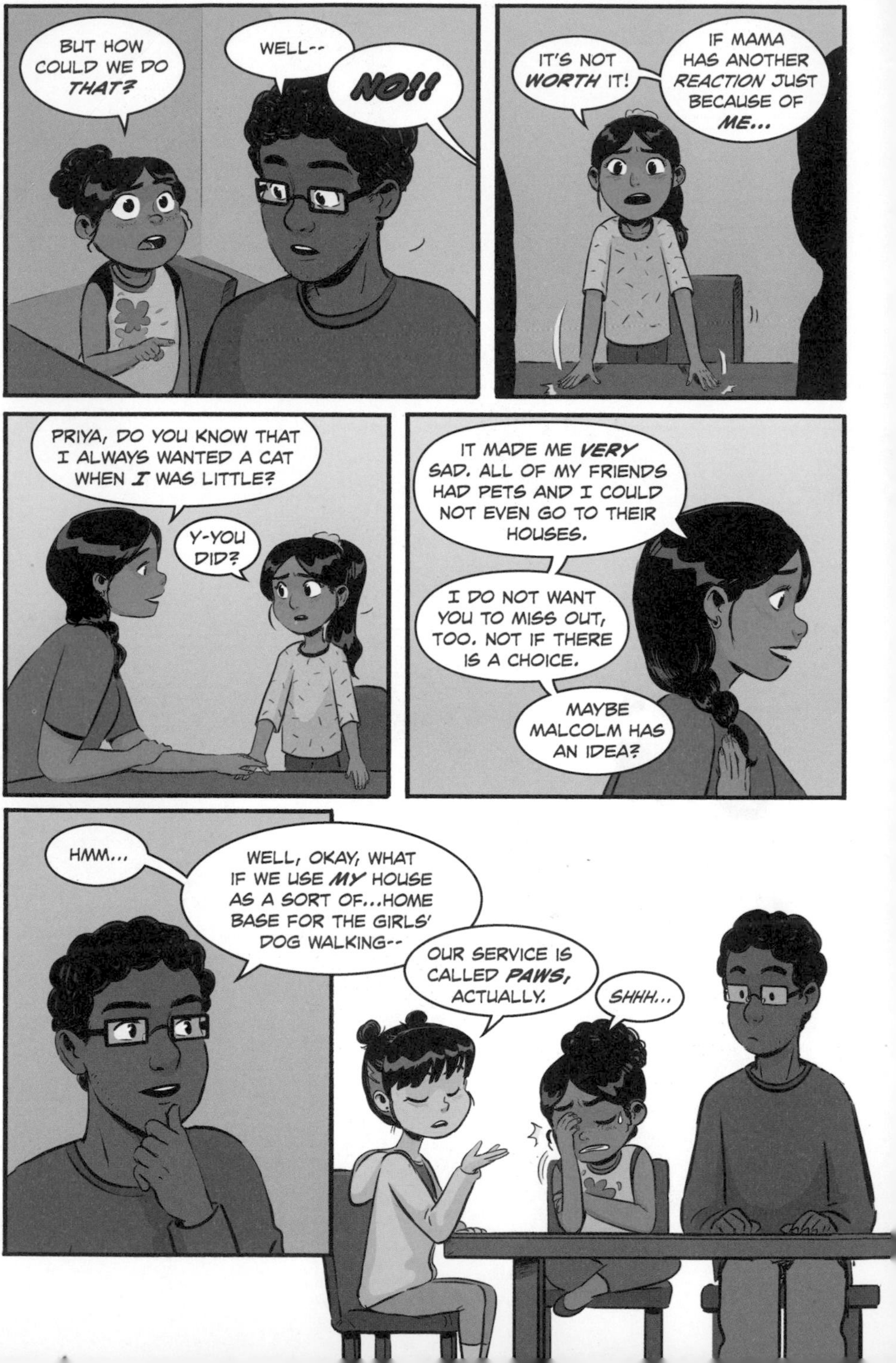

BUT HOW COULD WE DO *THAT?*
WELL--
NO!!
IT'S NOT *WORTH* IT!
IF MAMA HAS ANOTHER *REACTION* JUST BECAUSE OF *ME...*
PRIYA, DO YOU KNOW THAT I ALWAYS WANTED A CAT WHEN *I* WAS LITTLE?
Y-YOU DID?
IT MADE ME *VERY* SAD. ALL OF MY FRIENDS HAD PETS AND I COULD NOT EVEN GO TO THEIR HOUSES.
I DO NOT WANT YOU TO MISS OUT, TOO. NOT IF THERE IS A CHOICE.
MAYBE MALCOLM HAS AN IDEA?
HMM...
WELL, OKAY, WHAT IF WE USE *MY* HOUSE AS A SORT OF...HOME BASE FOR THE GIRLS' DOG WALKING--
OUR SERVICE IS CALLED *PAWS,* ACTUALLY.
SHHH...

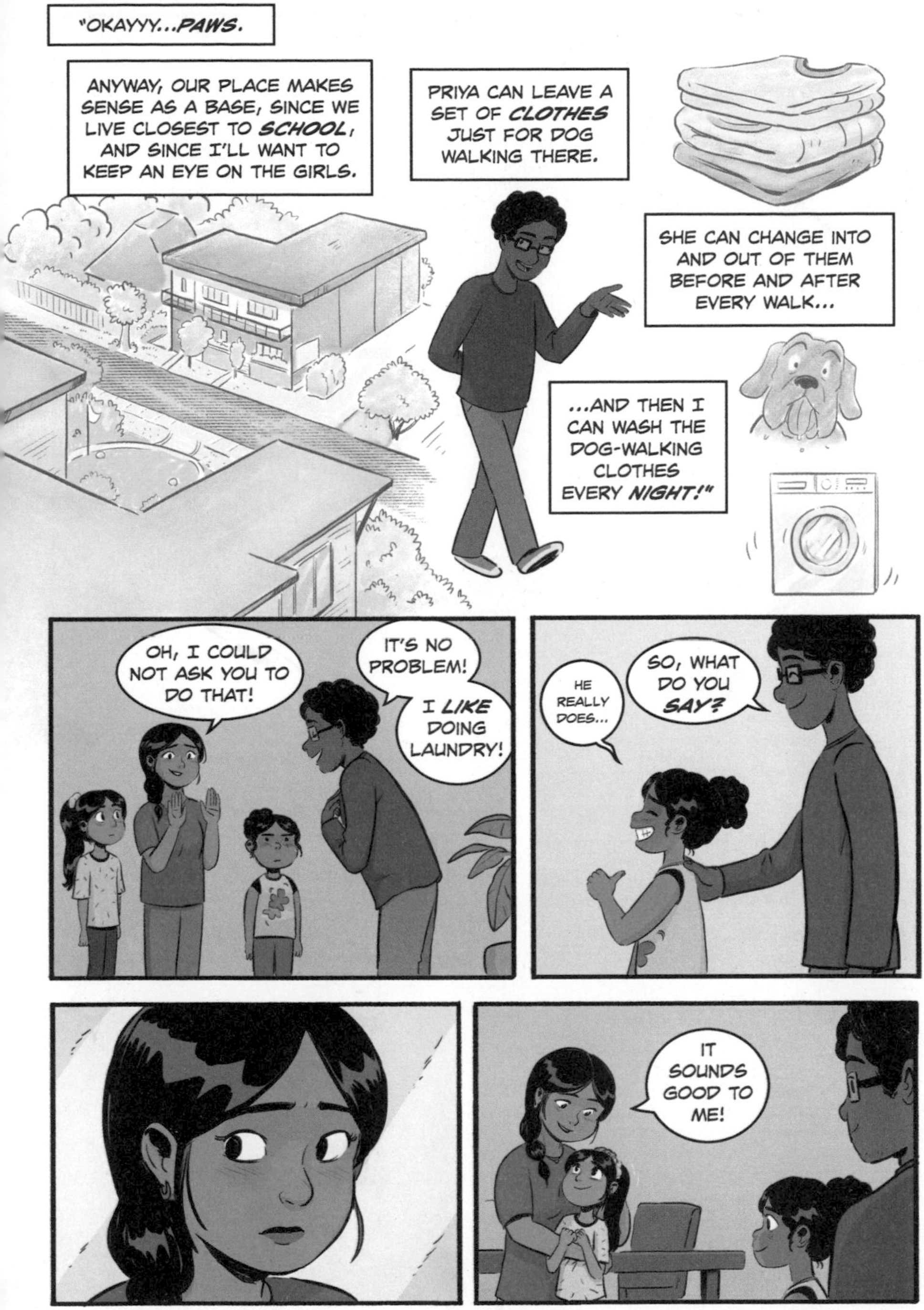
"OKAYYY...PAWS.
ANYWAY, OUR PLACE MAKES SENSE AS A BASE, SINCE WE LIVE CLOSEST TO SCHOOL, AND SINCE I'LL WANT TO KEEP AN EYE ON THE GIRLS.
PRIYA CAN LEAVE A SET OF CLOTHES JUST FOR DOG WALKING THERE.
SHE CAN CHANGE INTO AND OUT OF THEM BEFORE AND AFTER EVERY WALK...
...AND THEN I CAN WASH THE DOG-WALKING CLOTHES EVERY NIGHT!"
OH, I COULD NOT ASK YOU TO DO THAT!
IT'S NO PROBLEM!
I LIKE DOING LAUNDRY!
HE REALLY DOES...
SO, WHAT DO YOU SAY?
IT SOUNDS GOOD TO ME!

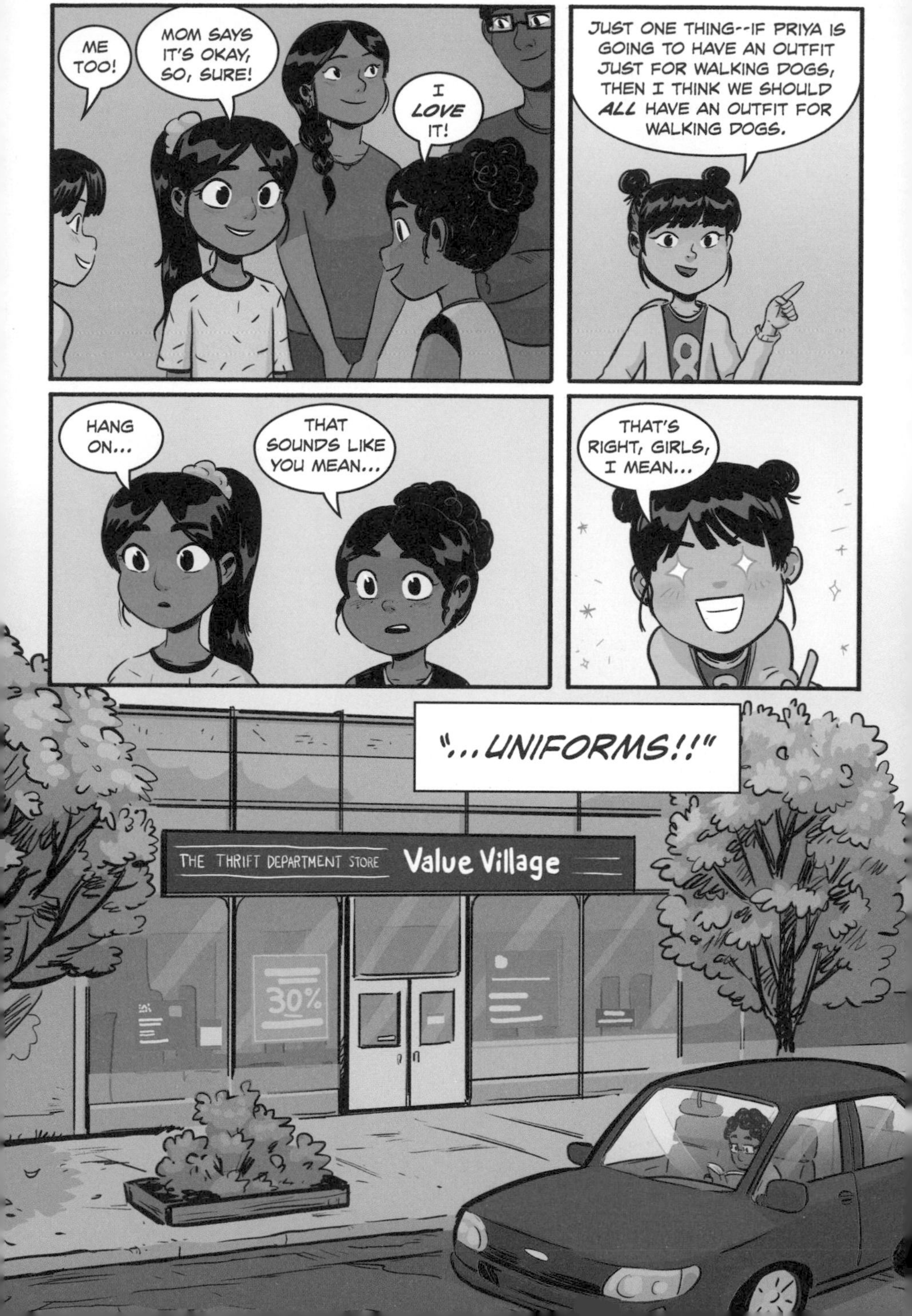
ME TOO!
MOM SAYS IT'S OKAY, SO, SURE!
I *LOVE* IT!
JUST ONE THING--IF PRIYA IS GOING TO HAVE AN OUTFIT JUST FOR WALKING DOGS, THEN I THINK WE SHOULD *ALL* HAVE AN OUTFIT FOR WALKING DOGS.
HANG ON...
THAT SOUNDS LIKE YOU MEAN...
THAT'S RIGHT, GIRLS, I MEAN...
"...UNIFORMS!!"
THE THRIFT DEPARTMENT STORE Value Village
30%

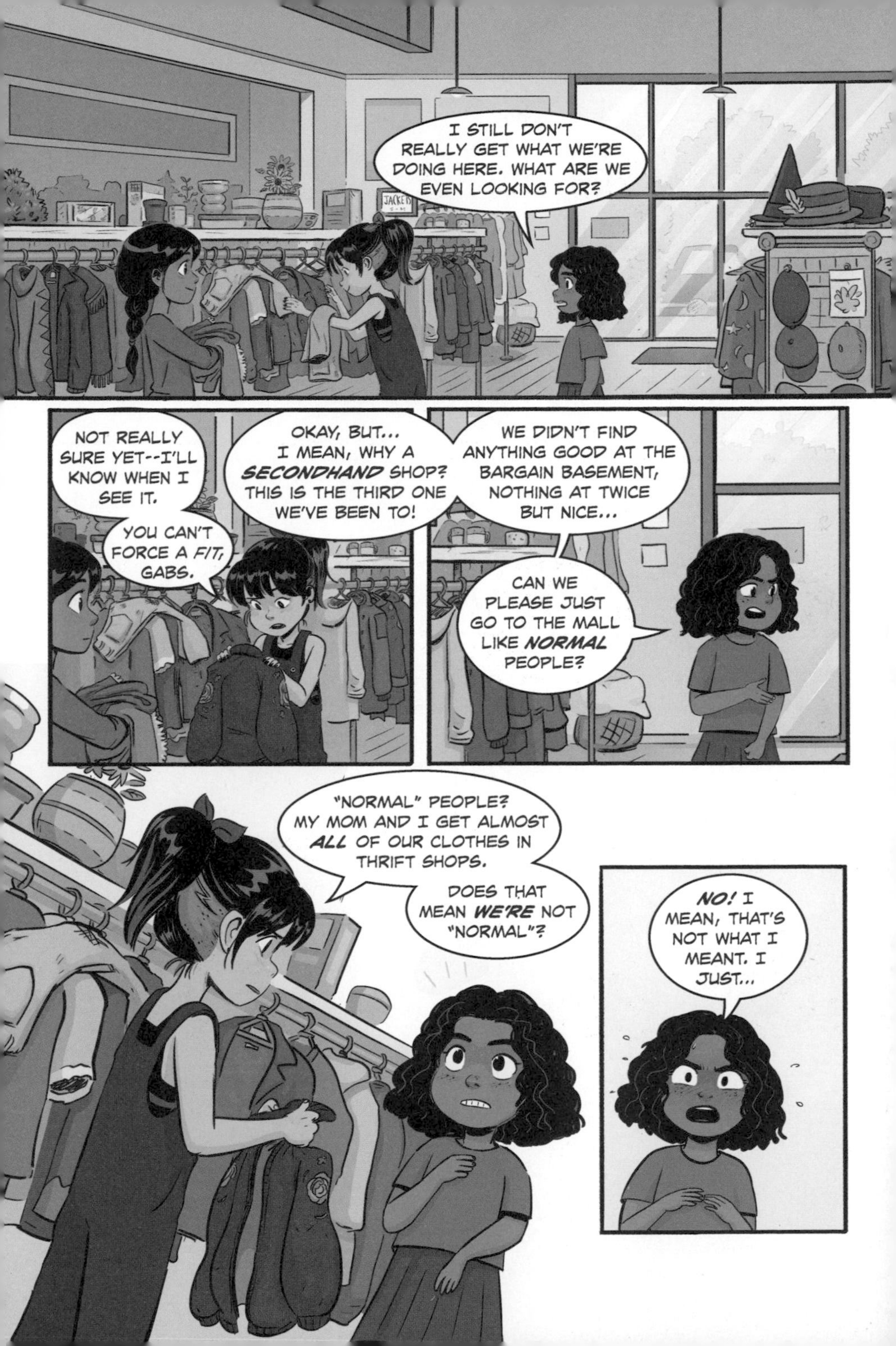

I STILL DON'T REALLY GET WHAT WE'RE DOING HERE. WHAT ARE WE EVEN LOOKING FOR?
NOT REALLY SURE YET--I'LL KNOW WHEN I SEE IT.
YOU CAN'T FORCE A *FIT*, GABS.
OKAY, BUT... I MEAN, WHY A ***SECONDHAND*** SHOP? THIS IS THE THIRD ONE WE'VE BEEN TO!
WE DIDN'T FIND ANYTHING GOOD AT THE BARGAIN BASEMENT, NOTHING AT TWICE BUT NICE...
CAN WE PLEASE JUST GO TO THE MALL LIKE ***NORMAL*** PEOPLE?
"NORMAL" PEOPLE? MY MOM AND I GET ALMOST ***ALL*** OF OUR CLOTHES IN THRIFT SHOPS.
DOES THAT MEAN ***WE'RE*** NOT "NORMAL"?
NO! I MEAN, THAT'S NOT WHAT I MEANT. I JUST...
JACKETS

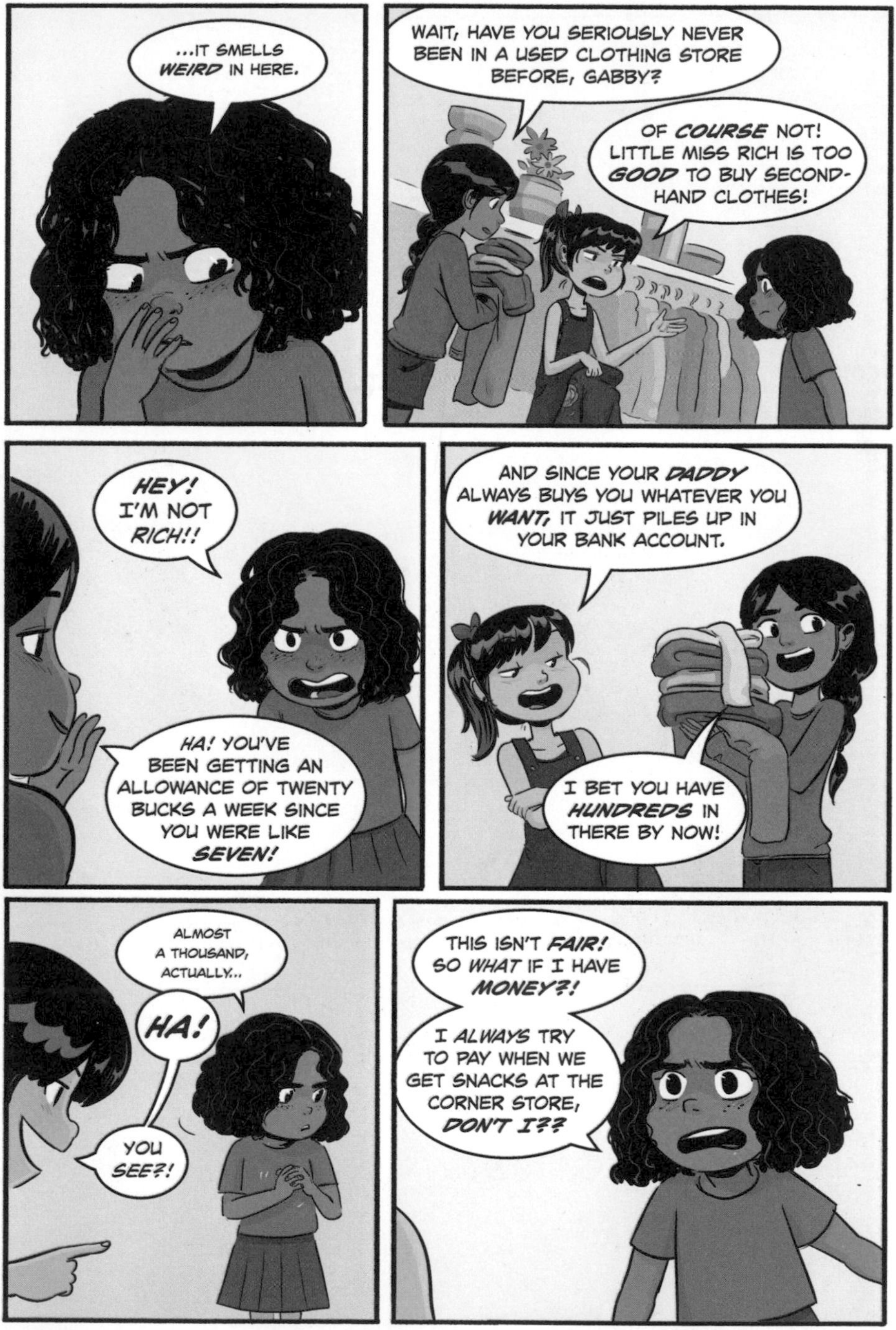
...IT SMELLS WEIRD IN HERE.
WAIT, HAVE YOU SERIOUSLY NEVER BEEN IN A USED CLOTHING STORE BEFORE, GABBY?
OF COURSE NOT! LITTLE MISS RICH IS TOO GOOD TO BUY SECOND-HAND CLOTHES!
HEY! I'M NOT RICH!!
HA! YOU'VE BEEN GETTING AN ALLOWANCE OF TWENTY BUCKS A WEEK SINCE YOU WERE LIKE SEVEN!
AND SINCE YOUR DADDY ALWAYS BUYS YOU WHATEVER YOU WANT, IT JUST PILES UP IN YOUR BANK ACCOUNT.
I BET YOU HAVE HUNDREDS IN THERE BY NOW!
ALMOST A THOUSAND, ACTUALLY...
HA!
YOU SEE?!
THIS ISN'T FAIR! SO WHAT IF I HAVE MONEY?!
I ALWAYS TRY TO PAY WHEN WE GET SNACKS AT THE CORNER STORE, DON'T I??

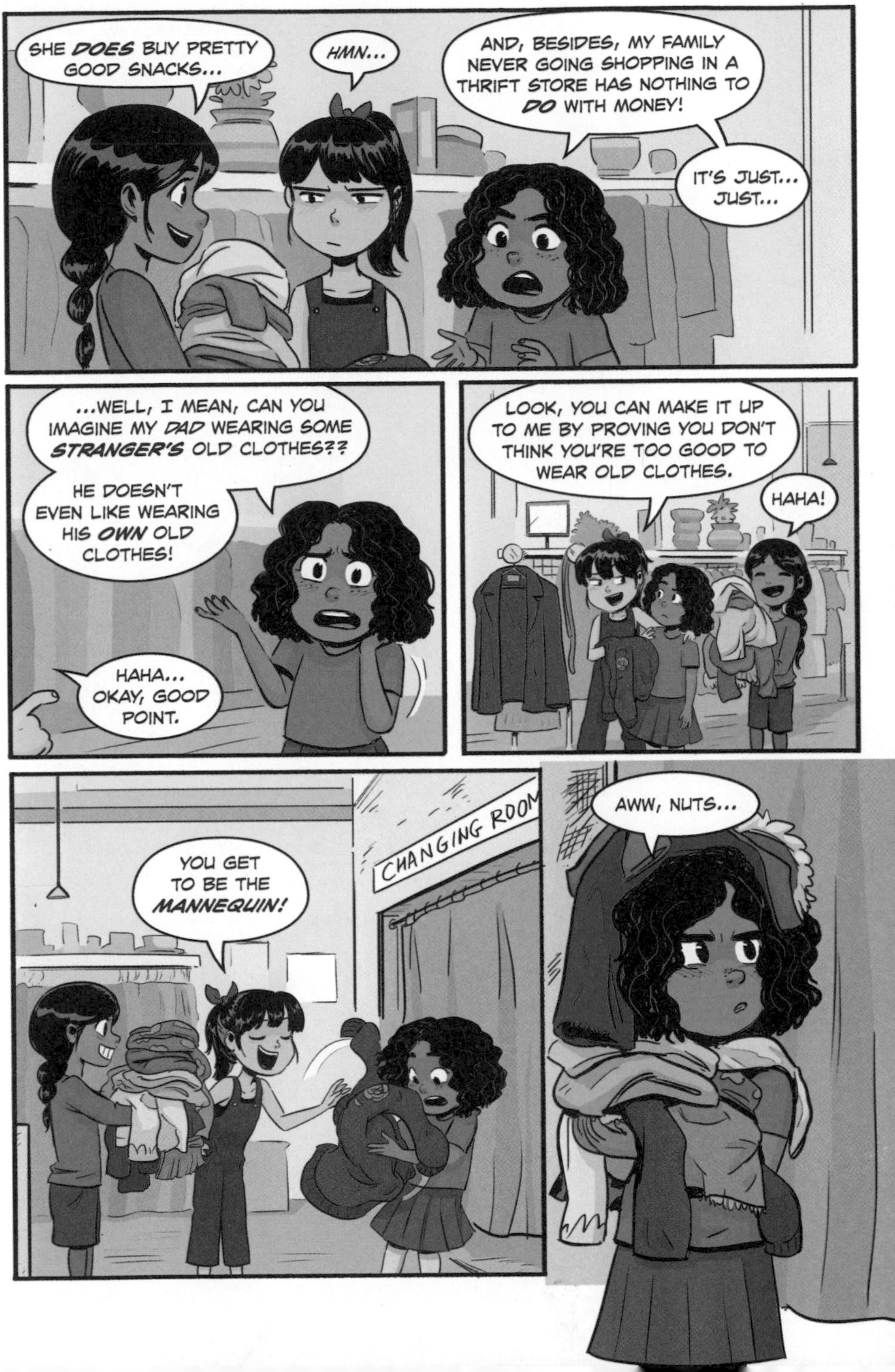
SHE DOES BUY PRETTY GOOD SNACKS...
HMN...
AND, BESIDES, MY FAMILY NEVER GOING SHOPPING IN A THRIFT STORE HAS NOTHING TO DO WITH MONEY!
IT'S JUST... JUST...
...WELL, I MEAN, CAN YOU IMAGINE MY DAD WEARING SOME STRANGER'S OLD CLOTHES??
HE DOESN'T EVEN LIKE WEARING HIS OWN OLD CLOTHES!
HAHA... OKAY, GOOD POINT.
LOOK, YOU CAN MAKE IT UP TO ME BY PROVING YOU DON'T THINK YOU'RE TOO GOOD TO WEAR OLD CLOTHES.
HAHA!
CHANGING ROOM
YOU GET TO BE THE MANNEQUIN!
AWW, NUTS...

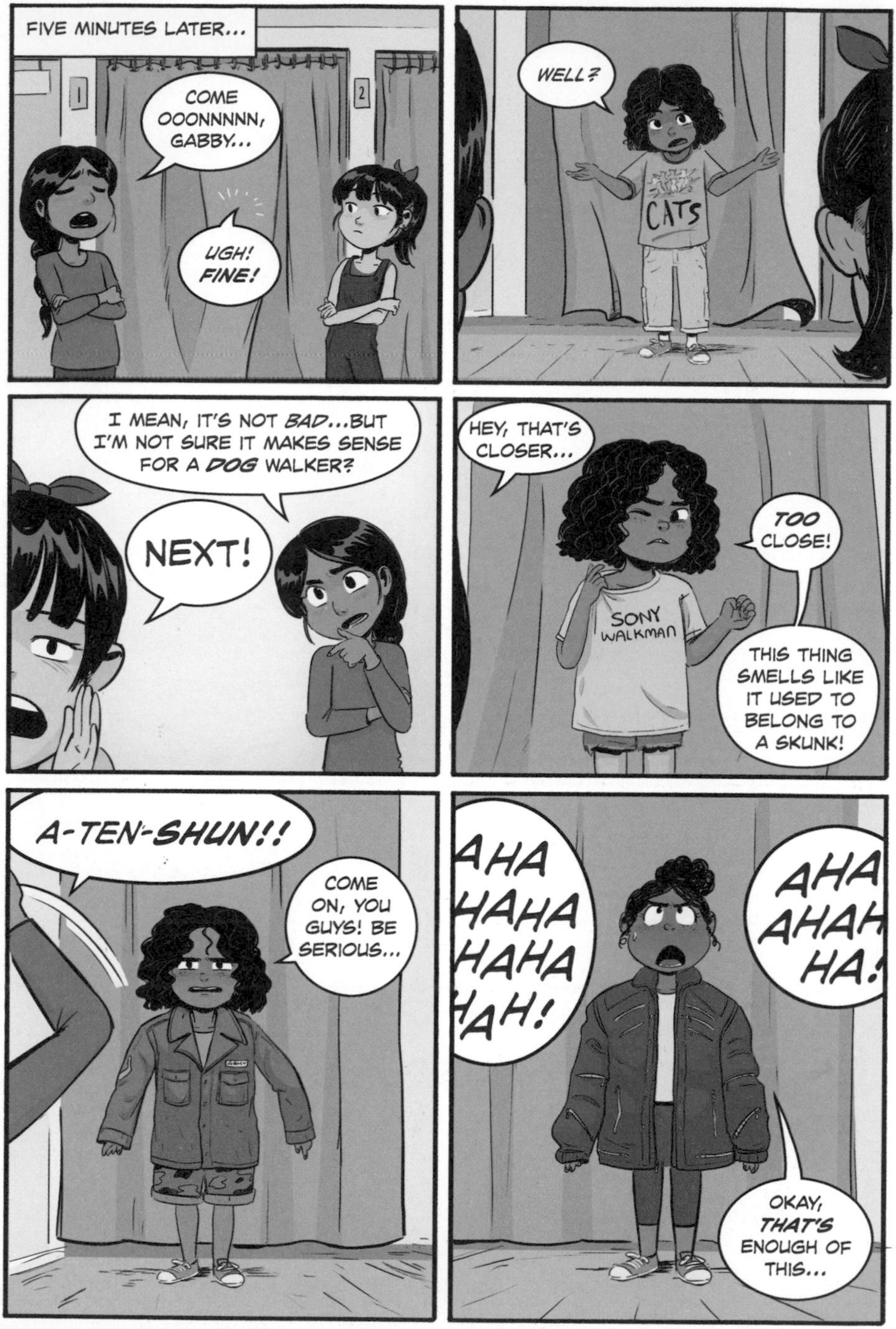
FIVE MINUTES LATER...
COME OOONNNNN, GABBY...
UGH! FINE!
WELL?
CATS
I MEAN, IT'S NOT BAD...BUT I'M NOT SURE IT MAKES SENSE FOR A DOG WALKER?
NEXT!
HEY, THAT'S CLOSER...
TOO CLOSE!
SONY WALKMAN
THIS THING SMELLS LIKE IT USED TO BELONG TO A SKUNK!
A-TEN-SHUN!!
COME ON, YOU GUYS! BE SERIOUS...
AHA HAHA HAHA HAH!
AHA AHAH HA!
OKAY, THAT'S ENOUGH OF THIS...

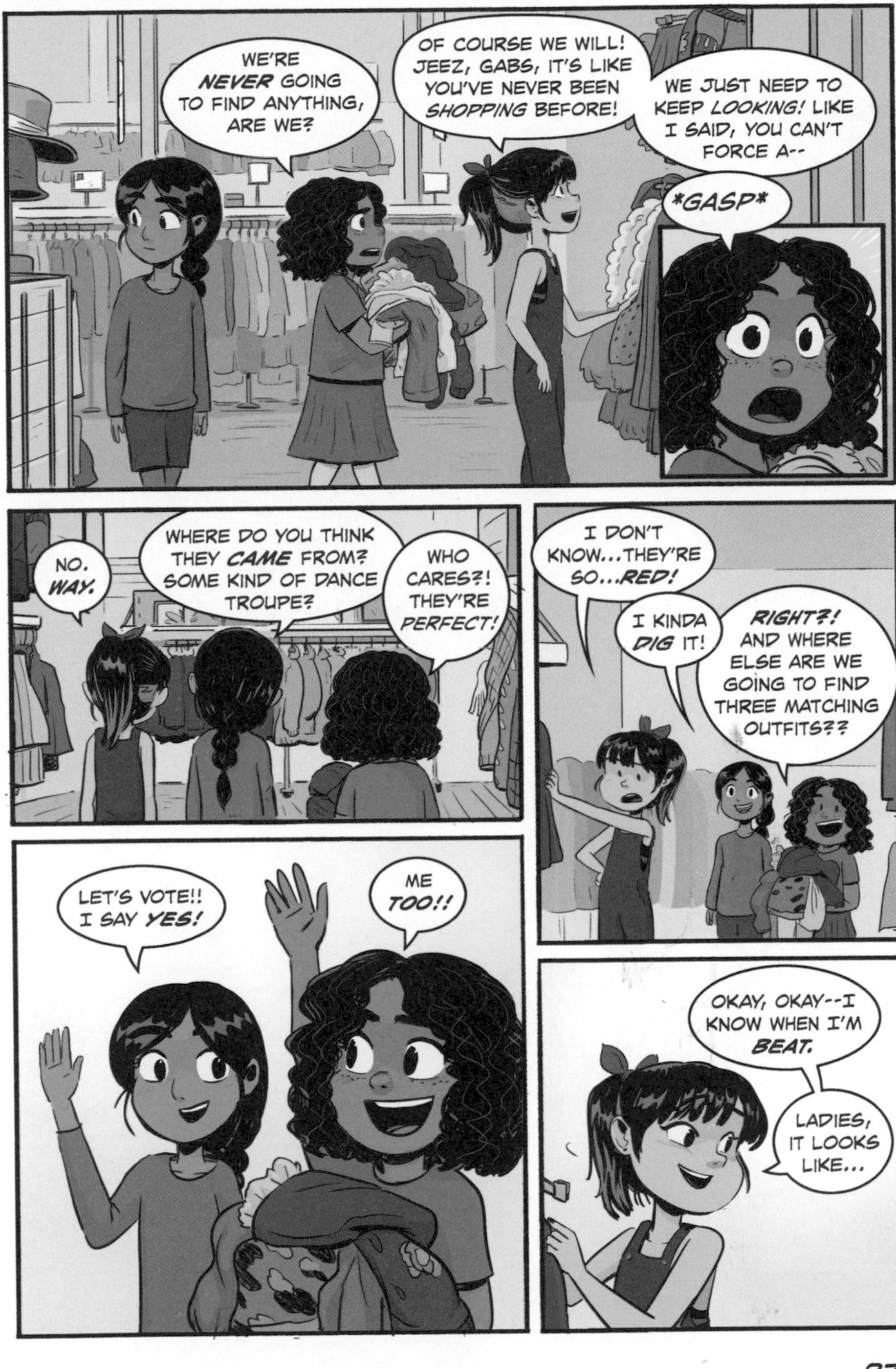
WE'RE NEVER GOING TO FIND ANYTHING, ARE WE?
OF COURSE WE WILL! JEEZ, GABS, IT'S LIKE YOU'VE NEVER BEEN SHOPPING BEFORE!
WE JUST NEED TO KEEP LOOKING! LIKE I SAID, YOU CAN'T FORCE A--
GASP
NO. WAY.
WHERE DO YOU THINK THEY CAME FROM? SOME KIND OF DANCE TROUPE?
WHO CARES?! THEY'RE PERFECT!
I DON'T KNOW...THEY'RE SO...RED!
I KINDA DIG IT!
RIGHT?! AND WHERE ELSE ARE WE GOING TO FIND THREE MATCHING OUTFITS??
LET'S VOTE!! I SAY YES!
ME TOO!!
OKAY, OKAY--I KNOW WHEN I'M BEAT.
LADIES, IT LOOKS LIKE...

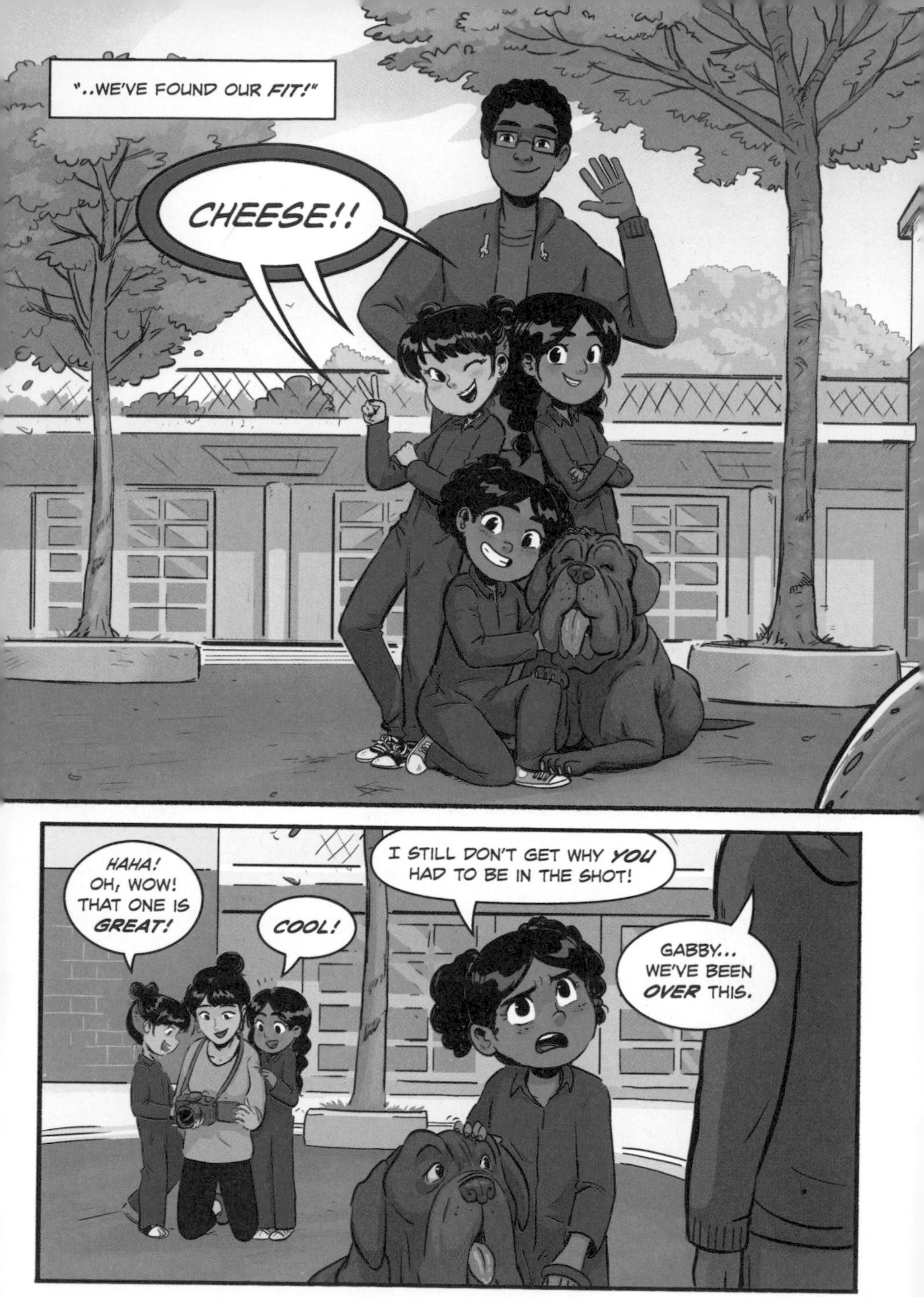
"..WE'VE FOUND OUR FIT!"
CHEESE!!
HAHA! OH, WOW! THAT ONE IS GREAT!
COOL!
I STILL DON'T GET WHY YOU HAD TO BE IN THE SHOT!
GABBY... WE'VE BEEN OVER THIS.

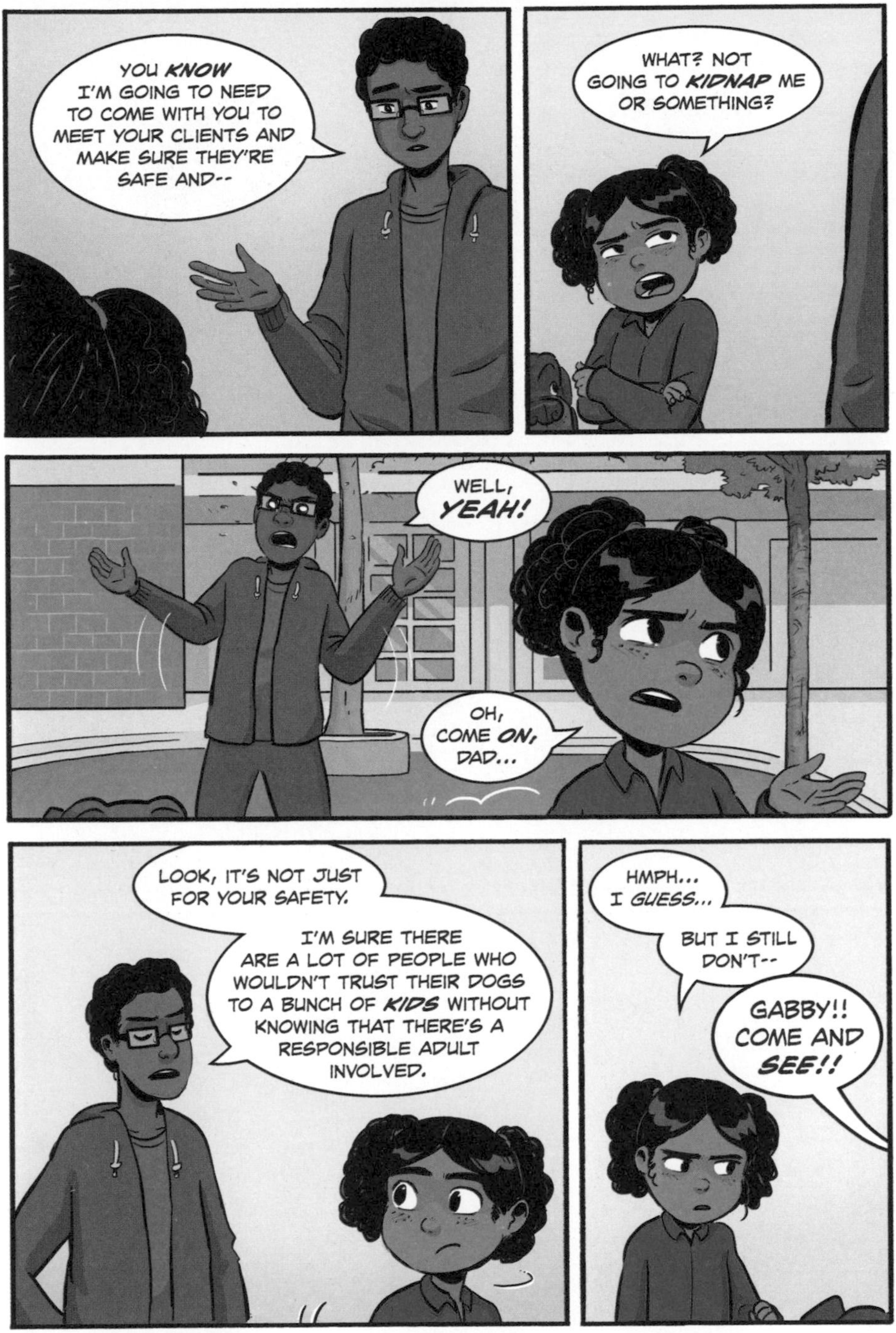
YOU KNOW I'M GOING TO NEED TO COME WITH YOU TO MEET YOUR CLIENTS AND MAKE SURE THEY'RE SAFE AND--
WHAT? NOT GOING TO KIDNAP ME OR SOMETHING?
WELL, YEAH!
OH, COME ON, DAD...
LOOK, IT'S NOT JUST FOR YOUR SAFETY.
I'M SURE THERE ARE A LOT OF PEOPLE WHO WOULDN'T TRUST THEIR DOGS TO A BUNCH OF KIDS WITHOUT KNOWING THAT THERE'S A RESPONSIBLE ADULT INVOLVED.
HMPH... I GUESS...
BUT I STILL DON'T--
GABBY!! COME AND SEE!!

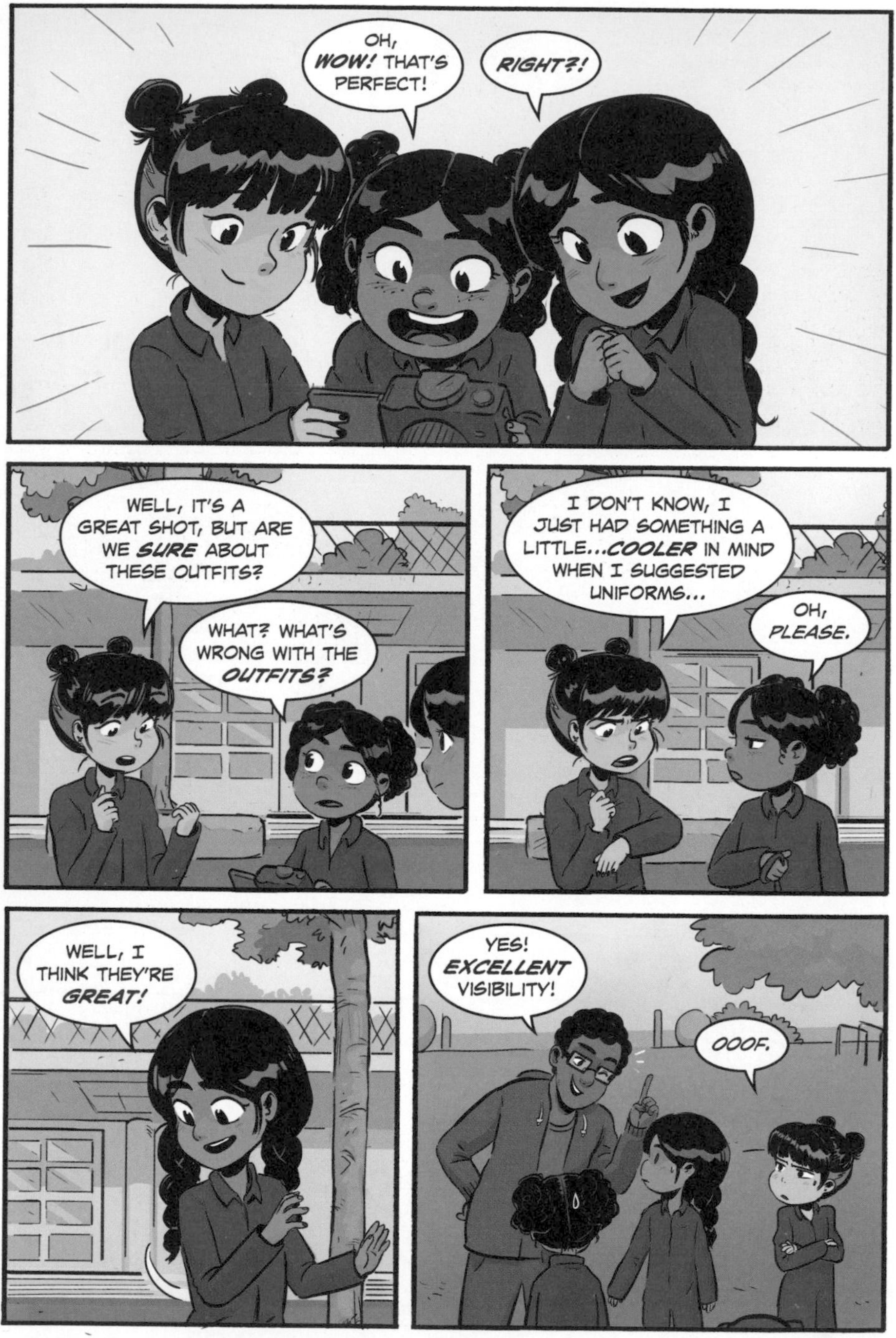
OH, WOW! THAT'S PERFECT!
RIGHT?!
WELL, IT'S A GREAT SHOT, BUT ARE WE SURE ABOUT THESE OUTFITS?
WHAT? WHAT'S WRONG WITH THE OUTFITS?
I DON'T KNOW, I JUST HAD SOMETHING A LITTLE...COOLER IN MIND WHEN I SUGGESTED UNIFORMS...
OH, PLEASE.
WELL, I THINK THEY'RE GREAT!
YES! EXCELLENT VISIBILITY!
OOOF.

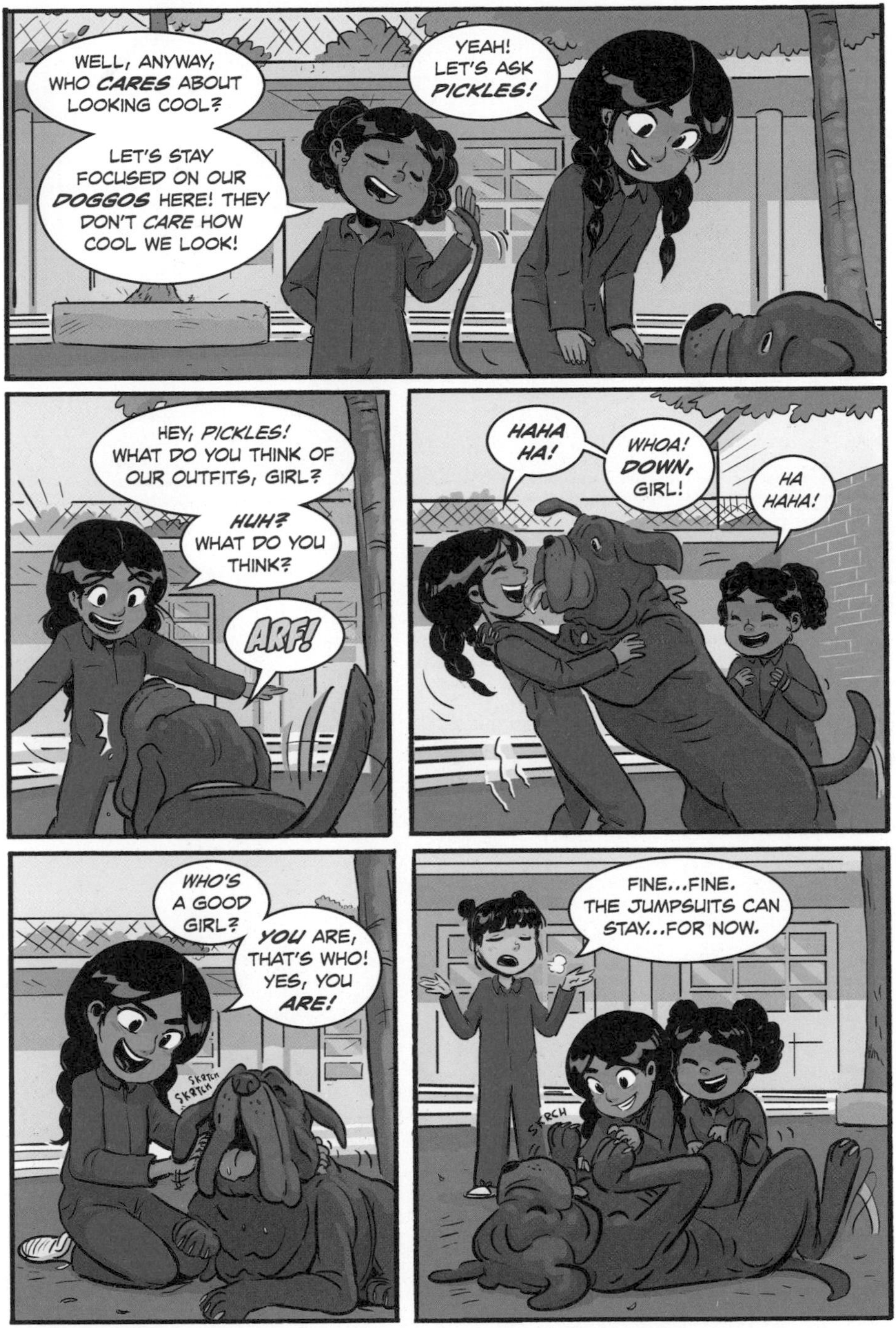
WELL, ANYWAY, WHO CARES ABOUT LOOKING COOL?
LET'S STAY FOCUSED ON OUR DOGGOS HERE! THEY DON'T CARE HOW COOL WE LOOK!
YEAH! LET'S ASK PICKLES!
HEY, PICKLES! WHAT DO YOU THINK OF OUR OUTFITS, GIRL?
HUH? WHAT DO YOU THINK?
ARF!
HAHA HA!
WHOA! DOWN, GIRL!
HA HAHA!
WHO'S A GOOD GIRL?
YOU ARE, THAT'S WHO! YES, YOU ARE!
SKRTCH SKRTCH
FINE...FINE. THE JUMPSUITS CAN STAY...FOR NOW.
SKRCH

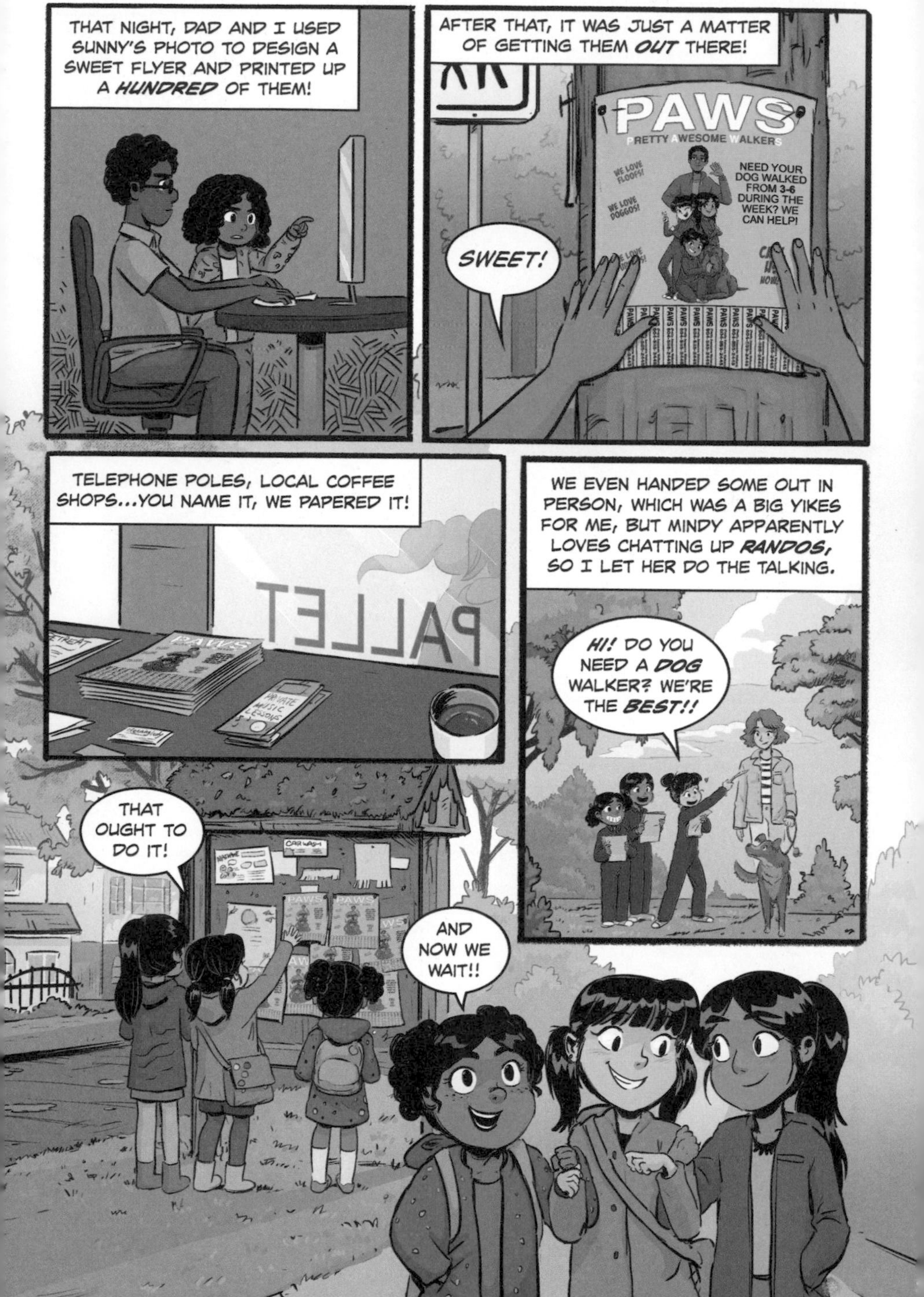

THAT NIGHT, DAD AND I USED SUNNY'S PHOTO TO DESIGN A SWEET FLYER AND PRINTED UP A *HUNDRED* OF THEM!
AFTER THAT, IT WAS JUST A MATTER OF GETTING THEM *OUT* THERE!
PAWS
PRETTY AWESOME WALKERS
WE LOVE FLOOFS!
WE LOVE DOGGOS!
NEED YOUR DOG WALKED FROM 3-6 DURING THE WEEK? WE CAN HELP!
SWEET!
TELEPHONE POLES, LOCAL COFFEE SHOPS...YOU NAME IT, WE PAPERED IT!
PALLET
PAWS
PRIVATE MUSIC LESSONS
WE EVEN HANDED SOME OUT IN PERSON, WHICH WAS A BIG YIKES FOR ME, BUT MINDY APPARENTLY LOVES CHATTING UP *RANDOS,* SO I LET HER DO THE TALKING.
HI! DO YOU NEED A *DOG* WALKER? WE'RE THE *BEST!!*
THAT OUGHT TO DO IT!
CAR WASH
PAWS
AND NOW WE WAIT!!

WE DIDN'T HAVE TO WAIT LONG--MY DAD'S PHONE STARTED RINGING RIGHT AWAY!

HELLO? *HUH?* OH, HAHA! YES, THIS IS *PAWS!* SORRY! YES, HOW CAN I HELP YOU?

PAWS (Pretty Awesome Walkers) 604-555-2445

PAWS (Pretty Awesome Walkers) 604-555-2445

PAWS (Pretty Awesome Walkers) 604-555-2445

PAWS (Pretty Awesome Walkers) 604-555-2445

PAWS (Pretty Awesome Walkers) 604-555-2445

PAWS (Pretty Awesome Walkers) 604-555-2445

PAWS (Pretty Awesome Walkers) 604-555-2445

THIS IS KEVIN! HE WORKS IN THE FILM INDUSTRY AS SOMETHING CALLED A *GRIP.* NO IDEA WHAT THAT IS, BUT IT SOUNDS PRETTY COOL.

THE PROBLEM WITH WORKING IN FILM, THOUGH, IS THE *SUPER-*LONG HOURS YOU HAVE TO WORK.

KEVIN WORRIES ABOUT LEAVING HIS GOOD BOI, *CARL,* ALONE ALL DAY...

...AND HE WANTED US TO CHECK IN WITH HIM AND TAKE HIM FOR WALKS!

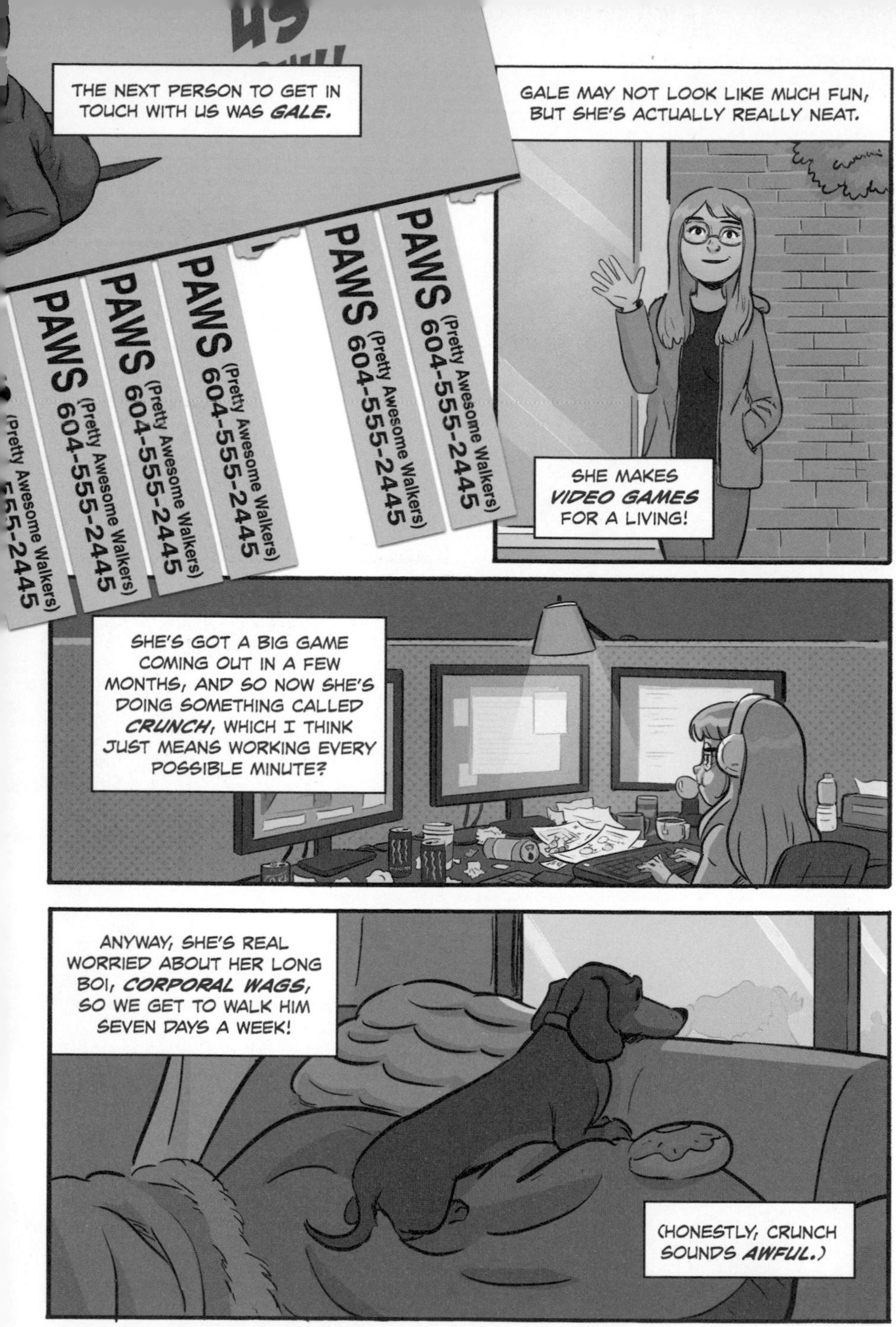

THE NEXT PERSON TO GET IN TOUCH WITH US WAS GALE.
PAWS (Pretty Awesome Walkers) 604-555-2445
PAWS (Pretty Awesome Walkers) 604-555-2445
PAWS (Pretty Awesome Walkers) 604-555-2445
PAWS (Pretty Awesome Walkers) 604-555-2445
PAWS (Pretty Awesome Walkers) 604-555-2445
(Pretty Awesome Walkers)
GALE MAY NOT LOOK LIKE MUCH FUN, BUT SHE'S ACTUALLY REALLY NEAT.
SHE MAKES VIDEO GAMES FOR A LIVING!
SHE'S GOT A BIG GAME COMING OUT IN A FEW MONTHS, AND SO NOW SHE'S DOING SOMETHING CALLED CRUNCH, WHICH I THINK JUST MEANS WORKING EVERY POSSIBLE MINUTE?
ANYWAY, SHE'S REAL WORRIED ABOUT HER LONG BOI, CORPORAL WAGS, SO WE GET TO WALK HIM SEVEN DAYS A WEEK!
(HONESTLY, CRUNCH SOUNDS AWFUL.)

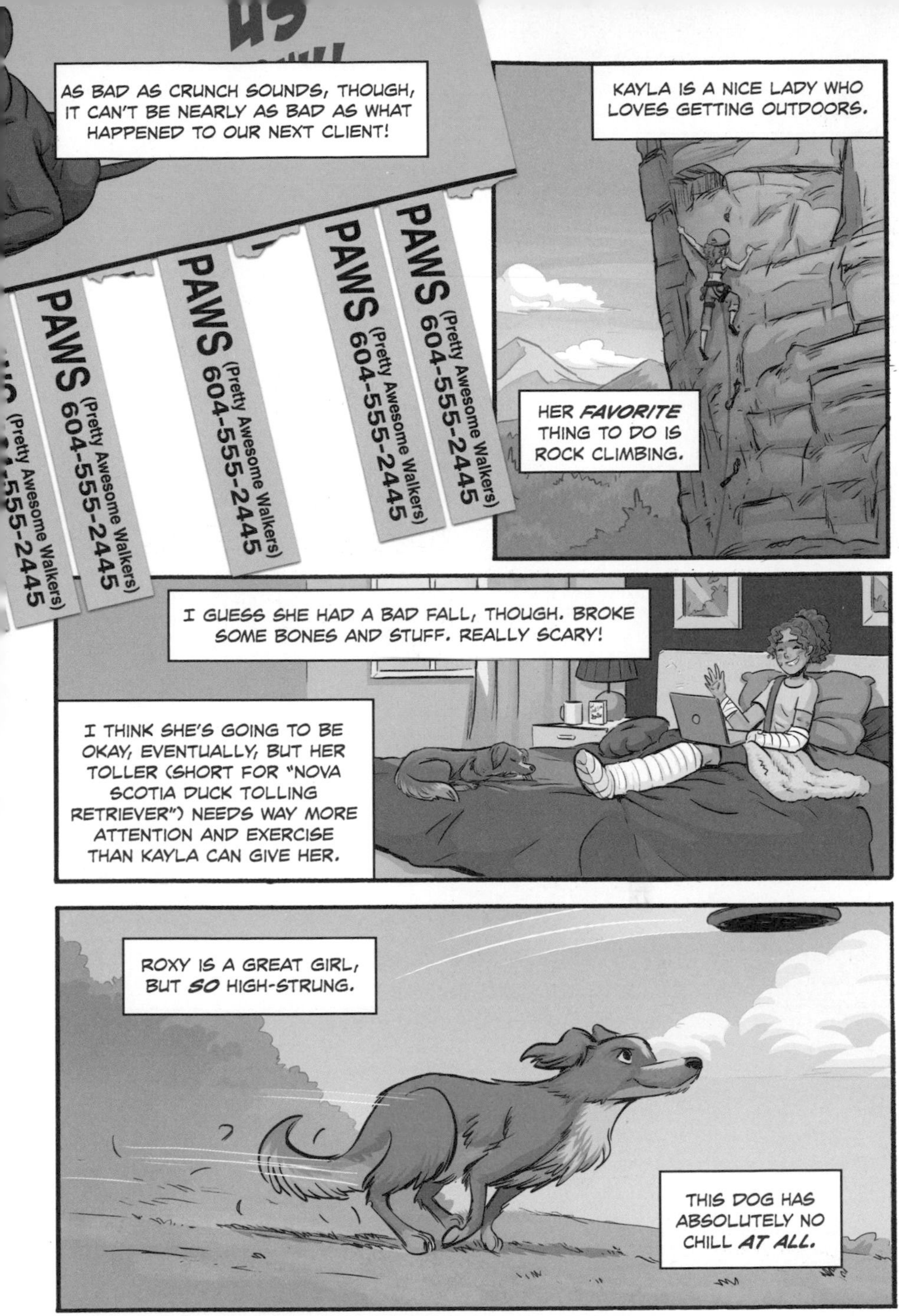

AS BAD AS CRUNCH SOUNDS, THOUGH, IT CAN'T BE NEARLY AS BAD AS WHAT HAPPENED TO OUR NEXT CLIENT!
PAWS (Pretty Awesome Walkers) 604-555-2445
PAWS (Pretty Awesome Walkers) 604-555-2445
PAWS (Pretty Awesome Walkers) 604-555-2445
PAWS (Pretty Awesome Walkers) 604-555-2445
KAYLA IS A NICE LADY WHO LOVES GETTING OUTDOORS.
HER *FAVORITE* THING TO DO IS ROCK CLIMBING.
I GUESS SHE HAD A BAD FALL, THOUGH. BROKE SOME BONES AND STUFF. REALLY SCARY!
I THINK SHE'S GOING TO BE OKAY, EVENTUALLY, BUT HER TOLLER (SHORT FOR "NOVA SCOTIA DUCK TOLLING RETRIEVER") NEEDS WAY MORE ATTENTION AND EXERCISE THAN KAYLA CAN GIVE HER.
ROXY IS A GREAT GIRL, BUT *SO* HIGH-STRUNG.
THIS DOG HAS ABSOLUTELY NO CHILL *AT ALL.*

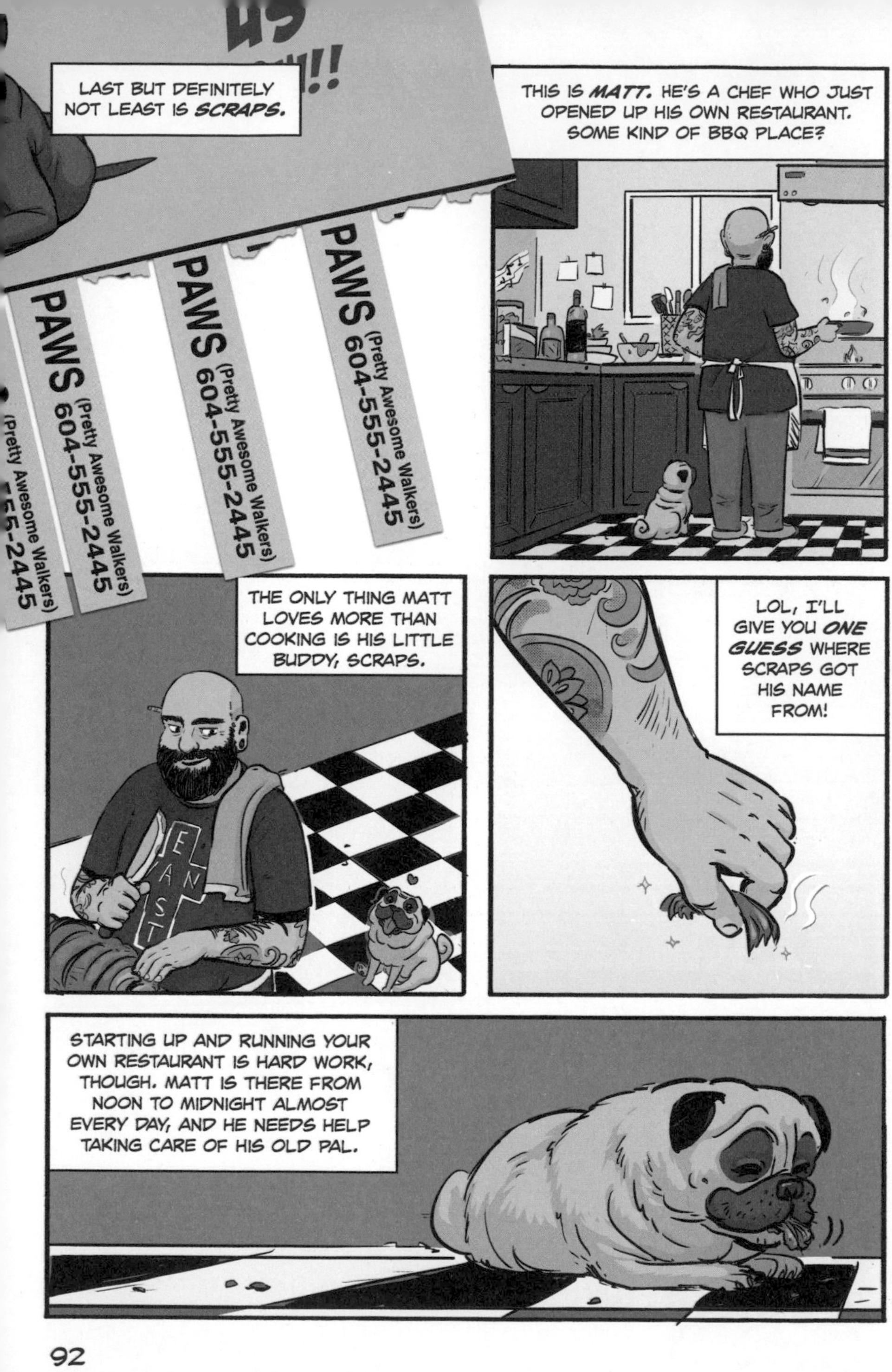
LAST BUT DEFINITELY NOT LEAST IS *SCRAPS.*
PAWS (Pretty Awesome Walkers) 604-555-2445
PAWS (Pretty Awesome Walkers) 604-555-2445
PAWS (Pretty Awesome Walkers) 604-555-2445
(Pretty Awesome Walkers)
THIS IS *MATT.* HE'S A CHEF WHO JUST OPENED UP HIS OWN RESTAURANT. SOME KIND OF BBQ PLACE?
THE ONLY THING MATT LOVES MORE THAN COOKING IS HIS LITTLE BUDDY, SCRAPS.
LOL, I'LL GIVE YOU *ONE GUESS* WHERE SCRAPS GOT HIS NAME FROM!
STARTING UP AND RUNNING YOUR OWN RESTAURANT IS HARD WORK, THOUGH. MATT IS THERE FROM NOON TO MIDNIGHT ALMOST EVERY DAY, AND HE NEEDS HELP TAKING CARE OF HIS OLD PAL.

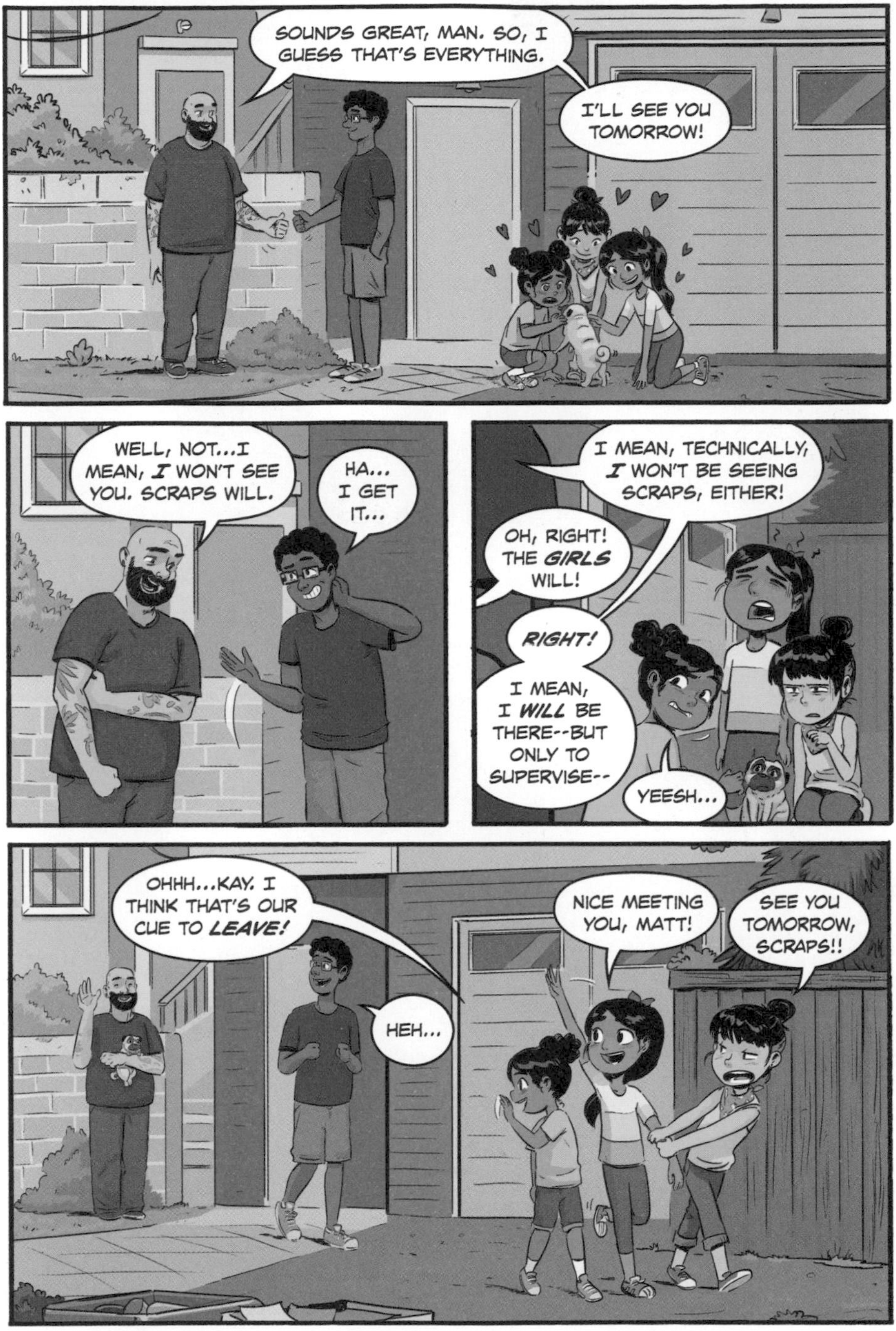
SOUNDS GREAT, MAN. SO, I GUESS THAT'S EVERYTHING.
I'LL SEE YOU TOMORROW!
WELL, NOT...I MEAN, *I* WON'T SEE YOU. SCRAPS WILL.
HA... I GET IT...
I MEAN, TECHNICALLY, *I* WON'T BE SEEING SCRAPS, EITHER!
OH, RIGHT! THE *GIRLS* WILL!
RIGHT!
I MEAN, I *WILL* BE THERE--BUT ONLY TO SUPERVISE--
YEESH...
OHHH...KAY. I THINK THAT'S OUR CUE TO *LEAVE!*
HEH...
NICE MEETING YOU, MATT!
SEE YOU TOMORROW, SCRAPS!!

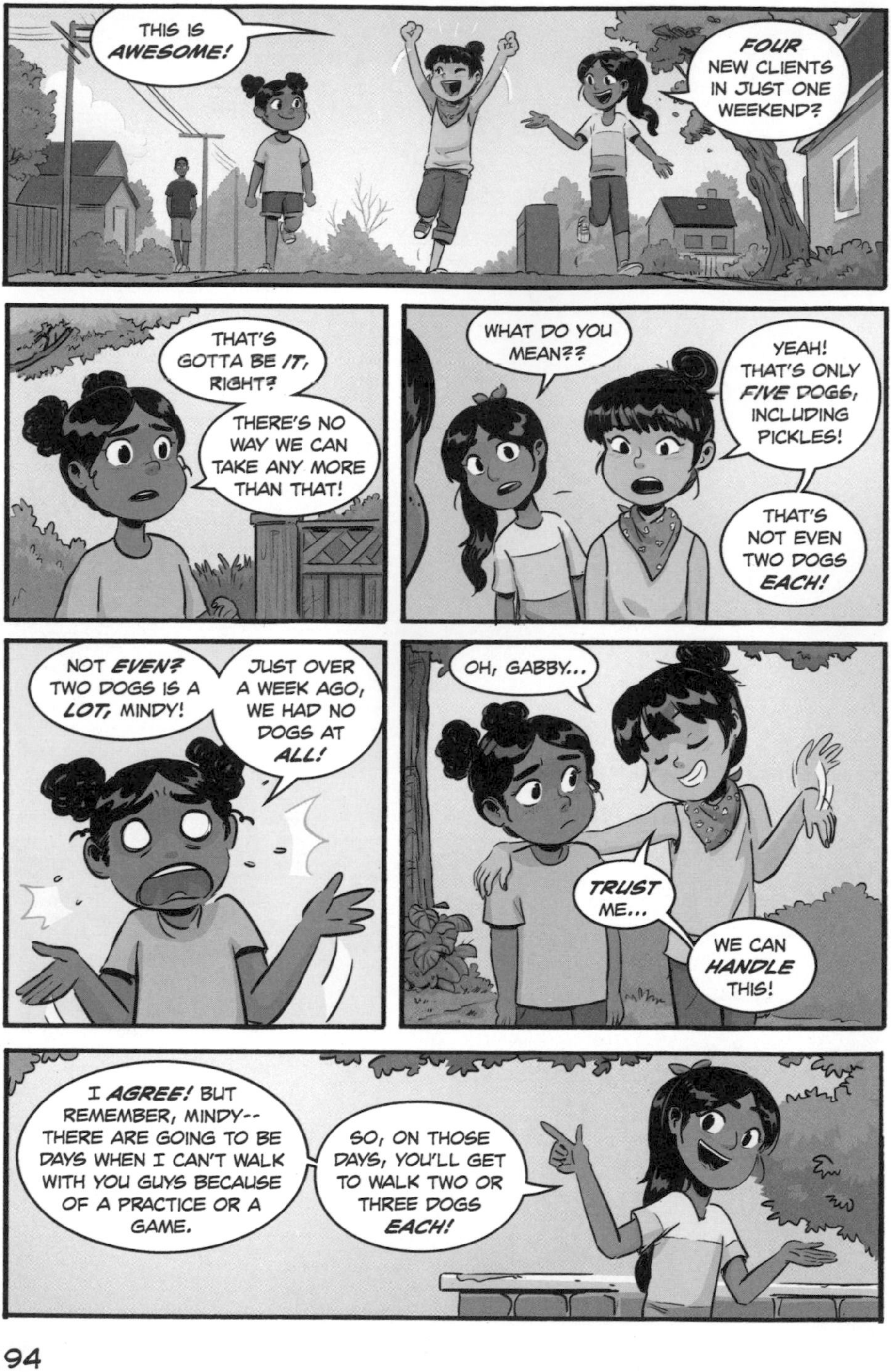
THIS IS AWESOME!
FOUR NEW CLIENTS IN JUST ONE WEEKEND?
THAT'S GOTTA BE IT, RIGHT?
THERE'S NO WAY WE CAN TAKE ANY MORE THAN THAT!
WHAT DO YOU MEAN??
YEAH! THAT'S ONLY FIVE DOGS, INCLUDING PICKLES!
THAT'S NOT EVEN TWO DOGS EACH!
NOT EVEN? TWO DOGS IS A LOT, MINDY!
JUST OVER A WEEK AGO, WE HAD NO DOGS AT ALL!
OH, GABBY...
TRUST ME...
WE CAN HANDLE THIS!
I AGREE! BUT REMEMBER, MINDY-- THERE ARE GOING TO BE DAYS WHEN I CAN'T WALK WITH YOU GUYS BECAUSE OF A PRACTICE OR A GAME.
SO, ON THOSE DAYS, YOU'LL GET TO WALK TWO OR THREE DOGS EACH!

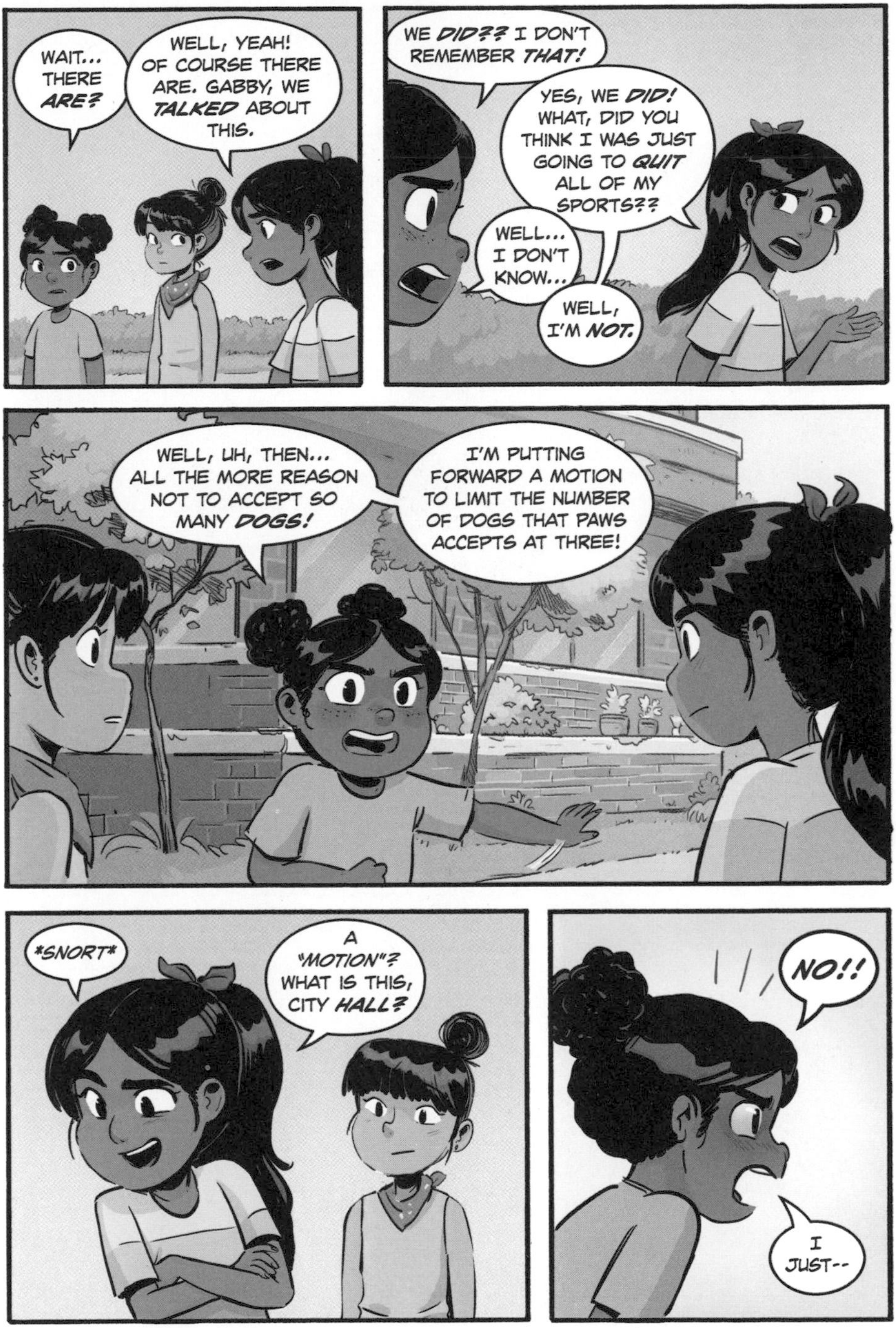
WAIT... THERE ARE?
WELL, YEAH! OF COURSE THERE ARE. GABBY, WE TALKED ABOUT THIS.
WE DID?? I DON'T REMEMBER THAT!
YES, WE DID! WHAT, DID YOU THINK I WAS JUST GOING TO QUIT ALL OF MY SPORTS??
WELL... I DON'T KNOW...
WELL, I'M NOT.
WELL, UH, THEN... ALL THE MORE REASON NOT TO ACCEPT SO MANY DOGS!
I'M PUTTING FORWARD A MOTION TO LIMIT THE NUMBER OF DOGS THAT PAWS ACCEPTS AT THREE!
SNORT
A "MOTION"? WHAT IS THIS, CITY HALL?
NO!!
I JUST--

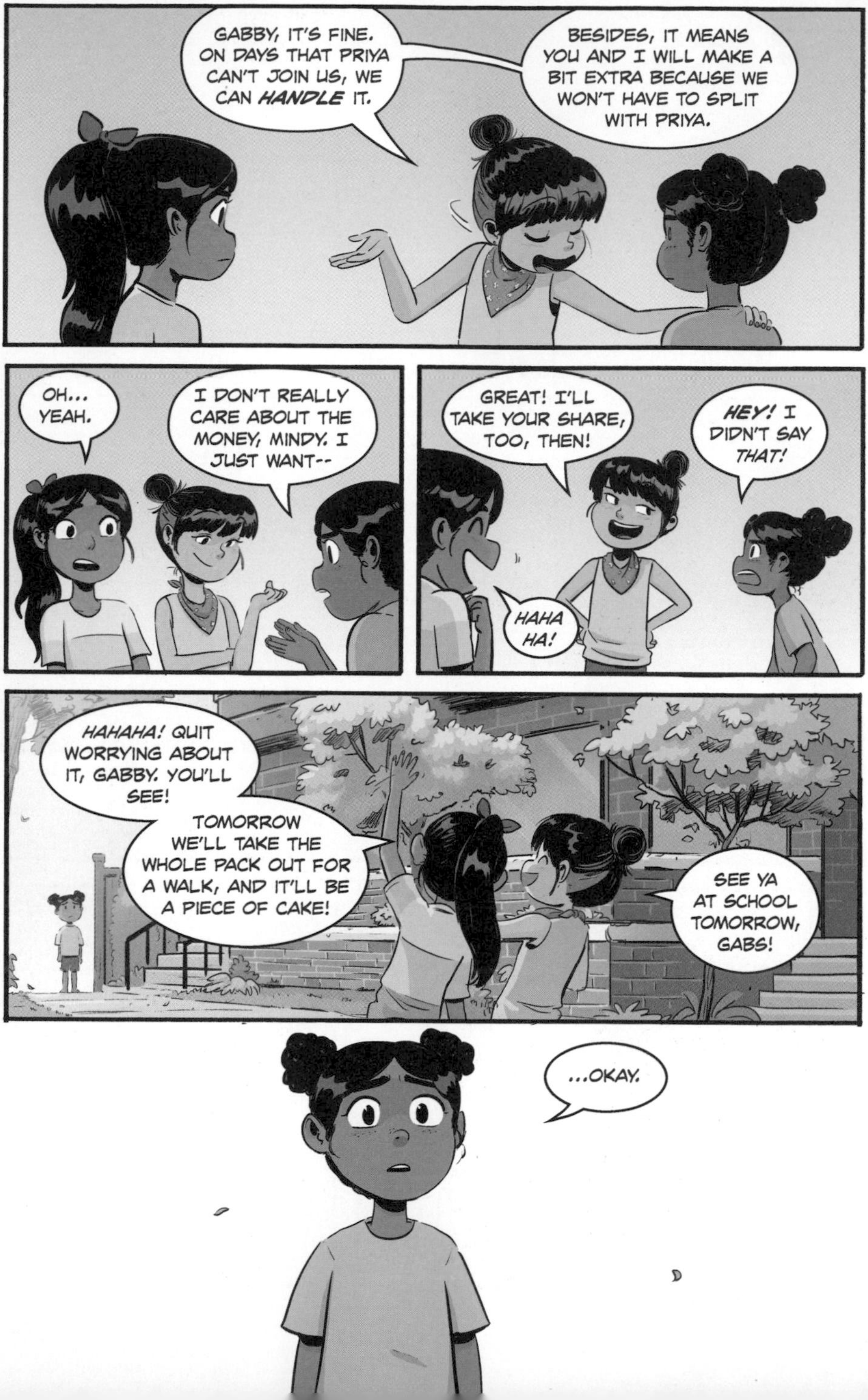
GABBY, IT'S FINE. ON DAYS THAT PRIYA CAN'T JOIN US, WE CAN *HANDLE* IT.
BESIDES, IT MEANS YOU AND I WILL MAKE A BIT EXTRA BECAUSE WE WON'T HAVE TO SPLIT WITH PRIYA.
OH... YEAH.
I DON'T REALLY CARE ABOUT THE MONEY, MINDY. I JUST WANT--
GREAT! I'LL TAKE YOUR SHARE, TOO, THEN!
HAHA HA!
HEY! I DIDN'T SAY *THAT!*
HAHAHA! QUIT WORRYING ABOUT IT, GABBY. YOU'LL SEE!
TOMORROW WE'LL TAKE THE WHOLE PACK OUT FOR A WALK, AND IT'LL BE A PIECE OF CAKE!
SEE YA AT SCHOOL TOMORROW, GABS!
...OKAY.

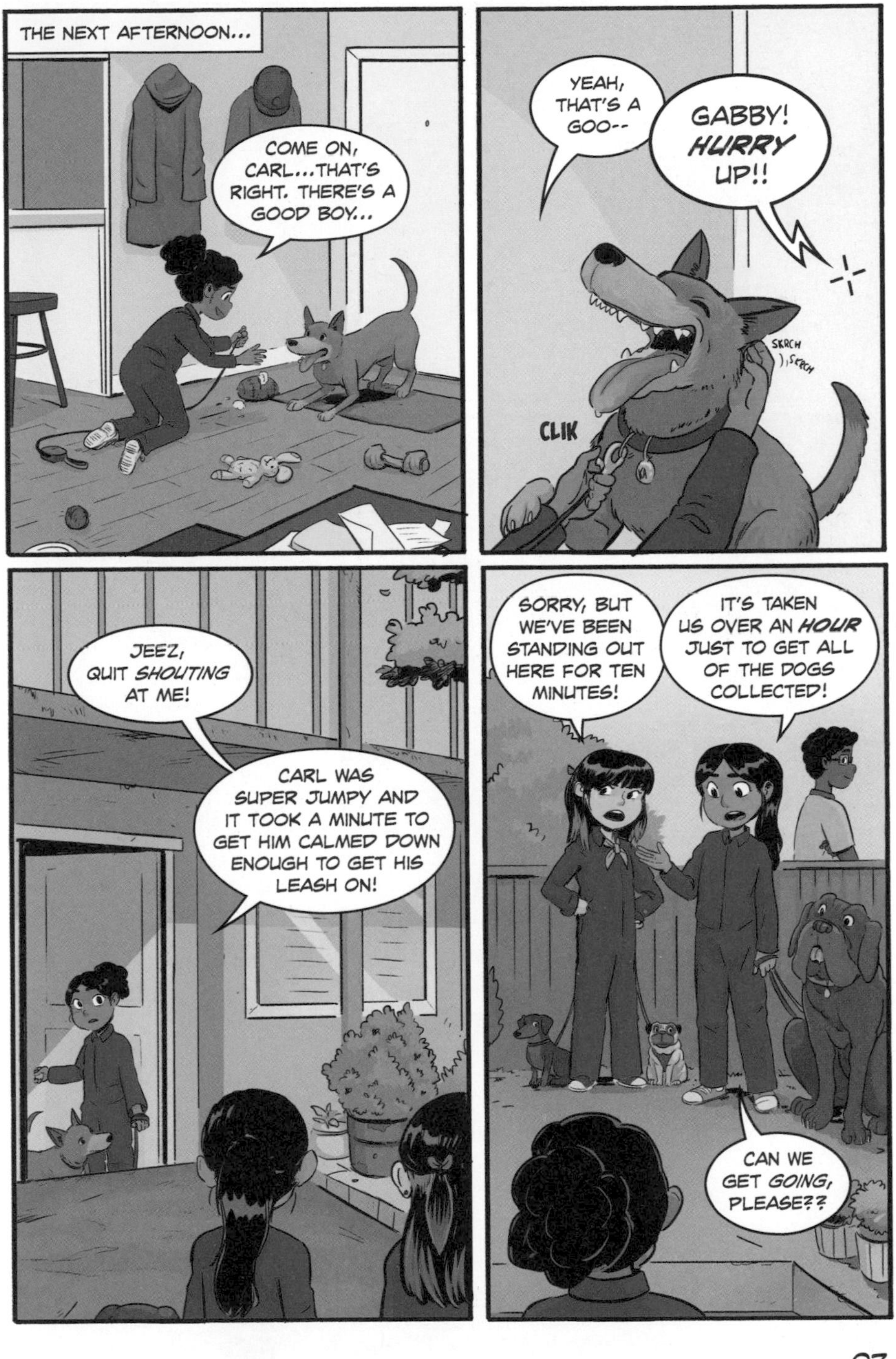
THE NEXT AFTERNOON...
COME ON, CARL...THAT'S RIGHT. THERE'S A GOOD BOY...
YEAH, THAT'S A GOO--
GABBY! HURRY UP!!
SKRCH SKRCH
CLIK
JEEZ, QUIT SHOUTING AT ME!
CARL WAS SUPER JUMPY AND IT TOOK A MINUTE TO GET HIM CALMED DOWN ENOUGH TO GET HIS LEASH ON!
SORRY, BUT WE'VE BEEN STANDING OUT HERE FOR TEN MINUTES!
IT'S TAKEN US OVER AN HOUR JUST TO GET ALL OF THE DOGS COLLECTED!
CAN WE GET GOING, PLEASE??

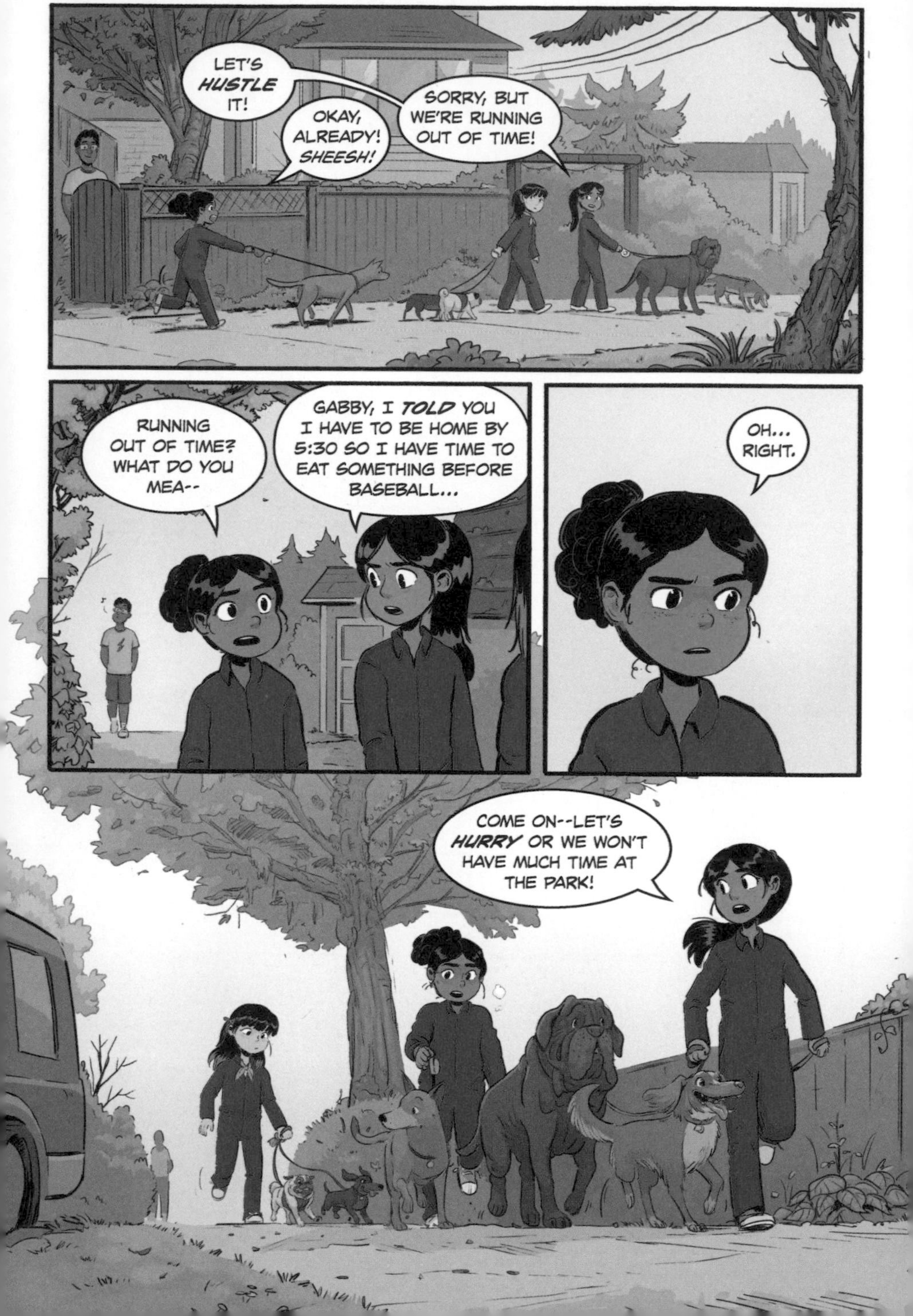
LET'S HUSTLE IT!
SORRY, BUT WE'RE RUNNING OUT OF TIME!
OKAY, ALREADY! SHEESH!
RUNNING OUT OF TIME? WHAT DO YOU MEA--
GABBY, I TOLD YOU I HAVE TO BE HOME BY 5:30 SO I HAVE TIME TO EAT SOMETHING BEFORE BASEBALL...
OH... RIGHT.
COME ON--LET'S HURRY OR WE WON'T HAVE MUCH TIME AT THE PARK!

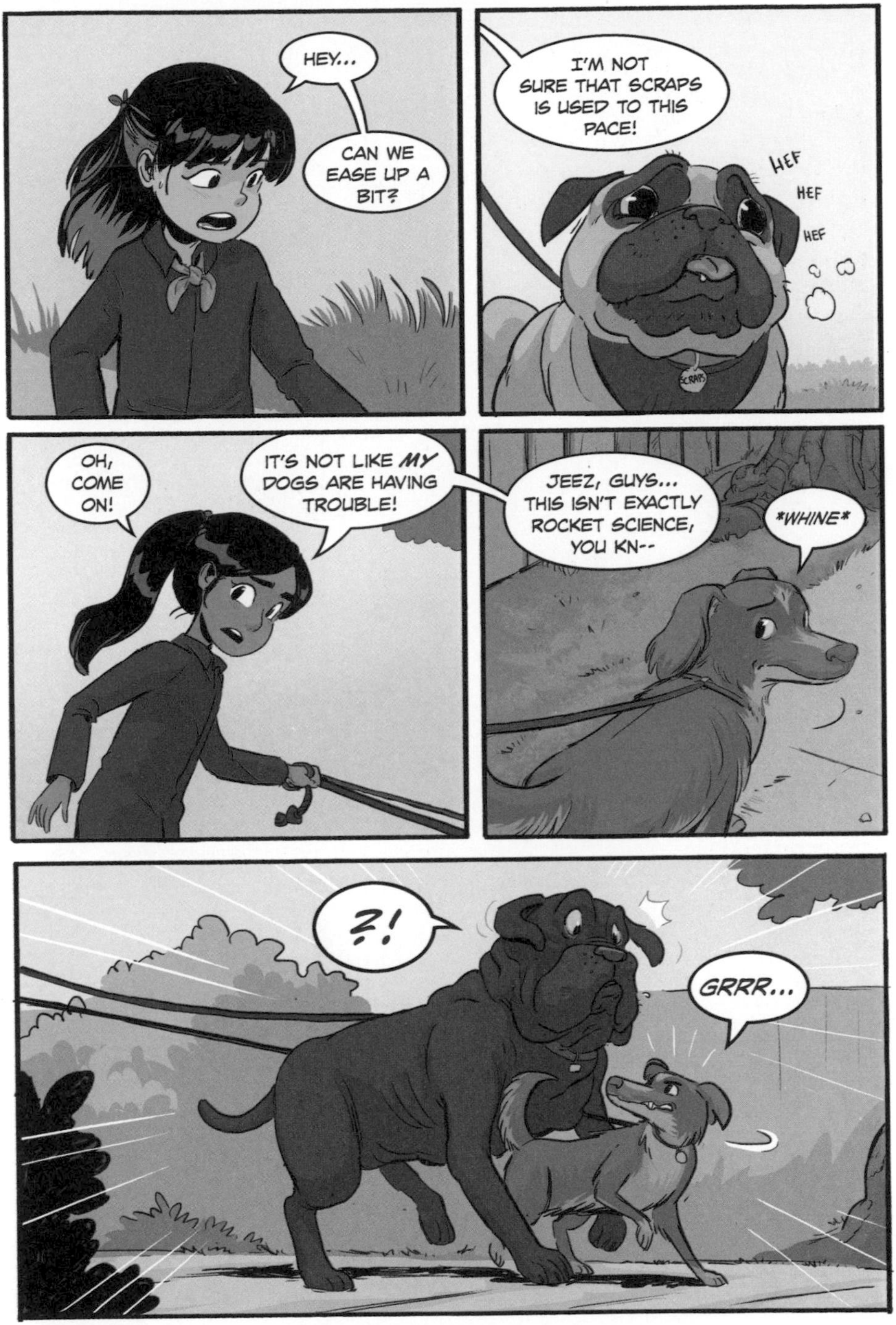
HEY...
CAN WE EASE UP A BIT?
I'M NOT SURE THAT SCRAPS IS USED TO THIS PACE!
HEF
HEF
HEF
SCRAPS
OH, COME ON!
IT'S NOT LIKE *MY* DOGS ARE HAVING TROUBLE!
JEEZ, GUYS... THIS ISN'T EXACTLY ROCKET SCIENCE, YOU KN--
WHINE
?!
GRRR...

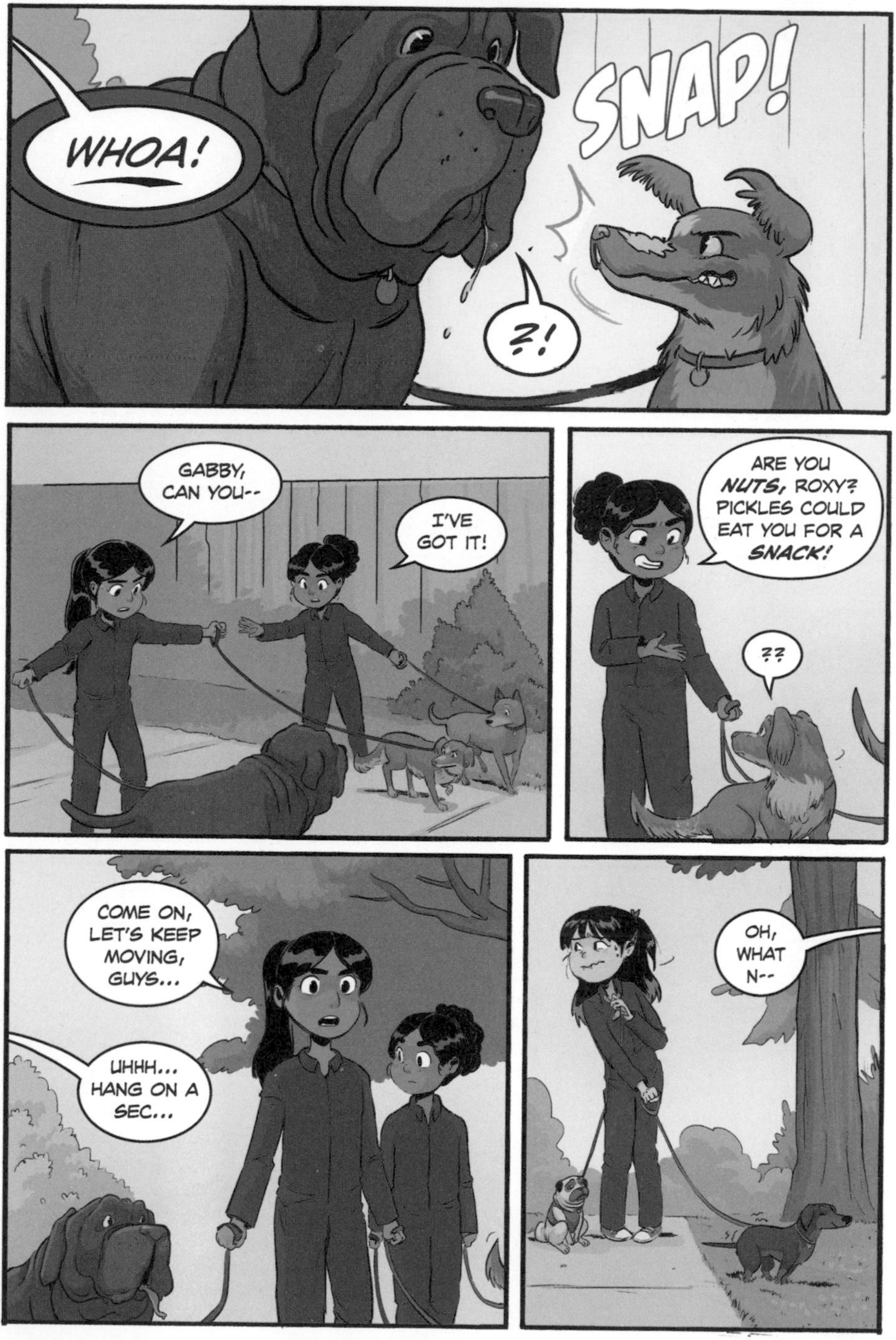
SNAP!
WHOA!
?!
GABBY, CAN YOU--
I'VE GOT IT!
ARE YOU **NUTS,** ROXY? PICKLES COULD EAT YOU FOR A **SNACK!**
??
COME ON, LET'S KEEP MOVING, GUYS...
UHHH... HANG ON A SEC...
OH, WHAT N--

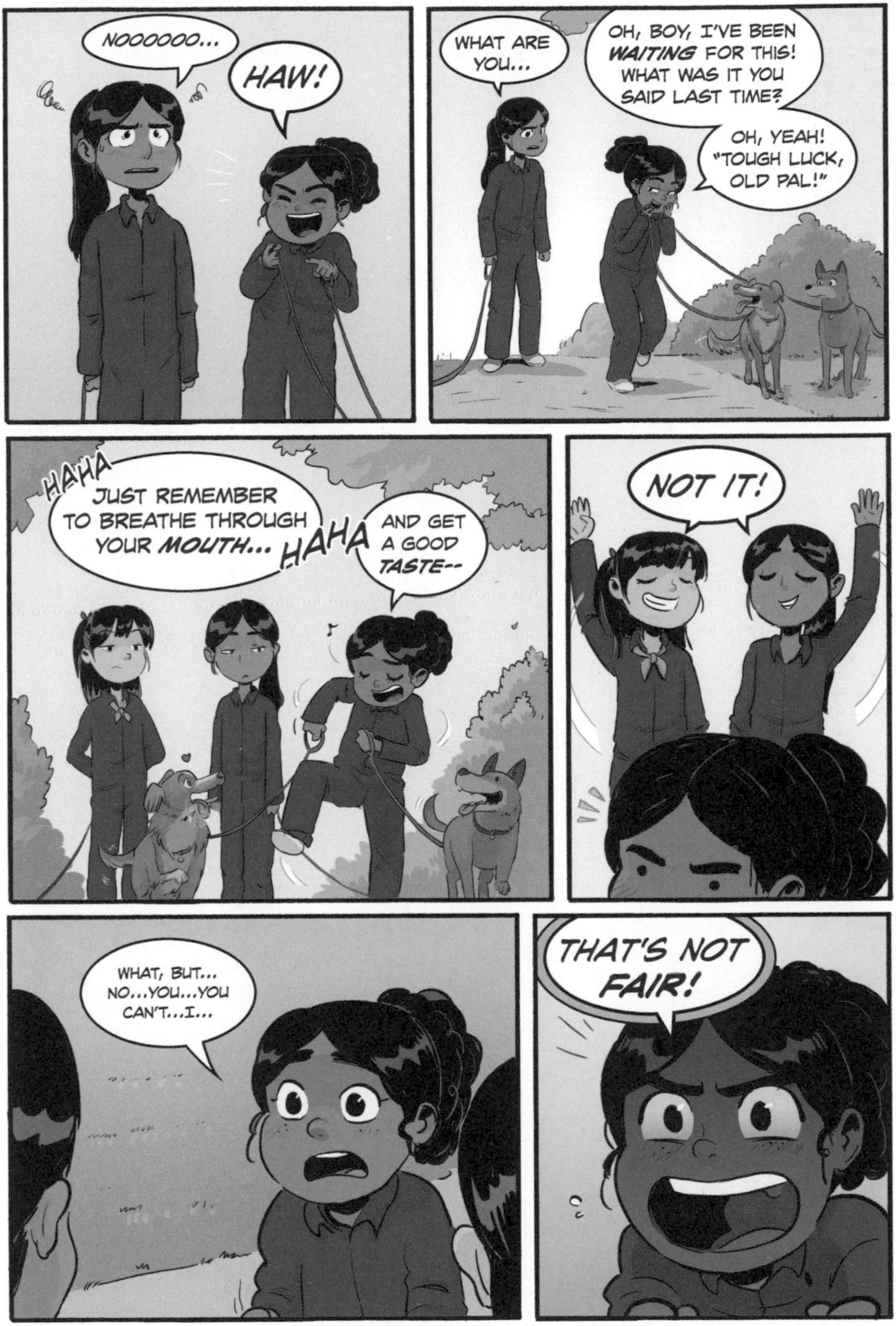
NOOOOOO...
HAW!
WHAT ARE YOU...
OH, BOY, I'VE BEEN WAITING FOR THIS! WHAT WAS IT YOU SAID LAST TIME?
OH, YEAH! "TOUGH LUCK, OLD PAL!"
HAHA
JUST REMEMBER TO BREATHE THROUGH YOUR MOUTH...
HAHA
AND GET A GOOD TASTE--
NOT IT!
WHAT, BUT... NO...YOU...YOU CAN'T...I...
THAT'S NOT FAIR!

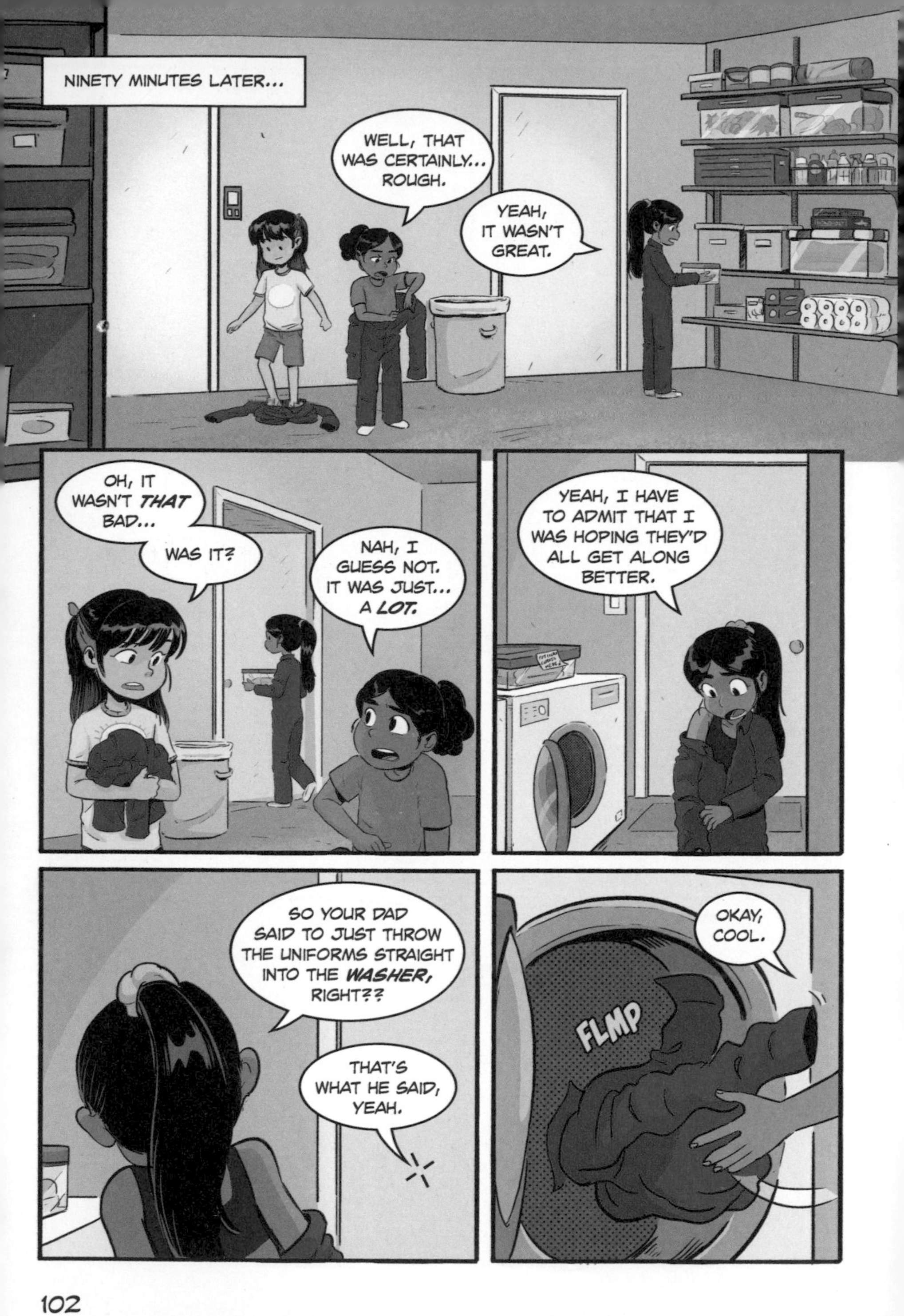
NINETY MINUTES LATER...
WELL, THAT WAS CERTAINLY... ROUGH.
YEAH, IT WASN'T GREAT.
OH, IT WASN'T *THAT* BAD...
WAS IT?
NAH, I GUESS NOT. IT WAS JUST... A *LOT.*
YEAH, I HAVE TO ADMIT THAT I WAS HOPING THEY'D ALL GET ALONG BETTER.
SO YOUR DAD SAID TO JUST THROW THE UNIFORMS STRAIGHT INTO THE *WASHER,* RIGHT??
THAT'S WHAT HE SAID, YEAH.
OKAY, COOL.
FLMP

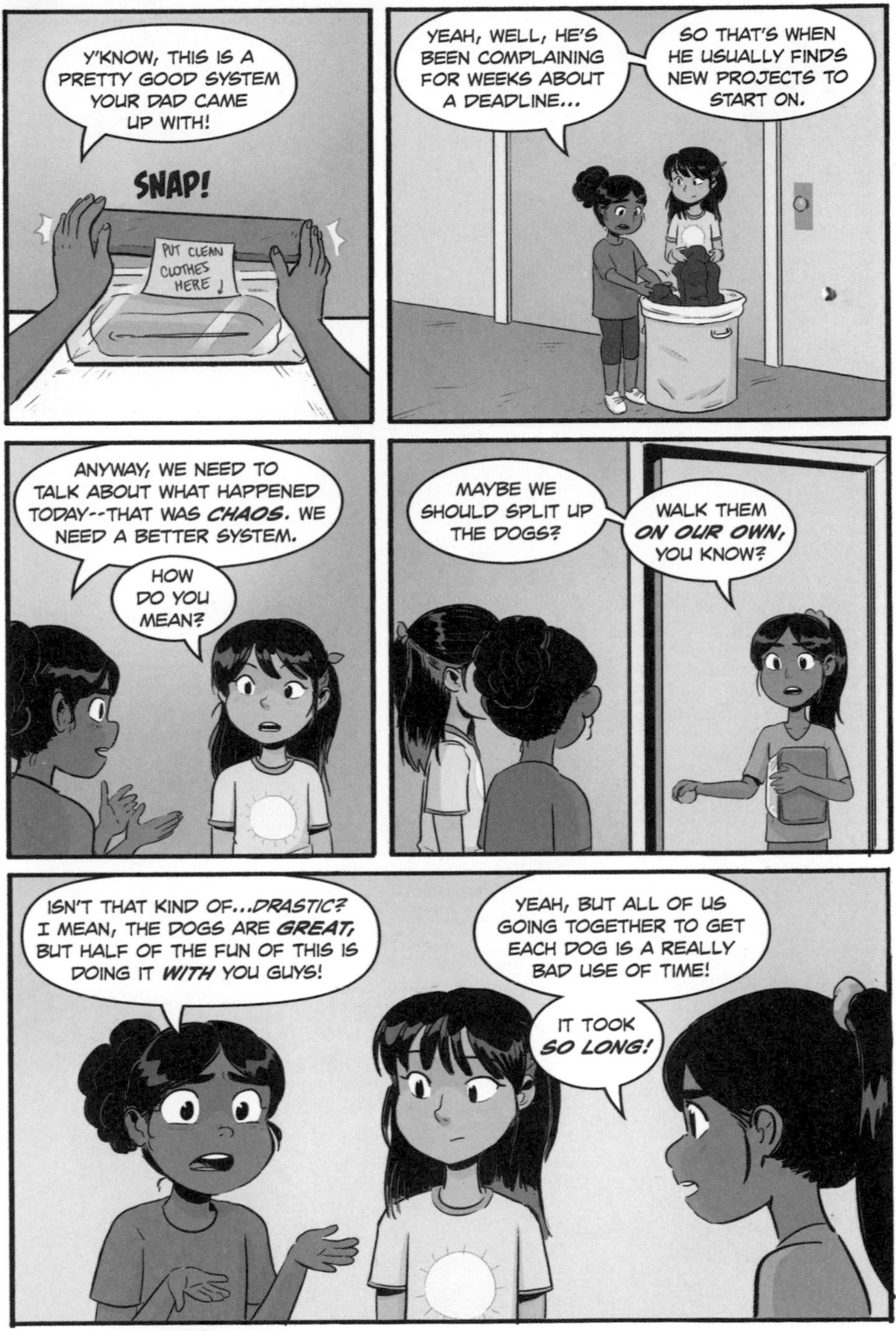
Y'KNOW, THIS IS A PRETTY GOOD SYSTEM YOUR DAD CAME UP WITH!
SNAP!
PUT CLEAN CLOTHES HERE
YEAH, WELL, HE'S BEEN COMPLAINING FOR WEEKS ABOUT A DEADLINE...
SO THAT'S WHEN HE USUALLY FINDS NEW PROJECTS TO START ON.
ANYWAY, WE NEED TO TALK ABOUT WHAT HAPPENED TODAY--THAT WAS *CHAOS*. WE NEED A BETTER SYSTEM.
HOW DO YOU MEAN?
MAYBE WE SHOULD SPLIT UP THE DOGS?
WALK THEM *ON OUR OWN,* YOU KNOW?
ISN'T THAT KIND OF...*DRASTIC?* I MEAN, THE DOGS ARE *GREAT,* BUT HALF OF THE FUN OF THIS IS DOING IT *WITH* YOU GUYS!
YEAH, BUT ALL OF US GOING TOGETHER TO GET EACH DOG IS A REALLY BAD USE OF TIME!
IT TOOK *SO LONG!*

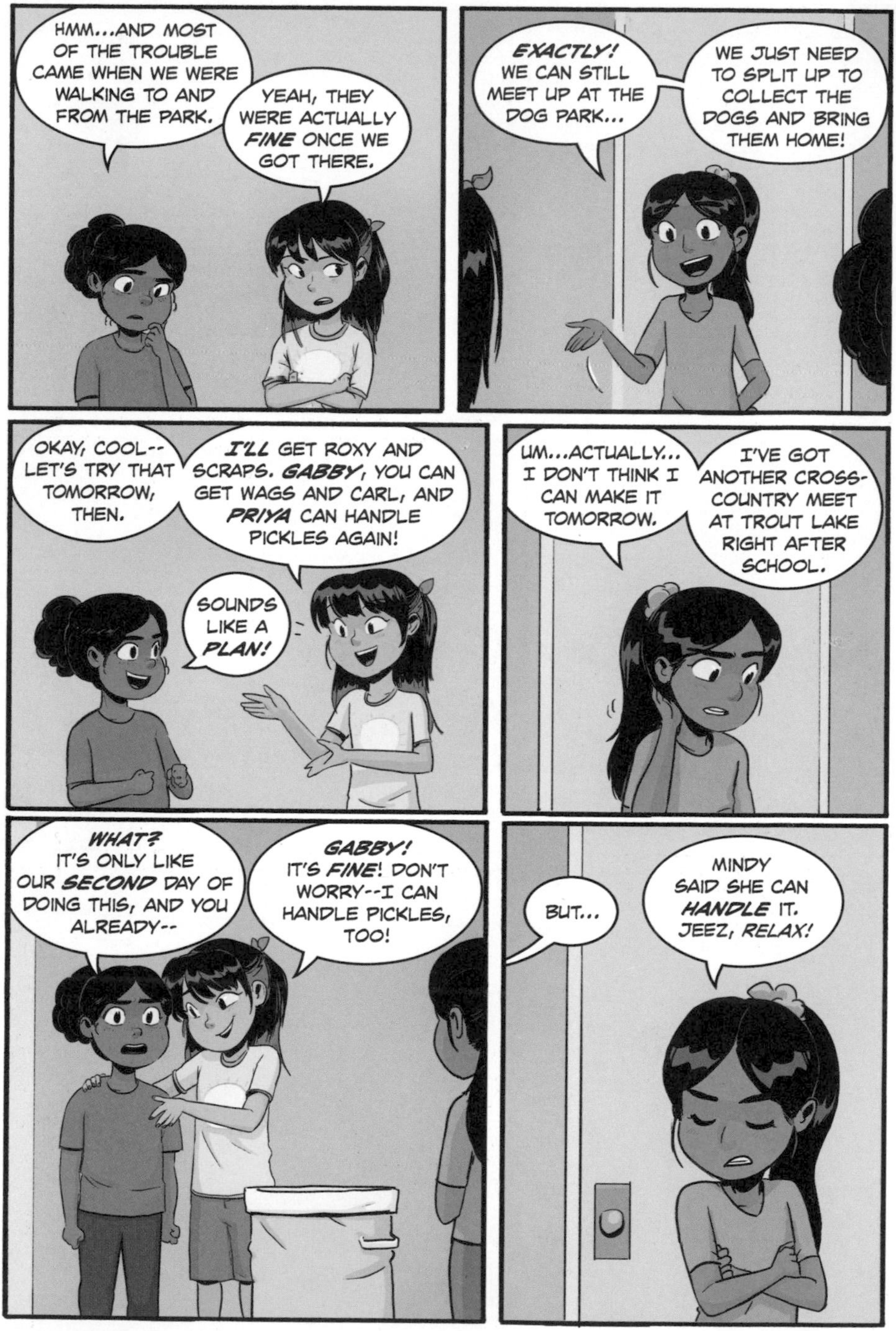
HMM...AND MOST OF THE TROUBLE CAME WHEN WE WERE WALKING TO AND FROM THE PARK.
YEAH, THEY WERE ACTUALLY FINE ONCE WE GOT THERE.
EXACTLY! WE CAN STILL MEET UP AT THE DOG PARK...
WE JUST NEED TO SPLIT UP TO COLLECT THE DOGS AND BRING THEM HOME!
OKAY, COOL--LET'S TRY THAT TOMORROW, THEN.
I'LL GET ROXY AND SCRAPS. GABBY, YOU CAN GET WAGS AND CARL, AND PRIYA CAN HANDLE PICKLES AGAIN!
SOUNDS LIKE A PLAN!
UM...ACTUALLY... I DON'T THINK I CAN MAKE IT TOMORROW.
I'VE GOT ANOTHER CROSS-COUNTRY MEET AT TROUT LAKE RIGHT AFTER SCHOOL.
WHAT? IT'S ONLY LIKE OUR SECOND DAY OF DOING THIS, AND YOU ALREADY--
GABBY! IT'S FINE! DON'T WORRY--I CAN HANDLE PICKLES, TOO!
BUT...
MINDY SAID SHE CAN HANDLE IT. JEEZ, RELAX!

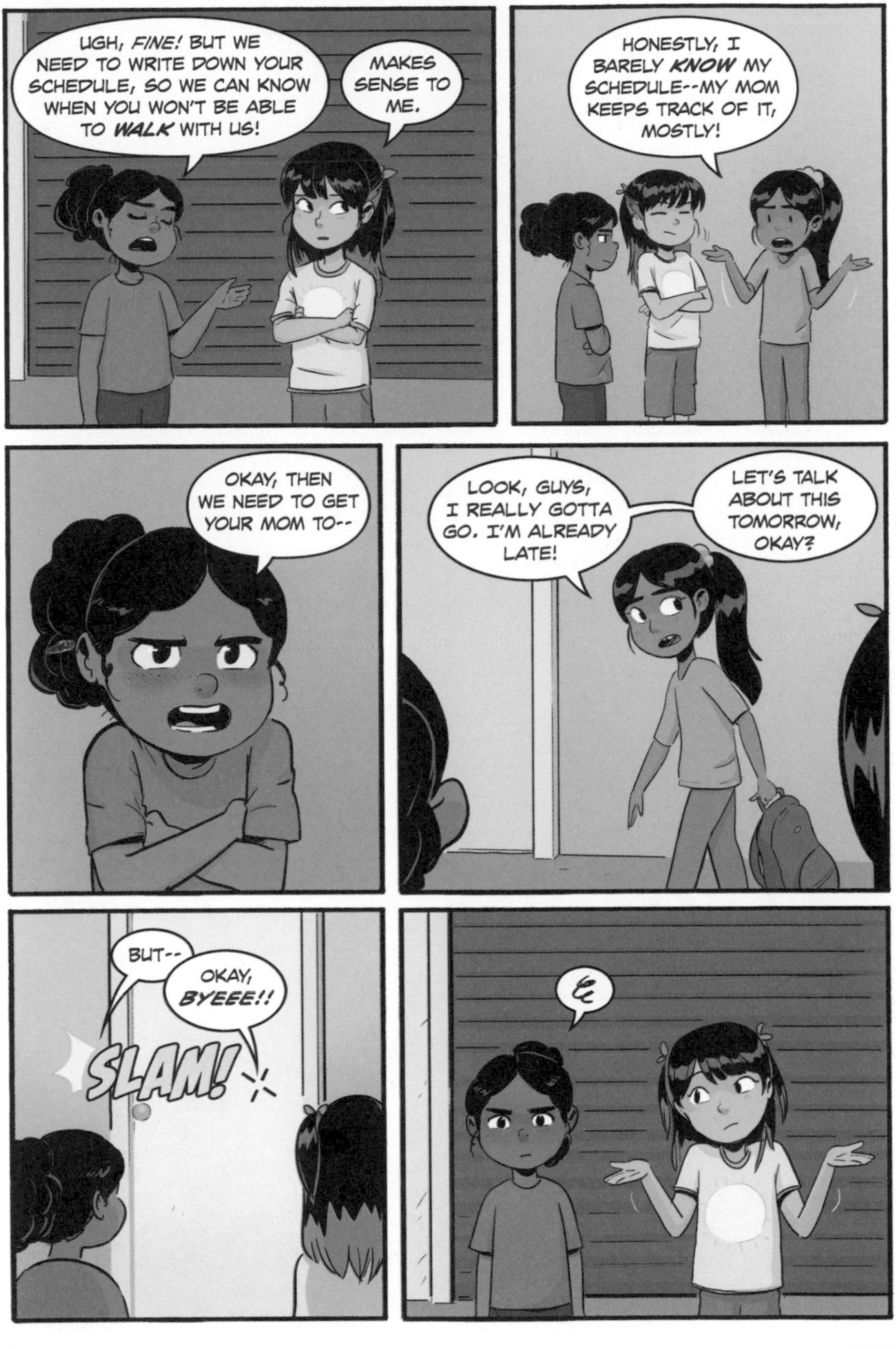
UGH, *FINE!* BUT WE NEED TO WRITE DOWN YOUR SCHEDULE, SO WE CAN KNOW WHEN YOU WON'T BE ABLE TO *WALK* WITH US!
MAKES SENSE TO ME.
HONESTLY, I BARELY *KNOW* MY SCHEDULE--MY MOM KEEPS TRACK OF IT, MOSTLY!
OKAY, THEN WE NEED TO GET YOUR MOM TO--
LOOK, GUYS, I REALLY GOTTA GO. I'M ALREADY LATE!
LET'S TALK ABOUT THIS TOMORROW, OKAY?
BUT--
OKAY, *BYEEE!!*
SLAM!

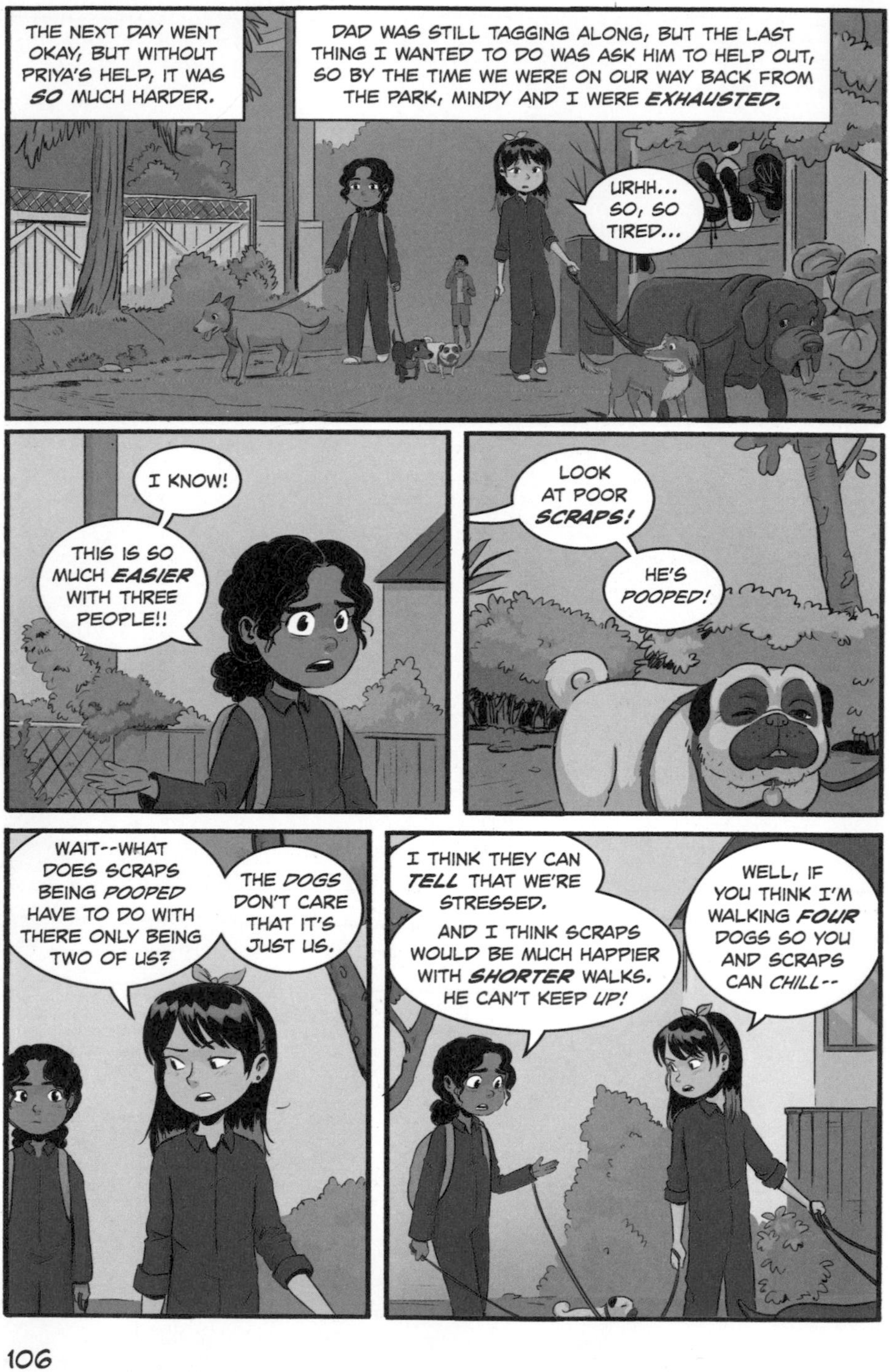
THE NEXT DAY WENT OKAY, BUT WITHOUT PRIYA'S HELP, IT WAS *SO* MUCH HARDER.
DAD WAS STILL TAGGING ALONG, BUT THE LAST THING I WANTED TO DO WAS ASK HIM TO HELP OUT, SO BY THE TIME WE WERE ON OUR WAY BACK FROM THE PARK, MINDY AND I WERE *EXHAUSTED.*
URHH... SO, SO TIRED...
I KNOW!
THIS IS SO MUCH *EASIER* WITH THREE PEOPLE!!
LOOK AT POOR *SCRAPS!*
HE'S *POOPED!*
WAIT--WHAT DOES SCRAPS BEING *POOPED* HAVE TO DO WITH THERE ONLY BEING TWO OF US?
THE *DOGS* DON'T CARE THAT IT'S JUST US.
I THINK THEY CAN *TELL* THAT WE'RE STRESSED.
AND I THINK SCRAPS WOULD BE MUCH HAPPIER WITH *SHORTER* WALKS. HE CAN'T KEEP *UP!*
WELL, IF YOU THINK I'M WALKING *FOUR* DOGS SO YOU AND SCRAPS CAN *CHILL*--

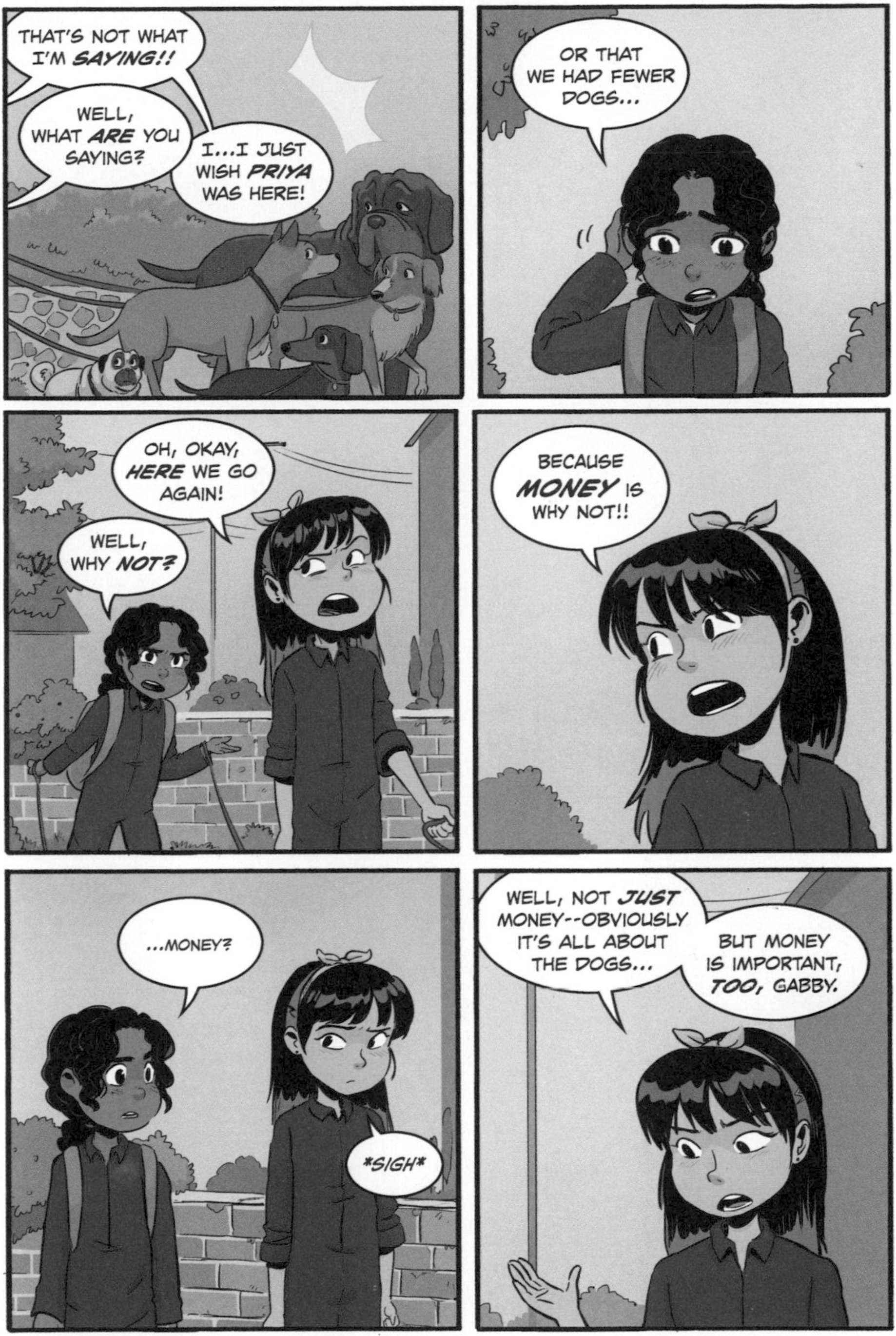
THAT'S NOT WHAT I'M SAYING!!
WELL, WHAT ARE YOU SAYING?
I...I JUST WISH PRIYA WAS HERE!
OR THAT WE HAD FEWER DOGS...
OH, OKAY, HERE WE GO AGAIN!
WELL, WHY NOT?
BECAUSE MONEY IS WHY NOT!!
...MONEY?
SIGH
WELL, NOT JUST MONEY--OBVIOUSLY IT'S ALL ABOUT THE DOGS...
BUT MONEY IS IMPORTANT, TOO, GABBY.

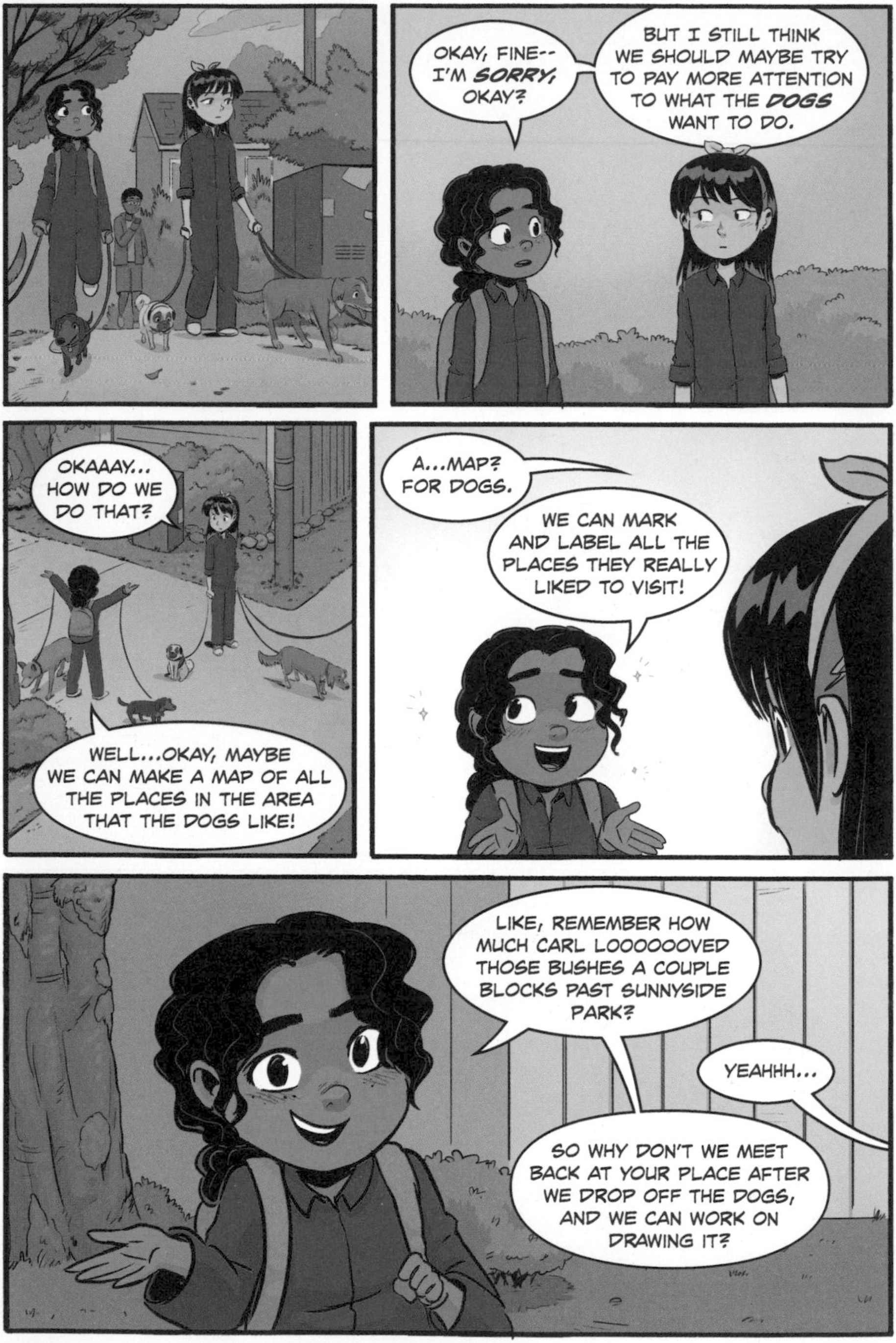
OKAY, FINE--
I'M SORRY, OKAY?
BUT I STILL THINK WE SHOULD MAYBE TRY TO PAY MORE ATTENTION TO WHAT THE DOGS WANT TO DO.
OKAAAY... HOW DO WE DO THAT?
WELL...OKAY, MAYBE WE CAN MAKE A MAP OF ALL THE PLACES IN THE AREA THAT THE DOGS LIKE!
A...MAP? FOR DOGS.
WE CAN MARK AND LABEL ALL THE PLACES THEY REALLY LIKED TO VISIT!
LIKE, REMEMBER HOW MUCH CARL LOOOOOOVED THOSE BUSHES A COUPLE BLOCKS PAST SUNNYSIDE PARK?
YEAHHH...
SO WHY DON'T WE MEET BACK AT YOUR PLACE AFTER WE DROP OFF THE DOGS, AND WE CAN WORK ON DRAWING IT?

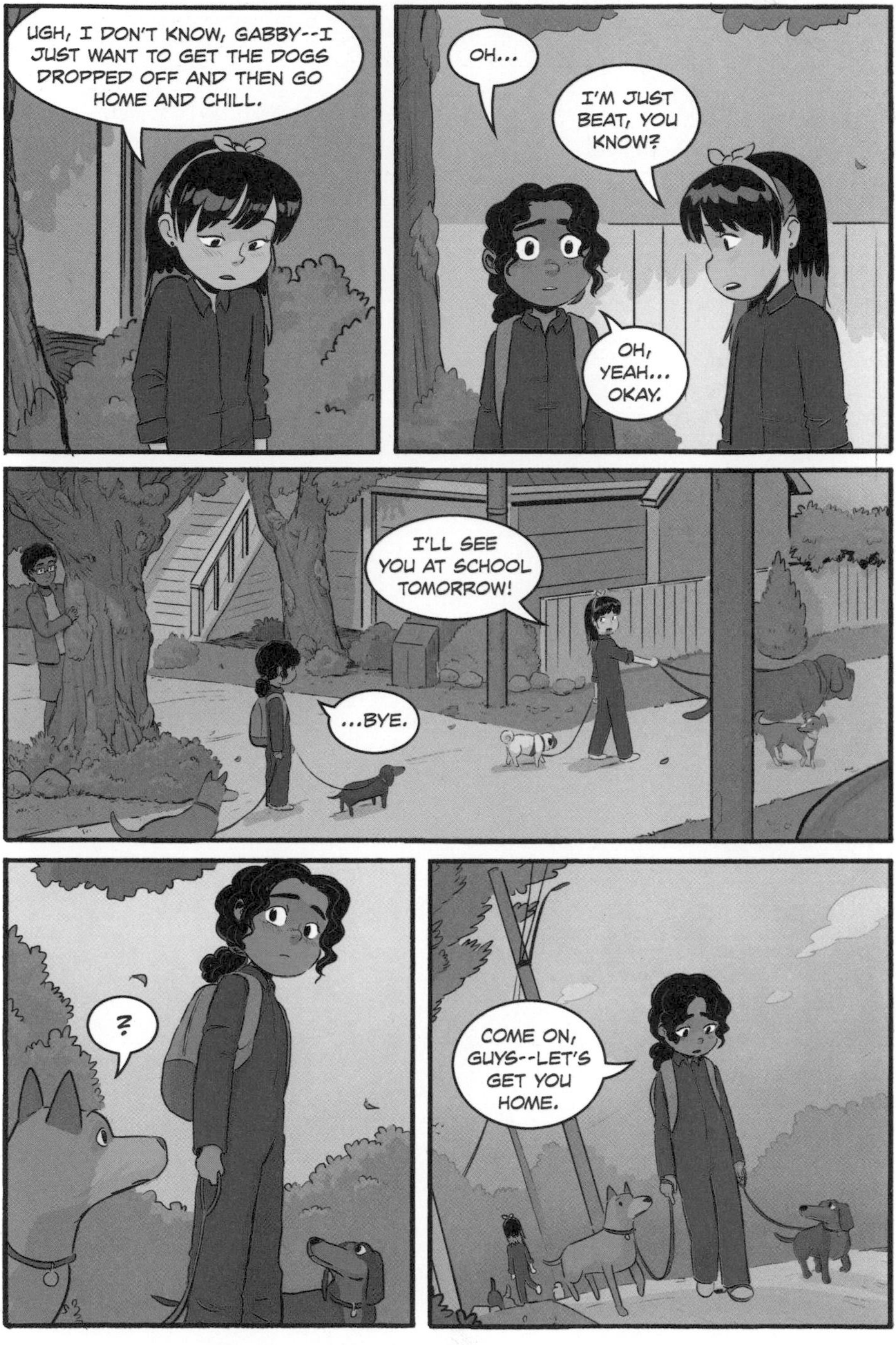
UGH, I DON'T KNOW, GABBY--I JUST WANT TO GET THE DOGS DROPPED OFF AND THEN GO HOME AND CHILL.
OH...
I'M JUST BEAT, YOU KNOW?
OH, YEAH... OKAY.
I'LL SEE YOU AT SCHOOL TOMORROW!
...BYE.
?
COME ON, GUYS--LET'S GET YOU HOME.

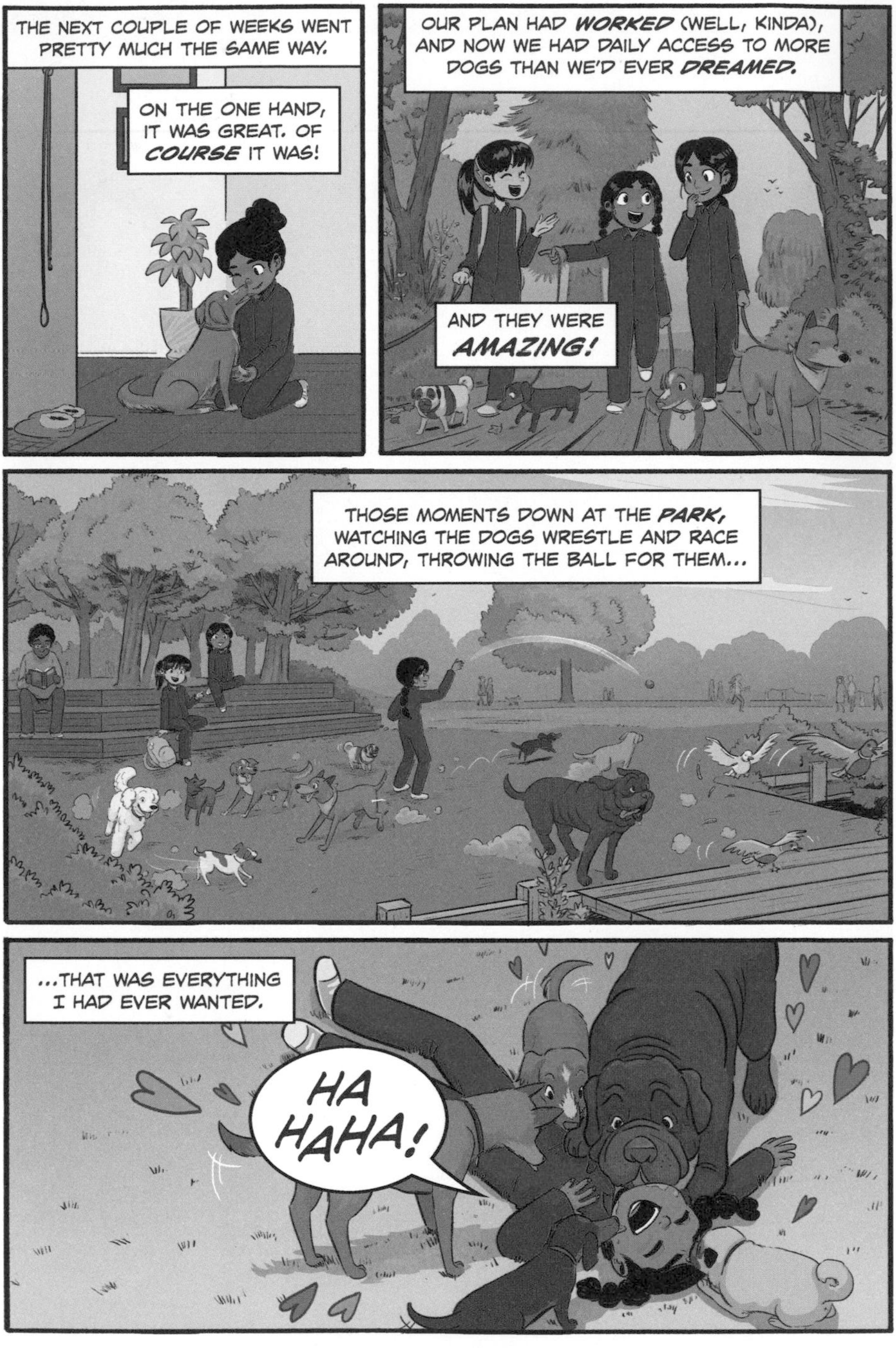
THE NEXT COUPLE OF WEEKS WENT PRETTY MUCH THE SAME WAY.
ON THE ONE HAND, IT WAS GREAT. OF *COURSE* IT WAS!
OUR PLAN HAD *WORKED* (WELL, KINDA), AND NOW WE HAD DAILY ACCESS TO MORE DOGS THAN WE'D EVER *DREAMED.*
AND THEY WERE *AMAZING!*
THOSE MOMENTS DOWN AT THE *PARK,* WATCHING THE DOGS WRESTLE AND RACE AROUND, THROWING THE BALL FOR THEM...
...THAT WAS EVERYTHING I HAD EVER WANTED.
HA HAHA!

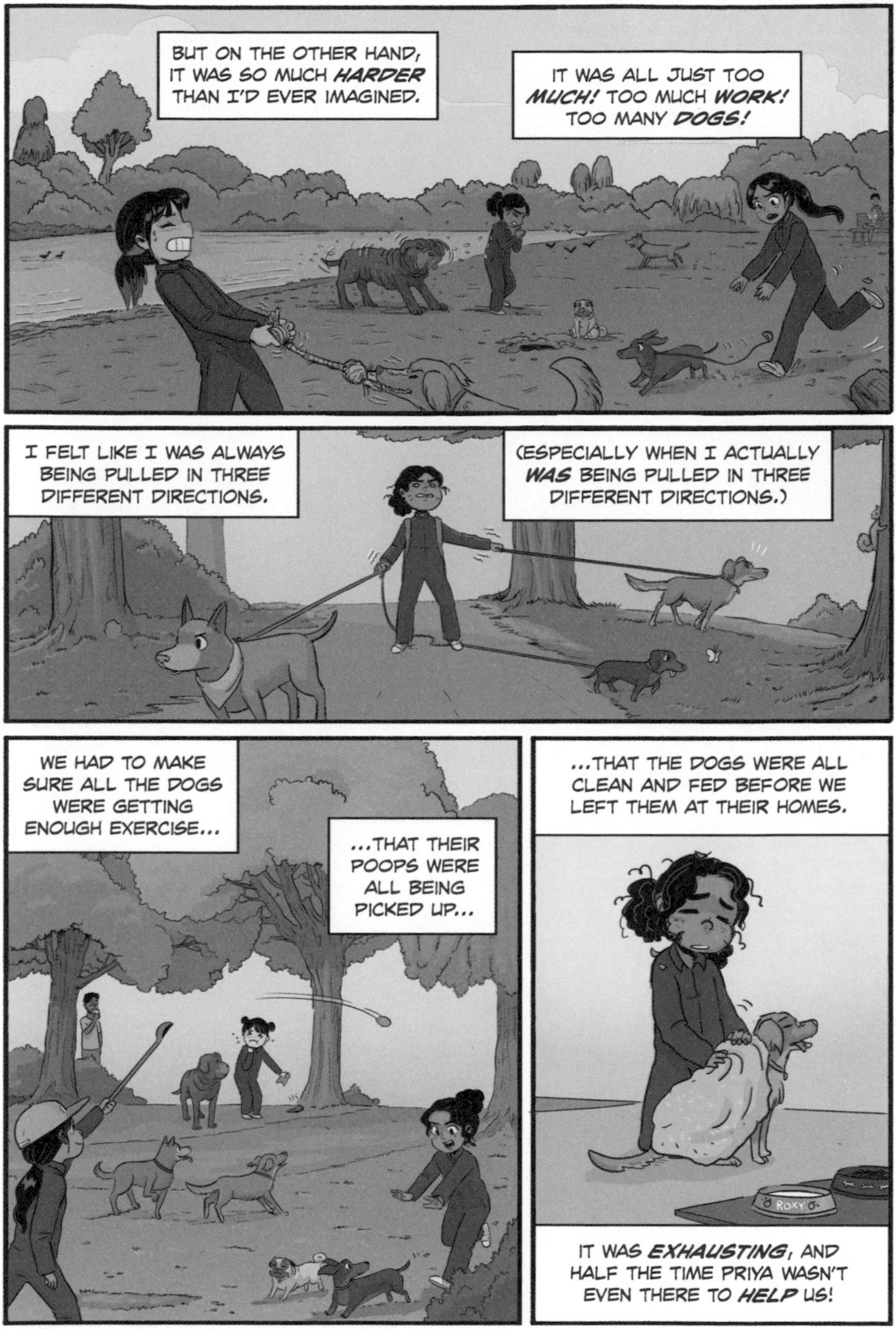
BUT ON THE OTHER HAND, IT WAS SO MUCH HARDER THAN I'D EVER IMAGINED.
IT WAS ALL JUST TOO MUCH! TOO MUCH WORK! TOO MANY DOGS!
I FELT LIKE I WAS ALWAYS BEING PULLED IN THREE DIFFERENT DIRECTIONS.
(ESPECIALLY WHEN I ACTUALLY WAS BEING PULLED IN THREE DIFFERENT DIRECTIONS.)
WE HAD TO MAKE SURE ALL THE DOGS WERE GETTING ENOUGH EXERCISE...
...THAT THEIR POOPS WERE ALL BEING PICKED UP...
...THAT THE DOGS WERE ALL CLEAN AND FED BEFORE WE LEFT THEM AT THEIR HOMES.
ROXY
IT WAS EXHAUSTING, AND HALF THE TIME PRIYA WASN'T EVEN THERE TO HELP US!

I KNOW HER SPORTS AND JUNK ARE *IMPORTANT* TO HER. I GET THAT.

(WELL, TO BE HONEST, I *DON'T* GET IT, BUT I KNOW THAT'S HOW SHE FEELS.)

BUT IT SEEMED LIKE THEY WERE ALWAYS *MORE* IMPORTANT TO HER THAN *PAWS.*

SOMETIMES SHE EVEN GOT PICKED UP IN THE MIDDLE OF OUR WALK TO GO...HIT A BALL WITH A STICK OR WHATEVER!

OH, SURE, SHE REARRANGED HER BASEBALL SCHEDULE A BIT--BIG *DEAL!* WE *STILL* HAD TO PICK UP HER SLACK *TWICE A WEEK!*

I DIDN'T EVEN GET A DAY *OFF* BECAUSE ROXY AND CORPORAL WAGS NEEDED WALKING ON THE WEEKEND, AND MINDY WAS BUSY, TOO!

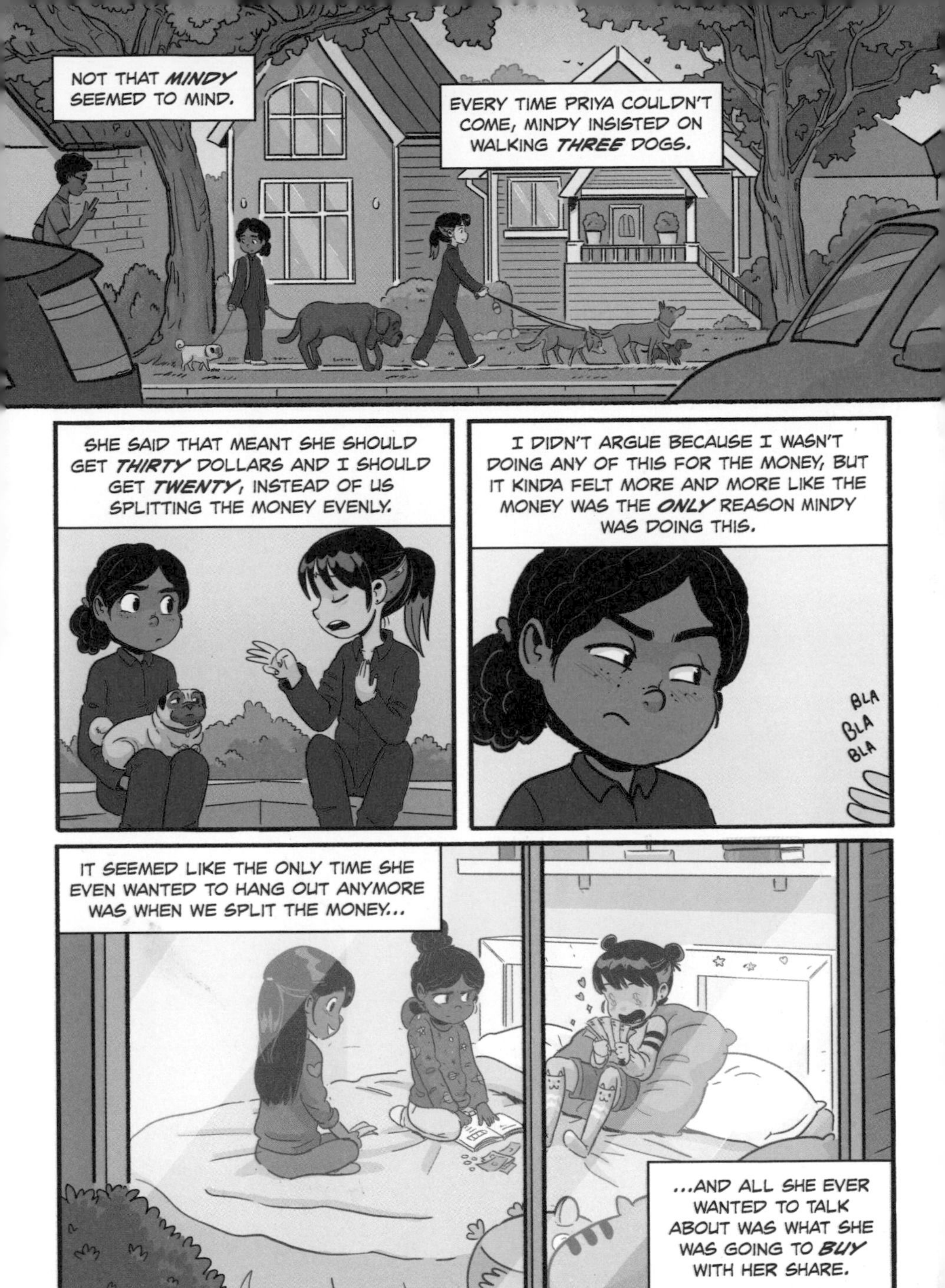
NOT THAT MINDY SEEMED TO MIND.
EVERY TIME PRIYA COULDN'T COME, MINDY INSISTED ON WALKING THREE DOGS.
SHE SAID THAT MEANT SHE SHOULD GET THIRTY DOLLARS AND I SHOULD GET TWENTY, INSTEAD OF US SPLITTING THE MONEY EVENLY.
I DIDN'T ARGUE BECAUSE I WASN'T DOING ANY OF THIS FOR THE MONEY, BUT IT KINDA FELT MORE AND MORE LIKE THE MONEY WAS THE ONLY REASON MINDY WAS DOING THIS.
BLA BLA BLA
IT SEEMED LIKE THE ONLY TIME SHE EVEN WANTED TO HANG OUT ANYMORE WAS WHEN WE SPLIT THE MONEY...
...AND ALL SHE EVER WANTED TO TALK ABOUT WAS WHAT SHE WAS GOING TO BUY WITH HER SHARE.

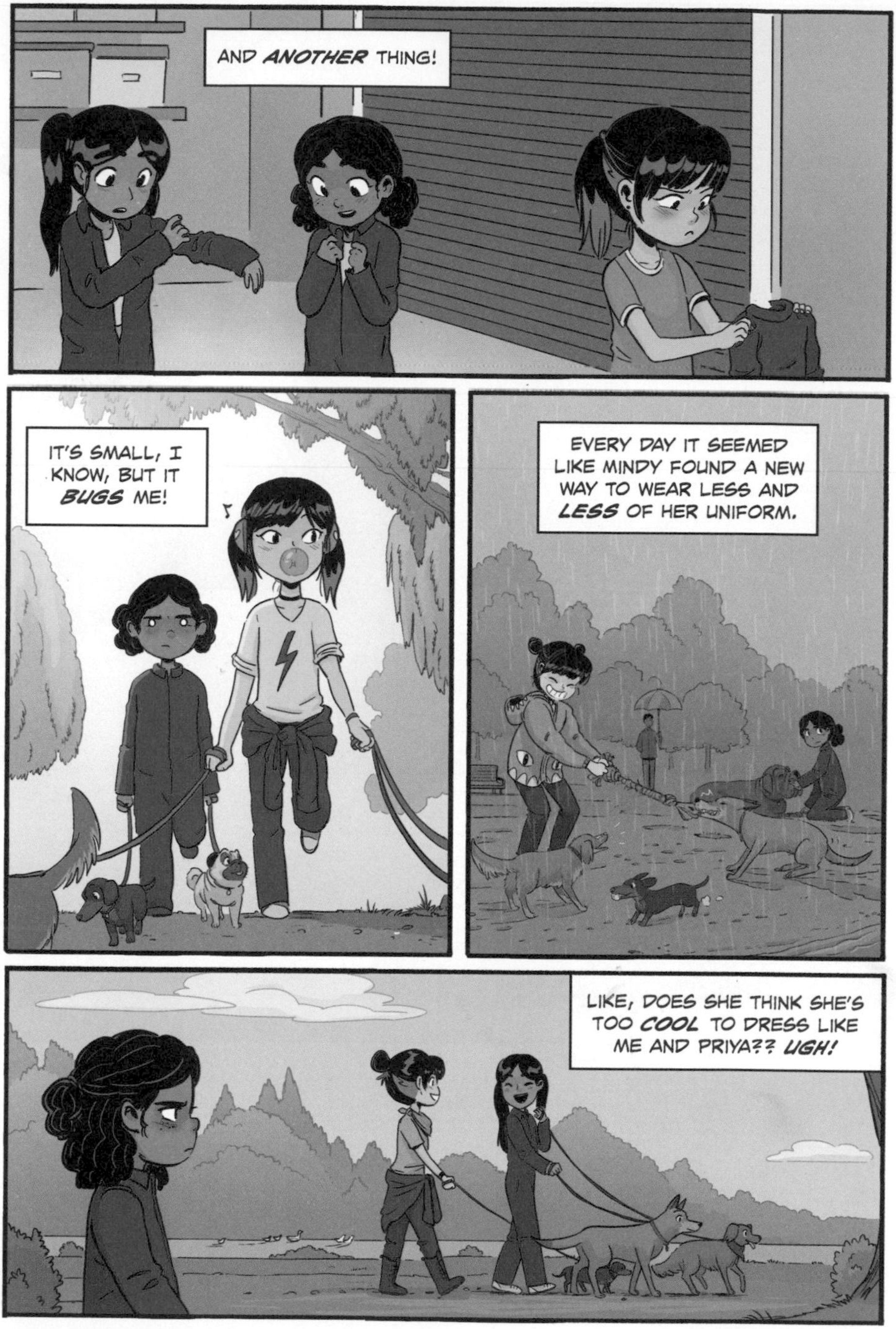
AND *ANOTHER* THING!
IT'S SMALL, I KNOW, BUT IT *BUGS* ME!
EVERY DAY IT SEEMED LIKE MINDY FOUND A NEW WAY TO WEAR LESS AND *LESS* OF HER UNIFORM.
LIKE, DOES SHE THINK SHE'S TOO *COOL* TO DRESS LIKE ME AND PRIYA?? *UGH!*

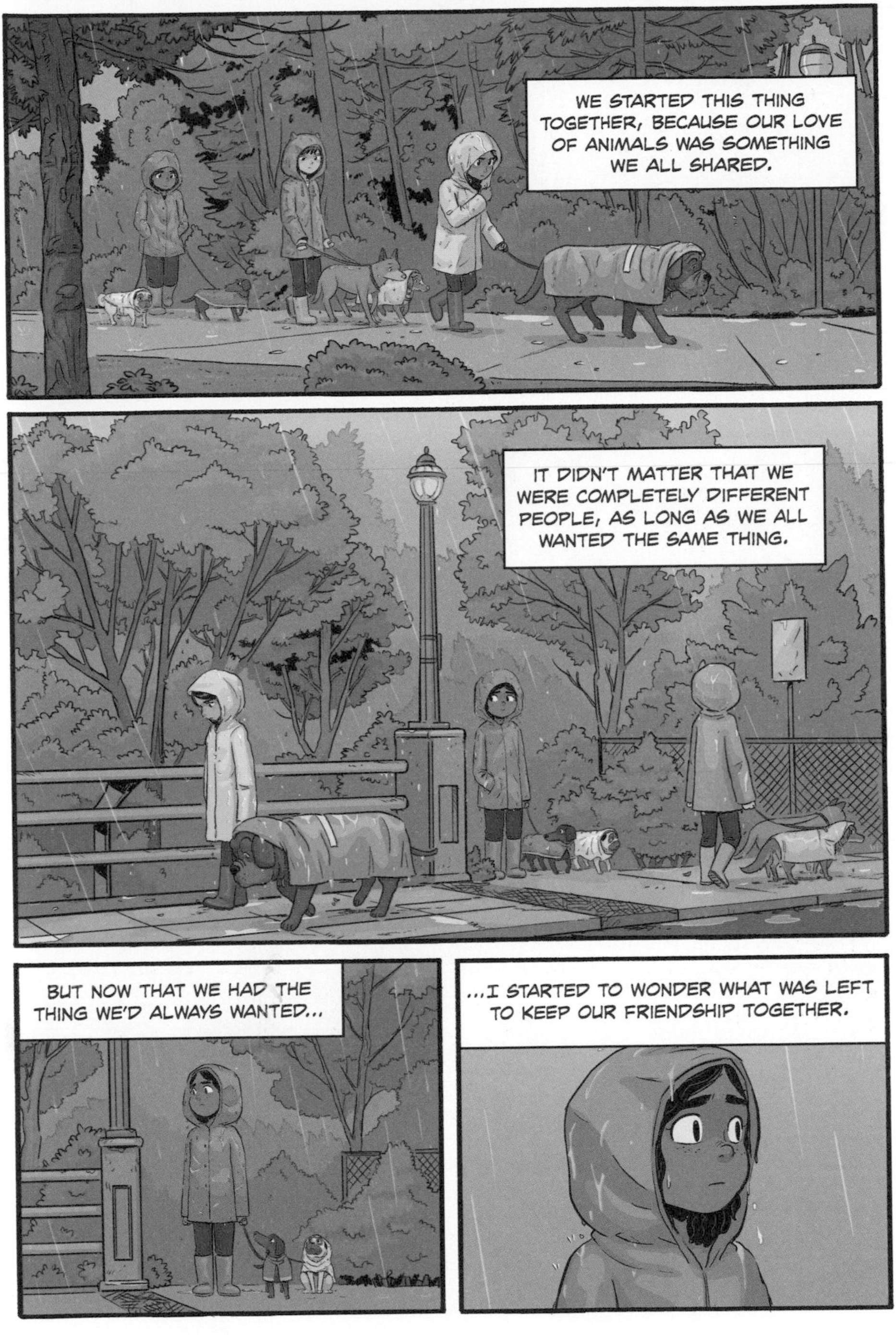
WE STARTED THIS THING TOGETHER, BECAUSE OUR LOVE OF ANIMALS WAS SOMETHING WE ALL SHARED.
IT DIDN'T MATTER THAT WE WERE COMPLETELY DIFFERENT PEOPLE, AS LONG AS WE ALL WANTED THE SAME THING.
BUT NOW THAT WE HAD THE THING WE'D ALWAYS WANTED...
...I STARTED TO WONDER WHAT WAS LEFT TO KEEP OUR FRIENDSHIP TOGETHER.

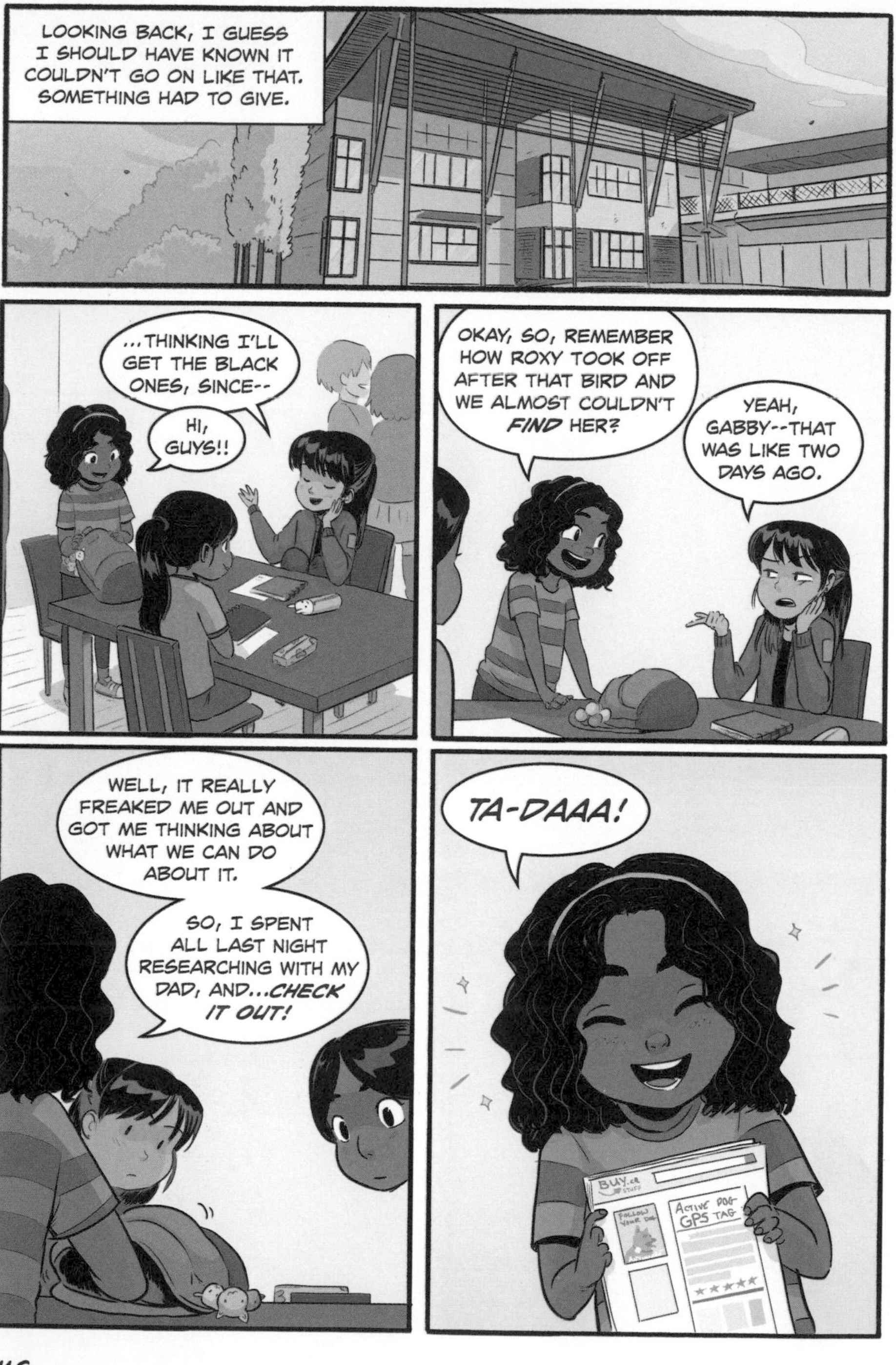
LOOKING BACK, I GUESS I SHOULD HAVE KNOWN IT COULDN'T GO ON LIKE THAT. SOMETHING HAD TO GIVE.
...THINKING I'LL GET THE BLACK ONES, SINCE--
HI, GUYS!!
OKAY, SO, REMEMBER HOW ROXY TOOK OFF AFTER THAT BIRD AND WE ALMOST COULDN'T *FIND* HER?
YEAH, GABBY--THAT WAS LIKE TWO DAYS AGO.
WELL, IT REALLY FREAKED ME OUT AND GOT ME THINKING ABOUT WHAT WE CAN DO ABOUT IT.
SO, I SPENT ALL LAST NIGHT RESEARCHING WITH MY DAD, AND...*CHECK IT OUT!*
TA-DAAA!
BUY.ca STUFF
FOLLOW YOUR DOG
ACTIVE DOG GPS TAG

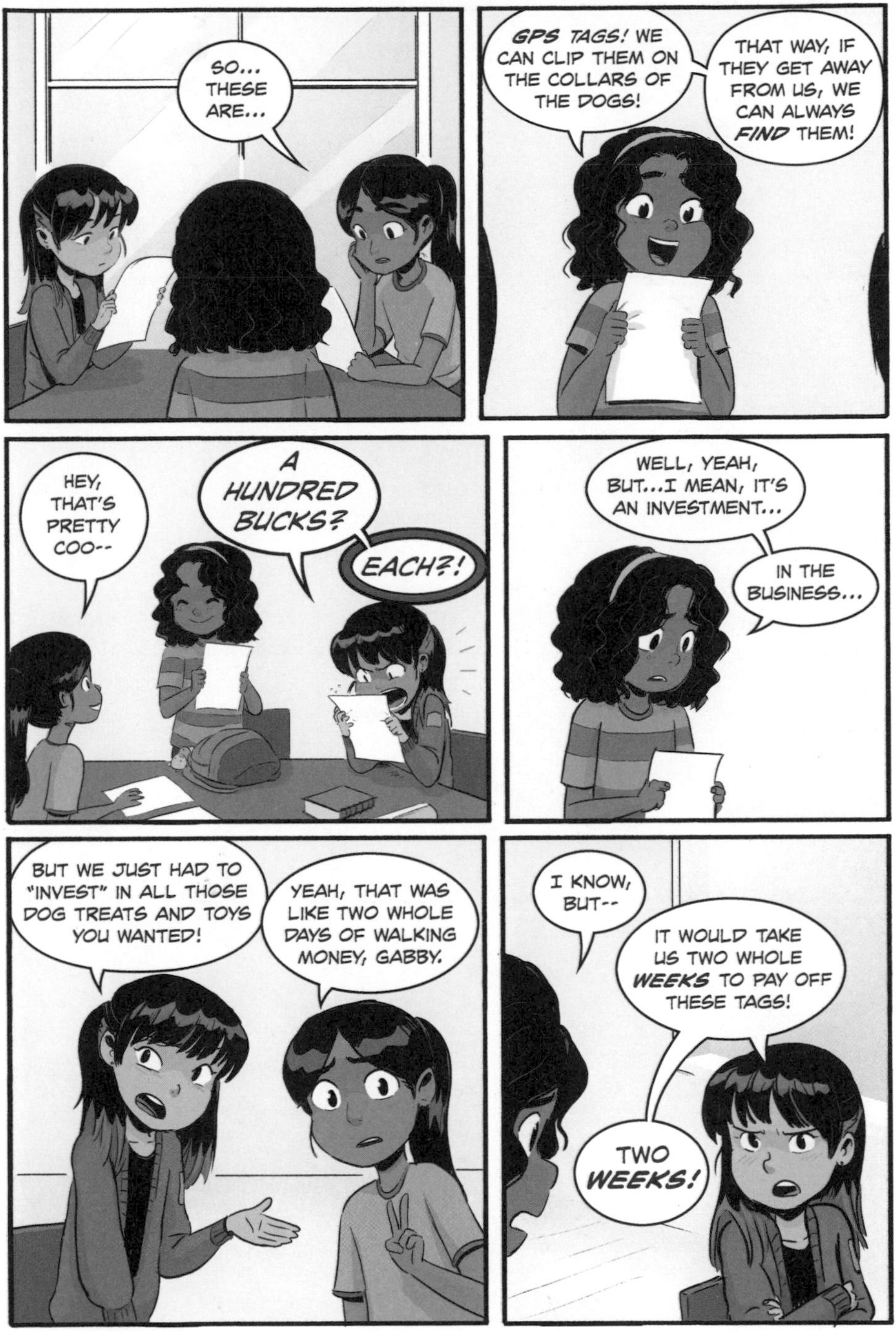
SO... THESE ARE...
GPS TAGS! WE CAN CLIP THEM ON THE COLLARS OF THE DOGS!
THAT WAY, IF THEY GET AWAY FROM US, WE CAN ALWAYS FIND THEM!
HEY, THAT'S PRETTY COO--
A HUNDRED BUCKS?
EACH?!
WELL, YEAH, BUT...I MEAN, IT'S AN INVESTMENT...
IN THE BUSINESS...
BUT WE JUST HAD TO "INVEST" IN ALL THOSE DOG TREATS AND TOYS YOU WANTED!
YEAH, THAT WAS LIKE TWO WHOLE DAYS OF WALKING MONEY, GABBY.
I KNOW, BUT--
IT WOULD TAKE US TWO WHOLE WEEKS TO PAY OFF THESE TAGS!
TWO WEEKS!

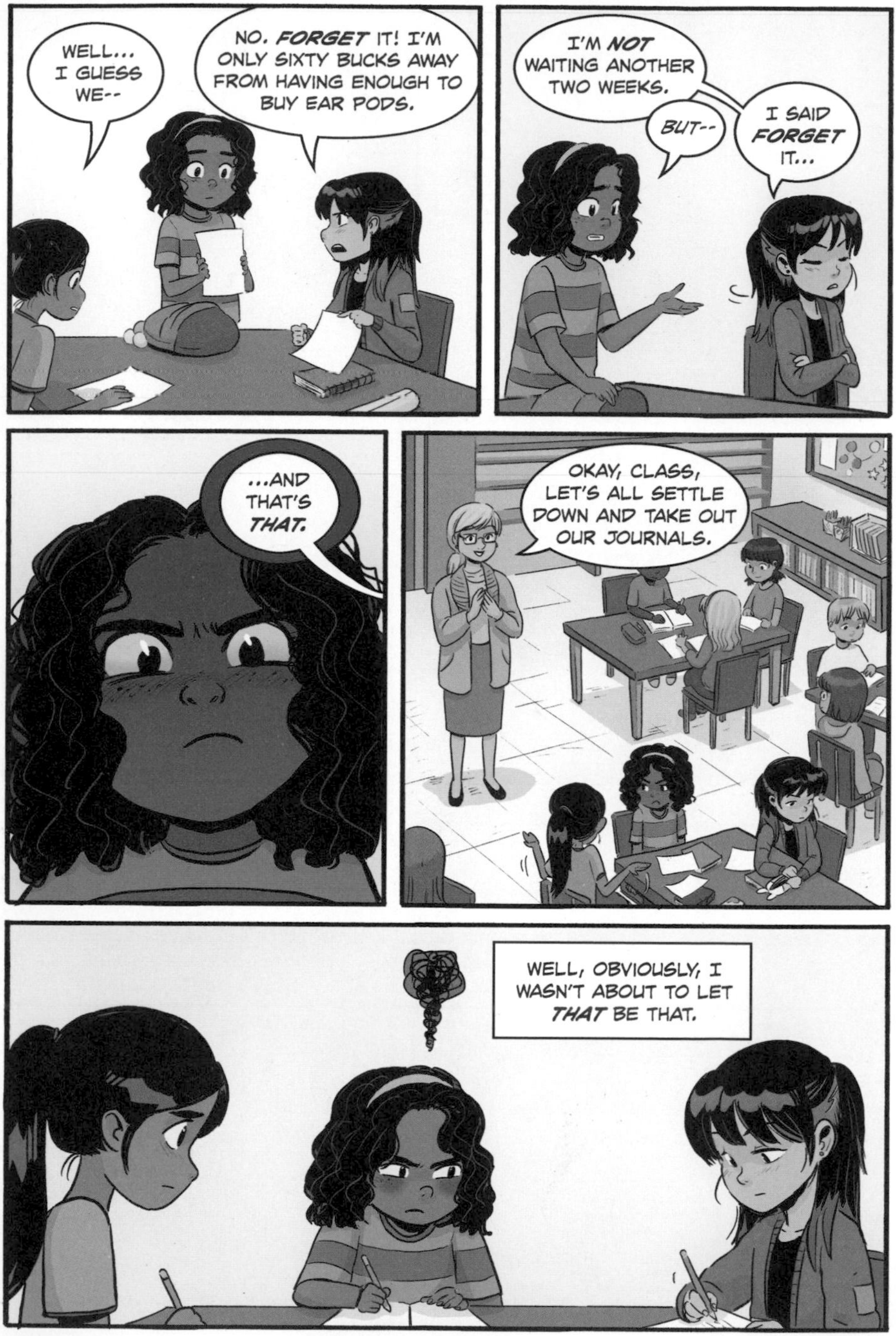
WELL... I GUESS WE--
NO. *FORGET* IT! I'M ONLY SIXTY BUCKS AWAY FROM HAVING ENOUGH TO BUY EAR PODS.
I'M *NOT* WAITING ANOTHER TWO WEEKS.
BUT--
I SAID *FORGET* IT...
...AND THAT'S *THAT.*
OKAY, CLASS, LET'S ALL SETTLE DOWN AND TAKE OUT OUR JOURNALS.
WELL, OBVIOUSLY, I WASN'T ABOUT TO LET *THAT* BE THAT.

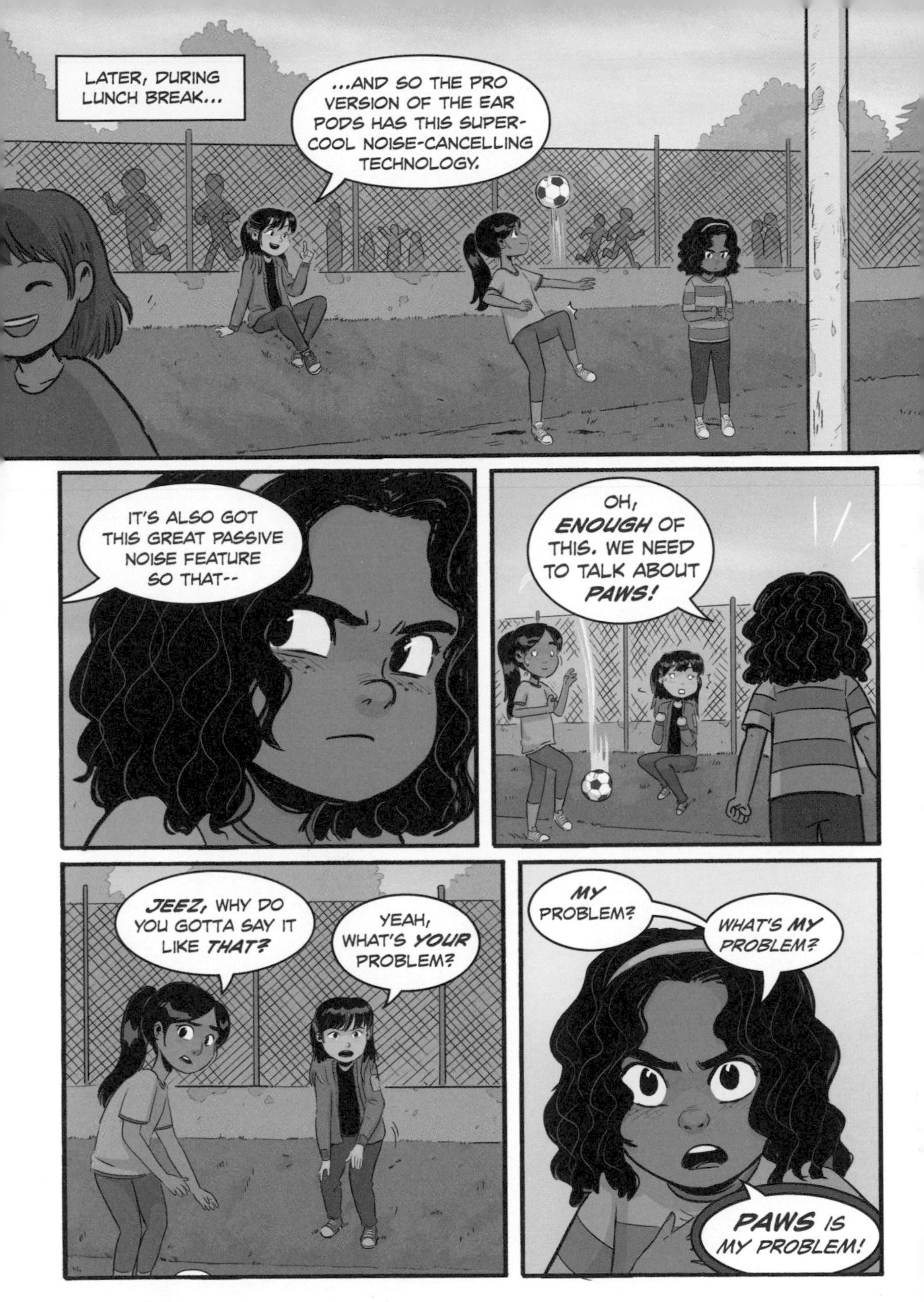

LATER, DURING LUNCH BREAK...
...AND SO THE PRO VERSION OF THE EAR PODS HAS THIS SUPER-COOL NOISE-CANCELLING TECHNOLOGY.
IT'S ALSO GOT THIS GREAT PASSIVE NOISE FEATURE SO THAT--
OH, ENOUGH OF THIS. WE NEED TO TALK ABOUT PAWS!
JEEZ, WHY DO YOU GOTTA SAY IT LIKE THAT?
YEAH, WHAT'S YOUR PROBLEM?
MY PROBLEM?
WHAT'S MY PROBLEM?
PAWS IS MY PROBLEM!

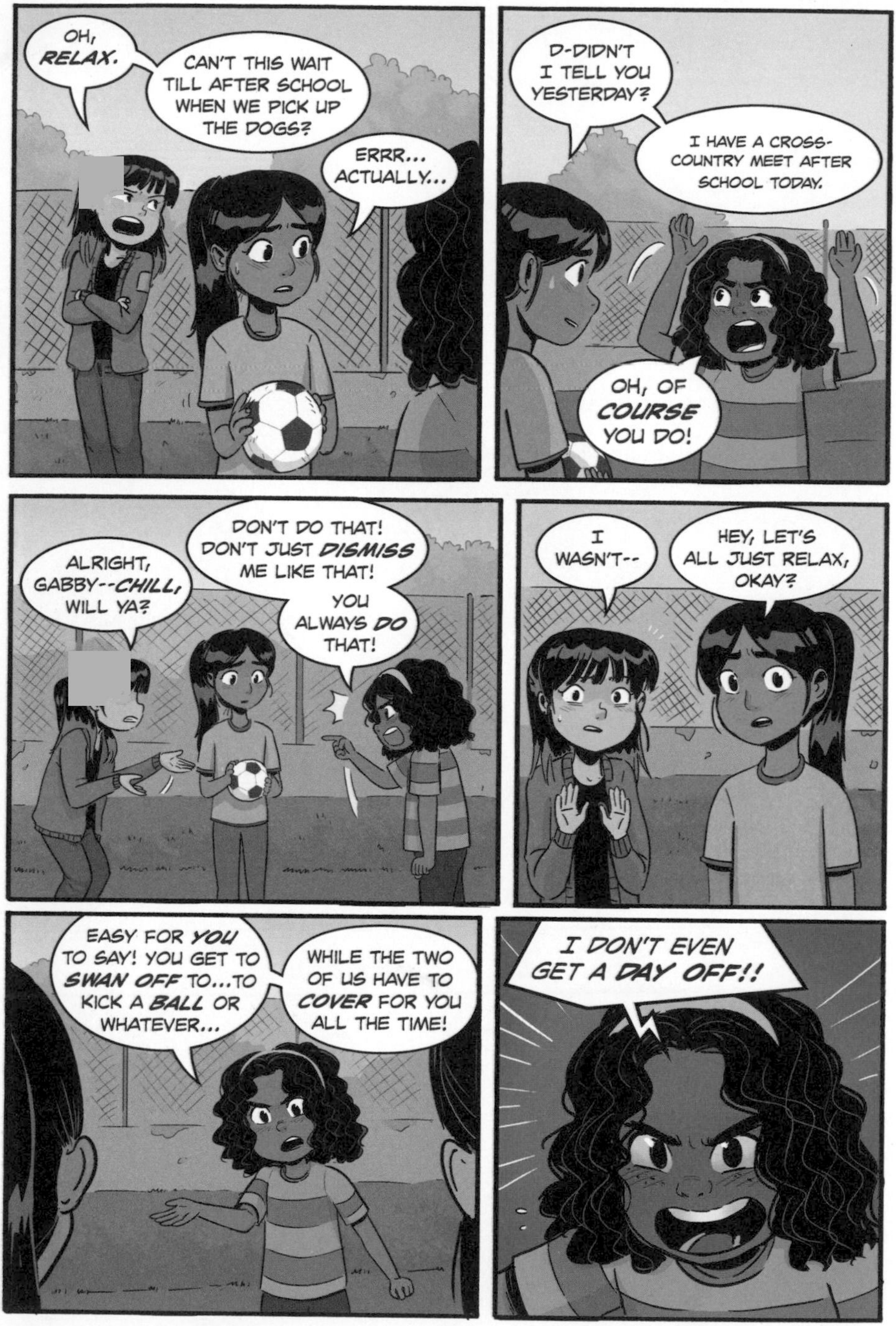
OH, RELAX.
CAN'T THIS WAIT TILL AFTER SCHOOL WHEN WE PICK UP THE DOGS?
ERRR... ACTUALLY...
D-DIDN'T I TELL YOU YESTERDAY?
I HAVE A CROSS-COUNTRY MEET AFTER SCHOOL TODAY.
OH, OF COURSE YOU DO!
ALRIGHT, GABBY--CHILL, WILL YA?
DON'T DO THAT! DON'T JUST DISMISS ME LIKE THAT!
YOU ALWAYS DO THAT!
I WASN'T--
HEY, LET'S ALL JUST RELAX, OKAY?
EASY FOR YOU TO SAY! YOU GET TO SWAN OFF TO...TO KICK A BALL OR WHATEVER...
WHILE THE TWO OF US HAVE TO COVER FOR YOU ALL THE TIME!
I DON'T EVEN GET A DAY OFF!!

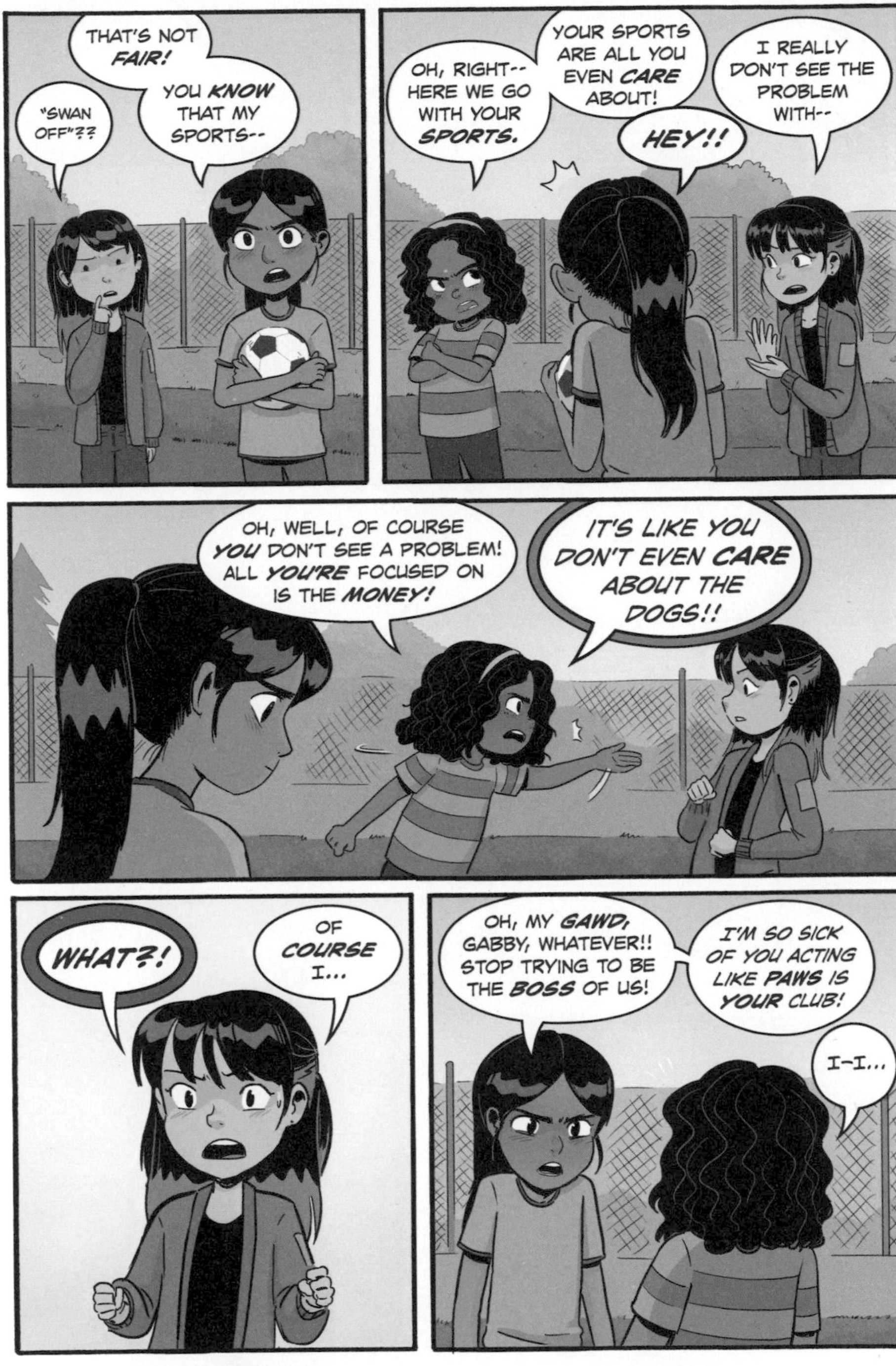
THAT'S NOT FAIR!
"SWAN OFF"??
YOU KNOW THAT MY SPORTS--
OH, RIGHT-- HERE WE GO WITH YOUR SPORTS.
YOUR SPORTS ARE ALL YOU EVEN CARE ABOUT!
HEY!!
I REALLY DON'T SEE THE PROBLEM WITH--
OH, WELL, OF COURSE YOU DON'T SEE A PROBLEM! ALL YOU'RE FOCUSED ON IS THE MONEY!
IT'S LIKE YOU DON'T EVEN CARE ABOUT THE DOGS!!
WHAT?!
OF COURSE I...
OH, MY GAWD, GABBY, WHATEVER!! STOP TRYING TO BE THE BOSS OF US!
I'M SO SICK OF YOU ACTING LIKE PAWS IS YOUR CLUB!
I-I...

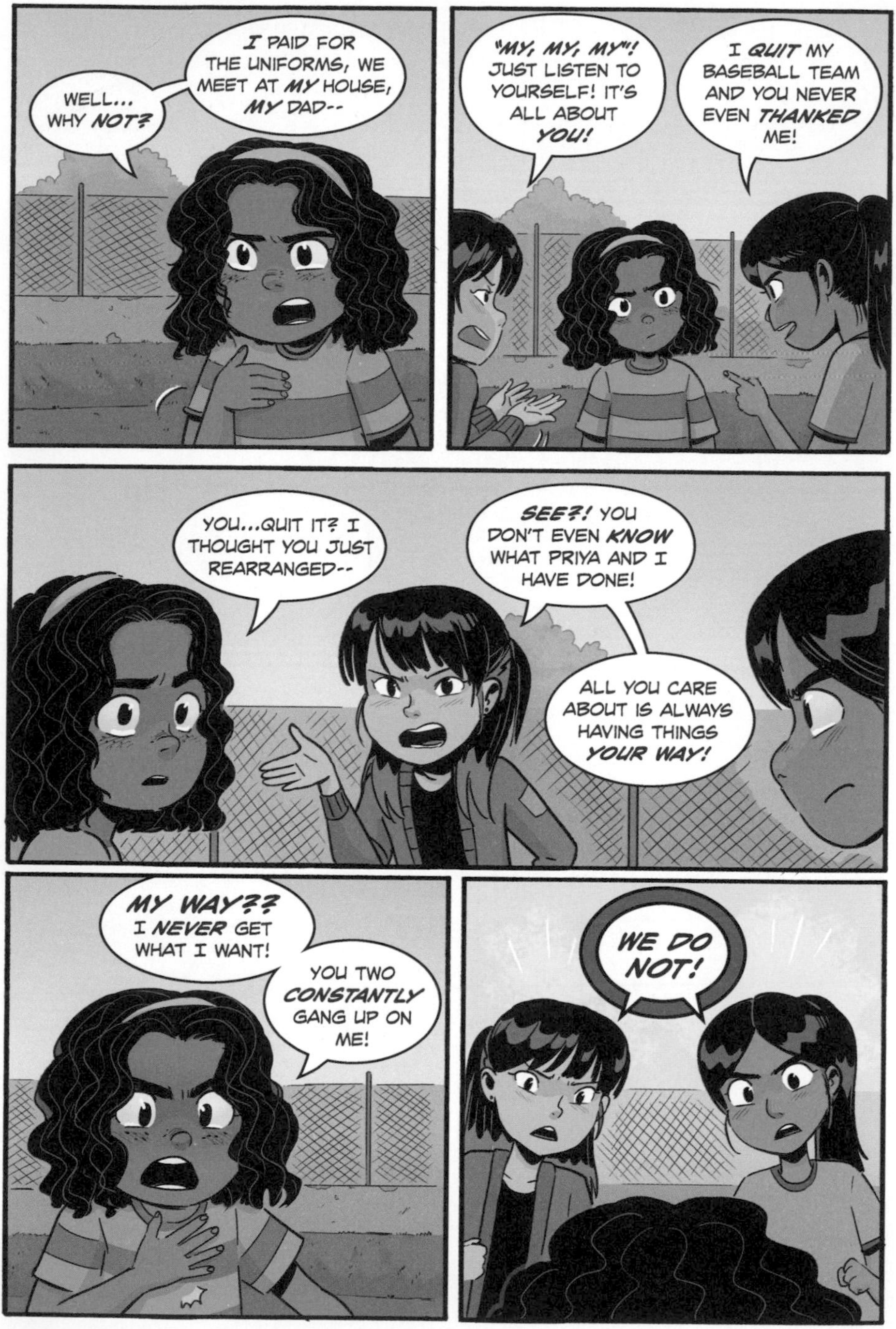

WELL... WHY NOT?
I PAID FOR THE UNIFORMS, WE MEET AT MY HOUSE, MY DAD--
"MY, MY, MY"! JUST LISTEN TO YOURSELF! IT'S ALL ABOUT YOU!
I QUIT MY BASEBALL TEAM AND YOU NEVER EVEN THANKED ME!
YOU...QUIT IT? I THOUGHT YOU JUST REARRANGED--
SEE?! YOU DON'T EVEN KNOW WHAT PRIYA AND I HAVE DONE!
ALL YOU CARE ABOUT IS ALWAYS HAVING THINGS YOUR WAY!
MY WAY?? I NEVER GET WHAT I WANT!
YOU TWO CONSTANTLY GANG UP ON ME!
WE DO NOT!

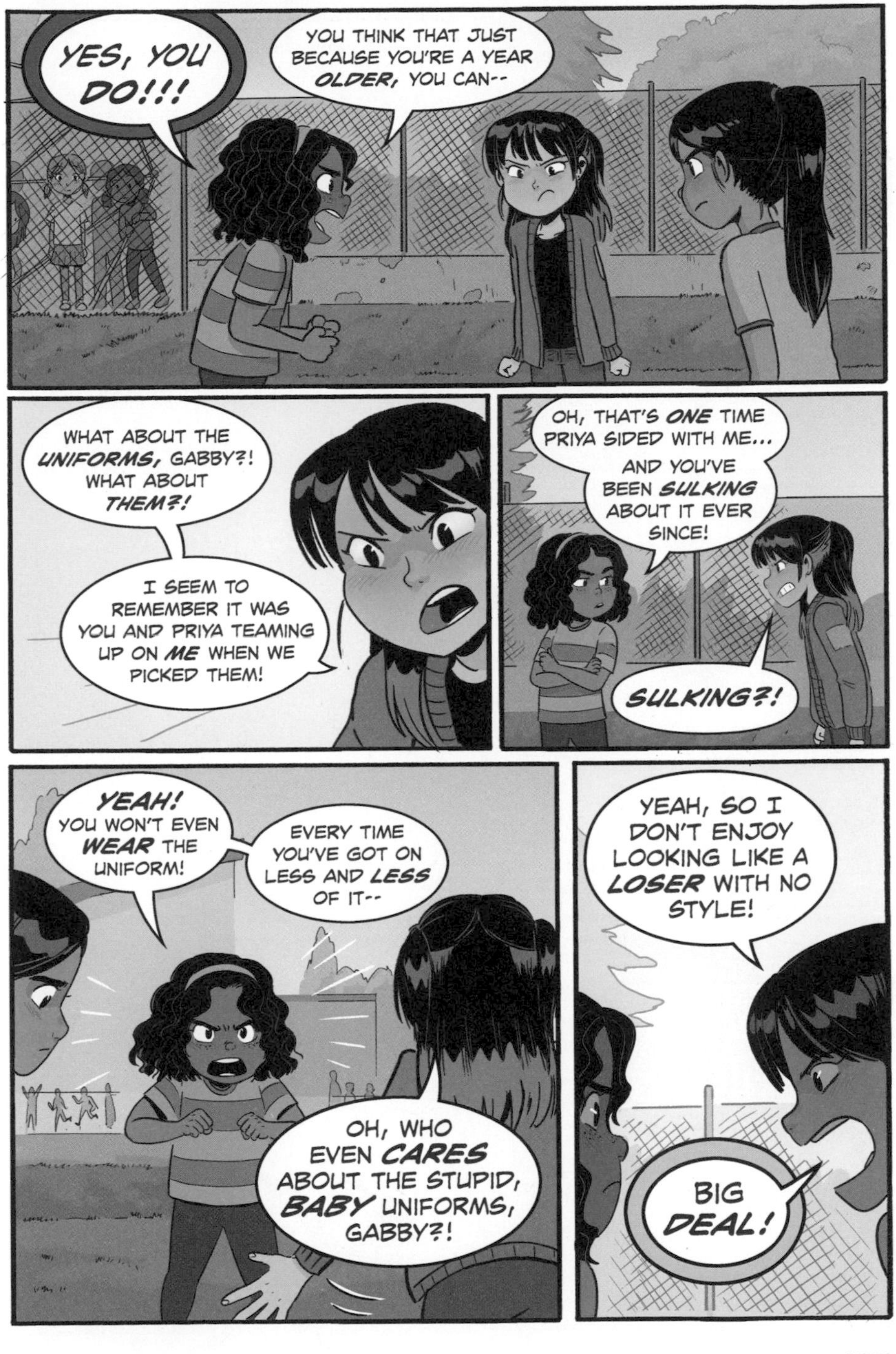
YES, YOU DO!!!
YOU THINK THAT JUST BECAUSE YOU'RE A YEAR OLDER, YOU CAN--
WHAT ABOUT THE UNIFORMS, GABBY?! WHAT ABOUT THEM?!
I SEEM TO REMEMBER IT WAS YOU AND PRIYA TEAMING UP ON ME WHEN WE PICKED THEM!
OH, THAT'S ONE TIME PRIYA SIDED WITH ME...
AND YOU'VE BEEN SULKING ABOUT IT EVER SINCE!
SULKING?!
YEAH! YOU WON'T EVEN WEAR THE UNIFORM!
EVERY TIME YOU'VE GOT ON LESS AND LESS OF IT--
OH, WHO EVEN CARES ABOUT THE STUPID, BABY UNIFORMS, GABBY?!
YEAH, SO I DON'T ENJOY LOOKING LIKE A LOSER WITH NO STYLE!
BIG DEAL!

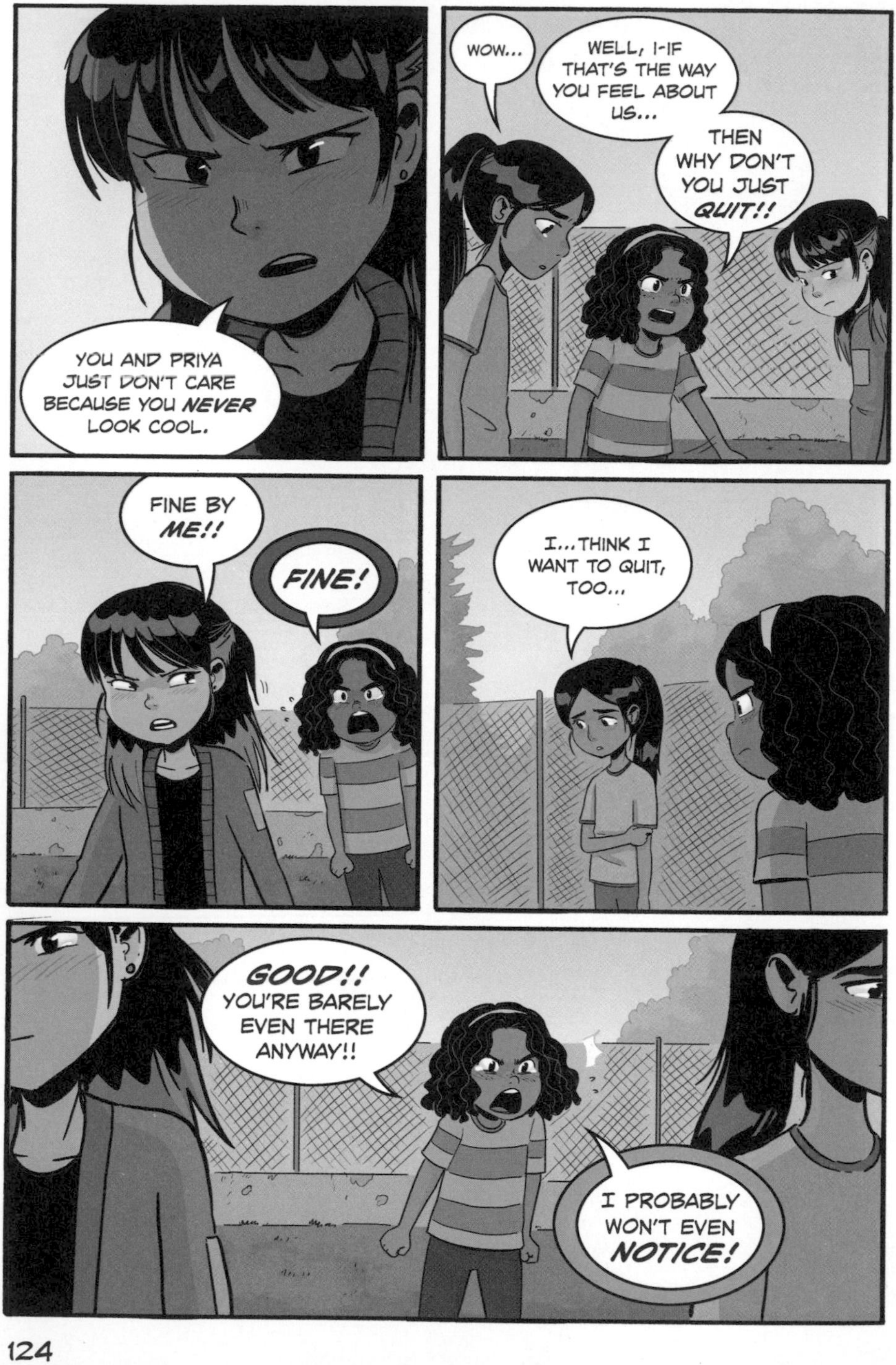
YOU AND PRIYA JUST DON'T CARE BECAUSE YOU NEVER LOOK COOL.
WOW...
WELL, I-IF THAT'S THE WAY YOU FEEL ABOUT US...
THEN WHY DON'T YOU JUST QUIT!!
FINE BY ME!!
FINE!
I...THINK I WANT TO QUIT, TOO...
GOOD!! YOU'RE BARELY EVEN THERE ANYWAY!!
I PROBABLY WON'T EVEN NOTICE!

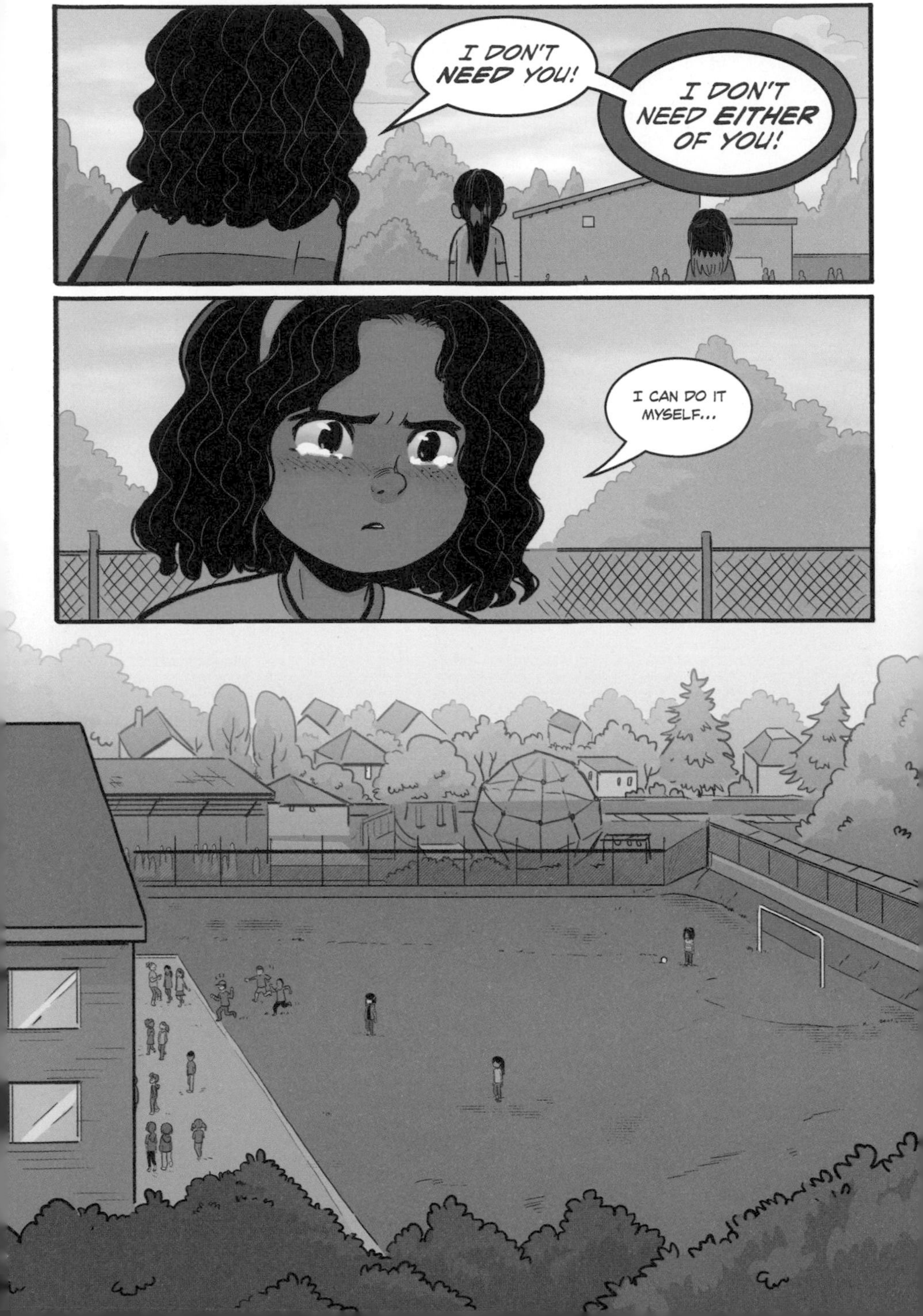
I DON'T NEED YOU!
I DON'T NEED EITHER OF YOU!
I CAN DO IT MYSELF...

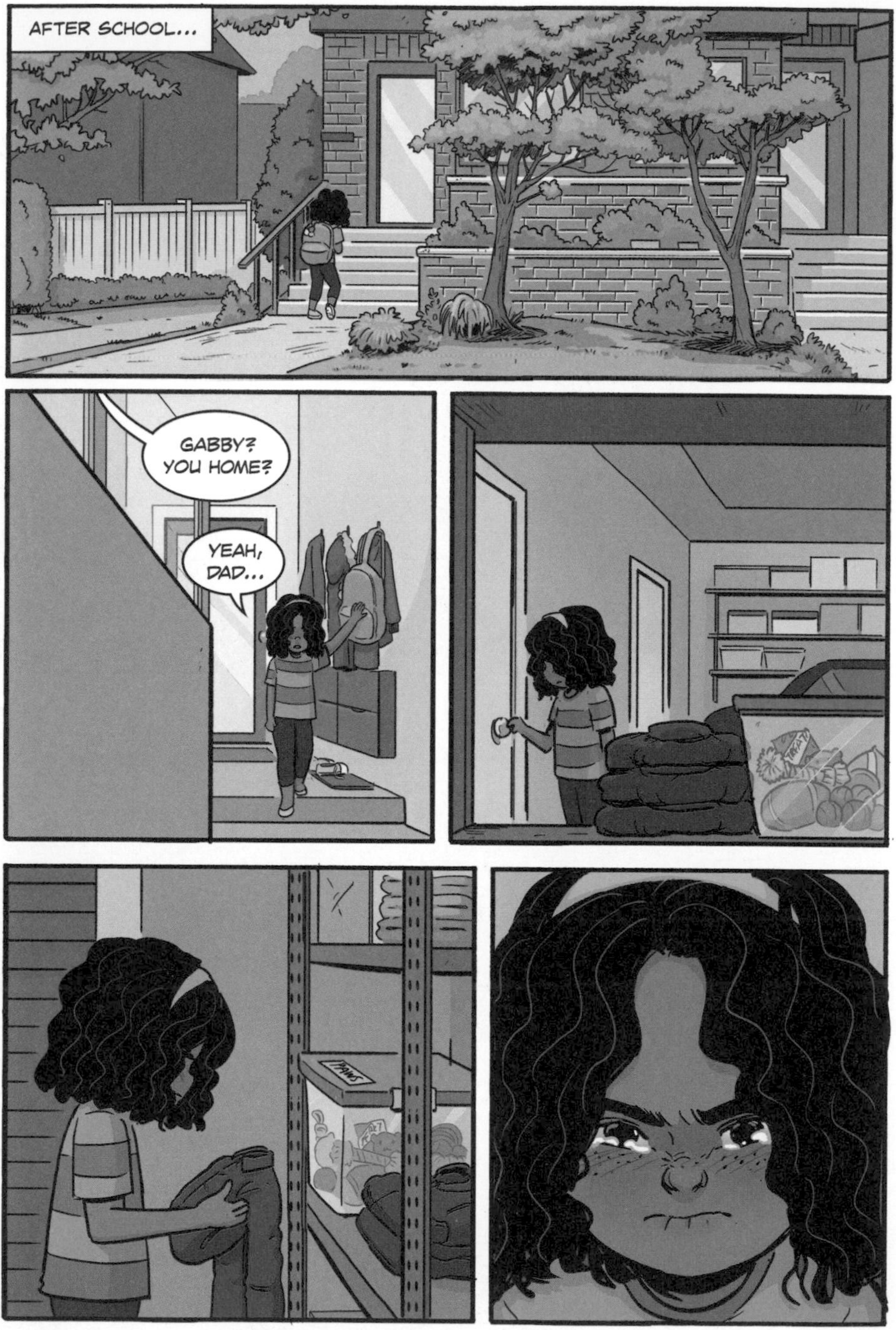
AFTER SCHOOL...
GABBY? YOU HOME?
YEAH, DAD...

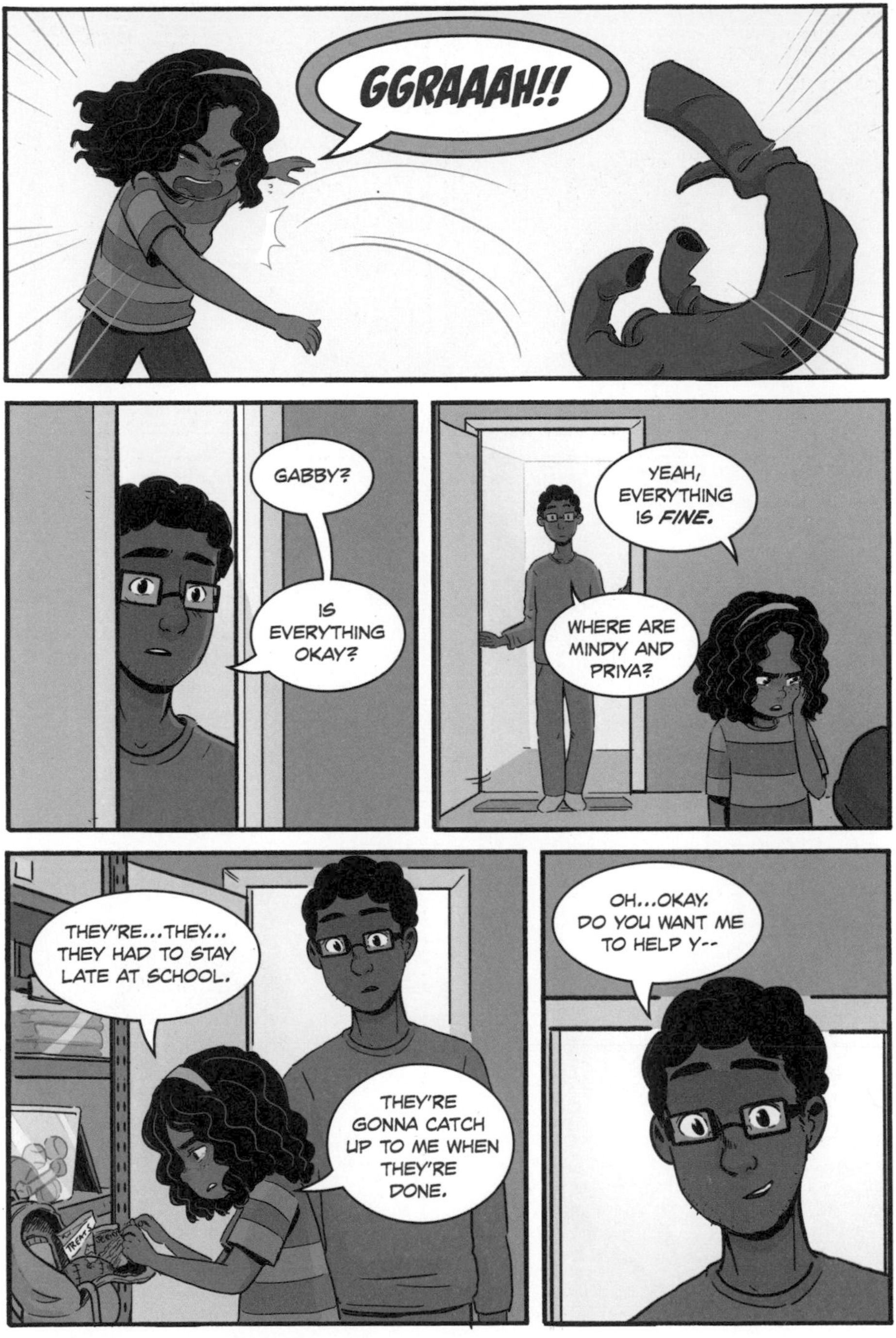
GGRAAAH!!
GABBY?
IS EVERYTHING OKAY?
YEAH, EVERYTHING IS *FINE.*
WHERE ARE MINDY AND PRIYA?
THEY'RE...THEY... THEY HAD TO STAY LATE AT SCHOOL.
THEY'RE GONNA CATCH UP TO ME WHEN THEY'RE DONE.
OH...OKAY. DO YOU WANT ME TO HELP Y--

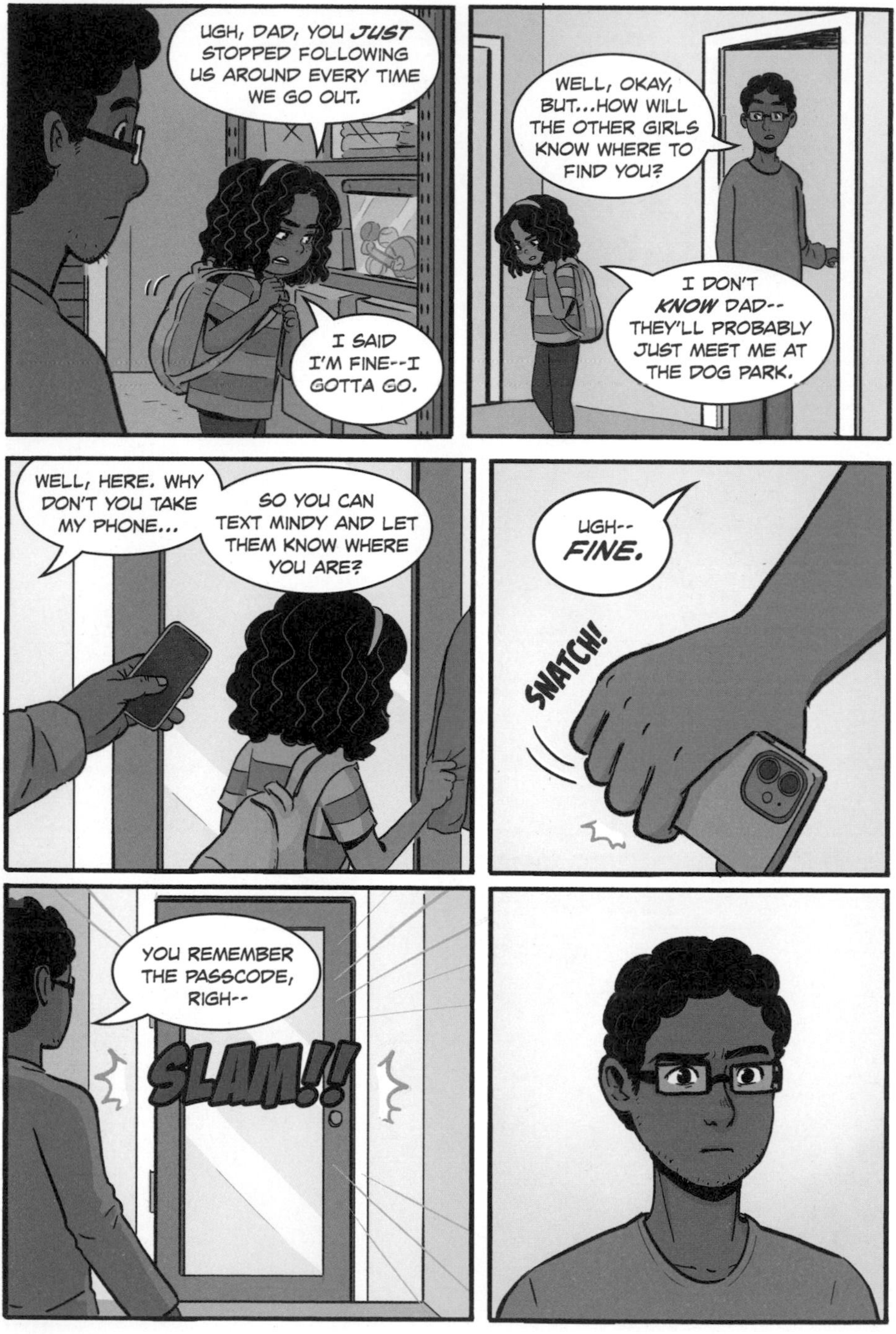
UGH, DAD, YOU JUST STOPPED FOLLOWING US AROUND EVERY TIME WE GO OUT.
I SAID I'M FINE--I GOTTA GO.
WELL, OKAY, BUT...HOW WILL THE OTHER GIRLS KNOW WHERE TO FIND YOU?
I DON'T KNOW DAD--THEY'LL PROBABLY JUST MEET ME AT THE DOG PARK.
WELL, HERE. WHY DON'T YOU TAKE MY PHONE...
SO YOU CAN TEXT MINDY AND LET THEM KNOW WHERE YOU ARE?
UGH--FINE.
SNATCH!
YOU REMEMBER THE PASSCODE, RIGH--
SLAM!!

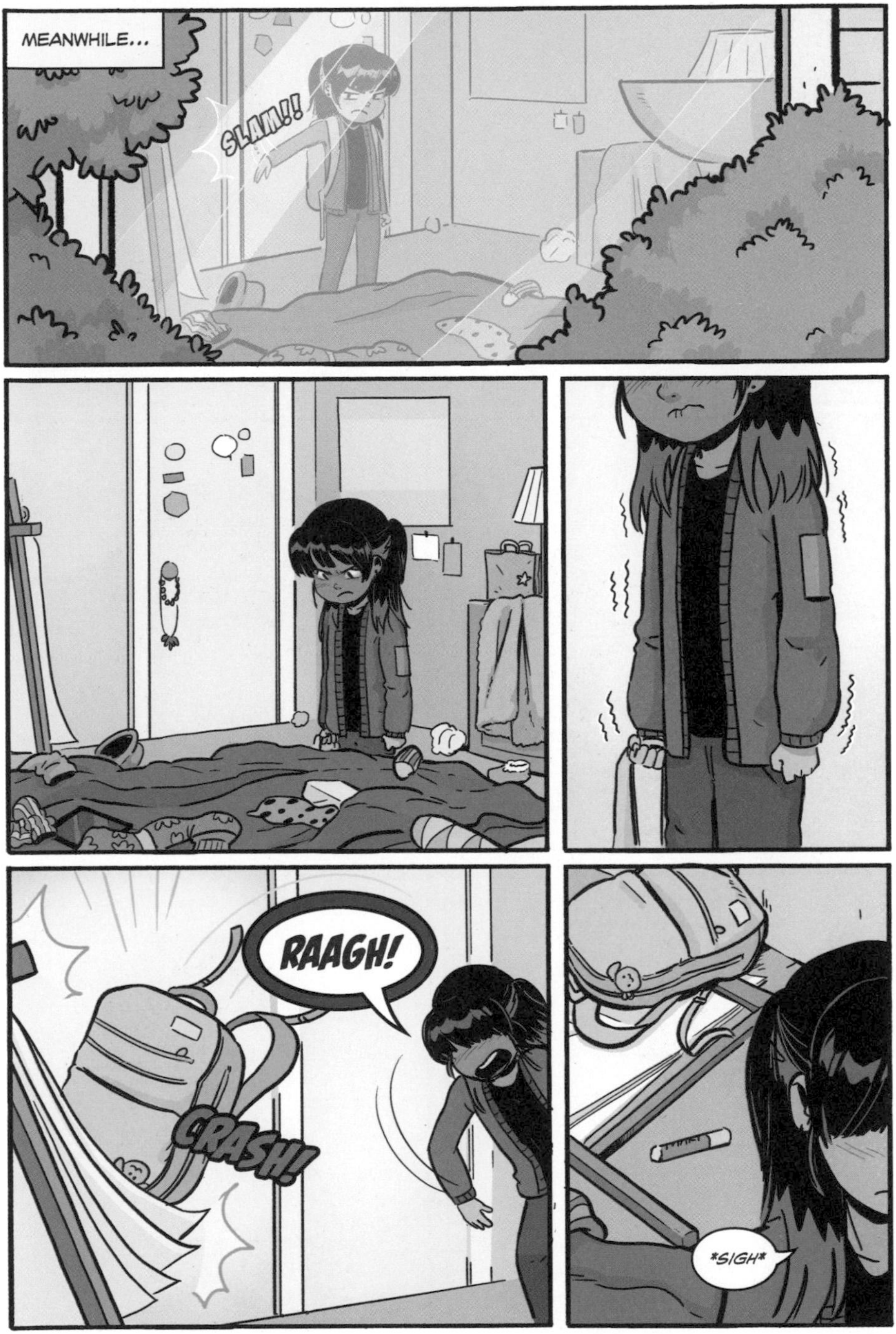
MEANWHILE...
SLAM!!
RAAGH!
CRASH!
SIGH

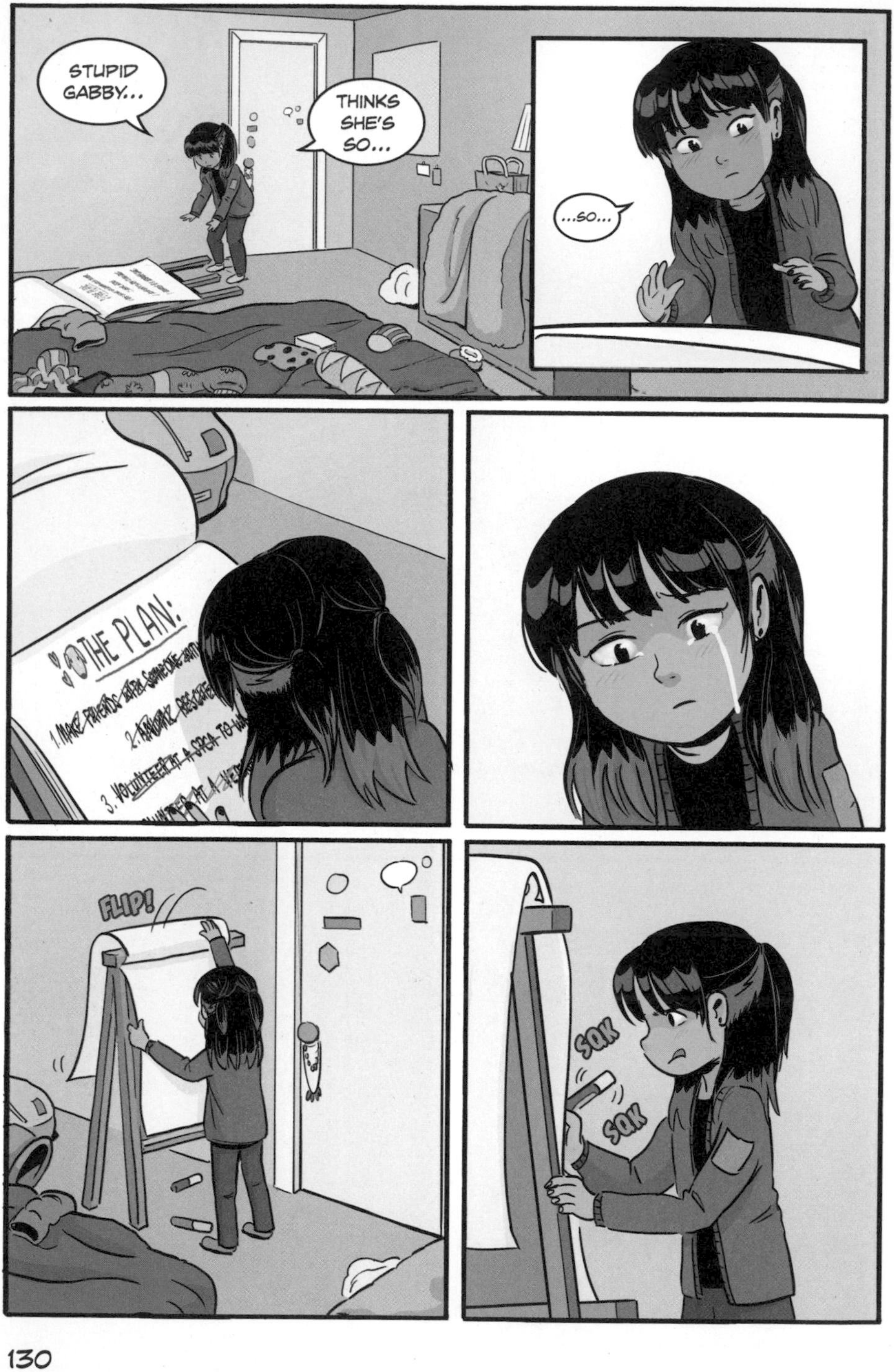
STUPID GABBY...
THINKS SHE'S SO...
...SO...
THE PLAN:
FLIP!
SQK
SQK

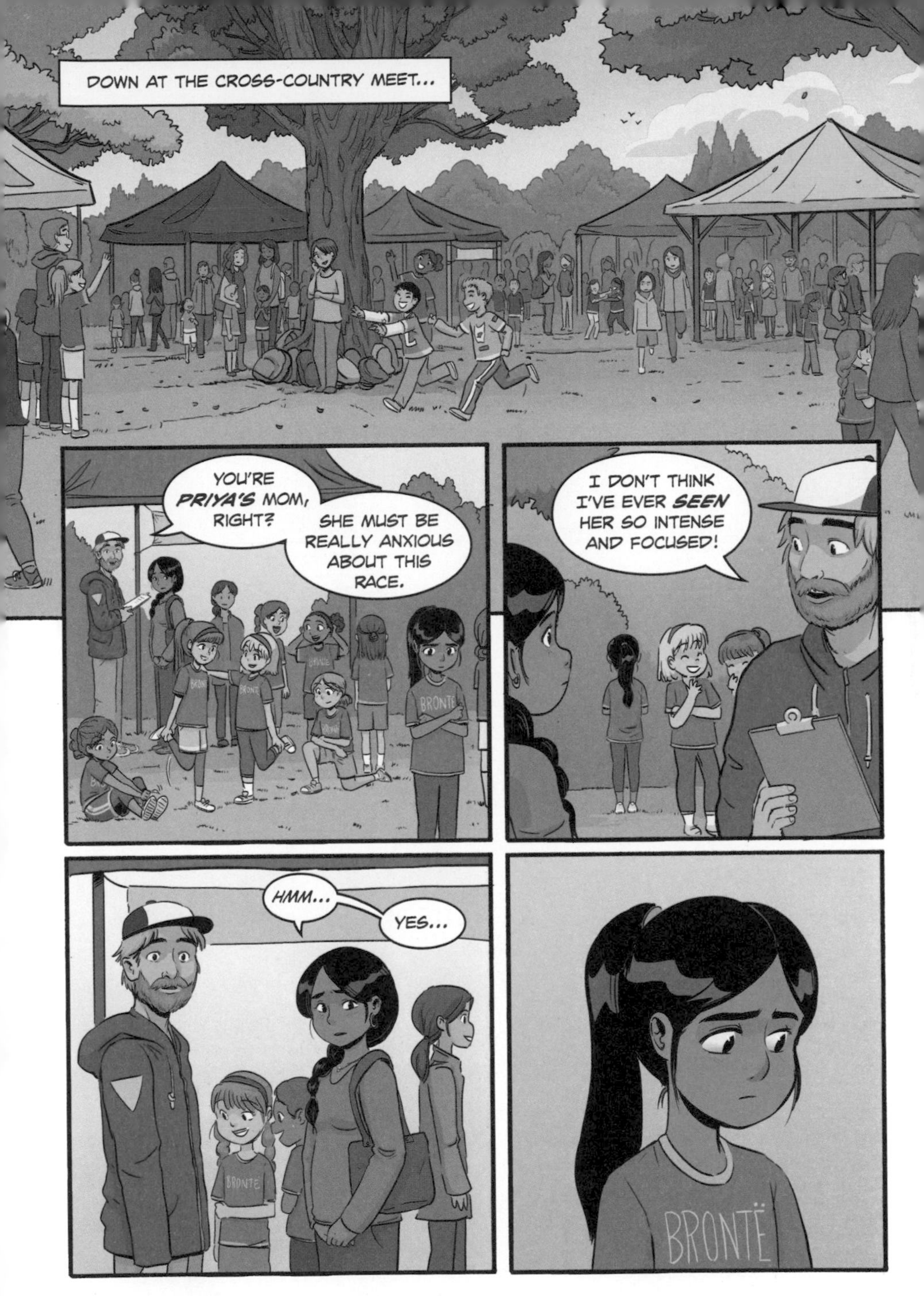
DOWN AT THE CROSS-COUNTRY MEET...
YOU'RE PRIYA'S MOM, RIGHT?
SHE MUST BE REALLY ANXIOUS ABOUT THIS RACE.
I DON'T THINK I'VE EVER SEEN HER SO INTENSE AND FOCUSED!
HMM...
YES...
BRONTË

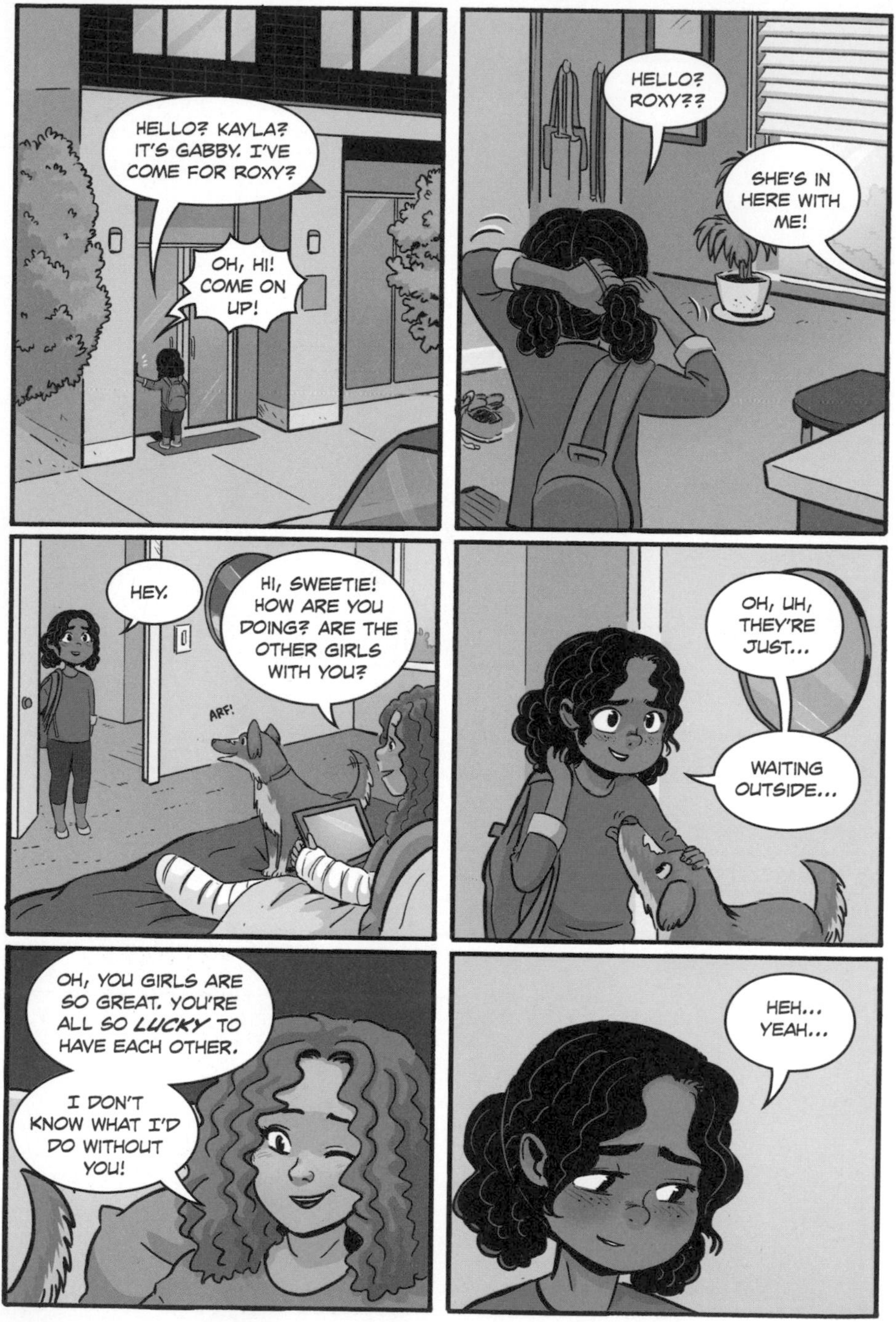
HELLO? KAYLA? IT'S GABBY. I'VE COME FOR ROXY?
OH, HI! COME ON UP!
HELLO? ROXY??
SHE'S IN HERE WITH ME!
HEY.
HI, SWEETIE! HOW ARE YOU DOING? ARE THE OTHER GIRLS WITH YOU?
ARF!
OH, UH, THEY'RE JUST...
WAITING OUTSIDE...
OH, YOU GIRLS ARE SO GREAT. YOU'RE ALL SO *LUCKY* TO HAVE EACH OTHER.
I DON'T KNOW WHAT I'D DO WITHOUT YOU!
HEH... YEAH...

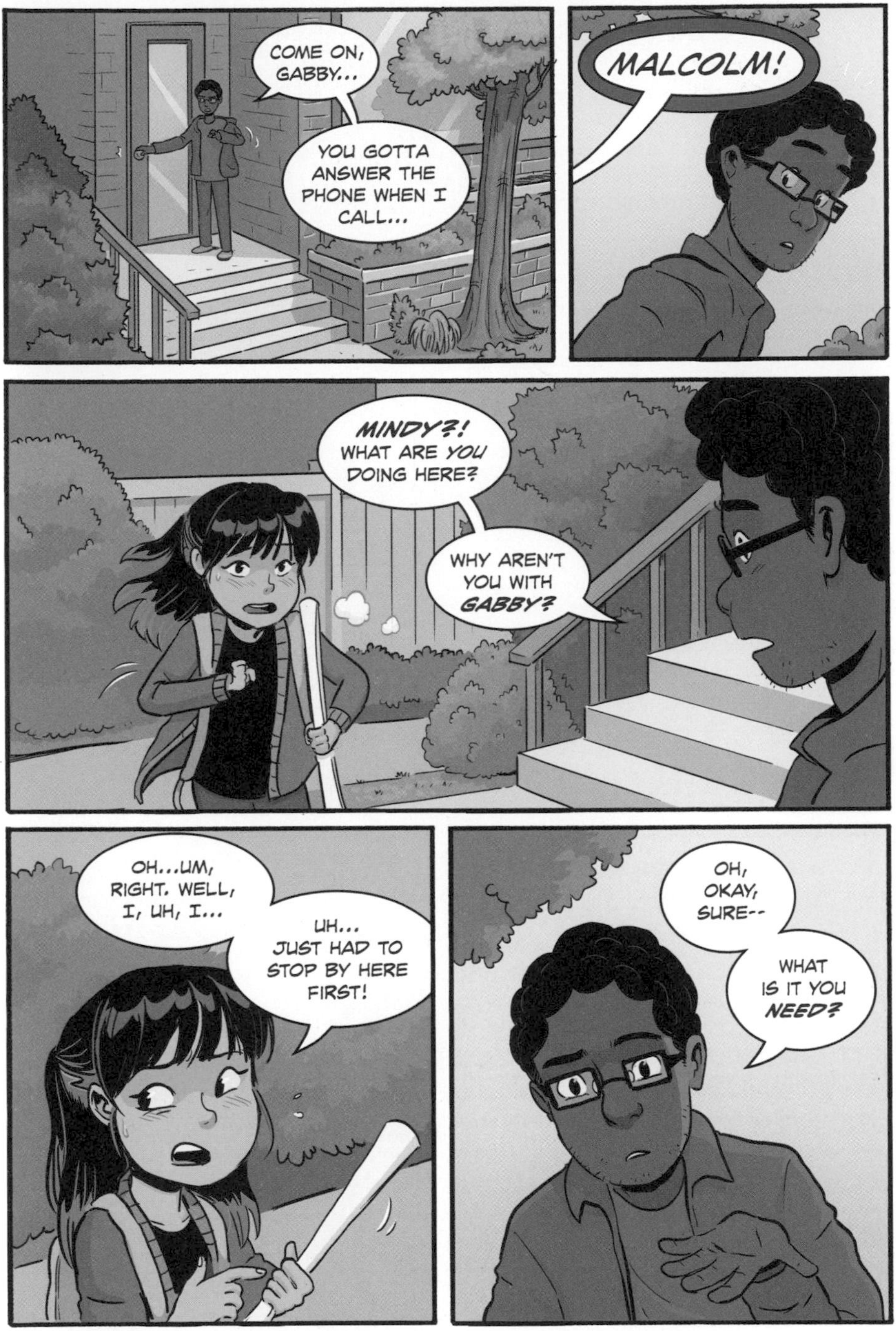
COME ON, GABBY...
YOU GOTTA ANSWER THE PHONE WHEN I CALL...
MALCOLM!
MINDY?! WHAT ARE YOU DOING HERE?
WHY AREN'T YOU WITH GABBY?
OH...UM, RIGHT. WELL, I, UH, I...
UH... JUST HAD TO STOP BY HERE FIRST!
OH, OKAY, SURE--
WHAT IS IT YOU NEED?

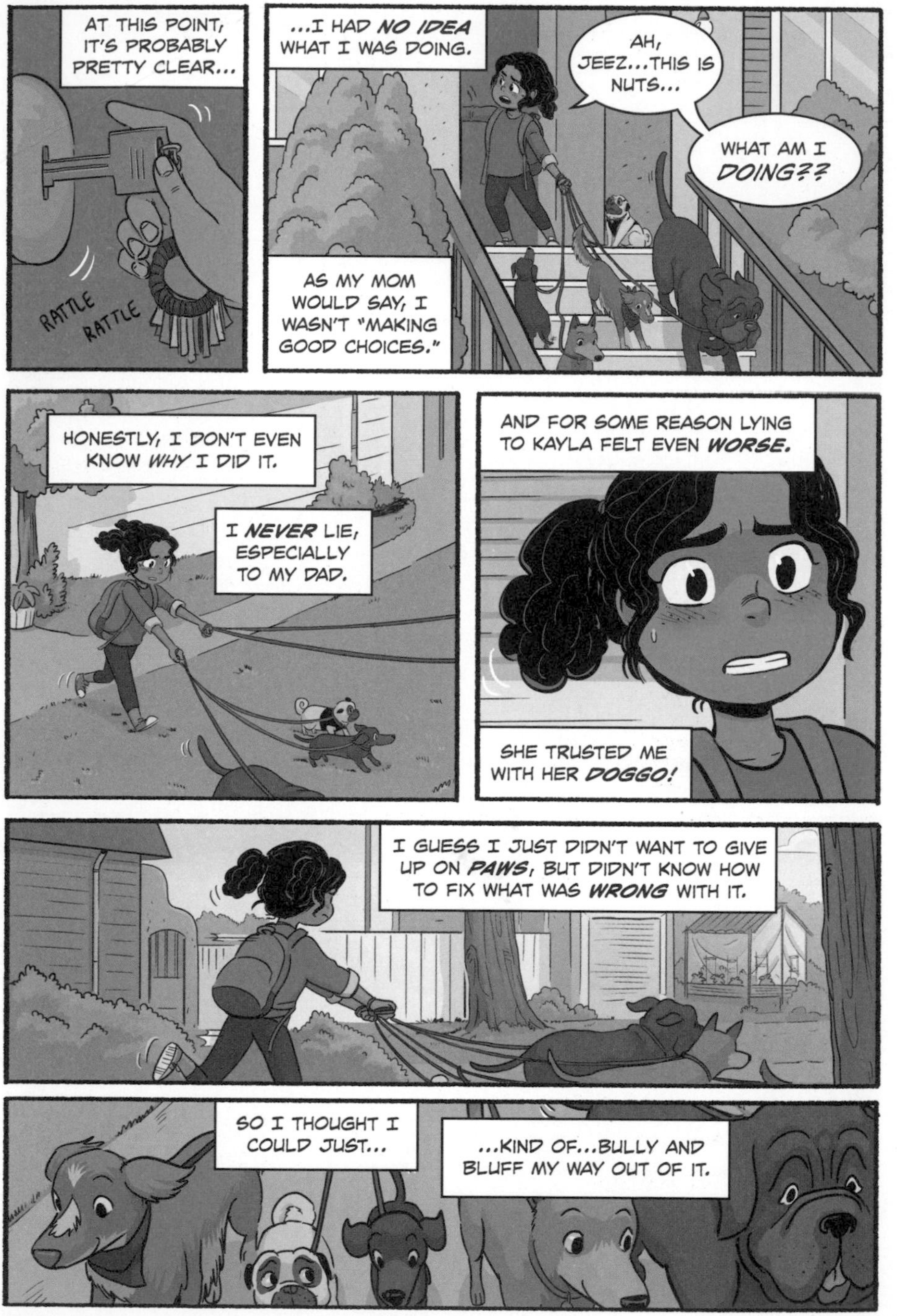
AT THIS POINT, IT'S PROBABLY PRETTY CLEAR...
RATTLE RATTLE
...I HAD NO IDEA WHAT I WAS DOING.
AH, JEEZ...THIS IS NUTS...
WHAT AM I DOING??
AS MY MOM WOULD SAY, I WASN'T "MAKING GOOD CHOICES."
HONESTLY, I DON'T EVEN KNOW WHY I DID IT.
I NEVER LIE, ESPECIALLY TO MY DAD.
AND FOR SOME REASON LYING TO KAYLA FELT EVEN WORSE.
SHE TRUSTED ME WITH HER DOGGO!
I GUESS I JUST DIDN'T WANT TO GIVE UP ON PAWS, BUT DIDN'T KNOW HOW TO FIX WHAT WAS WRONG WITH IT.
SO I THOUGHT I COULD JUST...
...KIND OF...BULLY AND BLUFF MY WAY OUT OF IT.

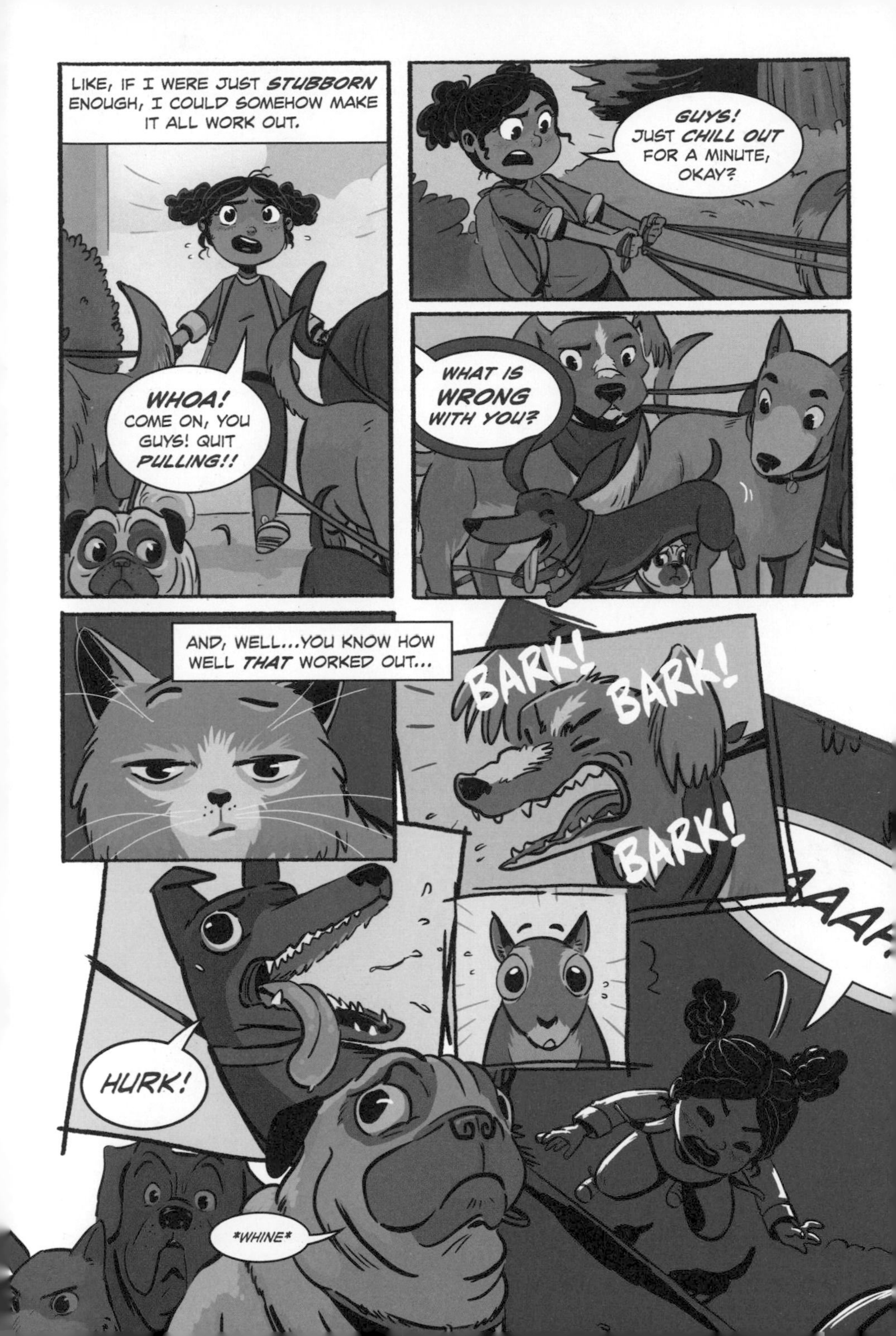
LIKE, IF I WERE JUST STUBBORN ENOUGH, I COULD SOMEHOW MAKE IT ALL WORK OUT.
GUYS! JUST CHILL OUT FOR A MINUTE, OKAY?
WHOA! COME ON, YOU GUYS! QUIT PULLING!!
WHAT IS WRONG WITH YOU?
AND, WELL...YOU KNOW HOW WELL THAT WORKED OUT...
BARK! BARK!
BARK!
HURK!
WHINE

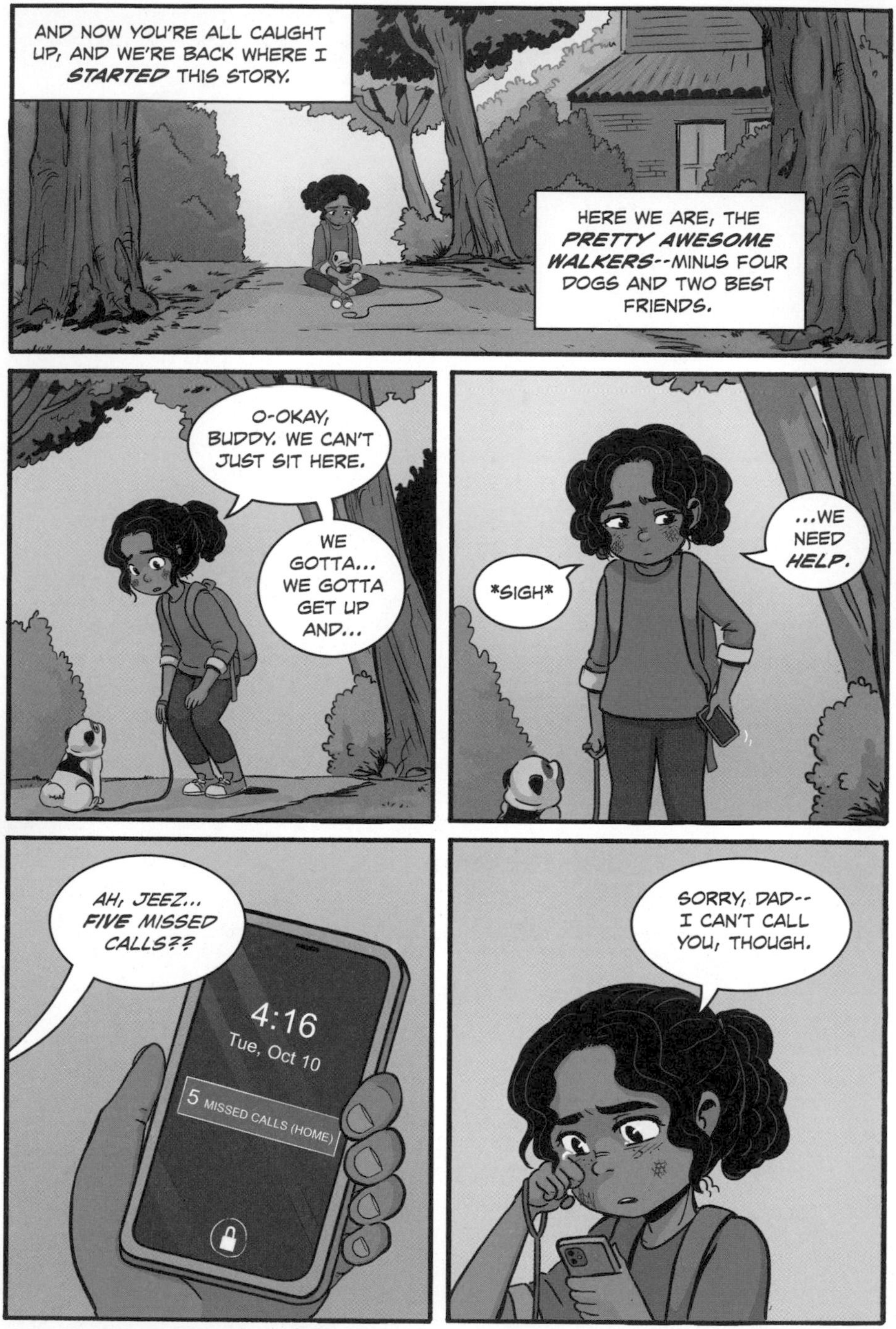
AND NOW YOU'RE ALL CAUGHT UP, AND WE'RE BACK WHERE I STARTED THIS STORY.
HERE WE ARE, THE PRETTY AWESOME WALKERS--MINUS FOUR DOGS AND TWO BEST FRIENDS.
O-OKAY, BUDDY. WE CAN'T JUST SIT HERE.
WE GOTTA... WE GOTTA GET UP AND...
SIGH
...WE NEED HELP.
AH, JEEZ... FIVE MISSED CALLS??
4:16
Tue, Oct 10
5 MISSED CALLS (HOME)
SORRY, DAD-- I CAN'T CALL YOU, THOUGH.

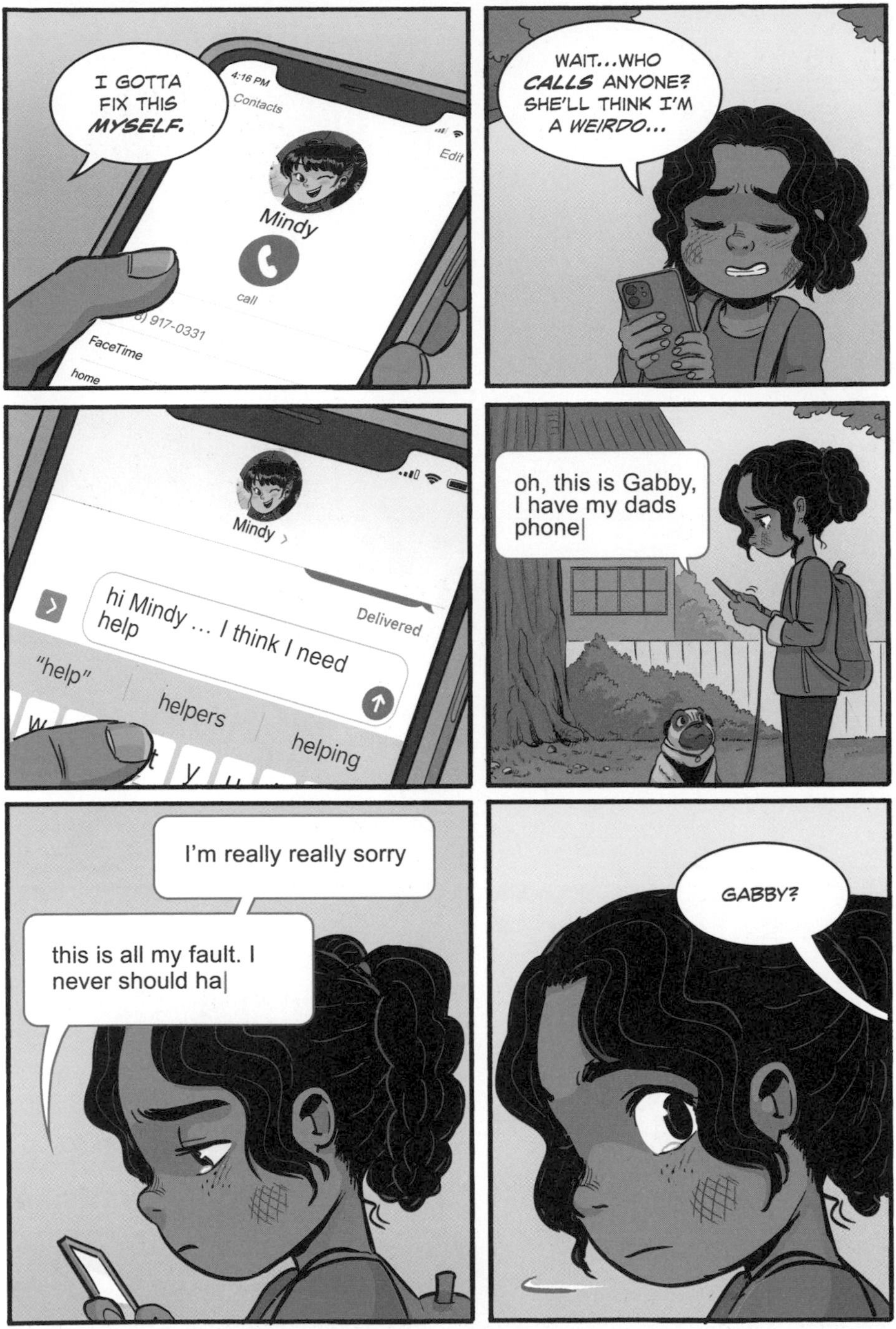
I GOTTA FIX THIS *MYSELF.*
4:16 PM
Contacts
Edit
Mindy
call
8) 917-0331
FaceTime
home
WAIT...WHO *CALLS* ANYONE? SHE'LL THINK I'M A *WEIRDO...*
Mindy
Delivered
hi Mindy … I think I need help
"help"
helpers
helping
oh, this is Gabby, I have my dads phone|
I'm really really sorry
this is all my fault. I never should ha|
GABBY?

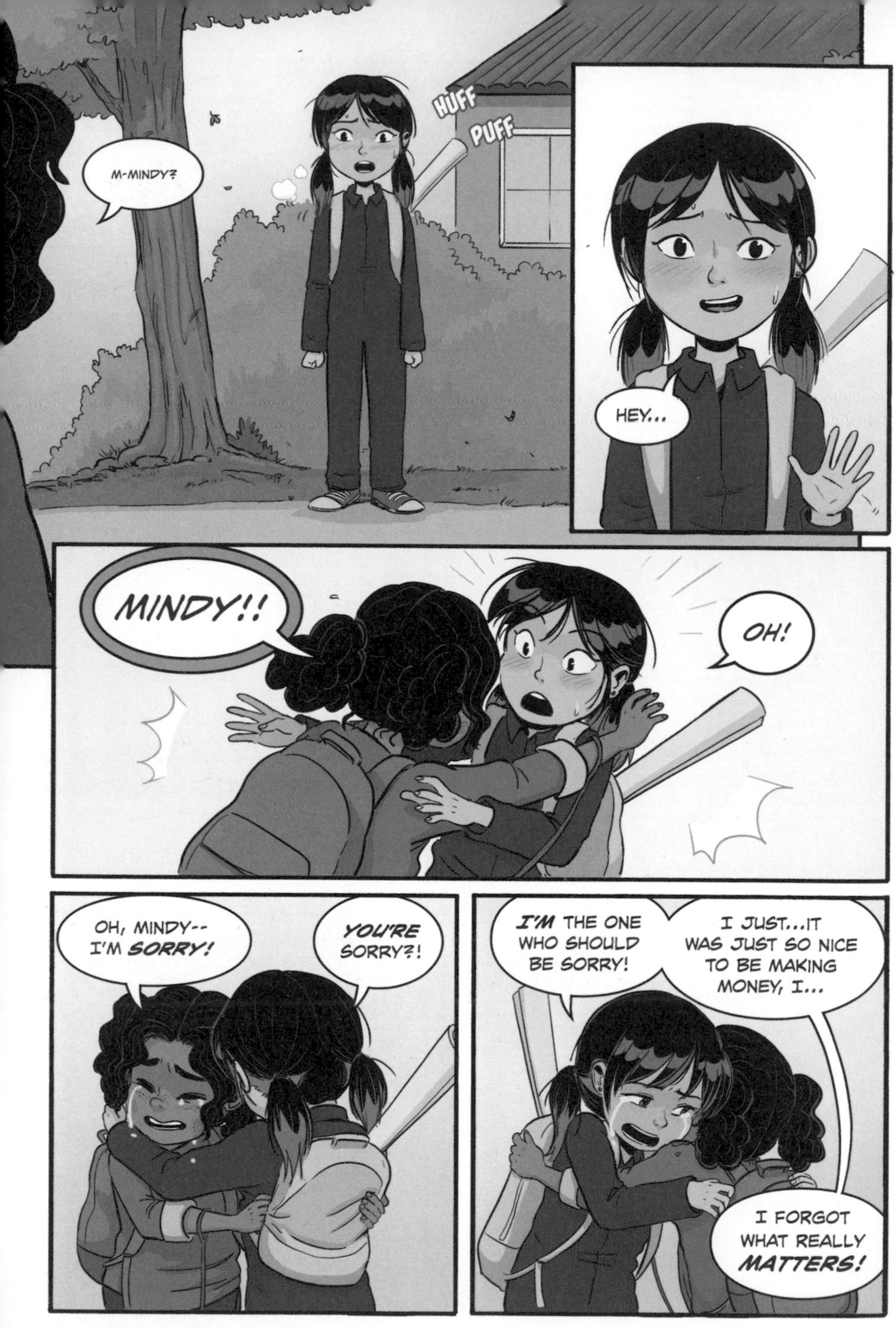
HUFF
PUFF
M-MINDY?
HEY...
MINDY!!
OH!
OH, MINDY-- I'M SORRY!
YOU'RE SORRY?!
I'M THE ONE WHO SHOULD BE SORRY!
I JUST...IT WAS JUST SO NICE TO BE MAKING MONEY, I...
I FORGOT WHAT REALLY MATTERS!

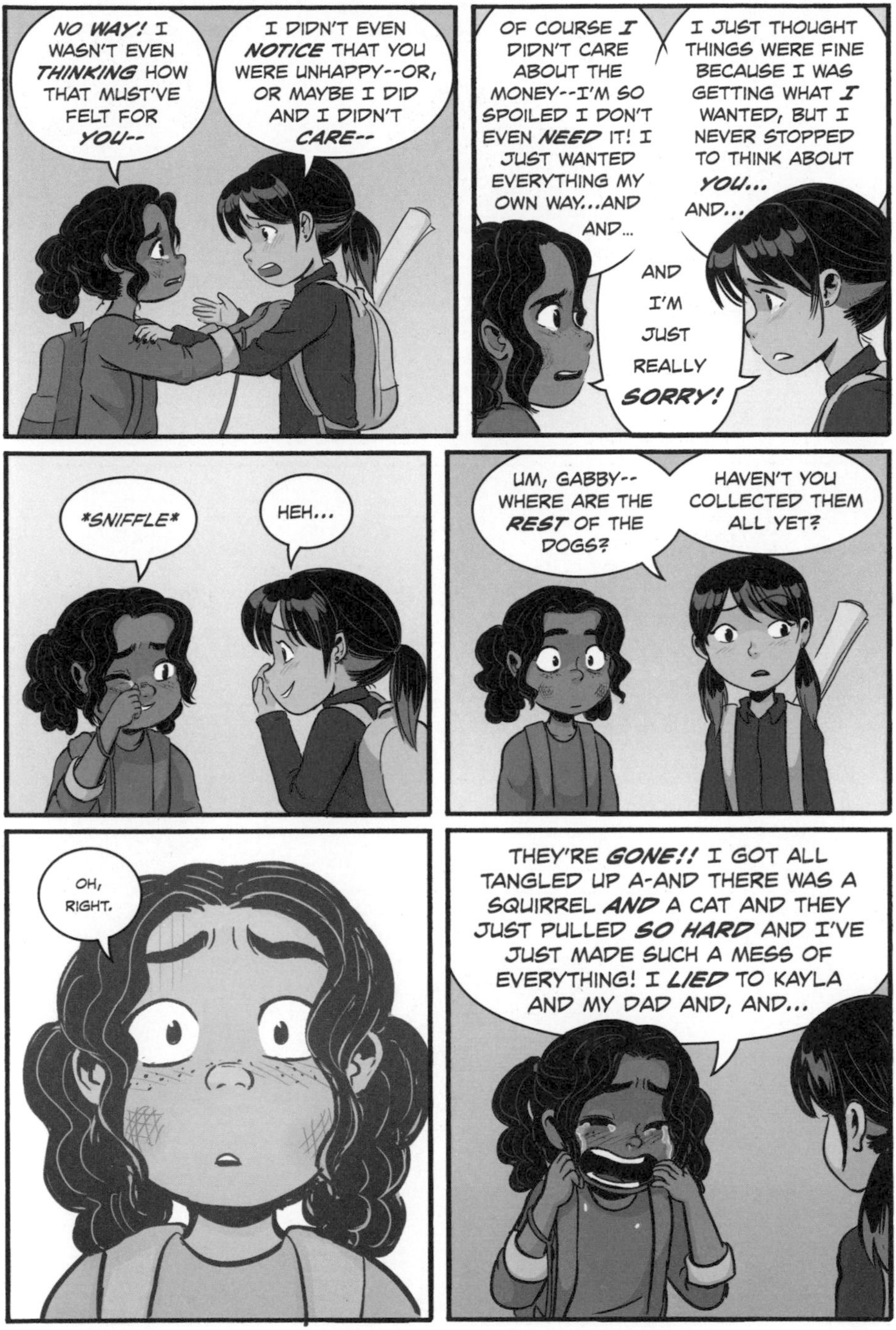
NO WAY! I WASN'T EVEN THINKING HOW THAT MUST'VE FELT FOR YOU--
I DIDN'T EVEN NOTICE THAT YOU WERE UNHAPPY--OR, OR MAYBE I DID AND I DIDN'T CARE--
OF COURSE I DIDN'T CARE ABOUT THE MONEY--I'M SO SPOILED I DON'T EVEN NEED IT! I JUST WANTED EVERYTHING MY OWN WAY...AND AND...
I JUST THOUGHT THINGS WERE FINE BECAUSE I WAS GETTING WHAT I WANTED, BUT I NEVER STOPPED TO THINK ABOUT YOU... AND...
AND I'M JUST REALLY SORRY!
SNIFFLE
HEH...
UM, GABBY--WHERE ARE THE REST OF THE DOGS?
HAVEN'T YOU COLLECTED THEM ALL YET?
OH, RIGHT.
THEY'RE GONE!! I GOT ALL TANGLED UP A-AND THERE WAS A SQUIRREL AND A CAT AND THEY JUST PULLED SO HARD AND I'VE JUST MADE SUCH A MESS OF EVERYTHING! I LIED TO KAYLA AND MY DAD AND, AND...

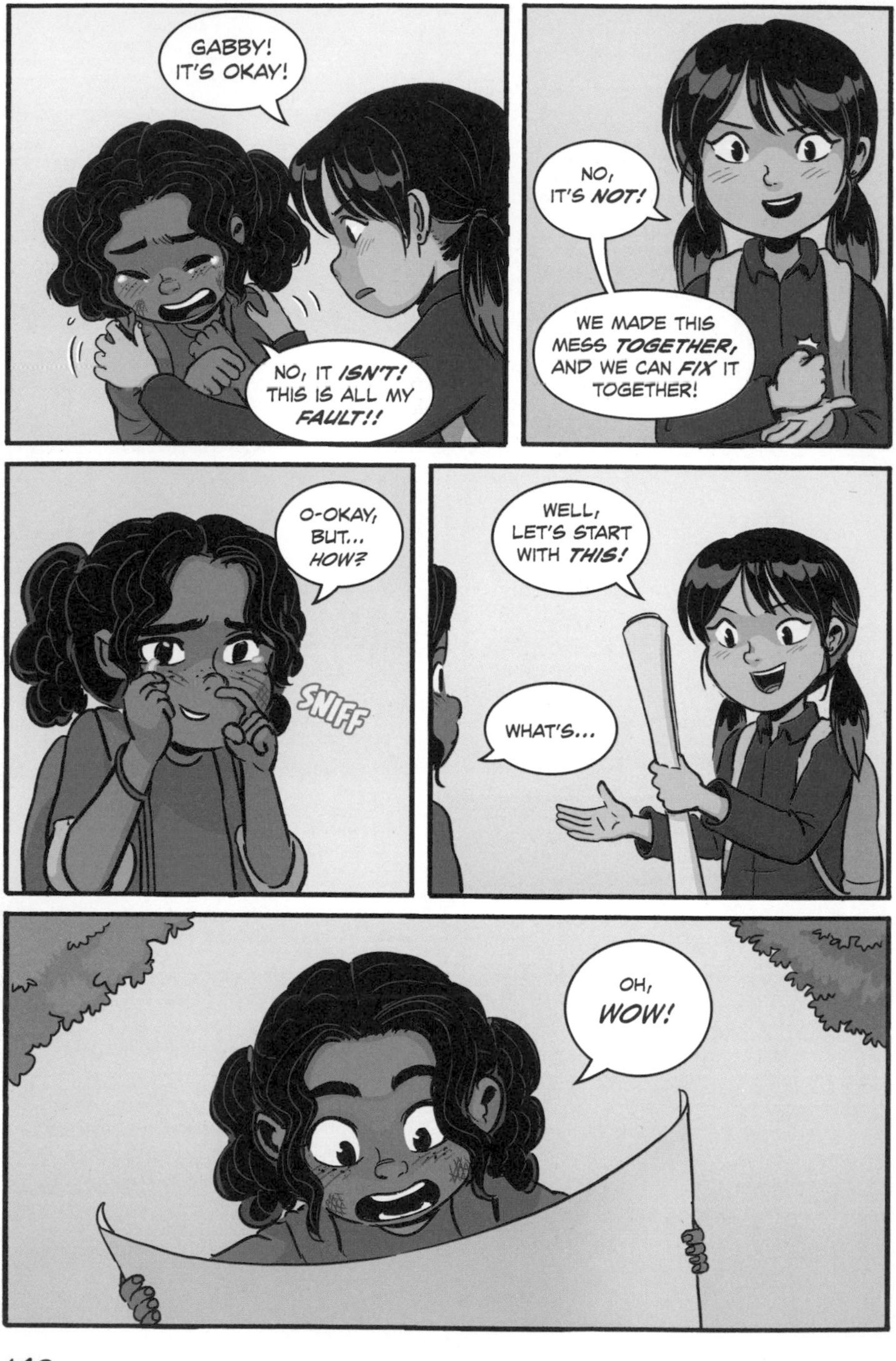
GABBY! IT'S OKAY!
NO, IT ISN'T! THIS IS ALL MY FAULT!!
NO, IT'S NOT!
WE MADE THIS MESS TOGETHER, AND WE CAN FIX IT TOGETHER!
O-OKAY, BUT... HOW?
SNIFF
WELL, LET'S START WITH THIS!
WHAT'S...
OH, WOW!

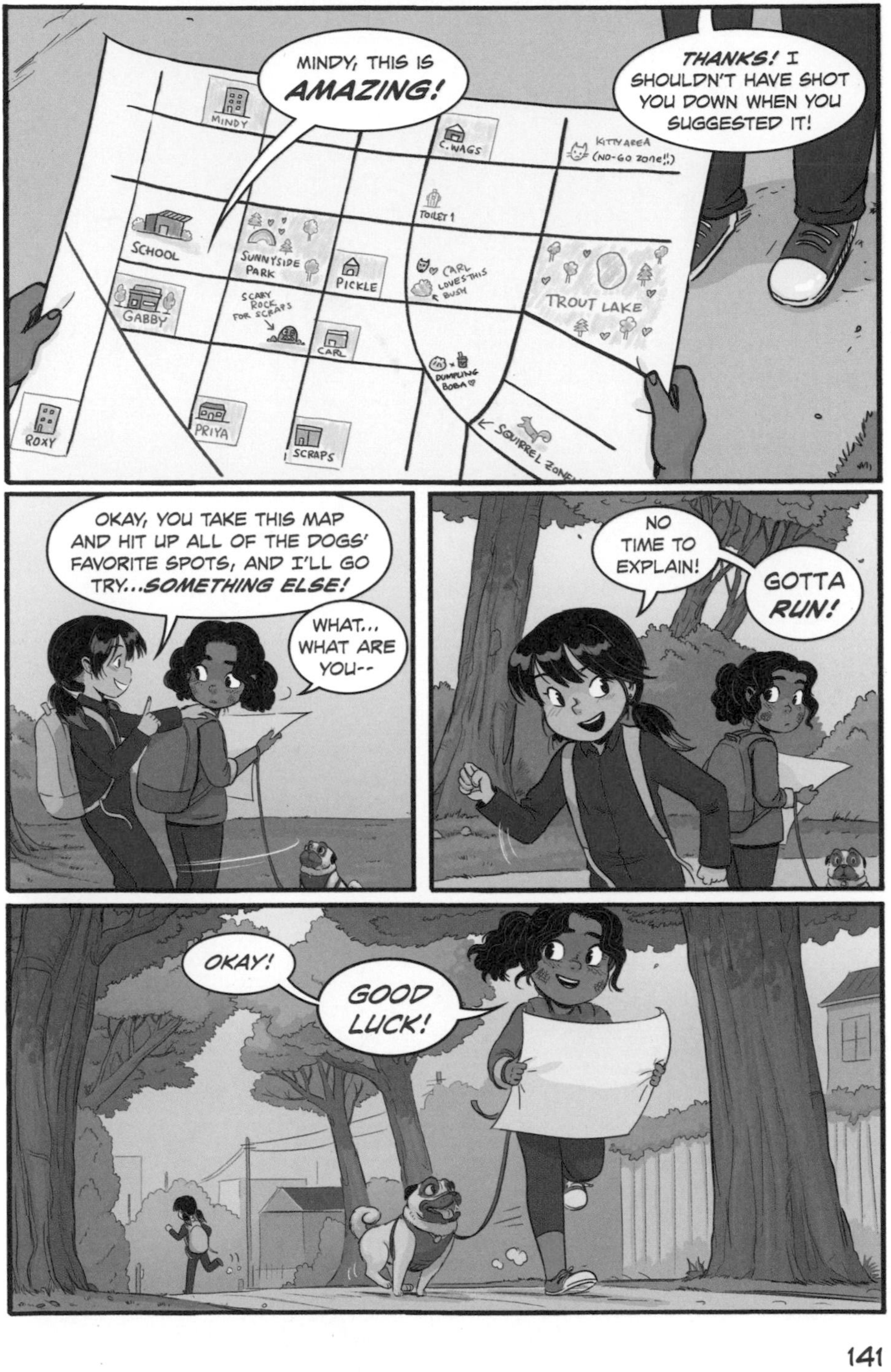
MINDY, THIS IS *AMAZING!*
THANKS! I SHOULDN'T HAVE SHOT YOU DOWN WHEN YOU SUGGESTED IT!
MINDY
C. WAGS
KITTY AREA (NO-GO zone!!)
TOILET 1
SCHOOL
SUNNYSIDE PARK
PICKLE
CARL LOVES THIS BUSH
TROUT LAKE
GABBY
SCARY ROCK FOR SCRAPS
CARL
DUMPLING BOBA
ROXY
PRIYA
SCRAPS
SQUIRREL ZONE
OKAY, YOU TAKE THIS MAP AND HIT UP ALL OF THE DOGS' FAVORITE SPOTS, AND I'LL GO TRY...*SOMETHING ELSE!*
WHAT... WHAT ARE YOU--
NO TIME TO EXPLAIN!
GOTTA *RUN!*
OKAY!
GOOD LUCK!

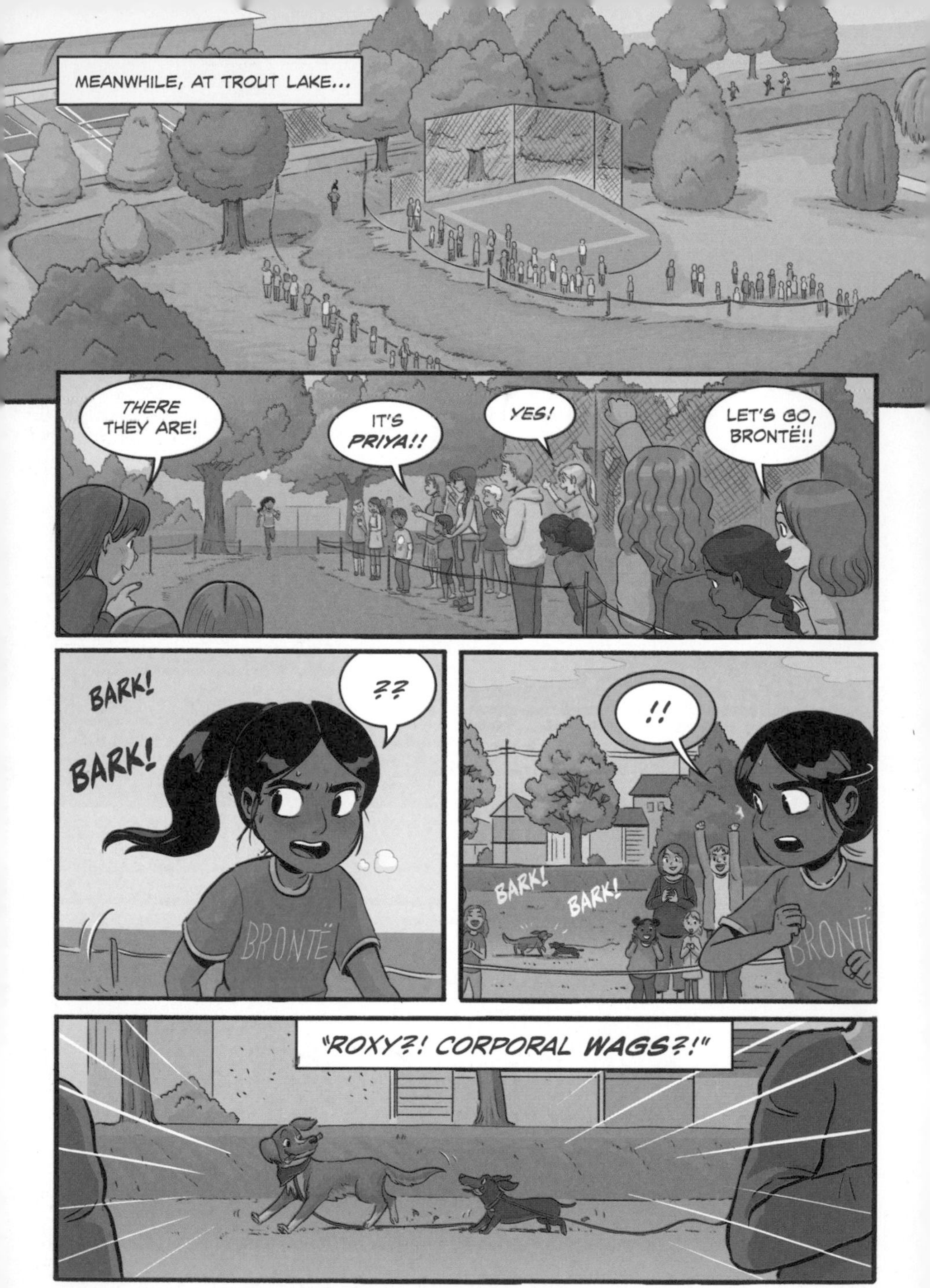
MEANWHILE, AT TROUT LAKE...
THERE THEY ARE!
IT'S PRIYA!!
YES!
LET'S GO, BRONTË!!
BARK!
BARK!
??
BRONTË
!!
BARK!
BARK!
BRONTË
"ROXY?! CORPORAL WAGS?!"

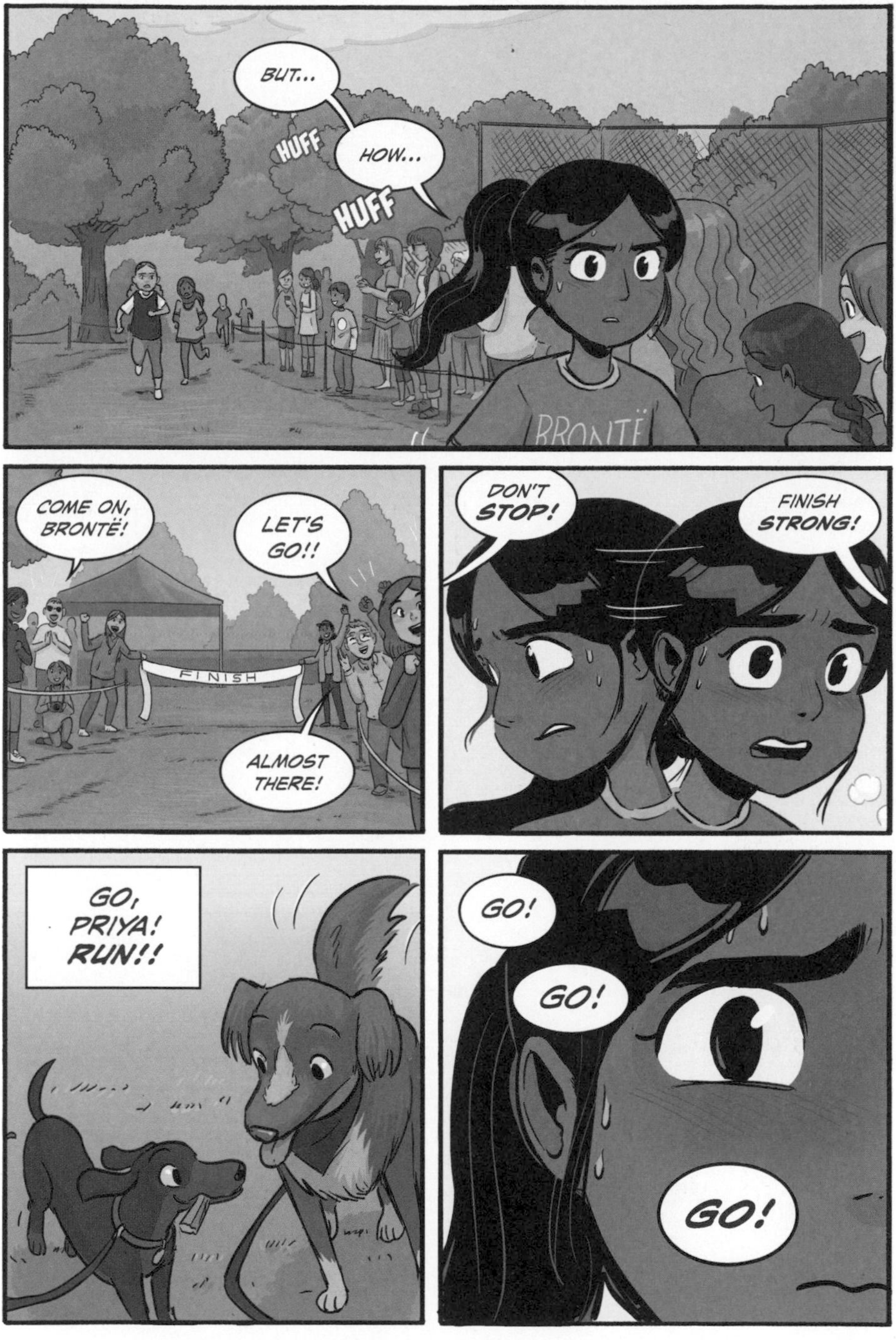
BUT...
HUFF
HOW...
HUFF
BRONTË
COME ON, BRONTË!
LET'S GO!!
FINISH
ALMOST THERE!
DON'T STOP!
FINISH STRONG!
GO, PRIYA! RUN!!
GO!
GO!
GO!

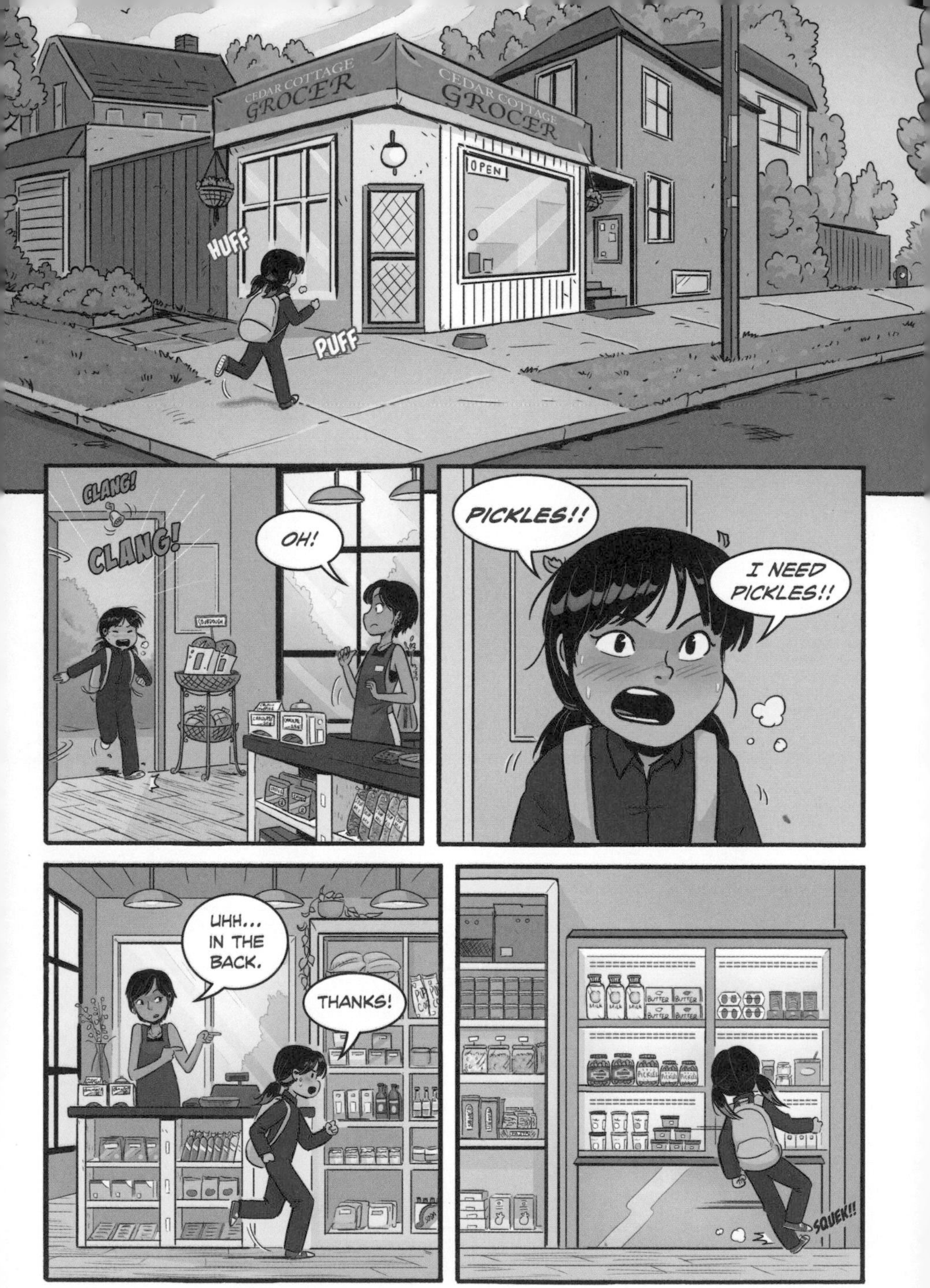
CEDAR COTTAGE GROCER
CEDAR COTTAGE GROCER
OPEN
HUFF
PUFF
CLANG!
CLANG!
OH!
PICKLES!!
I NEED PICKLES!!
UHH... IN THE BACK.
THANKS!
SQUEK!!

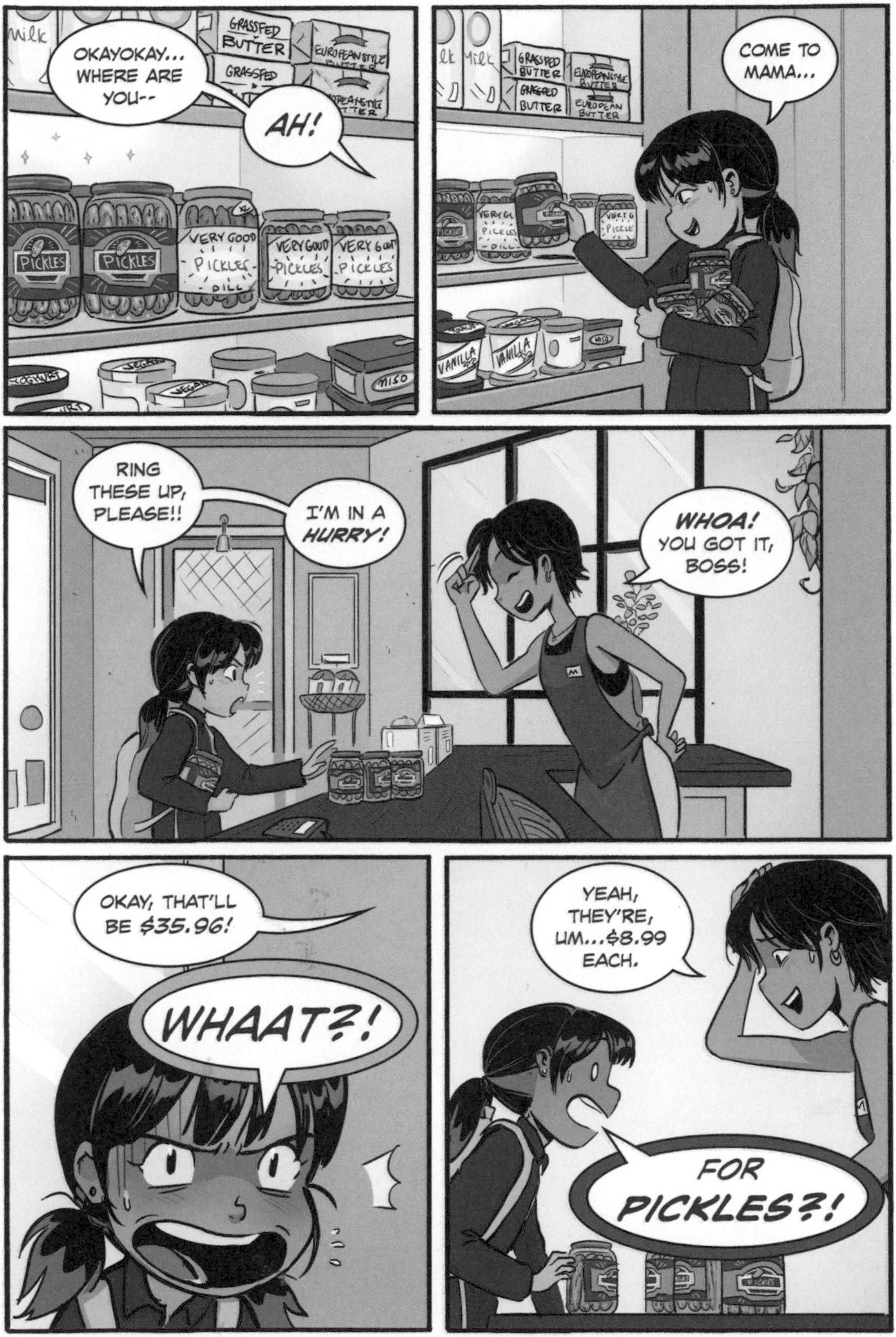
OKAYOKAY... WHERE ARE YOU--
AH!
GRASSFED BUTTER
EUROPEAN STYLE BUTTER
PICKLES
VERY GOOD PICKLES DILL
VERY GOOD PICKLES
MISO
COME TO MAMA...
VANILLA
RING THESE UP, PLEASE!!
I'M IN A HURRY!
WHOA! YOU GOT IT, BOSS!
OKAY, THAT'LL BE $35.96!
WHAAT?!
YEAH, THEY'RE, UM...$8.99 EACH.
FOR PICKLES?!

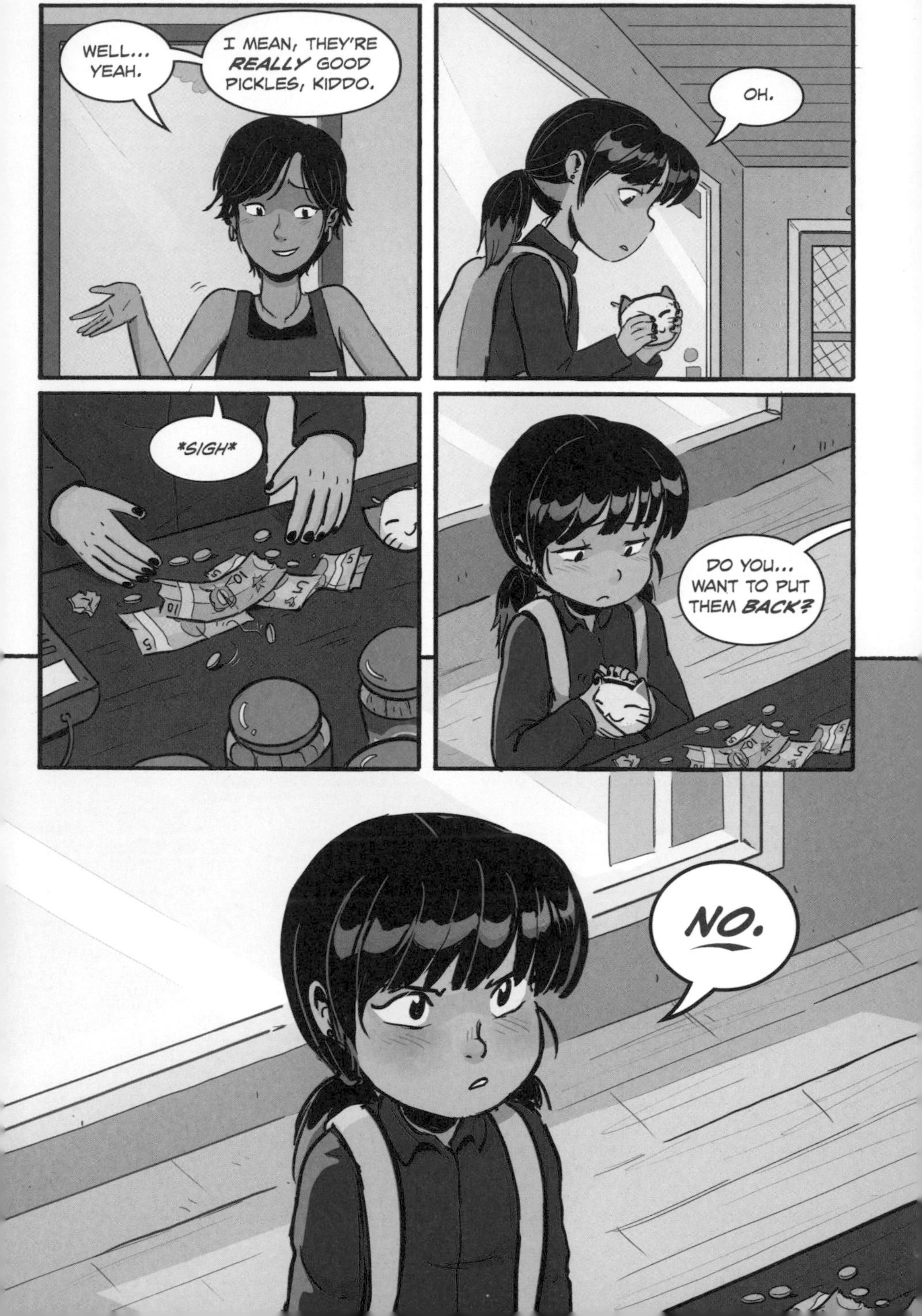
WELL... YEAH.
I MEAN, THEY'RE REALLY GOOD PICKLES, KIDDO.
OH.
SIGH
DO YOU... WANT TO PUT THEM BACK?
NO.

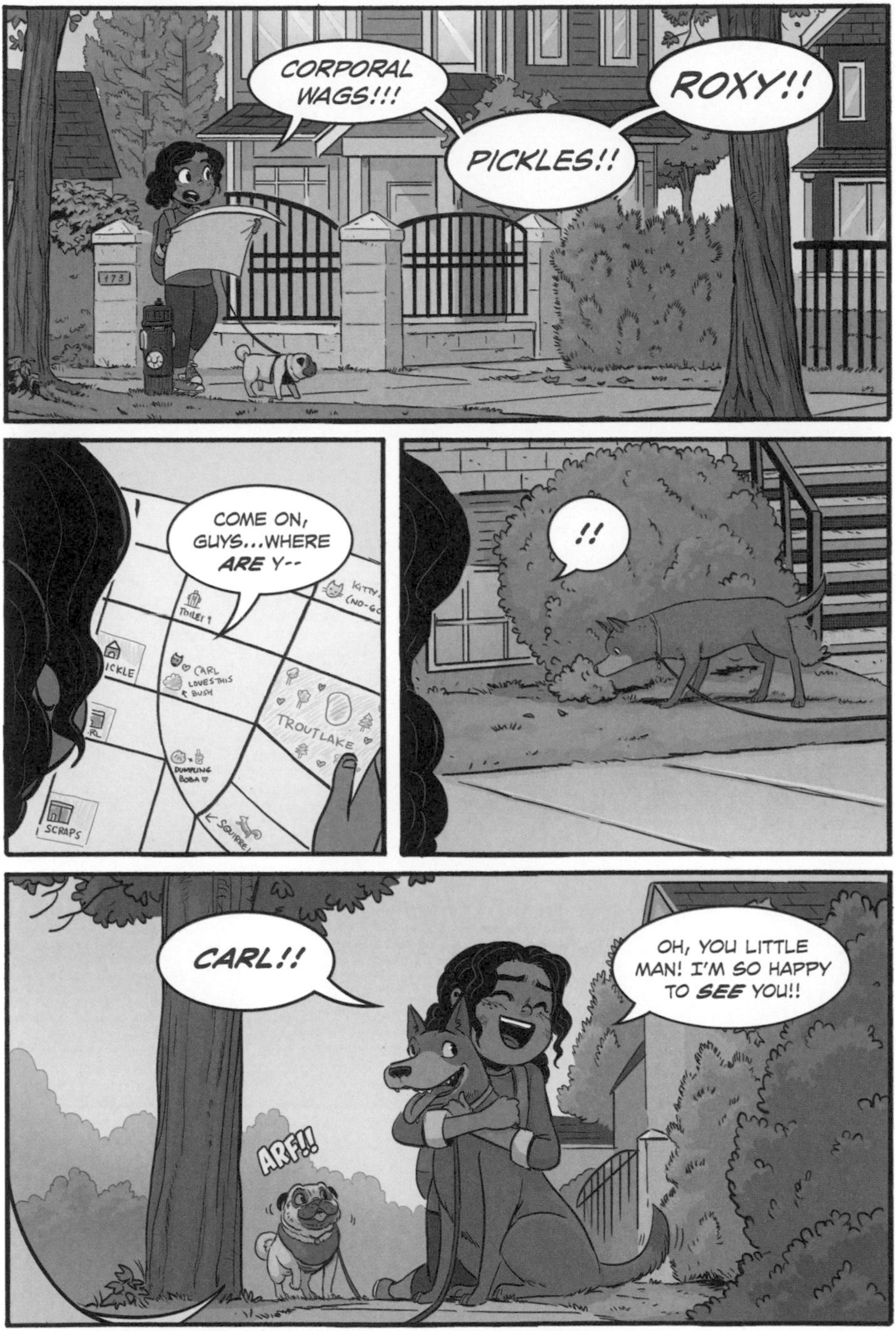
CORPORAL WAGS!!!
PICKLES!!
ROXY!!
COME ON, GUYS...WHERE *ARE* Y--
TROUT LAKE
CARL LOVES THIS BUSH
SCRAPS
!!
CARL!!
OH, YOU LITTLE MAN! I'M SO HAPPY TO *SEE* YOU!!
ARF!!

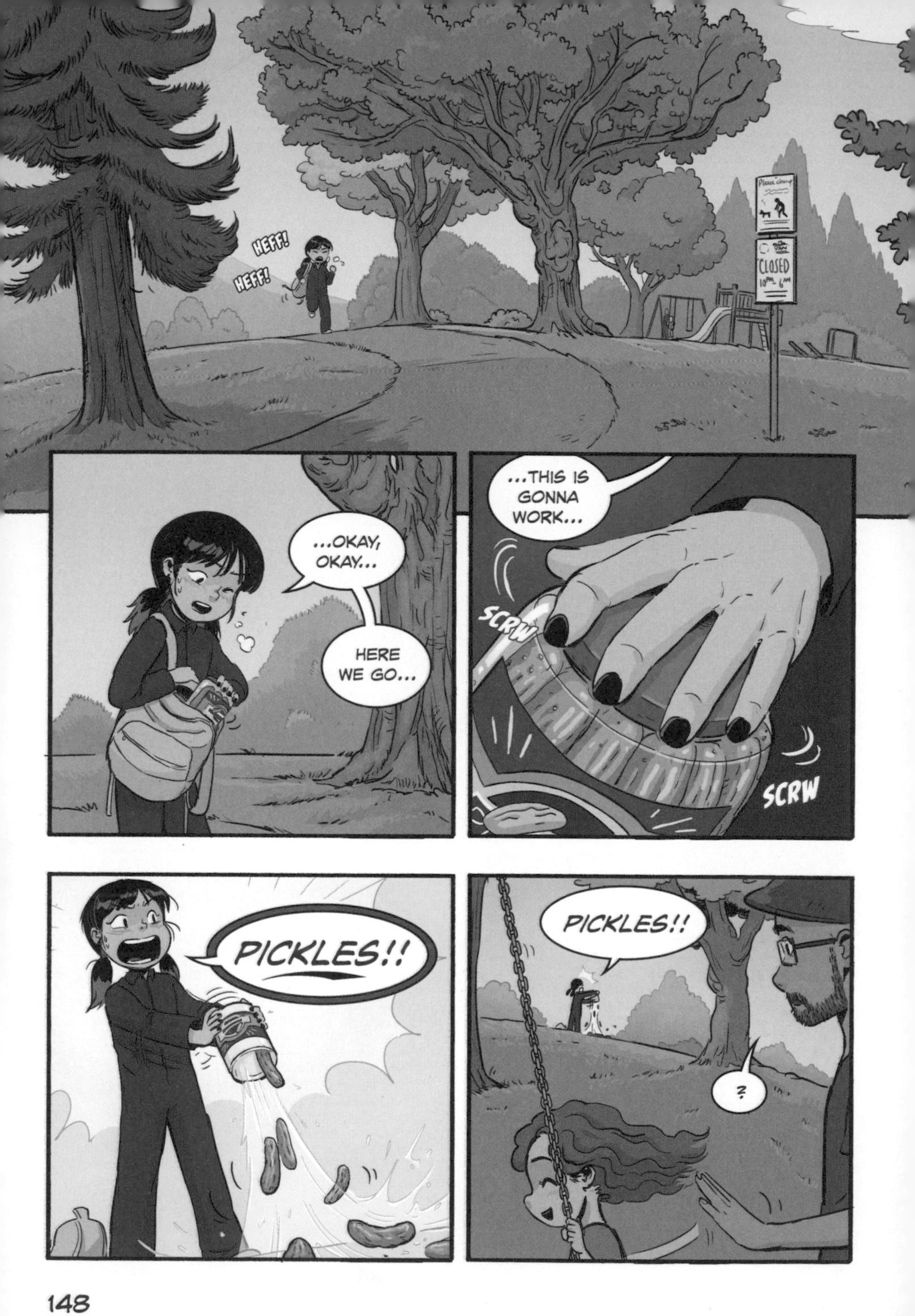
HEFF!
HEFF!
CLOSED
10PM-6AM
...OKAY, OKAY...
HERE WE GO...
...THIS IS GONNA WORK...
SCRW
SCRW
PICKLES!!
PICKLES!!
?

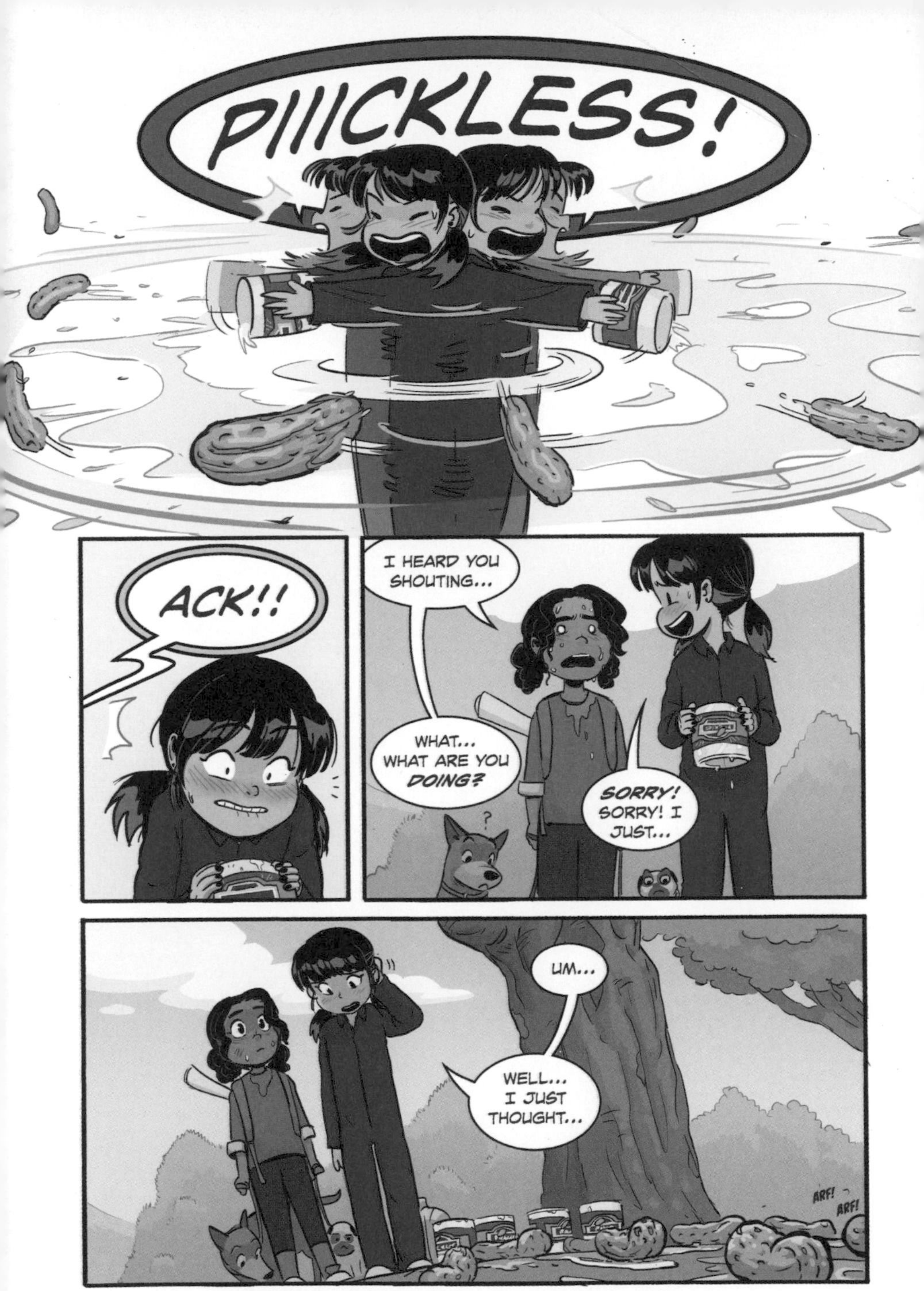
PIIICKLESS!
ACK!!
I HEARD YOU SHOUTING...
WHAT... WHAT ARE YOU DOING?
SORRY! SORRY! I JUST...
?
UM...
WELL... I JUST THOUGHT...
ARF! ARF!

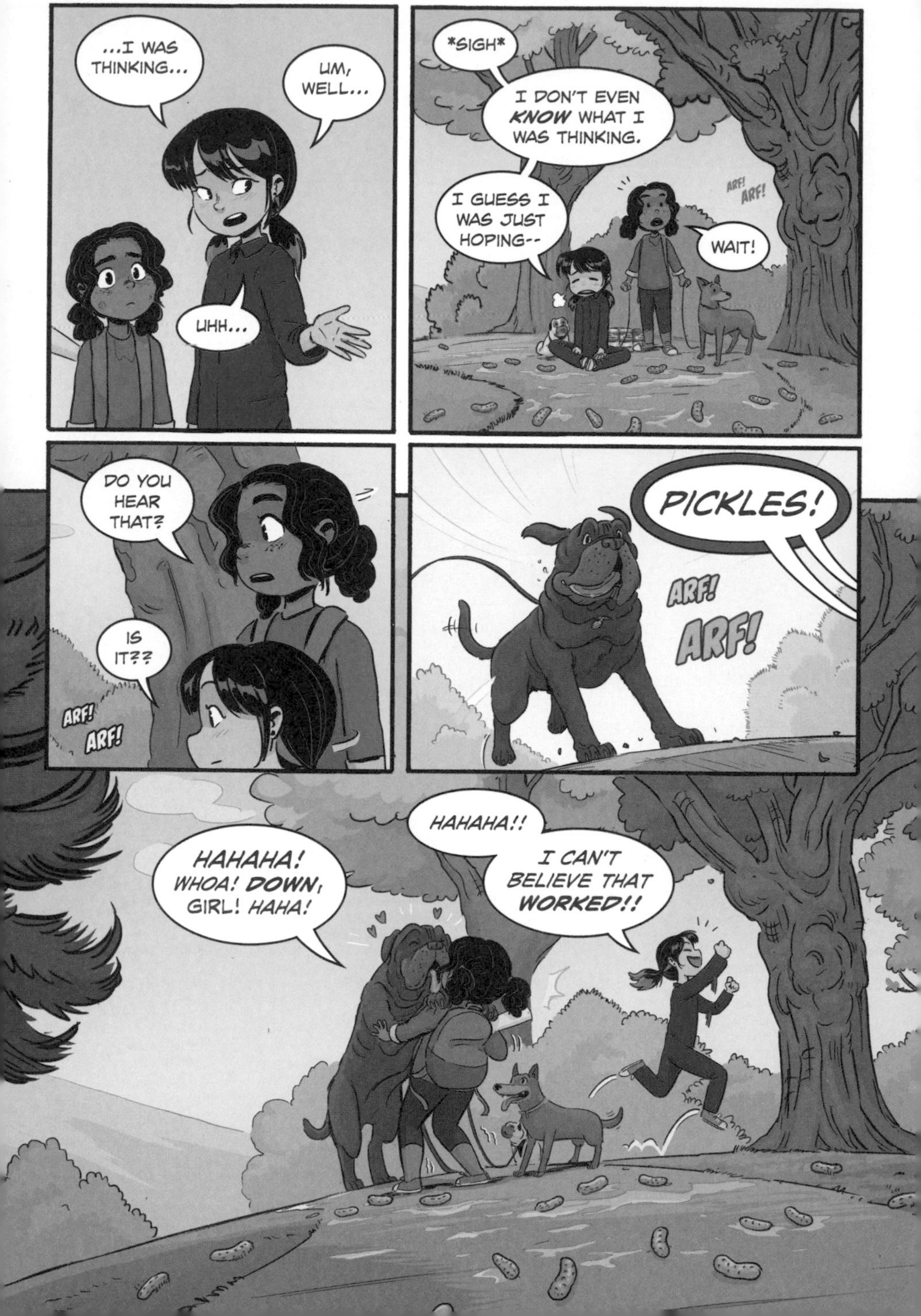
...I WAS THINKING...
UM, WELL...
UHH...
SIGH
I DON'T EVEN KNOW WHAT I WAS THINKING.
I GUESS I WAS JUST HOPING--
ARF! ARF!
WAIT!
DO YOU HEAR THAT?
IS IT??
ARF! ARF!
PICKLES!
ARF! ARF!
HAHAHA! WHOA! DOWN, GIRL! HAHA!
HAHAHA!!
I CAN'T BELIEVE THAT WORKED!!

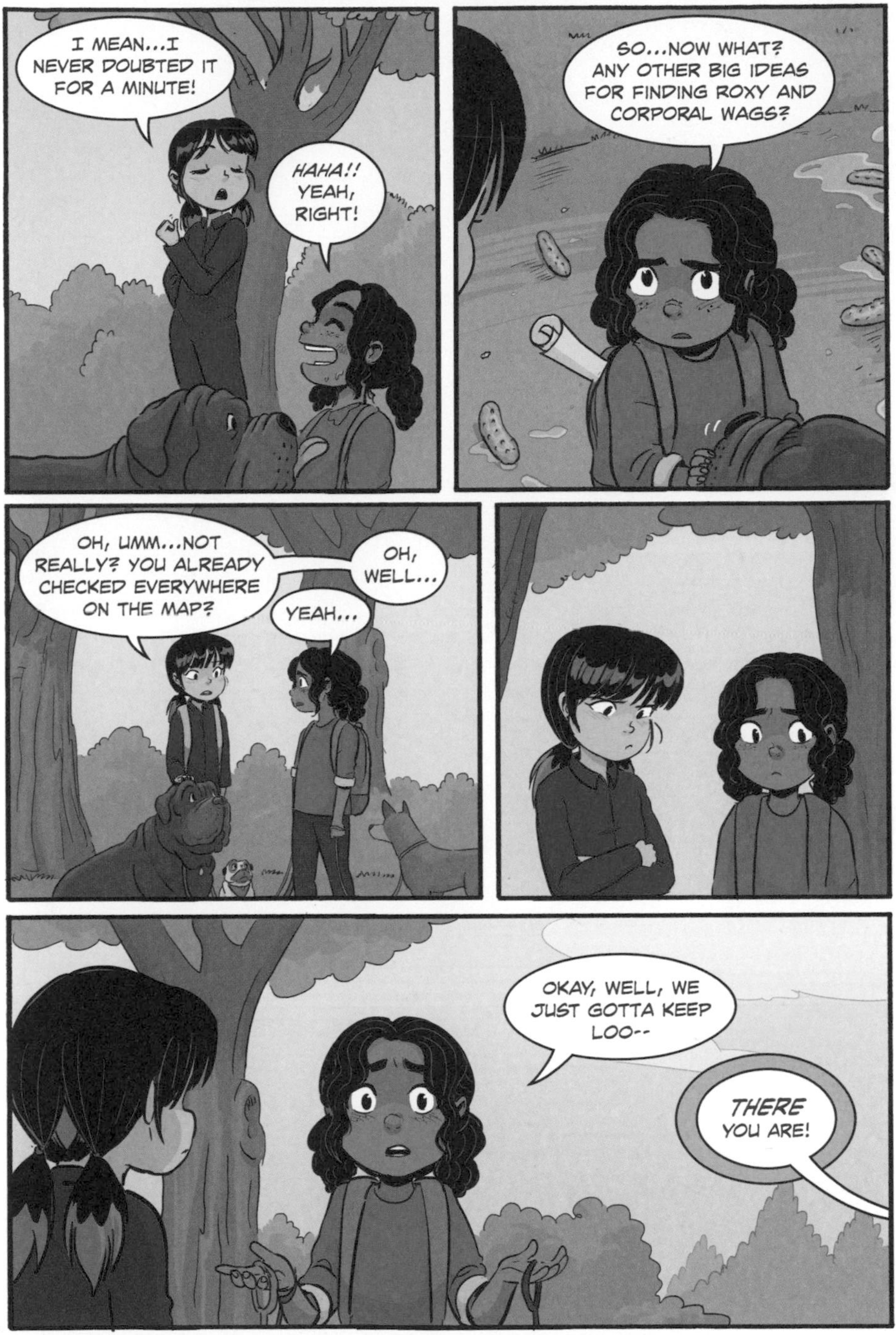
I MEAN...I NEVER DOUBTED IT FOR A MINUTE!
HAHA!! YEAH, RIGHT!
SO...NOW WHAT? ANY OTHER BIG IDEAS FOR FINDING ROXY AND CORPORAL WAGS?
OH, UMM...NOT REALLY? YOU ALREADY CHECKED EVERYWHERE ON THE MAP?
YEAH...
OH, WELL...
OKAY, WELL, WE JUST GOTTA KEEP LOO--
THERE YOU ARE!

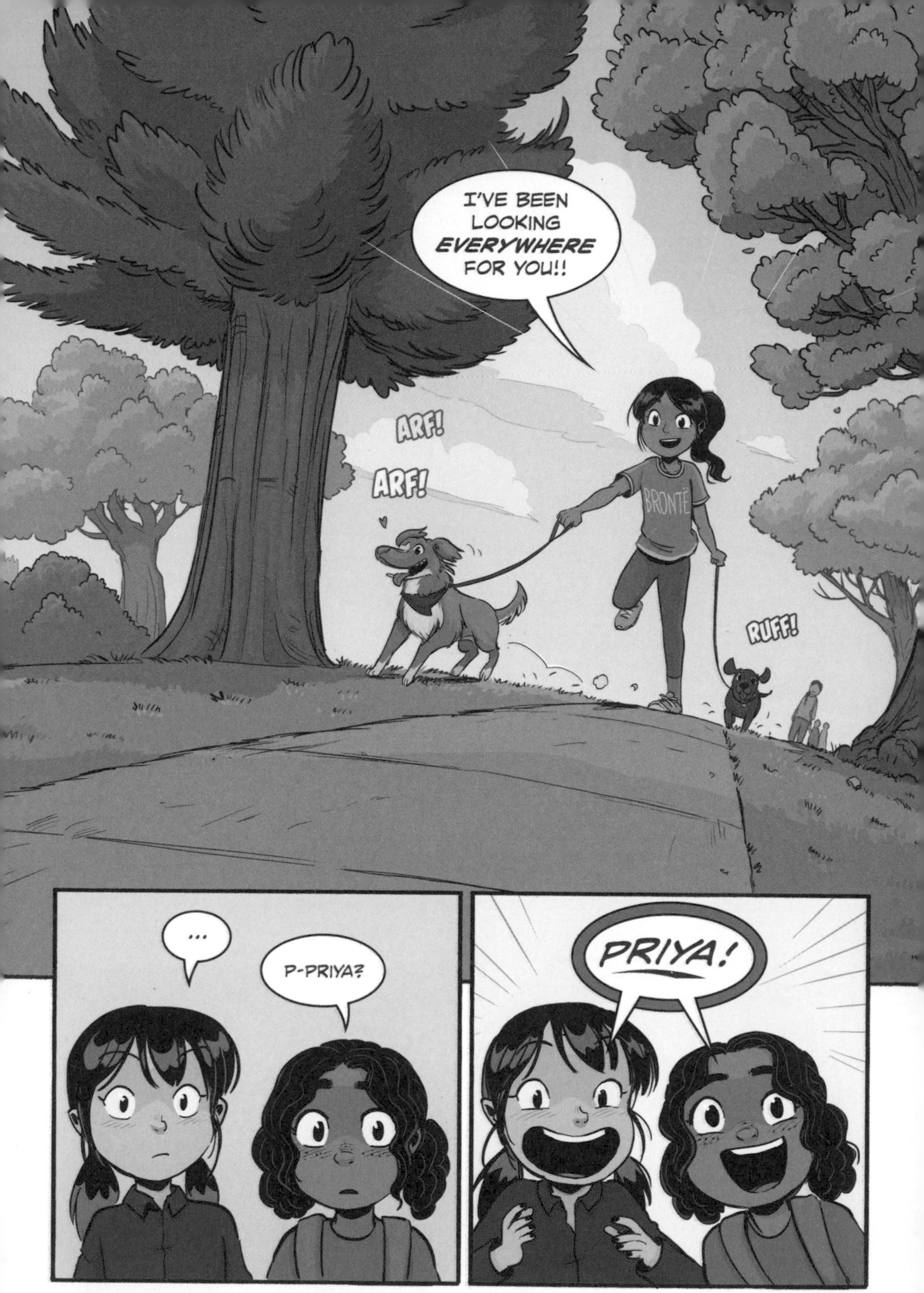
I'VE BEEN LOOKING EVERYWHERE FOR YOU!!
ARF!
ARF!
BRONTË
RUFF!
...
P-PRIYA?
PRIYA!

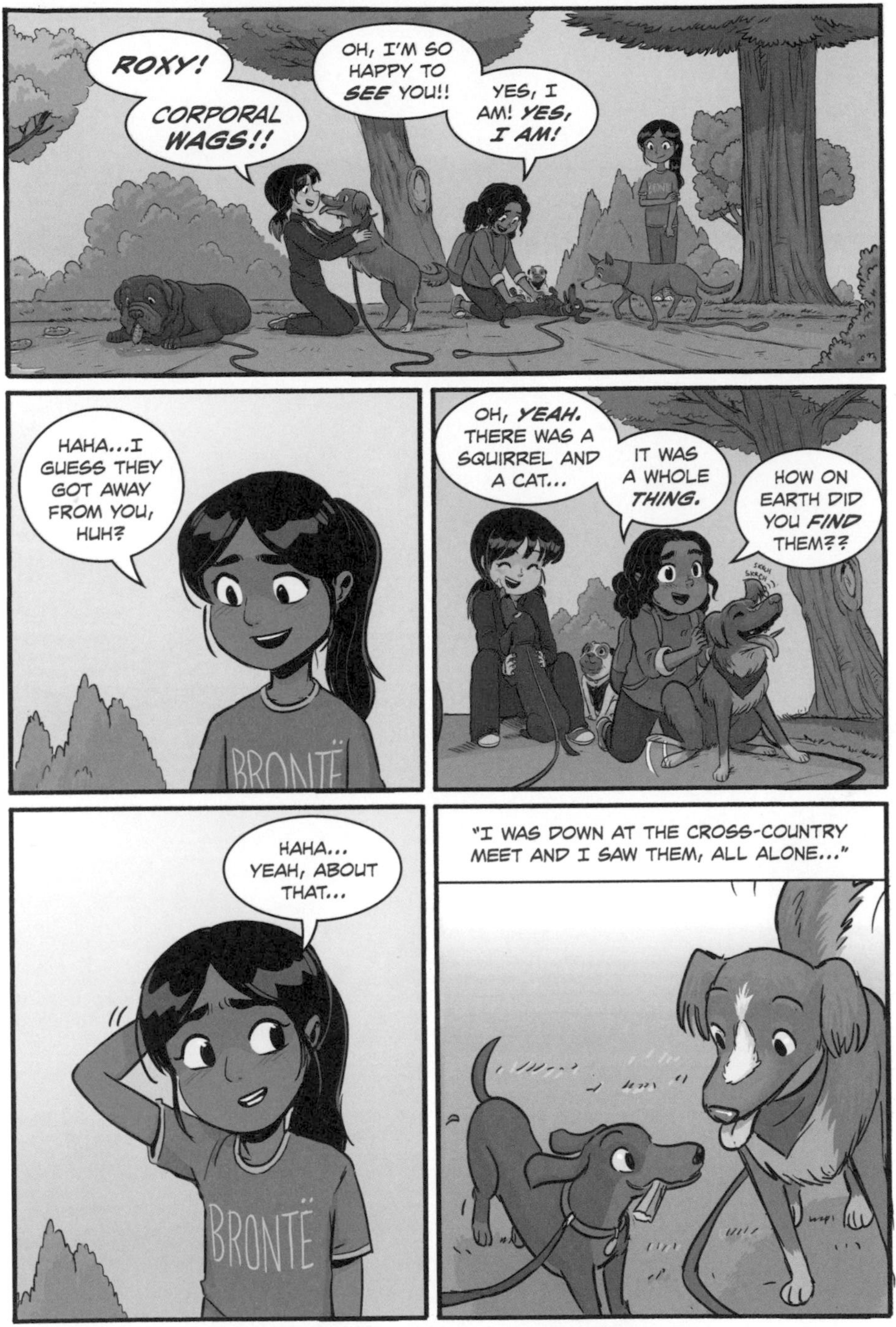
ROXY!
CORPORAL WAGS!!
OH, I'M SO HAPPY TO SEE YOU!!
YES, I AM! YES, I AM!
HAHA...I GUESS THEY GOT AWAY FROM YOU, HUH?
OH, YEAH. THERE WAS A SQUIRREL AND A CAT...
IT WAS A WHOLE THING.
HOW ON EARTH DID YOU FIND THEM??
BRONTË
HAHA... YEAH, ABOUT THAT...
"I WAS DOWN AT THE CROSS-COUNTRY MEET AND I SAW THEM, ALL ALONE..."
BRONTË

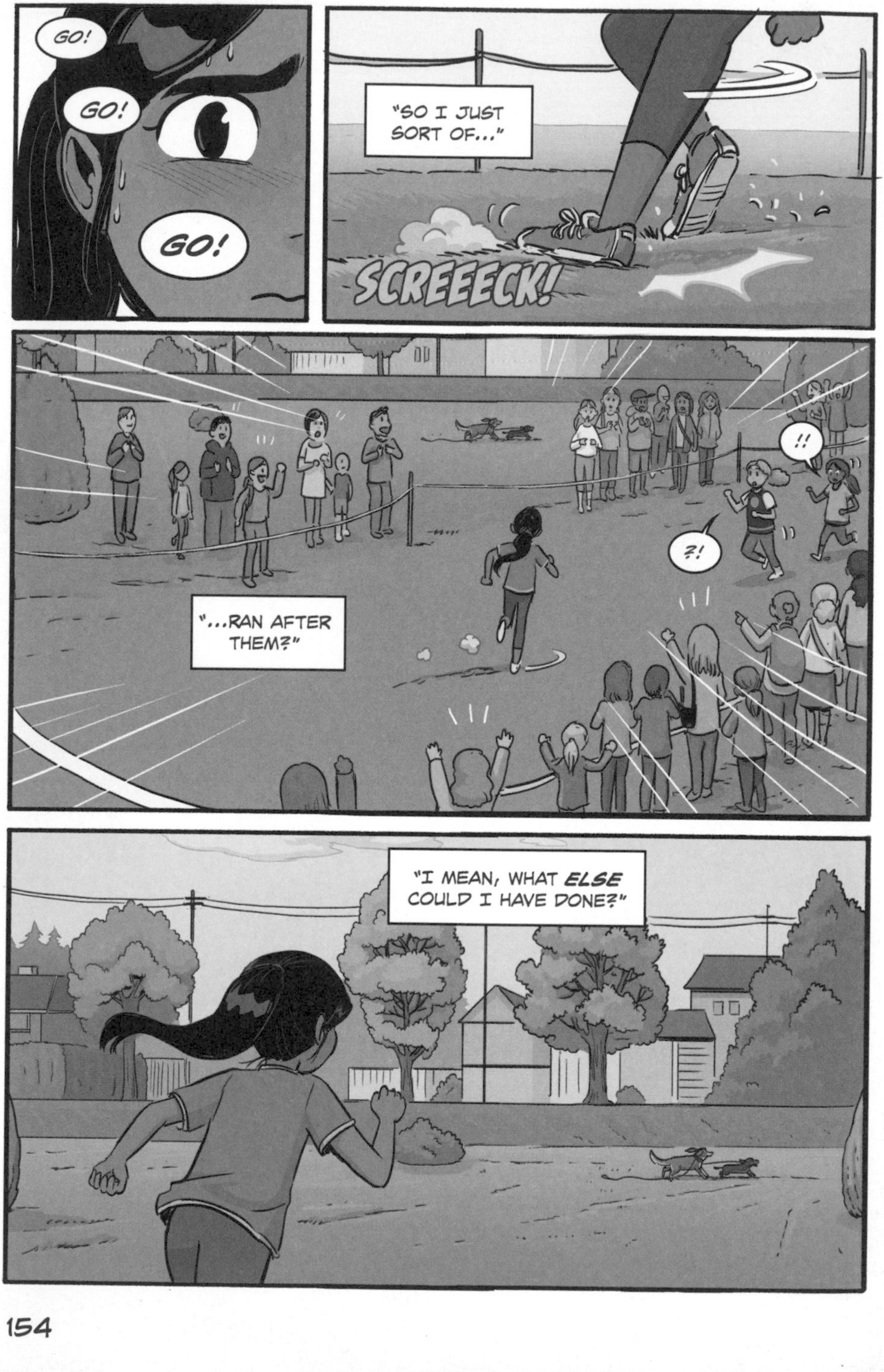
GO!
GO!
GO!
"SO I JUST SORT OF..."
SCREEECK!
!!
?!
"...RAN AFTER THEM?"
"I MEAN, WHAT ELSE COULD I HAVE DONE?"

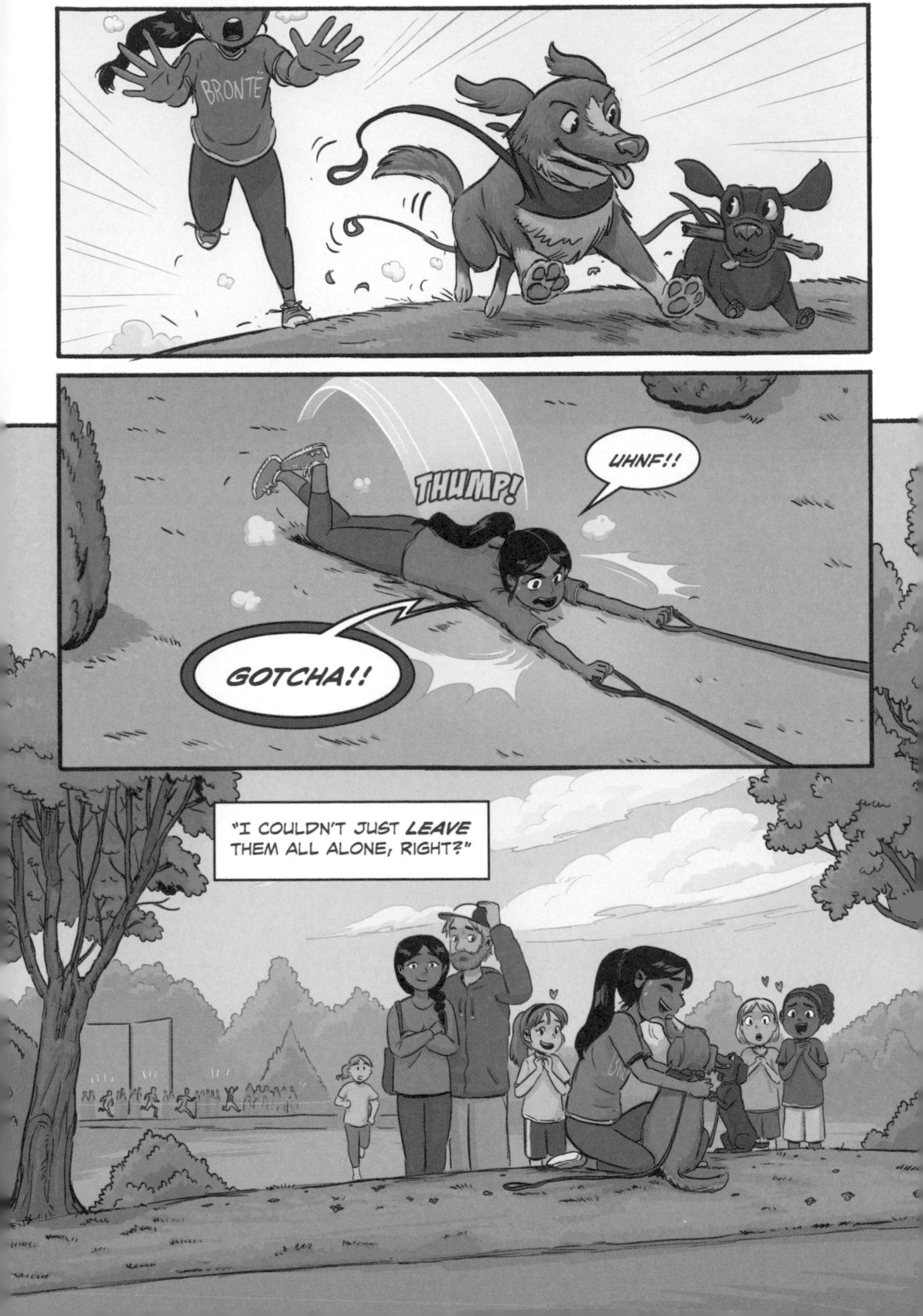
BRONTË
THUMP!
UHNF!!
GOTCHA!!
"I COULDN'T JUST *LEAVE* THEM ALL ALONE, RIGHT?"

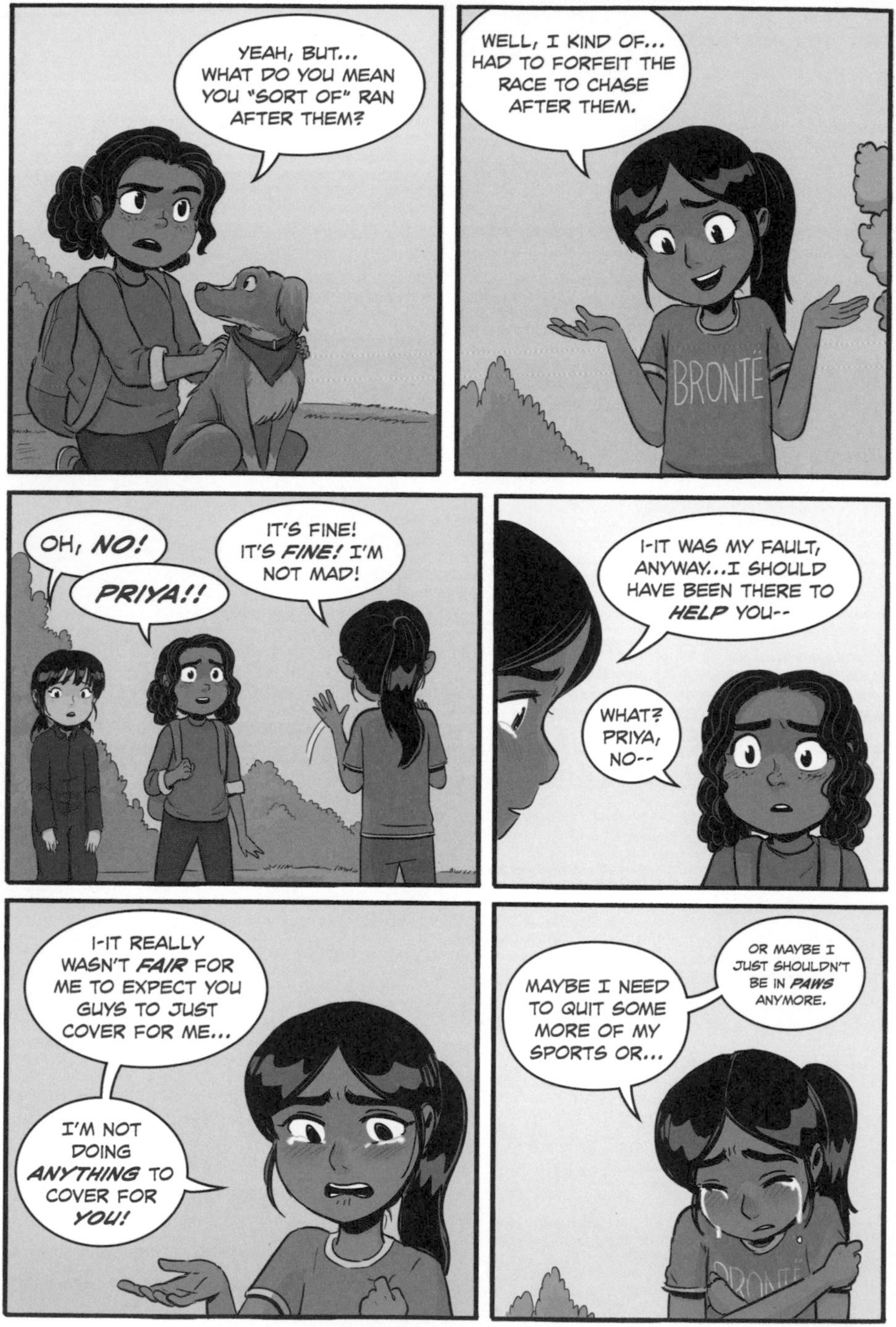

YEAH, BUT... WHAT DO YOU MEAN YOU "SORT OF" RAN AFTER THEM?
WELL, I KIND OF... HAD TO FORFEIT THE RACE TO CHASE AFTER THEM.
BRONTË
OH, NO!
PRIYA!!
IT'S FINE! IT'S FINE! I'M NOT MAD!
I-IT WAS MY FAULT, ANYWAY...I SHOULD HAVE BEEN THERE TO HELP YOU--
WHAT? PRIYA, NO--
I-IT REALLY WASN'T FAIR FOR ME TO EXPECT YOU GUYS TO JUST COVER FOR ME...
I'M NOT DOING ANYTHING TO COVER FOR YOU!
MAYBE I NEED TO QUIT SOME MORE OF MY SPORTS OR...
OR MAYBE I JUST SHOULDN'T BE IN PAWS ANYMORE.

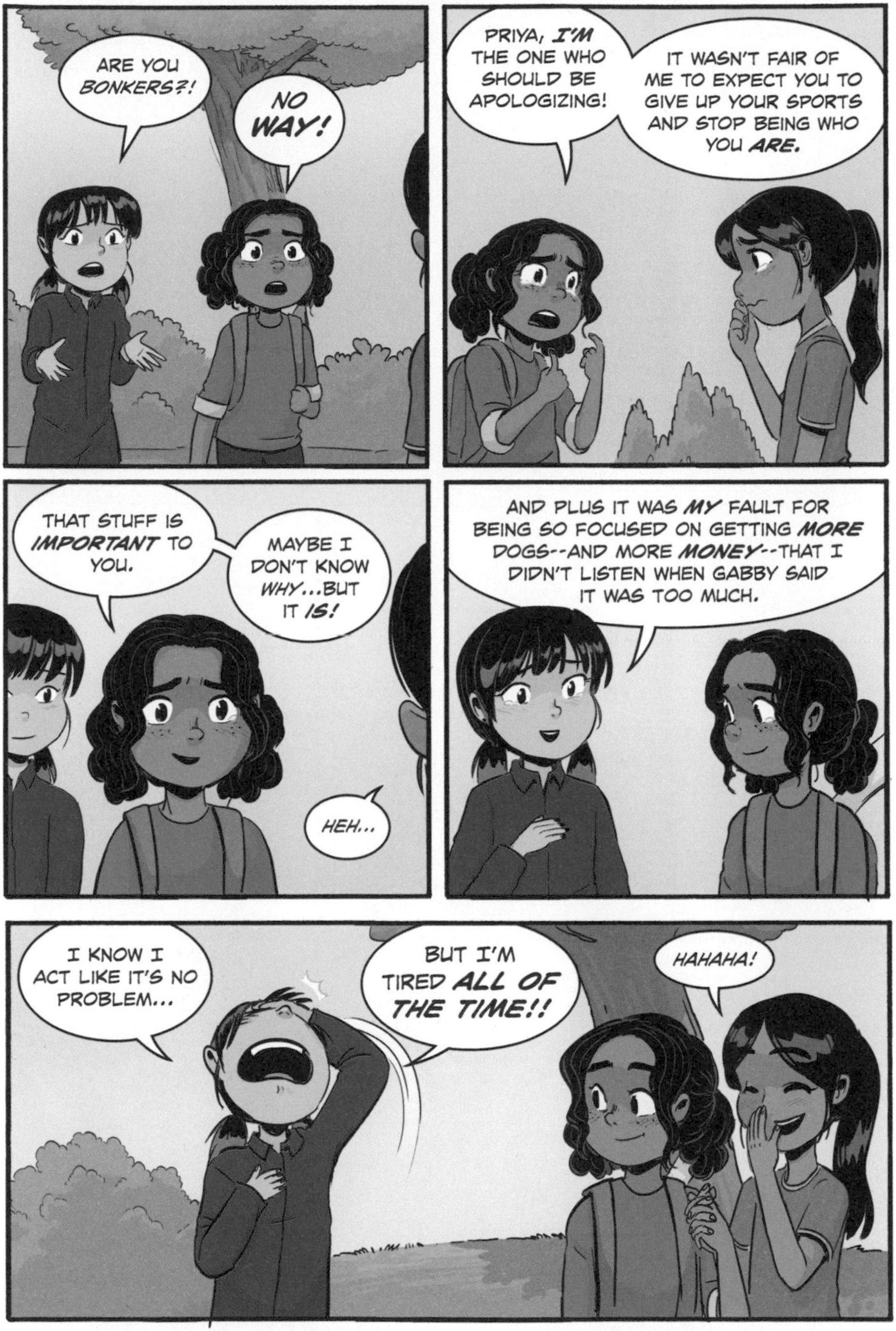
ARE YOU BONKERS?!
NO WAY!
PRIYA, I'M THE ONE WHO SHOULD BE APOLOGIZING!
IT WASN'T FAIR OF ME TO EXPECT YOU TO GIVE UP YOUR SPORTS AND STOP BEING WHO YOU ARE.
THAT STUFF IS IMPORTANT TO YOU.
MAYBE I DON'T KNOW WHY...BUT IT IS!
HEH...
AND PLUS IT WAS MY FAULT FOR BEING SO FOCUSED ON GETTING MORE DOGS--AND MORE MONEY--THAT I DIDN'T LISTEN WHEN GABBY SAID IT WAS TOO MUCH.
I KNOW I ACT LIKE IT'S NO PROBLEM...
BUT I'M TIRED ALL OF THE TIME!!
HAHAHA!

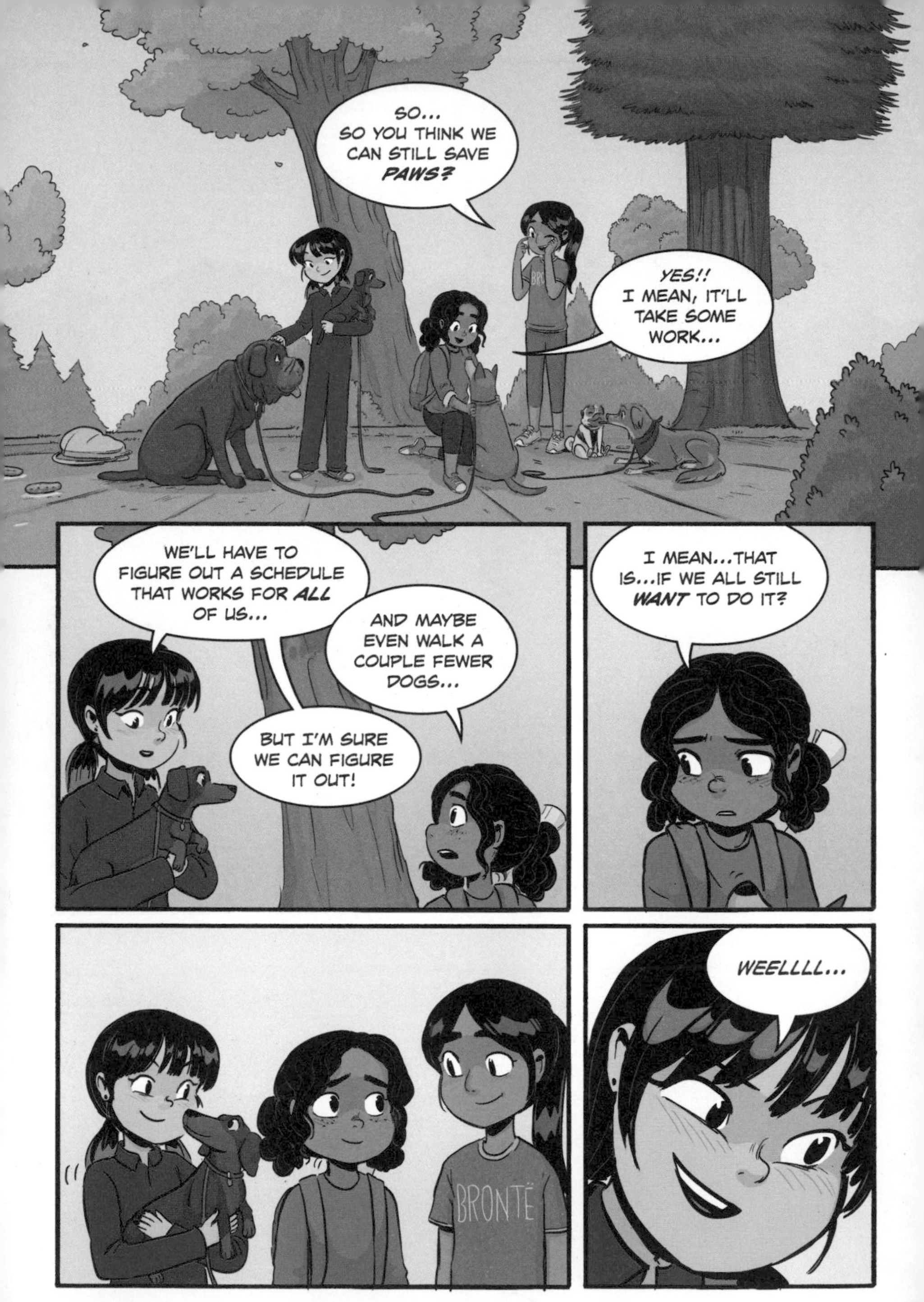
SO... SO YOU THINK WE CAN STILL SAVE PAWS?
YES!! I MEAN, IT'LL TAKE SOME WORK...
WE'LL HAVE TO FIGURE OUT A SCHEDULE THAT WORKS FOR ALL OF US...
BUT I'M SURE WE CAN FIGURE IT OUT!
AND MAYBE EVEN WALK A COUPLE FEWER DOGS...
I MEAN...THAT IS...IF WE ALL STILL WANT TO DO IT?
BRONTË
WEELLLL...

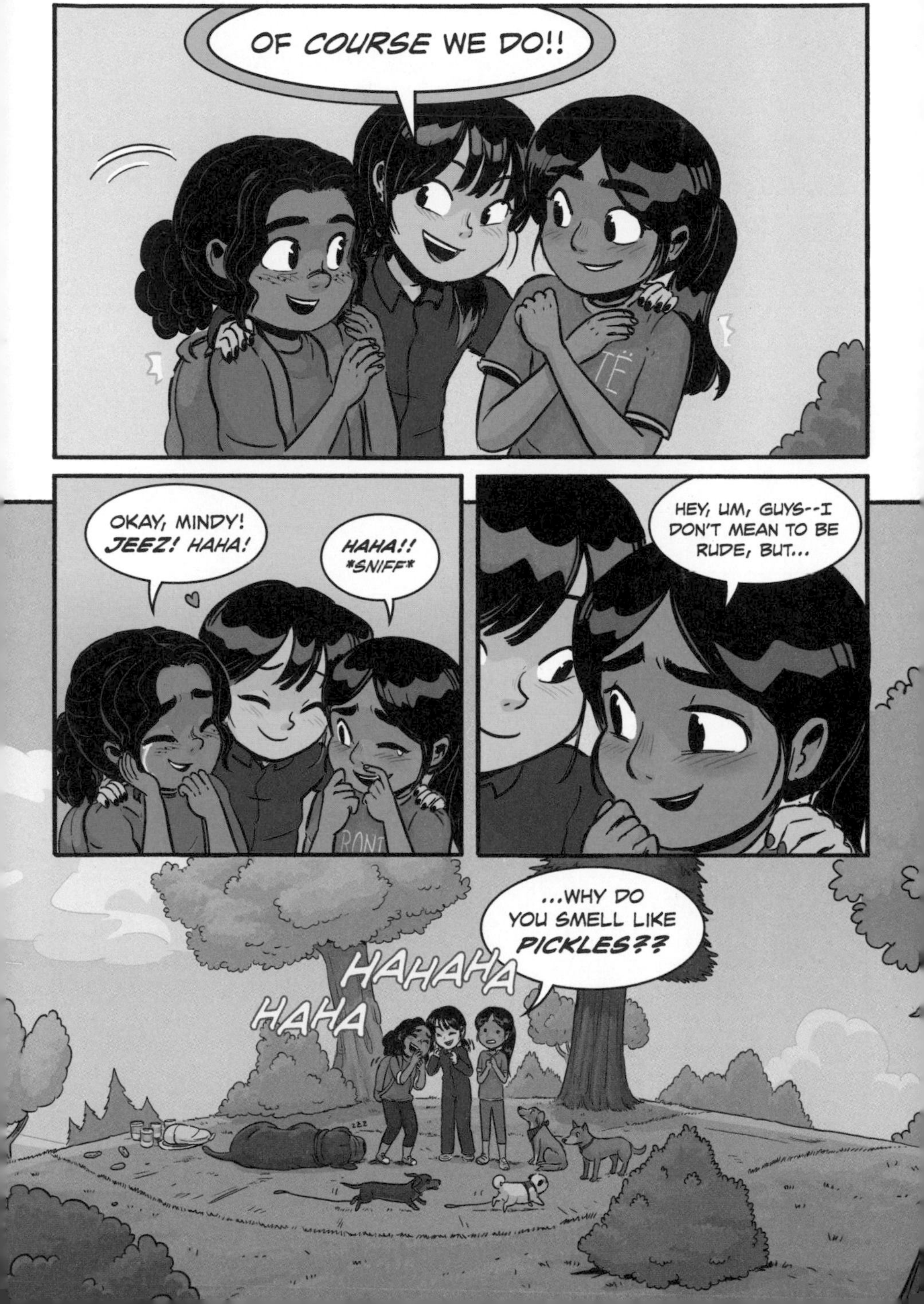
OF *COURSE* WE DO!!
OKAY, MINDY! ***JEEZ!*** HAHA!
HAHA!! **SNIFF**
HEY, UM, GUYS--I DON'T MEAN TO BE RUDE, BUT...
...WHY DO YOU SMELL LIKE ***PICKLES??***
HAHAHA
HAHA

AFTER THAT, EVERYTHING JUST BECAME A LOT EASIER. NOT *EASY;* BUT EASIER, ANYWAY.

WE STILL HAD LOTS TO WORK OUT, BUT THE FACT THAT WE WERE WORKING IT OUT *TOGETHER* MADE IT SEEM DOABLE.

WE HAD A BIG FAMILY MEETING TO MAKE SURE EVERYONE WAS ALL ON THE SAME PAGE AND THERE'D BE NO MORE MISUNDERSTANDINGS.

AND MY DAD WAS ACTUALLY PRETTY GOOD AT HELPING US SORT OUT ALL OF OUR *SCHEDULES.*

WE DECIDED WE SHOULD HAVE JUST ONE DOG PER WALKER, WHICH MEANT WE COULD ONLY WALK EACH DOG *TWO OR THREE* TIMES A WEEK.

WE WERE A *BIT* WORRIED ABOUT TELLING OUR CLIENTS WE COULDN'T WALK THEIR DOGS EVERY DAY...

...BUT THEY WERE ALL *SUPER COOL* ABOUT IT!

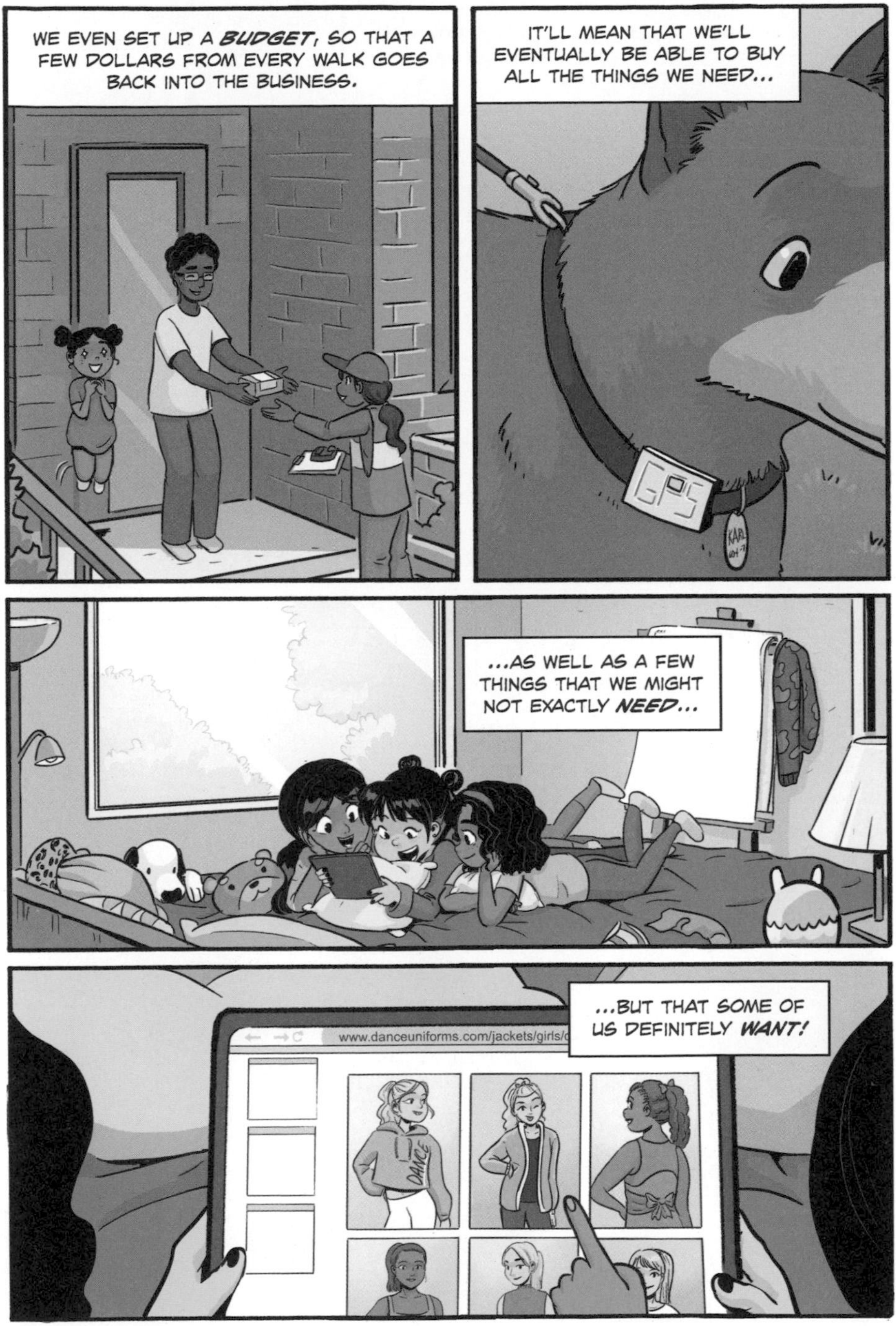
WE EVEN SET UP A *BUDGET*, SO THAT A FEW DOLLARS FROM EVERY WALK GOES BACK INTO THE BUSINESS.
IT'LL MEAN THAT WE'LL EVENTUALLY BE ABLE TO BUY ALL THE THINGS WE NEED...
GPS
KARL
...AS WELL AS A FEW THINGS THAT WE MIGHT NOT EXACTLY *NEED*...
...BUT THAT SOME OF US DEFINITELY *WANT!*
www.danceuniforms.com/jackets/girls/
DANCE

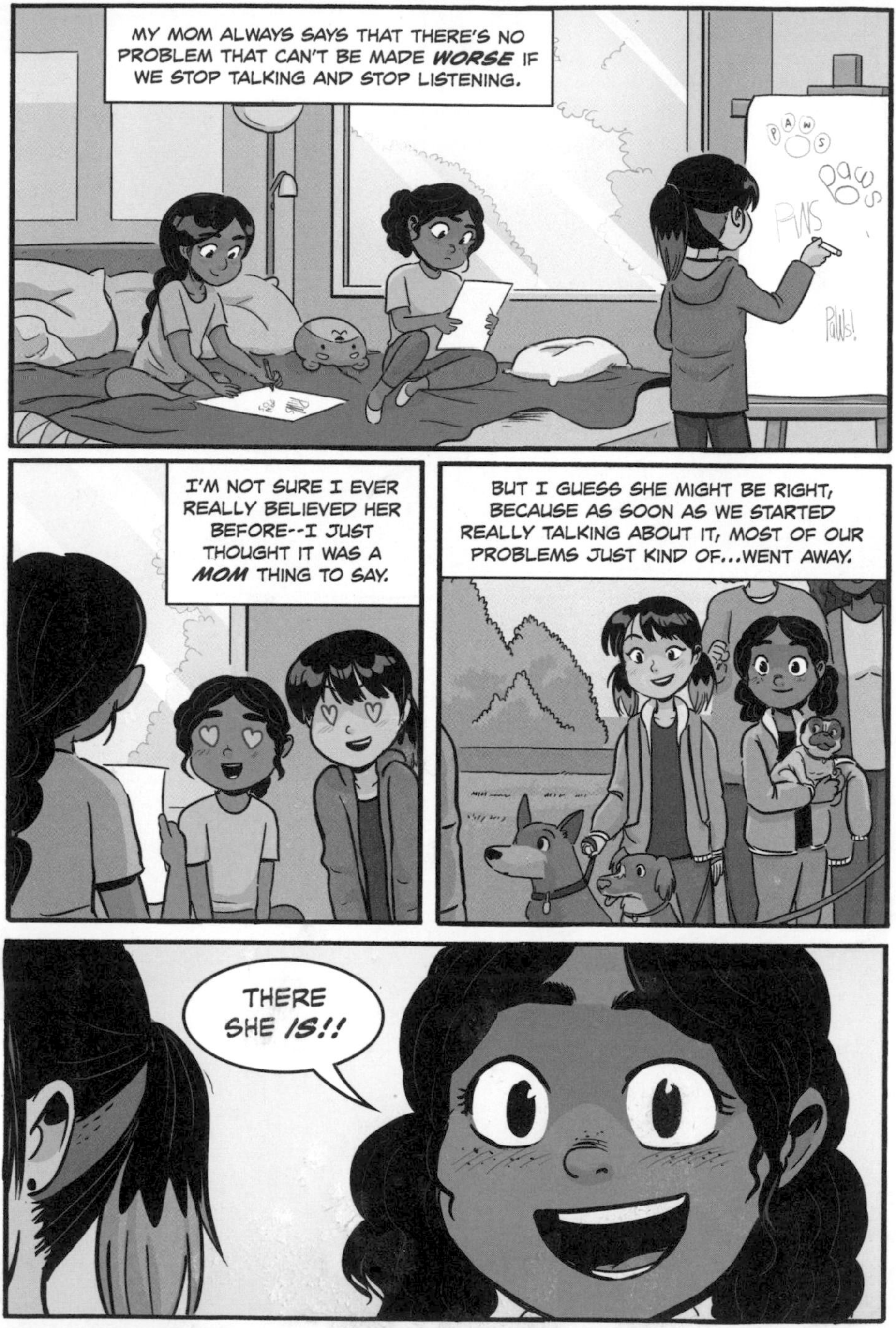
MY MOM ALWAYS SAYS THAT THERE'S NO PROBLEM THAT CAN'T BE MADE *WORSE* IF WE STOP TALKING AND STOP LISTENING.
PAWS
PAWS
PAWS
PAWS!
I'M NOT SURE I EVER REALLY BELIEVED HER BEFORE--I JUST THOUGHT IT WAS A *MOM* THING TO SAY.
BUT I GUESS SHE MIGHT BE RIGHT, BECAUSE AS SOON AS WE STARTED REALLY TALKING ABOUT IT, MOST OF OUR PROBLEMS JUST KIND OF...WENT AWAY.
THERE SHE *IS!!*

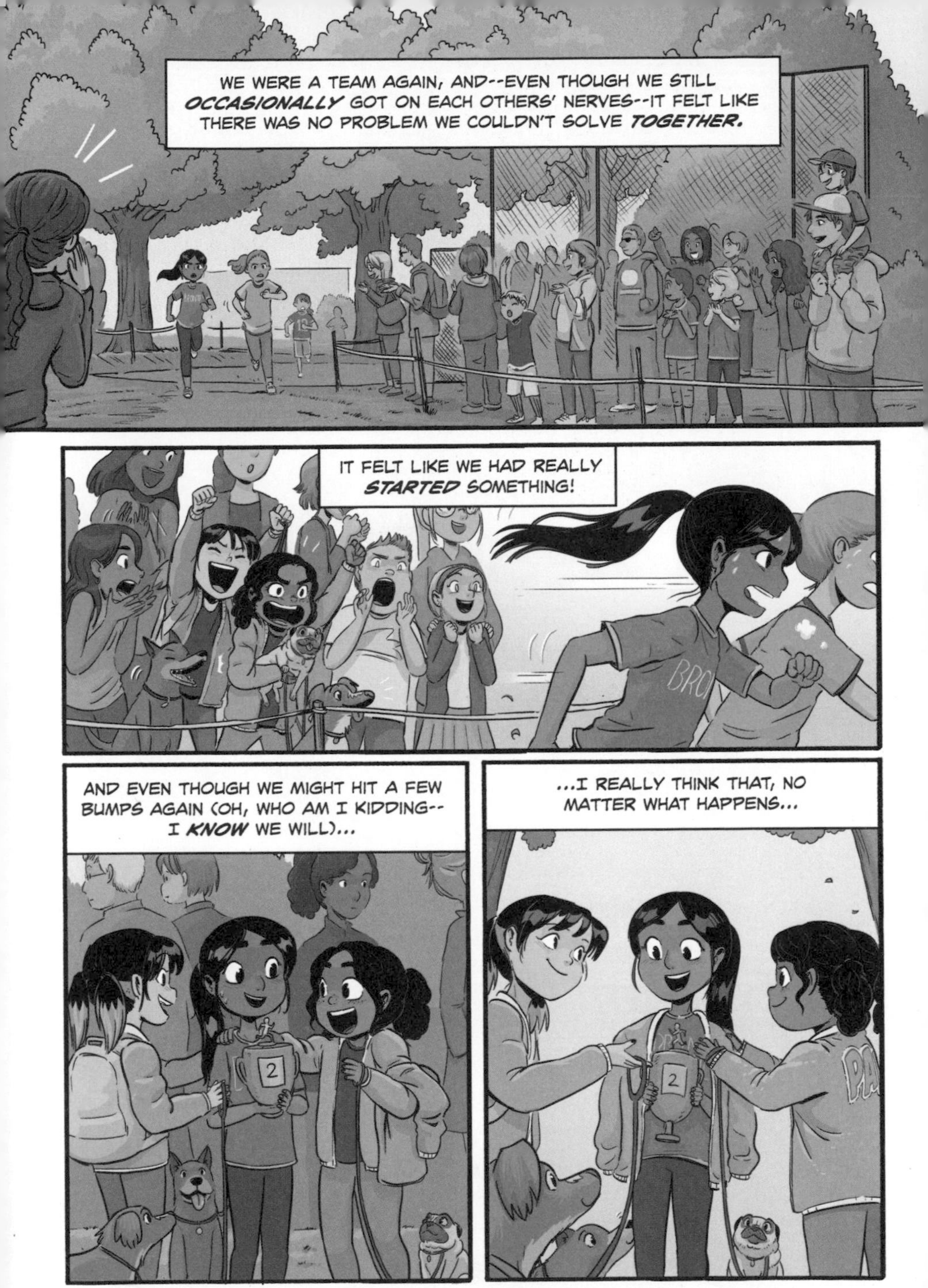
WE WERE A TEAM AGAIN, AND--EVEN THOUGH WE STILL OCCASIONALLY GOT ON EACH OTHERS' NERVES--IT FELT LIKE THERE WAS NO PROBLEM WE COULDN'T SOLVE TOGETHER.
IT FELT LIKE WE HAD REALLY STARTED SOMETHING!
AND EVEN THOUGH WE MIGHT HIT A FEW BUMPS AGAIN (OH, WHO AM I KIDDING--I KNOW WE WILL)...
...I REALLY THINK THAT, NO MATTER WHAT HAPPENS...

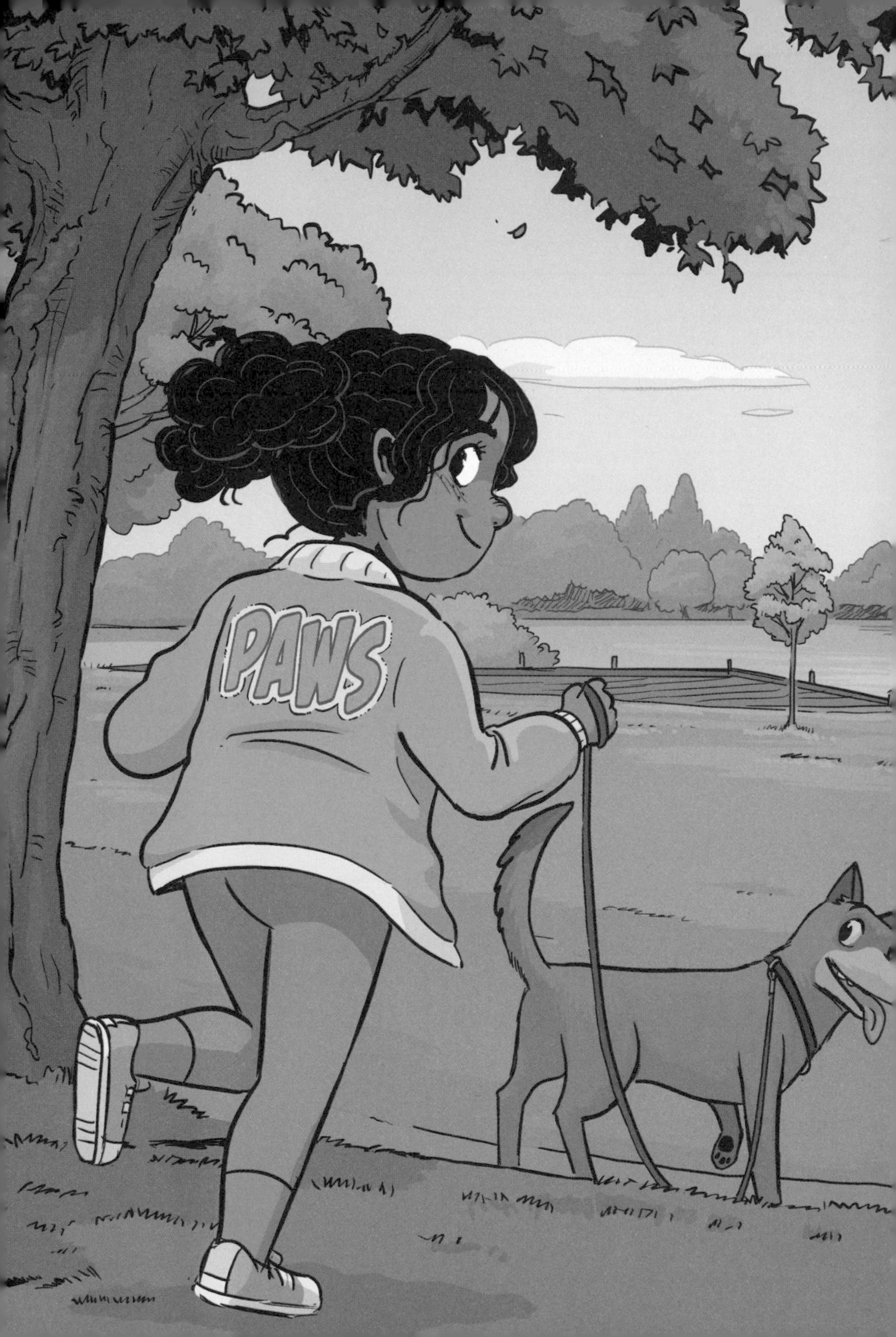
PAWS

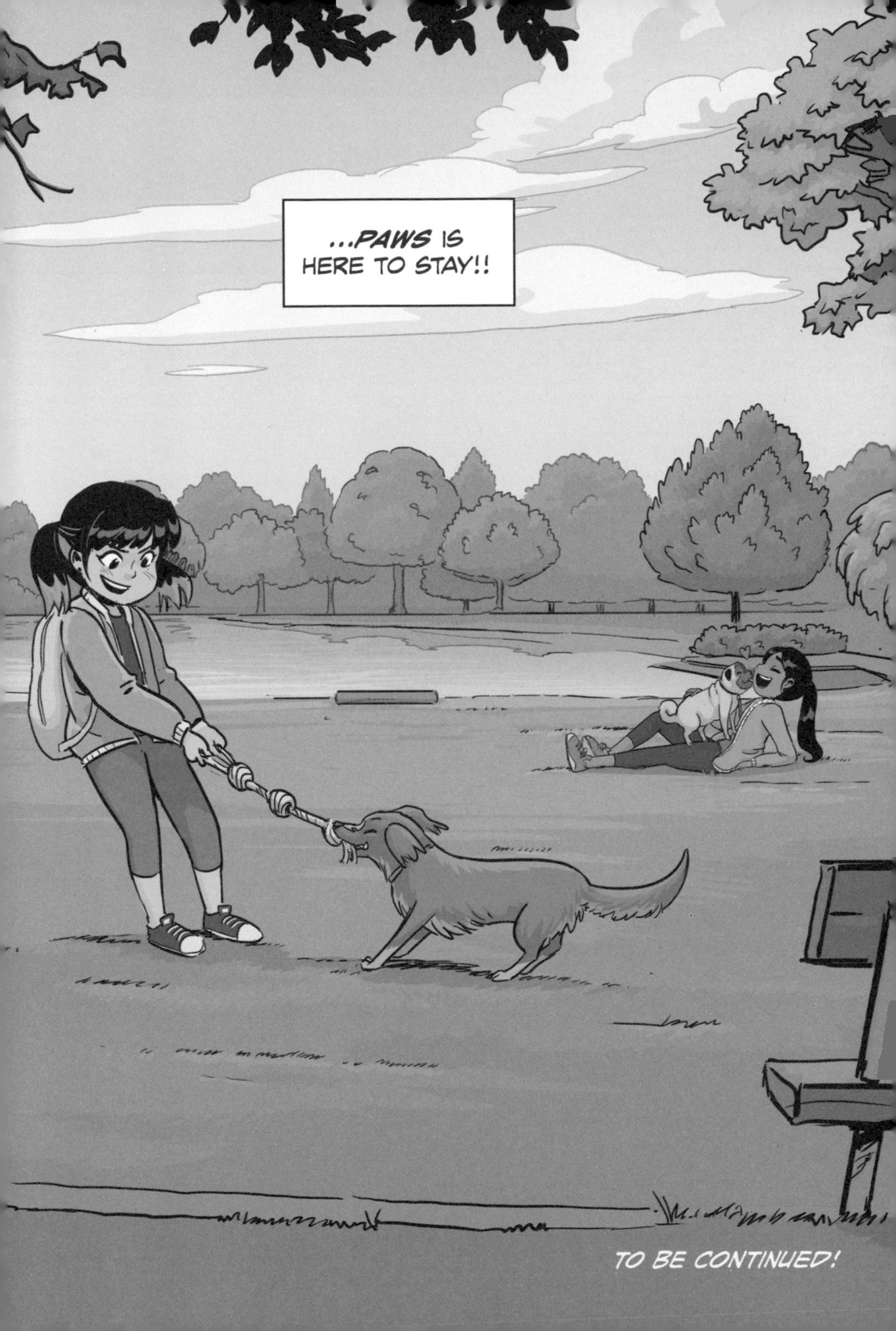
...PAWS IS HERE TO STAY!!
TO BE CONTINUED!

Acknowledgments

It's been fourteen years since I decided to uproot my life to a new country and pursue a career in my passion. I am grateful to countless people for where I am in my life, but I want to give special thanks to these people for being the main reason why I'm able to do this today.

Thank you to Mom, Dad, and Nick for nurturing and encouraging my passion and letting me follow my dreams in a new country.

Than you to Adam, my partner in life, who has been the greatest mentor and most consistent wind behind my sails.

Thank you to Karl Kerschl, Brenden Fletcher, and Becky Cloonan for kick-starting my career as a comic book colorist on Gotham Academy.

Fianlly, thank you to the Canada Council for the Arts. Without their generous support, this project would have never gotten off the ground. —M. A.

A book like this doesn't get made without a lot of help from a lot of people.

Thank you to my loving parents, who brought comics and pets into my life, and started this whole ball rolling.

Thank you to my wife, Rachel, who has always believed in me and supported me in whatever I wanted to do.

Thank you to my kids, especially Lily, who helped me so, so much in figuring out this story. There is so much of her in this book, I feel like her name should be on it.

Thank you to generous peers like Faith Erin Hicks, Gale Galligan, and Aditya Bidikar for their invaluable advice and encouragement along the way.

Thank you to Chris Hernandez and the whole team at Razorbill for their interest in our story and faith in our ability to tell it. —N. F.

Michele Assarasakorn grew up glued to manga and animation. She soon began drawing for herself, and at the age of eighteen she left her home in Bangkok, Thailand, to pursue her art education in Toronto, Canada. She studied concept design for film and video games, and after graduation spent some time as a junior concept artist before landing a gig coloring a comic for one of her idols. Since then she has had the pleasure of coloring books for such publishers as DC, Marvel, Image, and Dark Horse.

In her free time, Michele likes going on adventures around the world with her partner and often catalogues their escapades in illustration. This habit kept her drawing, and caught the interest of her current writer, Nathan Fairbairn, so she pivoted again and took the plunge into comic illustration!

Michele currently lives and draws in Vancouver, Canada, with her husband, Adam, her daughter, and two cats.

Nathan Fairbairn moved around a lot as a kid, but no matter where he moved to, there were always pets and comics lying around the house, so he was happy.

Nathan loves making comics. He has colored all kinds of comics—big superhero books like Spider-Man and Wonder Woman, and fun indie books like Scott Pilgrim. In addition to a lot of coloring, Nathan has also done a bit of writing. He once wrote a graphic novel called *Lake of Fire*, which was about a bunch of knights fighting aliens. He really likes writing, and hopes to do lots more of it in the future.

Nathan now lives in Vancouver, Canada, and tries to move around as little as possible.

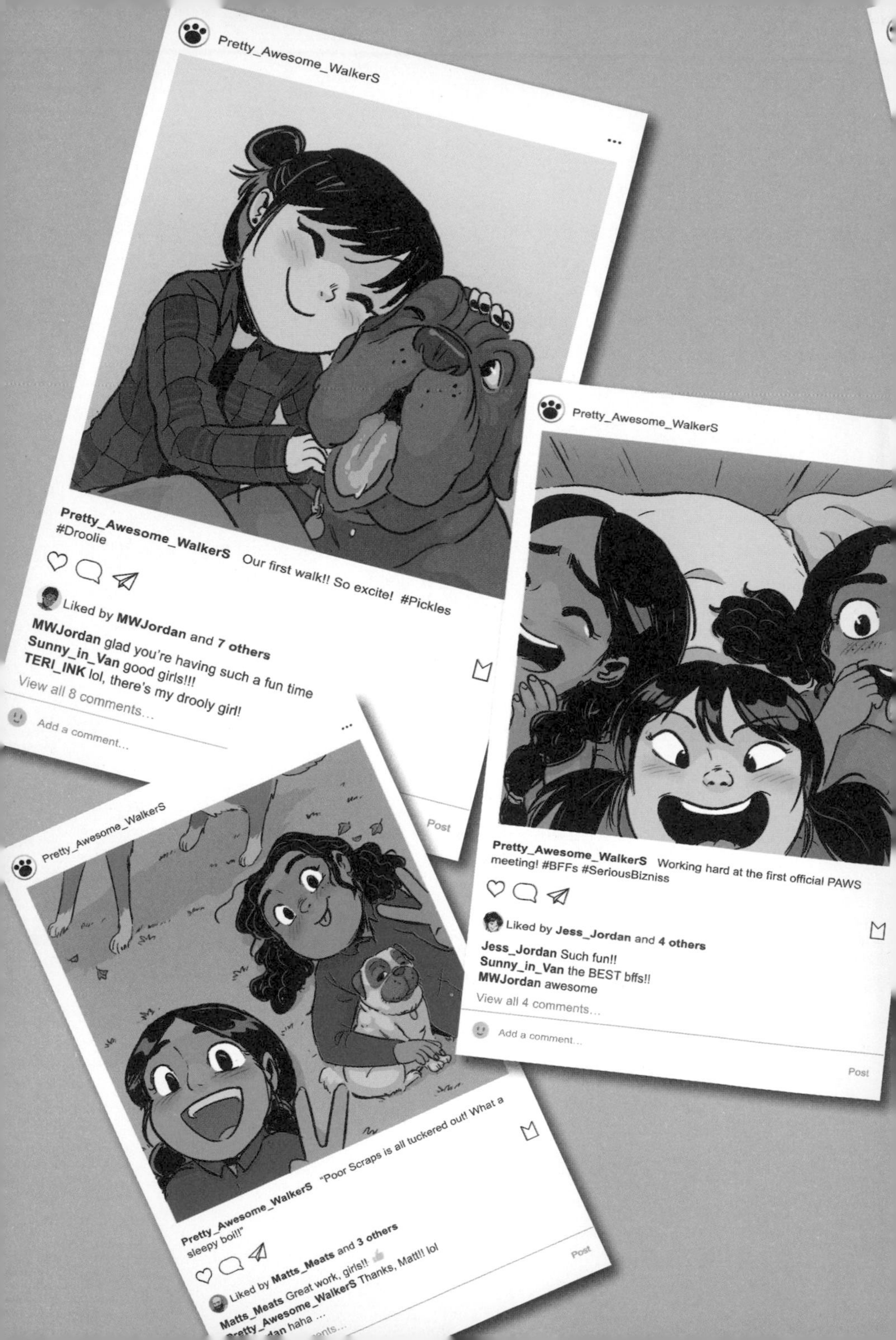
Pretty_Awesome_WalkerS
Pretty_Awesome_WalkerS Our first walk!! So excite! #Pickles #Droolie
Liked by MWJordan and 7 others
MWJordan glad you're having such a fun time
Sunny_in_Van good girls!!!
TERI_INK lol, there's my drooly girl!
View all 8 comments...
Add a comment...
Post
Pretty_Awesome_WalkerS
Pretty_Awesome_WalkerS Working hard at the first official PAWS meeting! #BFFs #SeriousBizniss
Liked by Jess_Jordan and 4 others
Jess_Jordan Such fun!!
Sunny_in_Van the BEST bffs!!
MWJordan awesome
View all 4 comments...
Add a comment...
Post
Pretty_Awesome_WalkerS
Pretty_Awesome_WalkerS "Poor Scraps is all tuckered out! What a sleepy boi!!"
Liked by Matts_Meats and 3 others
Matts_Meats Great work, girls!!
Pretty_Awesome_WalkerS Thanks, Matt!! lol
Post

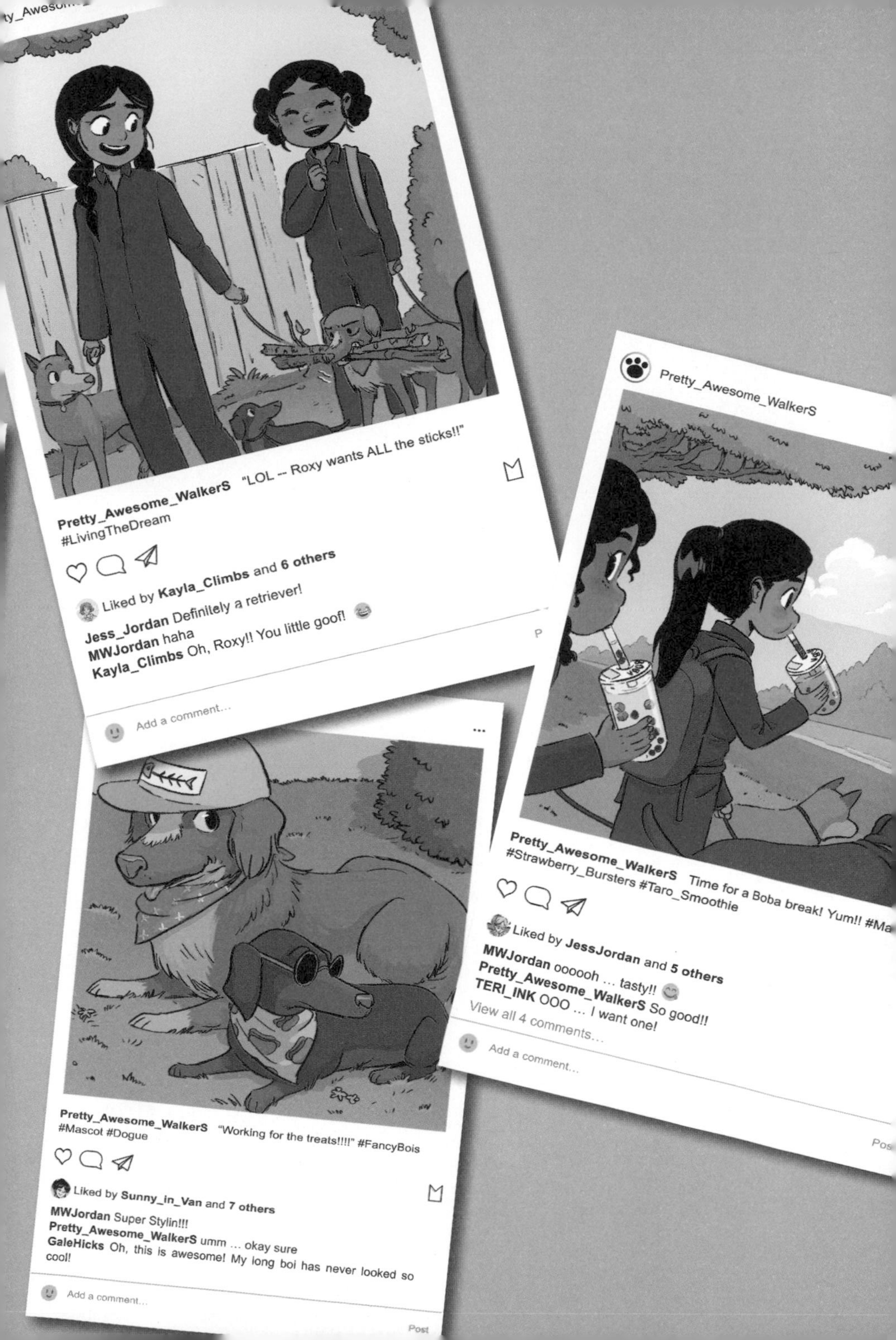

ty_Awesom
Pretty_Awesome_WalkerS "LOL -- Roxy wants ALL the sticks!!" #LivingTheDream
Liked by Kayla_Climbs and 6 others
Jess_Jordan Definitely a retriever!
MWJordan haha
Kayla_Climbs Oh, Roxy!! You little goof!
Add a comment...
P
Pretty_Awesome_WalkerS
Pretty_Awesome_WalkerS Time for a Boba break! Yum!! #Ma #Strawberry_Bursters #Taro_Smoothie
Liked by JessJordan and 5 others
MWJordan oooooh … tasty!!
Pretty_Awesome_WalkerS So good!!
TERI_INK OOO … I want one!
View all 4 comments…
Add a comment...
Pos
...
Pretty_Awesome_WalkerS "Working for the treats!!!!" #FancyBois #Mascot #Dogue
Liked by Sunny_in_Van and 7 others
MWJordan Super Stylin!!!
Pretty_Awesome_WalkerS umm … okay sure
GaleHicks Oh, this is awesome! My long boi has never looked so cool!
Add a comment...
Post

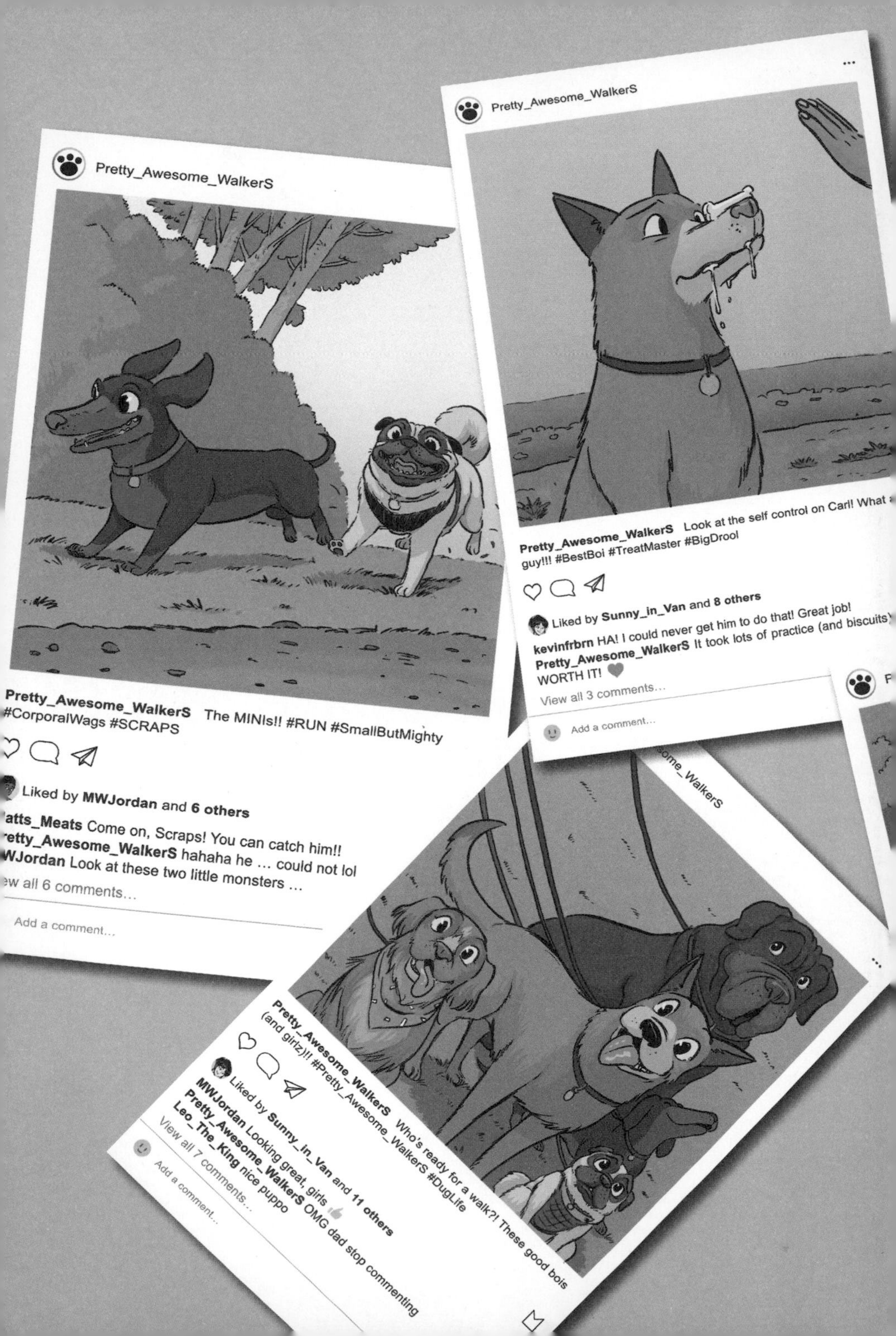

Pretty_Awesome_WalkerS
Pretty_Awesome_WalkerS The MINIs!! #RUN #SmallButMighty #CorporalWags #SCRAPS
Liked by MWJordan and 6 others
atts_Meats Come on, Scraps! You can catch him!!
retty_Awesome_WalkerS hahaha he … could not lol
WJordan Look at these two little monsters …
ew all 6 comments…
Add a comment…
Pretty_Awesome_WalkerS
Pretty_Awesome_WalkerS Look at the self control on Carl! What a guy!!! #BestBoi #TreatMaster #BigDrool
Liked by Sunny_in_Van and 8 others
kevinfrbrn HA! I could never get him to do that! Great job!
Pretty_Awesome_WalkerS It took lots of practice (and biscuits) WORTH IT!
View all 3 comments…
Add a comment…
ome_WalkerS
Pretty_Awesome_WalkerS Who's ready for a walk?! These good bois (and girlz)!! #Pretty_Awesome_WalkerS #DugLife
Liked by Sunny_in_Van and 11 others
MWJordan Looking great, girls
Pretty_Awesome_WalkerS OMG dad stop commenting
Leo_The_King nice puppo
View all 7 comments…
Add a comment…

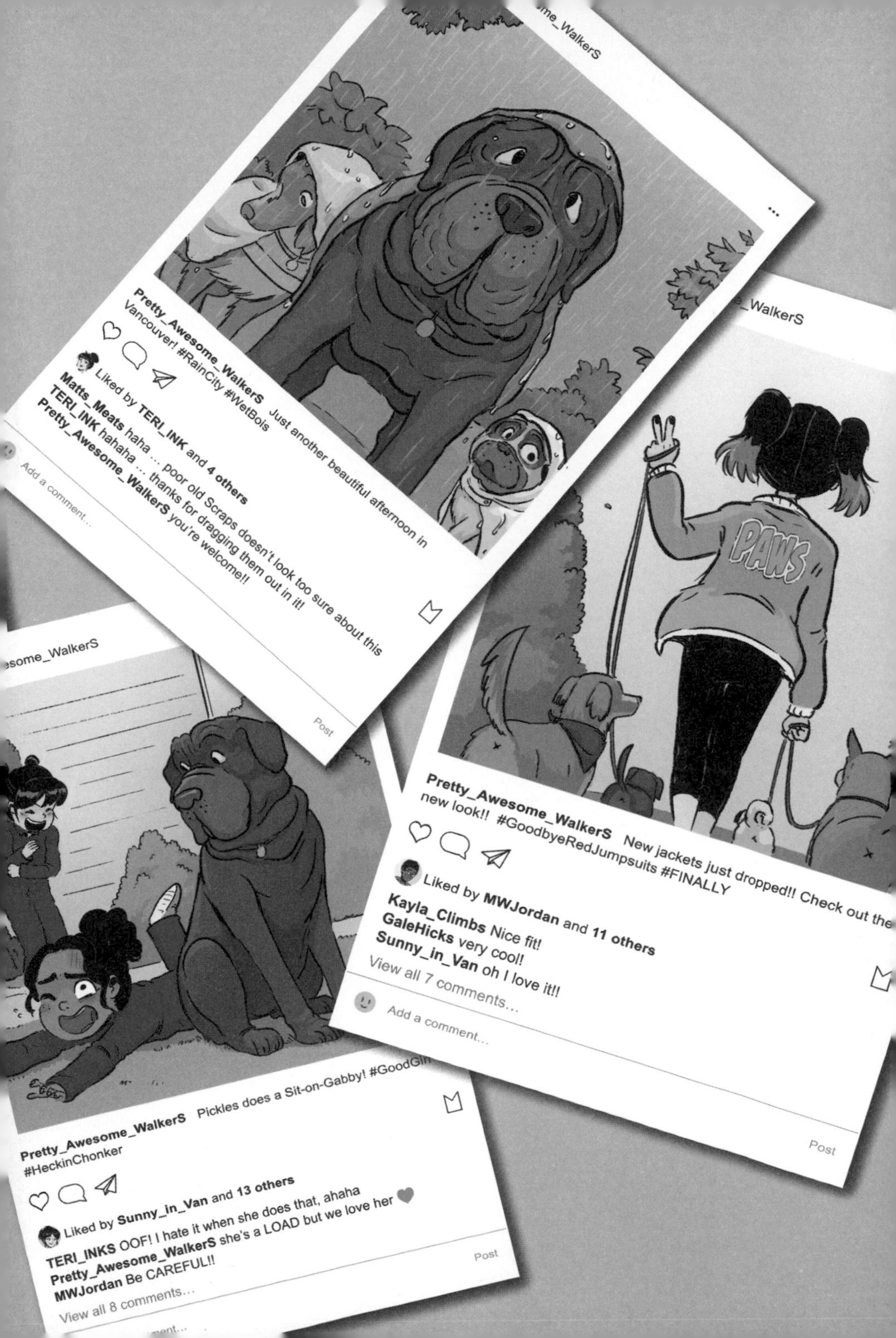

me_WalkerS
Pretty_Awesome_WalkerS Just another beautiful afternoon in Vancouver! #RainCity #WetBois
Liked by TERI_INK and 4 others
Matts_Meats haha … poor old Scraps doesn't look too sure about this
TERI_INK hahaha … thanks for dragging them out in it!
Pretty_Awesome_WalkerS you're welcome!!
Add a comment...
Post
_WalkerS
PAWS
Pretty_Awesome_WalkerS New jackets just dropped!! Check out the new look!! #GoodbyeRedJumpsuits #FINALLY
Liked by MWJordan and 11 others
Kayla_Climbs Nice fit!
GaleHicks very cool!
Sunny_in_Van oh I love it!!
View all 7 comments...
Add a comment...
Post
esome_WalkerS
Pretty_Awesome_WalkerS Pickles does a Sit-on-Gabby! #GoodGir
#HeckinChonker
Liked by Sunny_in_Van and 13 others
TERI_INKS OOF! I hate it when she does that, ahaha
Pretty_Awesome_WalkerS she's a LOAD but we love her
MWJordan Be CAREFUL!!
View all 8 comments...
Post

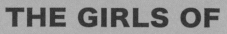

THE GIRLS OF PAWS WILL RETURN!

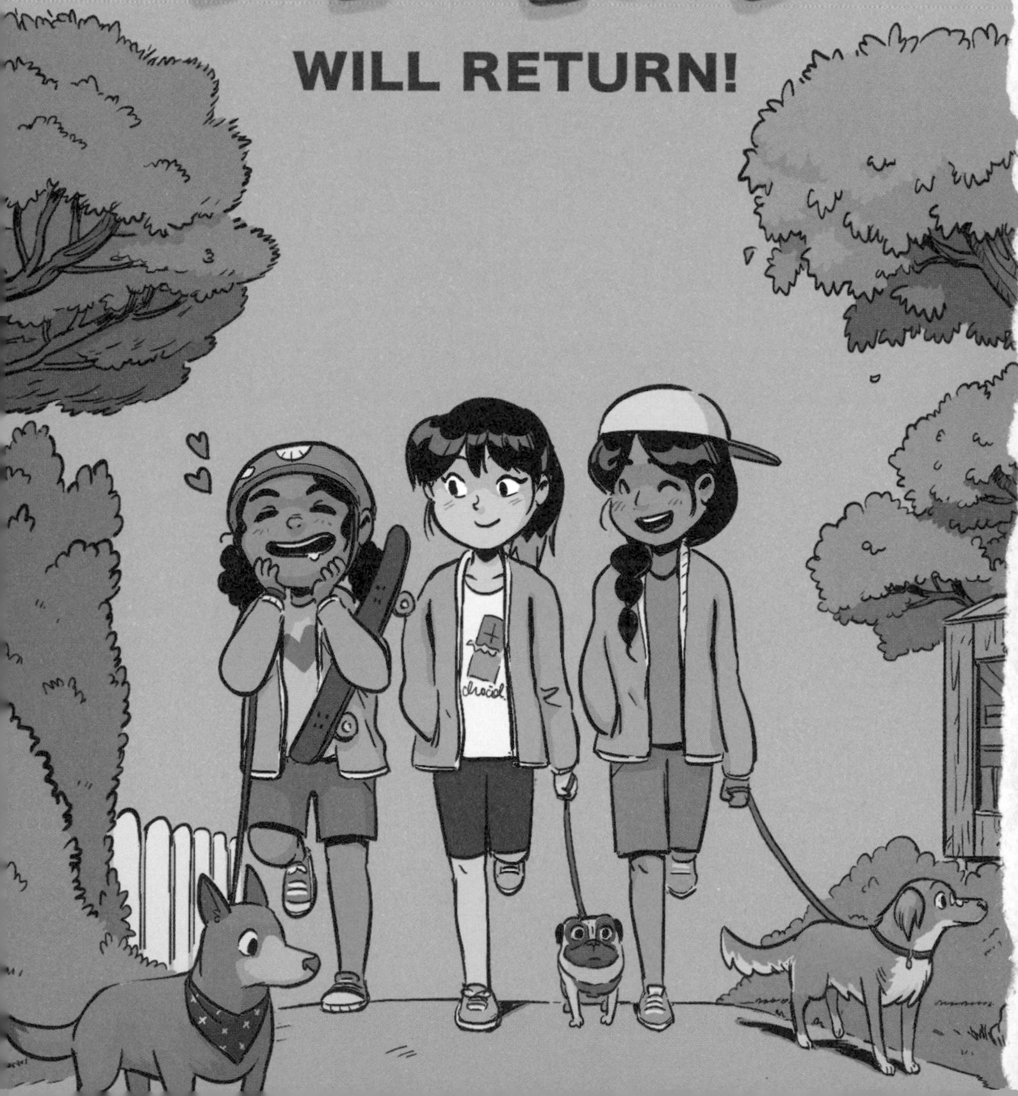